Linda Fairstein is a former prosecutor and one of America's foremost legal experts on crimes of violence against women and children. For three decades she served in the office of the New York Country District Attorney, where she was Chief of the Sex Crimes Prosecution Unit. In 2010 she was presented with the Silver Bullet Award from the International Thriller Writers Association. Fairstein's Alexandra Cooper novels have been translated into more than a dozen languages and have debuted on the *Sunday Times* and the *New York Times* bestseller lists, among others. She lives in Manhattan and on Martha's Vineyard.

You can discover more about the author at www.lindafairstein.com
Follow her on Twitter @LindaFairstein

DEVIL'S BRIDGE

The Manhattan waterfront is one of New York City's most magnificent vistas, boasting both the majestic Statue of Liberty and the busy George Washington Bridge. But Detective Mike Chapman is about to become far too well acquainted with the dangerous side of the Hudson River and its islands when he takes on his most personal case yet: the disappearance of Alex Cooper. Coop is missing — but there are so many leads and terrifying complications: scores of enemies she has made after a decade of putting criminals behind bars; a recent security breach with dangerous repercussions; and a new intimacy in her relationship with Mike, causing the police commissioner himself to be wary of the methods Mike will use to get Coop back . . . if he can.

LINDA FAIRSTEIN

◆

DEVIL'S BRIDGE

Complete and Unabridged

CHARNWOOD
Leicester

First published in Great Britain in 2015 by
Little, Brown
an imprint of
Little, Brown Book Group
London

First Charnwood Edition
published 2017
by arrangement with
Little, Brown Book Group
An Hachette UK Company
London

Map by David Cain

A catalogue record for this book is available
from the British Library.

For Michael Goldberg

Sway with me

All detectives might be called investigators, but not all investigators can be called detectives. Investigators need a trail of facts which might eventually lead to a successful conclusion of their inquiry. If there are no investigative leads to pursue, then they are finished. This is where a detective comes in — a person who can paint a landscape he has never seen from inside a darkened room, which is actually the crime scene. That's the difference between the craft and the art.

Former chief inspector, Scotland Yard

COOP

1

'Are the People ready for trial, Ms. Cooper?' Judge Fleming took off her glasses and pointed them in my direction.

I was slower than usual to get to my feet, stalling for time as I waited for another prosecutor from my office to walk into court with information that would determine my answer.

'Actually, Your Honor, I'd be grateful if you would put this matter over until tomorrow.'

'That wasn't your attitude yesterday when you were urging me — pushing me, actually — to clear my calendar so we could start jury selection this afternoon.'

'I'm sorry, Judge. Something was brought to my attention this morning and I'm trying to ascertain the truth of the facts before I move the case to trial.' I started the sentence by facing the court but had turned my head to the back of the room, trying to will the door to open.

Gino Moretti could barely suppress a smile, sensing my vulnerability. 'We're ready to proceed, Judge. My client is eager to get on with clearing his good name,' my adversary said. 'Alex has twisted her neck so many times this afternoon that I figure she's either looking over her shoulder for a stalker, or she's waiting until the guys in the press room get wind that she's about to start performing for them.'

'Cut me a break, Gino,' I said, turning my attention back to the bench.

'Coop hates playing to an empty house, Judge.'

Judge Fleming knew that a convicted rapist was in fact stalking me, and had been since his escape from a psych facility months earlier. Raymond Tanner was not actually on my mind in the secure surrounds of her courtroom, but he'd been a tremendous source of anxiety since he had threatened my life in August.

'What did you say about your client's good name?' Fleming asked, replacing her glasses and scrolling through the rap sheet attached to the arraignment papers in her file.

'Just that the sooner he can clear himself of these ridiculous charges — '

Fleming didn't brook nonsense in her courtroom. 'Antonio Carlito Estevez. Nice enough name. Going to be pretty hard to clear it, though, Mr. Moretti, no matter what happens with this case. Looks like nine misdemeanor convictions, a murder rap that he beat — '

'He was innocent, Your Honor. He didn't beat anything.'

'A conviction for manslaughter and — '

'That was a YO, Judge.'

'The fact that he was a youthful offender doesn't change much, Moretti. Just meant he wasn't a predicate felon when a jury found him guilty of second-degree assault four years ago. It explains why he did such a short stint for such a serious crime.'

Antonio Estevez gave Janet Fleming his iciest

4

stare. But she met it head-on and returned it with an equally frigid gaze. It was a look I had seen many times on the face of this former Legal Aid attorney who'd been appointed to the bench a decade earlier. She was tougher on perps than most judges who'd come up as assistant district attorneys.

'Can we bring the panel in, Your Honor?' Moretti asked.

'Have you and Ms. Cooper exhausted the possibility of a plea for Mr. Estevez?'

'The only offer is a plea to the charge,' I said.

The top count of the indictment was Sex Trafficking, a crime — added to the New York State Penal Law less than a decade ago — with a maximum penalty of twenty-five years, the same level of punishment as first-degree rape.

'You like the cold, Mr. Estevez?' Fleming asked, waving her right hand at the stenographer, telling her to go off the record and stop recording the proceedings.

'You don't have to answer that,' Moretti said, catching the move.

' 'Scuse me?' Estevez cocked his head and smiled at the judge.

'I see you're born in the Dominican Republic, moved to Miami, which is where you served time.'

'Yes, ma'am.'

Gino Moretti leaned over and whispered into his client's ear. Estevez brushed him away.

'Dannemora's where you're going to end up, if Ms. Cooper is right,' Fleming said. 'Clinton Correctional Facility in Dannemora — not that

5

they correct many of the guys I send there.'

'Let's have this on the record, Judge,' Moretti said, rising to his feet and tapping his pen on the old oak counsel table.

Janet Fleming shook her head at the stenographer. 'I'm just trying to make progress before the jury panel gets here, Gino. Trying to talk plea. Get a disposition.'

'Not happening, I promise you. Ms. Cooper's got her holier-than-thou posture going on.'

Fleming leaned in and talked straight at Estevez. 'They don't call that prison Siberia for nothing, Antonio. Rubs right up against the Canadian border. I get a chill just thinking about you being holed up there till you're fifty years old.'

'I'm glad you're thinking about me, Judge, is all I got to say,' the defendant said, almost leering at her. 'I didn't do nothing wrong.'

'Can we please — ?' The conversation was going in a bad direction.

'Stay seated, Ms. Cooper,' Fleming said, holding her arm out toward me. 'Clinton is full up with guys who didn't do nothing wrong, Antonio. It's a helluva lot warmer in Shawan-gunk. They have special classes for men like you.'

The prison in Shawangunk was one of the few with a sex offender program, but Estevez — who was also charged with physical assault — had refused all plea discussions that involved accepting sex offender status, and I wasn't caving to anything less.

'What you know about men like me?' Estevez asked, jabbing his finger in the air, toward the judge. The smile disappeared and a hint of his temper was about to boil to the surface.

Gino Moretti grabbed his client's arm and flattened it on counsel table.

'Ms. Cooper says you abuse women,' Fleming went on, flipping through the eight-count indictment. 'She says you take pimping to a new level.'

'I'm on the record now, Your Honor,' I said, standing up to address the court. 'What *I* say has no relevance. Those are the charges against Mr. Estevez. I get your point, Judge. I'll move the case to trial.'

'She don't know shit about me,' Estevez said, now focusing his anger on me as the court officers moved closer to surround him. 'I got a wife; I got a baby — '

'No more, Antonio,' Moretti said to him. 'Keep your mouth shut.'

'You just wait and see if that bitch who ran her mouth shows up to testify. She took back everything she said about me. The lady DA knows that.'

Janet Fleming stuck her glasses on top of her head. 'So you're stalling this operation till you figure out whether you've got a witness or not, Ms. Cooper? Any truth to that rumor?'

It wasn't unusual for victims who'd been threatened by a perp to change their minds about their willingness to testify in open court by the time the case came to trial. Tiffany Glover had texted me three days ago that she no longer wanted to cooperate, but just yesterday Mercer Wallace — a detective from the Special Victims

7

Squad and one of my closest friends — found her and brought her to my office.

'Ms. Glover will be here when we need her.'

'Perhaps she recanted her recantation, Judge,' Moretti said, one hand on his client's shoulder, snickering at me across the aisle.

'Which will make your cross even more devastating than I've been prepping for,' I said to Moretti, not loud enough for the judge to hear. 'The threats didn't work, Gino. Just FYI.'

'What did you say, Ms. Cooper?' Fleming cupped her hand to her ear.

'I apologize, Your Honor. I had forgotten to tell Gino something I wanted him to know before we got started.'

My adversary and I went back a long way together. I was sure he was aware that Estevez had sent threats to his former girlfriend through someone who had visited him at Rikers Island, but I didn't want to burn Moretti by putting that on the record.

'Did I hear the word *threat?*' Fleming asked.

'Ms. Cooper couldn't help herself, Judge,' Moretti said. 'She's been threatening to have her favorite detectives break my legs if I show her up in the courtroom. Looks like I'm in for the big hurt. That's all that was.'

Fleming's scowl suggested she didn't believe Moretti. 'Do you want to move the case, Ms. Cooper?'

'The People are ready for trial,' I said.

'The defense is ready.'

Fleming nodded to the captain of the court officers. 'I've got a panel of a hundred and fifty prospective jurors waiting in the hallway. Any other housekeeping before I bring them in?'

Gino Moretti and I both shook our heads.

I settled into my chair, resisting the opportunity to turn and look over the dozens of citizens who had responded to their jury duty summons. There would be no more than ten or so in business clothes, another thirty in casual dress, and the majority wearing gear so sloppy and threadbare — and often so odorous — that it appeared court proceedings had lost all the dignity in which they had been cloaked for centuries.

Moretti had turned his chair almost a hundred and eighty degrees, less for the purpose of sizing up the jury pool than for trying to charm them with a welcoming grin, a cheesy suggestion that he wouldn't be seated next to anyone except an innocent man.

'Nothing to eat or drink in the courtroom,' the captain called out from the railing behind me. 'Except for water. All newspapers and materials must be put away. Turn off your cell phones and devices. No e-mailing, calling, or texting. Take your seats, please.'

Moretti stood up and positioned himself behind Antonio Estevez, using the moment to give him a friendly pat on the back, leaning to whisper into his ear. The faked intimacy would feed jurors the idea that my adversary really liked his client — touched him and talked to him and shared a secret from the rest of us. He'd probably just told the experienced criminal to keep his mouth shut from this moment on and resist the temptation to do anything stupid in front of the people who would decide his fate.

'Good afternoon, ladies and gentlemen. My name is Janet Fleming. I'm a justice of the Supreme Court of the State of New York, presiding in Part 53 of the criminal term.'

The judge rose, circled her chair, and leaned on its high leather back as she addressed the prospective jurors. She compensated for her short stature by wearing stiletto heels, which got everyone's attention whenever she walked on the elevated wooden platform that held the bench. Fleming pulled back one side of her black robe — placing her hand on her hip — to make sure the group saw the colorful dress that clung to the outline of her body.

I glanced at my watch. Almost three o'clock and I'd had no word from anyone in my office. Fleming was going to steamroll forward with selection. Jeopardy would not attach until the twelfth juror was sworn in, but that could happen by noon tomorrow.

I zoned out on the judge's introductory remarks and came back to the case at hand only when she told the group that her clerk would now read the names of prospective jurors to take their seats in the jury box.

The clerk cranked the handle of the metal cylinder on the corner of her desk. The stub of each summons had been placed inside, and all were mixed together as they rolled over and over again. She let go of the handle, reached in, and removed a piece of paper, calling the name of the first individual and following it with thirteen others — which filled even the seats allotted for two alternates.

The usual commotion ensued. Those who had just settled into the long pews and heard their names announced picked up their backpacks and tote bags and scuttled past their neighbors to get to the center aisle and head for the jury box.

A middle-aged woman carrying four shopping bags and dressed for anything but success tried to detour away from the path set by the court officers to approach the bench. One of them put his arm out to stop her.

'But I have to tell the judge something.'

'I'll take you in turn, madam,' Fleming called out in her sternest voice. She liked to keep tight control of her courtroom.

'But I don't want to say what I'm going to say to you in public,' the woman whined.

'I'll give you the opportunity to talk to us privately. Do as we tell you for now.'

The woman reluctantly trudged to the box and took her seat in the number eight position.

Fleming began her general jury instructions. She introduced Gino and me, directing each of us to stand and spin around so that everyone in the room could see us.

She told them that the indictment contained eight counts, but that it was just a piece of paper, and that the defendant's innocence was presumed at this point.

I could hear juror number eight murmur to the group, 'Where there's smoke, there's fire. That's what an indictment means.' I assumed that she was on a mission to get herself excused and knew exactly which buttons to push.

'The top count with which Mr. Estevez is charged,' Fleming continued, 'is Section 230.34 of the Penal Law: Sex Trafficking.'

Prospective juror number eight gasped audibly and slumped down in her seat. 'Oh, my God. I knew he looked like a pervert. He oughta get the chair.'

This time, Gino Moretti heard her.

'Judge Fleming, I'd like to approach the bench with Ms. Cooper.'

He reached there before I could push back and get to my feet.

'What is it with you, Moretti?' the judge asked, cupping her hand over her mouth so the jurors couldn't hear her.

'You've got a whack job in the box and she's going to poison the well if you don't remove her right now,' he said. 'Didn't you hear her?'

He repeated the second statement she made and I filled in the first.

Fleming slammed her gavel on the desktop. 'The lady in the number eight seat, you're excused.'

'Who, me? But I want to see you, Your Honor. I want to tell you what my issue is.'

'Just follow the court officer. Before you wind up with a bigger problem than you think you have now. And zip your mouth while you're on your way out.'

Fleming took the summons stub from the clerk, looked at the name, and ordered her to have the woman removed from all future service.

'You ladies and gentlemen in the audience,

raise your hand if you heard anything that woman said,' the judge said.

Not one hand went up.

'Those of you in the jury box,' she said, waving her glasses back and forth over the two rows of stunned spectators who had been within earshot of the woman, 'you're all excused with my gratitude. See you in six years.'

Before they could gather their belongings and follow the crazy lady out of the room, the heavy doors creaked open again.

'You caught a break, Alex,' Fleming said to me. 'Did you coach her? Is she part of your stalling-for-time routine?'

'Beyond my doing, Your Honor, but I like her thinking.'

'Well, speak of the devil,' Moretti said. 'Detective Michael Chapman, Manhattan North Homicide. We got a body I don't know about?'

I spun around and saw Mike standing at the back of the large room. He was holding the door open for the exiting line of prospective jurors.

'Speak of what?' Fleming asked.

'I told you Alex had detectives lined up to break my legs. Seems not to be an idle threat if she's got Chapman on board.'

'Did your man Estevez kill somebody?' the judge said to Moretti as she motioned to Mike to approach the bench.

'Chapman has nothing to do with this case,' I said. 'I have no idea why he's here.'

'Don't get flustered, Alex,' Moretti said to me. 'I think we all have a good idea why he's here, or haven't you heard, Judge Fleming?'

13

'Can we take a break, Your Honor?' I asked. 'I can assure you it's nothing personal.'

'Ten-minute recess, ladies and gentlemen. You're not to leave this room, but you're free to check your messages and talk among yourselves,' Fleming said. Then she snapped at the captain as she stepped down from the bench. 'Make Mr. Estevez comfortable in his office.'

The fact that any defendant on trial was a prisoner at Rikers Island was supposed to be withheld from the jury. They dressed in civilian clothes, and but for being escorted back to the holding pen behind the courtroom surrounded by four armed men, most jurors would have to guess the fact that Estevez was actually incarcerated.

'Let's see what Chapman's got,' Fleming said. 'We'll go to my robing room.'

'Don't you have a *dis*robing room for them?' Moretti asked.

I walked ahead of Fleming and Moretti, into the short hallway that connected her robing room to the courtroom. Mike caught up with us, offering apologies to the judge, greeting Moretti and me, and closing the door behind him.

'Sorry to break up your trial, Judge. Commissioner Scully asked me to come over to deliver the news to Ms. Cooper face-to-face. Let you know there'll be a passel of reporters swarming around her when she leaves your courtroom.'

'I have no intention of letting her leave till the close of business, Mr. Chapman. Now, what's the story?'

My heart was racing. I couldn't make a connection between Mike and this defendant. I couldn't think of a reason for Mike to interrupt the middle of my working day, especially since our relationship had now become an intimate one. I was embarrassed by his presence.

'Bad news first. We had an attempted murder early this morning. Rape and stabbing of a teenager in Riverside Park. Likely to die when I got the call, but she seems to be coming around.'

'You're not getting Ms. Cooper on this one,' Fleming said.

'Not a problem,' I said, avoiding eye contact with both Mike Chapman and the judge. 'He's not here for me. I had a call on this case at nine A.M., before I knew there was anyone in custody, and assigned it to Marissa Bourges.'

Bourges was one of the best lawyers in my unit.

'The commissioner wanted me to deliver good news for a change, and make a plan with the judge about the media. We nailed the bastard who did the girl in the park an hour ago, Coop. It's Raymond Tanner. You're out of harm's way.'

2

'Sit down before you fall over,' the judge said to me. 'Take a deep breath.'

'I'm fine, Your Honor. Really I am. This is great news.' I was shaken by the mention of Tanner's latest attack, and the reality that I would now have to face him from the witness stand.

'Maybe he needs a good lawyer,' Moretti said. 'You might whisper my name in his ear, Chapman.'

'This is the scumbag — excuse me, Judge — that's got KILL COOP inked on his hand, Gino. I'm looking to do more to him than whisper in his ear. Some of his other body parts have my more immediate attention.'

'Don't tell me anything else about him,' Fleming said, clapping her hands over her ears. 'I don't want to have to recuse myself if this guy winds up in my courtroom. Siberia might not be cold enough for him.'

'The commissioner wants to know whether your court officers can take Alex down to her office at the end of the day. Just so the press guys don't throw microphones in her face.'

'Sure. We can put her right on the judges' elevator. Nobody has access to that bank.'

The tiny elevator kept the judiciary away from the great unwashed, so they didn't have to ride up and down with perps and witnesses, snitches and scoundrels of all sorts. It opened directly

16

into the back room of the office of District Attorney Paul Battaglia on the eighth floor of the massive courthouse.

'Perfect,' I said, trying to control the tremor in my hand by steadying it on the judge's desk. 'Where's Tanner now?'

'Look,' Fleming said. 'Why don't you two take five minutes in here? Answer all her questions, Detective, so she can get back to concentrating on the business at hand.'

Gino Moretti winked at me as he followed Janet Fleming out of the robing room, a stark space with only a desk, three chairs, and an empty bookcase. There were no curtains on the windows that overlooked the narrow passage of Hogan Place. Elsewhere in the courthouse the judge had chambers with a large office, well decorated and watched over by her secretary.

'You're okay now, Coop,' Mike said, bracing his back against the door to the room.

I bit my lip and nodded.

'This is weird, don't you think, kid? That you're just standing there staring at me?'

'What's weird about it? I'm not staring.' I shifted my eyes from Mike's face, focusing on a button on his navy blazer.

'Six months ago, if the same thing had happened, the judge would have walked out and you'd be clinging to me for dear life, asking me to tell you details and stop you from shaking.'

'It's different now.'

'Yeah, it's different,' he said, brushing back a shock of dark hair. 'It's supposed to be better. C'mere.'

I walked toward Mike and let him wrap his arms around me. Inside that embrace had always felt like the safest place to be. We had started working together more than a decade ago, and throughout those years had become best friends. Just two months earlier, in August, we had crossed the line and turned our friendship into a romance. I still wasn't clear on how that would affect things on the job — at crime scenes, the morgue, my office, or his squad room.

Mike took my chin in his hand and tipped my face up to look into his. 'It's over for Tanner, Coop.'

'Don't kiss — '

'You think I was going to kiss you? Get over yourself, girl. I know where we are.' Mike threw his hands up in the air and walked to the window.

'Sorry for being so awkward,' I said. 'Where's Tanner now?'

'The lieutenant's going to hold him up uptown at the squad till you leave the building tonight. Whatever time that is. He just doesn't want you under the same roof at the same time.'

'Crazy to slow down his arraignment for that reason.' I walked to one of the chairs and sat down. 'Is he talking?'

'As in a confession? Not a word,' Mike said, walking to the desk, leaning on it as he looked into my eyes. 'We don't need anything from Tanner. Put together all the stuff he's been doing since he slipped out of his work release program and his rap sheet will reach to Cleveland.'

'The girl, Mike. The likely from this morning. How's she doing?'

'Collapsed lung from the stab wound, but

18

she's out of surgery and expected to make it.'

'No lead pipe?' The lethal weapon had been his signature in several cases.

'Except for the crater in this vic's head, you'd hardly know it was Tanner. Yeah, he had a pipe. Yeah, he tried to smash her skull with it. The guys just haven't found it yet.'

'Who collared him?' I asked, over my own reaction and interested now in the details. 'Please tell me it was Mercer.'

'That's a better attitude. Show me those whites, Coop.'

I smiled at him, reaching out and covering his hand with one of mine.

'Call it rookie luck. A kid on patrol heard screams, but they stopped so abruptly that he couldn't find the location. Tanner apparently laid low for a couple of hours, hiding in one of those huge rock formations in the park till the cops scoured the area and cleared out. This kid asks his boss if he could stay on the scene for a while, guessing Tanner hadn't made it far. Good instincts. And he asked for the K9 Unit to give him a dog to sniff around. The rookie eventually broke with the rules — let the dog off the leash to hunt on his own — and the animal actually rousted the rapist from his spot. The kid saw Tanner running down a grassy slope toward the river. Gave chase and caught up with a blood-spattered perp.'

'Sounds impressive,' I said. 'The knife?'

'Yeah. Tanner dropped it during the chase.'

'They'll get prints off it? Or submit it for touch D — ?'

'You know what?' Mike said, straightening up and adjusting his tie as he walked to open the door. 'They'll do everything they're supposed to without you breathing down their necks. They're pros, kid. Just like you think you are. You get back to Mr. Estevez.'

'When do we celebrate? I mean, not us, but the team.'

'You do what you gotta do for the rest of the afternoon. A few of us will be lifting a glass to that rookie a little later this evening. You'll be the first to know where.'

I headed for the door. 'The lieutenant call you in on this today?'

'No, no. Mercer gave me the heads-up first, and the commissioner knew I had a keen interest in the motherfucker's arrest.'

'So you're still doing a midnight?'

'That's what the Loo tells me. Lets you get a good night's sleep.'

'The weekend can't come soon enough.'

'Scoot, Coop.'

One of the court officers was waiting for me in the hallway. Mike walked past us and we entered the courtroom. Fleming nodded at the captain to return the defendant from the small cell that held him during these proceedings to his place at counsel table.

Janet Fleming gaveled the group back to order and asked the clerk to put fourteen more citizens in the box. 'And if I didn't tell you earlier, folks, once you leave here tonight, there will be no tweeting, no Facebooking, no Instagramming your buddies about what goes on in here. For the forty dollars a day the state pays you, you get your train fare and your hot dog from the umbrella man in front of the building. No selfies with me or my staff. You don't get to link in or friend me, understood?'

She rose again to project her voice to the entire room. 'This is just to remind you that the unexpected interruption had absolutely nothing to do with the case at trial. You are not to speculate about anything you see or hear the parties do. The only evidence will come from that witness box, or from physical evidence and exhibits introduced during the trial,' she said, going on with the general instructions.

Fleming liked to control the voir dire of the panel as well. She would allow Moretti and me to ask a limited number of questions, but it wasn't like the old days when a lawyer could free-form and inquire about magazine subscriptions or favorite television shows, hoping to glean a bias that would make a juror's exclusion automatic.

After the judge finished forty-five minutes of questioning and entertaining three requests to be excused from the case, Fleming nodded to me for my turn. I carried an old green felt board, eighteen inches long, with two slotted tiers that held the summons for each of the individuals seated in front of me, so that I had their names and addresses at the ready. I rested it on the wooden flap that served as a mini podium attached to the side of the jury box.

'Good afternoon, Mr. Riley,' I said to the man in the first seat. An unemployed electrical engineer, he had tried in vain to have Fleming let him go. He didn't answer me but stared straight ahead, determined — it seemed to me — to make himself unlikeable to Moretti and me so as not to make the cut.

The second juror was my age — thirty-eight — and a professor of women's studies at Columbia College. I was quick with her, too, for the opposite reason. Human trafficking had become a hot-button issue with feminists and academics, and I had the gut instinct that she would be sympathetic to my victim, despite the witness's history of prostitution. No need for me to open any doors for Moretti to slip in and knock her off.

Prospective juror number three was a challenge. An African-American male in his early thirties, he seemed affable and engaged in the proceedings, but a bit too eager to get the attention of the defendant, who looked over at the box from time to time. His black T-shirt featured a small logo of a pizza in the center of his chest, although I found the large neon green letters above it — EAT ME — to be not only off-putting but also totally inappropriate for the occasion.

'Mr. How-ton,' I said, phonetically breaking up the name that I read on the summons. It was spelled *Houghton*. 'Am I pronouncing it correctly?'

'Nope. No, you're not. My people say Huff-ton.'

Strike one for me.

'Could you tell us a little more about the work

you do at Metropolitan Hospital?' He had his sneakered feet up against the wall of the jury box. His hands were clasped together and he was twiddling his thumbs somewhat nervously.

'I'm, like, a phlebotomist, you know?'

'So you're trained to draw blood.'

'I'm in a tech program right now. I'm being trained,' Houghton said, looking over at Antonio Estevez. 'I'm not quite Dracula yet.'

Estevez pulled back one side of his mouth in half a smile and Houghton laughed. Half of the prospective jurors laughed with him, at my expense.

Strike two for me.

'Is there anything you've heard so far that might make you uncomfortable sitting on a case of this nature?' I asked.

'Nah. You gotta prove what you gotta prove.'

'One of the charges here is that Mr. Estevez used force to compel a young woman to engage in acts of prostitution. You understand that?'

'I'm good.'

I walked toward the railing at the end of the well of the courtroom. 'Do you know who Jason Voorhees is, Mr. Houghton?'

He sat up straight and dropped his feet to the floor. 'You kidding me? Of course I do.'

Jurors number two and four looked at him, puzzled by either the question or his answer.

'Miss Cooper,' Judge Fleming said, glancing up from her notebook, 'I hope you're going somewhere with this.'

'I am, Your Honor.' I continued talking with Mr. Houghton. 'And who is Jason Voorhees?'

23

'He's the guy — the creepy one with that kind of full-face hockey mask — in the *Friday the 13th* movies.'

Gino Moretti was on his feet. 'I'm going to object to this line of questioning, Your Honor.'

'What's your point, Ms. Cooper?' the judge asked.

'We intend to present evidence that — '

'Wait a minute,' Moretti said, losing his cool. 'May we approach? She can present her evidence when she's got witnesses in the box.'

I wanted to give the prospective jurors a taste of the People's case. Houghton, after his Dracula reference, seemed a likely candidate to know the horror-movie genre. I thought I could see whether anyone in the room would be freaked-out by a description of Estevez, whose victims claimed he wore the distinctive goalie mask, punctuated by holes and painted with red triangles — and wielded the same machete Jason did — when he threatened them to go to work for him. Better to find out they had weak stomachs now than midtrial.

'It's not about the evidence, Judge. I'd like to — '

'I know what you'd like to do, Ms. Cooper. Don't even think about it. Next question, please.'

'Mr. Houghton, is there anything about your familiarity with the fictional movie character Jason Voorhees that would prevent you from analyzing the facts in this case, independent of — '

'I object,' Moretti said, practically shouting at the judge.

24

'Sustained, Ms. — '

But Houghton was ready to take his shot. 'Mr. Estevez isn't charged with hacking his old lady's head off like in the movie, is he? I didn't hear that count.'

The judge had to gavel the courtroom back to order, while Houghton basked in the amusement he had provoked with his response.

'Approach the bench, both of you,' Fleming said, making her displeasure clear when we got within earshot. 'Over and out, Alex. You're done. Move on to the next seat and ask a few questions and then Gino takes it from there.'

'Understood.'

'Do you want a curative instruction, Gino?' she asked.

'Are you crazy, Judge? Call a little more attention to it? Spare me a 'No, ladies and gentleman, Mr. Estevez is neither a vampire nor a homicidal maniac.''

'He's just a pumped-up pimp,' I said, whispering to Moretti, 'who uses masks and machetes to coerce young women — to scare them to death — so they turn tricks from which he profits.'

'Your choice,' the judge said.

'If you're not going to allow me to ask anything else,' I said, 'I'd like you to go a little deeper into the meaning of sex trafficking, Judge. It's not a familiar statute to most jurors.'

The sex-trade profession may be the oldest on earth, but the crime was a very new one on the books, ramped up recently in recognition of the brutal nature of sex slavery and the inadequacy of the old 'promoting prostitution' laws.

'I'll entertain some questions from you, Alex, but keep them within reason.'

The door creaked open at the rear of the room. I didn't bother to turn this time as I tried to suggest a punch list for Fleming to use.

Her law assistant assiduously made notes of my comments, while the judge had her eyes on whoever had entered the room.

When I did glance back, I saw a neatly turned-out twenty-something-year-old striding down the aisle, making for the first pew, a row kept empty for press and for family and friends of the accused, directly behind Gino Moretti's seat. She looked familiar to me. I had seen her recently, in the corridor near my office.

'Keep going, Alex,' the judge said to me, chewing on the arm of her eyeglasses. 'That's not the colleague you've been waiting for, is it?'

'No.'

' 'Cause if it was, you might want to tell her she's sitting on the wrong side of the courtroom.'

'She's new. She's a paralegal in the Child Abuse Unit, I think.'

'Cute kid. She could give some cred to Mr. Estevez, sitting at his back, fluttering her eyelashes over here at Gino.'

'She's in the right place, Your Honor,' Moretti said. 'Seated on the side of the angels.'

'You must mean my side, Gino,' I said, smiling at him. 'That's why she's working in my office. Maybe I'll scoop her up for the Special Victims Unit.'

'You're missing my point, Alexandra. That

young woman is married to Antonio Estevez.'

'She's *what?*'

Fleming was on her feet again. 'Lower your voice, Alex. I don't need a situation here.'

'I don't think she's been in the office a month,' I said, my jaw clenched. 'I'll bet she didn't put that fact on her job application. I can't imagine the hiring administrator — '

'Of course it's not on her application,' Moretti said, one eye on me and one on the attractive young woman who was trying to get the attention of the defendant. 'The wedding was at Rikers Island last weekend. I was the best man.'

I was steaming mad. 'I'd like a recess, Judge. I need to find out — '

'Don't try to stall this anymore, Alex,' Moretti said. 'Shit happens. There's nothing illegal about marrying an inmate.'

Antonio Estevez looked back and saw his bride. She mouthed words to him, but I couldn't read her lips. He nodded. Then she blew him a kiss and got up to leave.

'Excuse me, Judge, but I've got to talk to her. I'll be right back,' I said.

Most of the prospective jurors were riveted by this bit of courtroom drama. Gino and I were having a standoff in front of the judge and the young paralegal was sashaying her way out of court. The jurors were staring at us as I took off after the new Mrs. Estevez.

'You've got no business, Alex,' Moretti yelled after me.

'Hold it right there, Ms. Cooper,' the judge said as she banged her gavel on the bench.

'Captain, don't let the DA out of here.'

The door slammed behind the paralegal and the captain of the court officers squared himself in front of it.

'I'd like to see you both in the robing room,' Fleming said to Moretti and me. 'Ladies and gentlemen, I apologize for the lack of decorum in my courtroom. You're excused from service for the next six years, with the thanks of the court.'

I walked past the judge on my way to the side door next to the jury box.

'You may have been looking for a mistrial, Ms. Cooper,' Fleming said, 'but you are far more likely to have me find you in contempt right now, cooling down in a jail cell next to Mr. Estevez, before I give you the chance to pull that kind of stunt on me again.'

3

'So what's the story, Alex?' the judge asked. She parked herself behind the bare wooden desk and invited Moretti and me to sit opposite her. 'You started this afternoon's session by saying that you were waiting for someone from your office to come up with information. Was Señora Estevez your courier? You knew this whole charade was about to happen? Showtime for the prospective jurors?'

'Absolutely not, Judge.'

'What, then?'

I hesitated. 'May we go ex parte on this for a few minutes? Would you mind stepping out, Gino, while I explain the problem?'

'You bet I'd mind. I'm as curious as the judge.'

'That's a new legal standard?' Fleming asked. 'Curiosity? There'd be a lot of dead cats in this courthouse.'

'I'd rather answer the question you asked out of the presence of counsel, Your Honor. It's a confidential matter,' I said.

'What news were you waiting for, Alex?' the judge pressed.

'Just so you understand, there's an internal investigation in progress. When it was launched,' I said, looking at my adversary, 'it had nothing to do with your client. And I assure you that work will go on.'

'See, Judge?' Moretti said. 'Another threat.'

'It's not a threat, Gino. It's a fact. When I got into my office this morning, I was notified by the head of the IT team that someone outside my unit had tried to hack into my computer file on this case.'

'Oh, the drama in your world is — '

Judge Fleming silenced Moretti with one slam of her hand on the desk. 'From outside the office, you mean?'

'No, no. Someone unauthorized to see my trial documents, but with access to the DANY system, logged in and tried to get through the firewall that was set up for my staff only.'

'Nice touch, Gino,' Janet Fleming said, nodding as she stared straight through Moretti's blank face. 'The virgin bride, perhaps?'

'Hold on, Judge. No pointing fingers at me,' he said, bracing both hands on his chest.

'And just a minute ago you were best man. Short honeymoon, Gino,' Fleming said with a sneer. 'Go on, Alex.'

'When I came up to court this afternoon, Your Honor, we had no suspect and no reason to think anyone in the office had a connection to Mr. Estevez. Maybe someone was surfing and accidentally punched the wrong docket number into the database. I was hoping to get an answer to stop the spread of some sensitive information — hopefully find some virtual fingerprints of an inexperienced colleague before you impaneled a jury. That's why I was so anxious and, frankly, trying to stall you.'

'Nothing yet?'

'I'd say I can tell my team to narrow the list of suspects to just one young woman, don't you think?' There are five hundred prosecutors in the Manhattan District Attorney's Office and a support staff twice that size. 'Would you mind if I called the investigators with the wedding news?'

Fleming dug her cell phone out of her pocket and handed it to me.

'What's her name, Gino?' I asked him as I dialed.

'She's Mrs. Estevez now.' He shrugged his shoulders. 'How the hell should I know what it was two weeks ago?'

Fleming slammed her hand down again. 'Do better than that, Gino.'

'Her first name is Josie. It's Josie.'

'Laura?' I said when my secretary answered the phone. 'As fast as you can move, okay? Call the squad and tell whoever is closest to the door to come down and grab on to — '

'No!' Moretti shouted.

'Step into the hallway, Gino,' Fleming said. 'Now you're out of order.'

'They need to grab that new kid down the corridor. Josie is her name and — '

'Bring her right up to me,' Fleming said, talking over me.

'Laura? Still there? That's the judge speaking. I don't know who Josie works for exactly, but they can cuff her if necessary and bring her up to Part 53. We're in the robing room.'

'Cuff her?' Moretti said. 'You two are going overboard. There's an innocent view of this that you haven't even considered. My client isn't — '

'Move faster, Gino.'

'But, Judge — ?'

I put one hand over my ear while Fleming laced into my adversary.

'You know, when I was in your shoes and stood up in court for a client,' she said, 'I was the client. I thought for him, I talked for him, I bled for him if necessary. I was going to be cleaner than a hound's tooth so no one could hold any of my conduct against a guy who was already behind the eight ball. But you? You're just gaming me. You're gaming the system. And that's the lowest type of animal life in my courtroom.'

'I'm not gaming anybody. I had no idea.' Moretti couldn't bring himself to walk out. 'Like it's okay for a prosecutor and a cop to hook up, right, but not for anybody else? For a paralegal or even the accused, who is still presumed innocent even though you're the one presiding, Judge Fleming. At least that's my guess. You don't think that kind of incestuous relationship between Cooper and her homicide hotshot compromises how an investigation gets worked?'

'Don't go there, Gino,' I said.

'Close the door behind you,' Fleming added, waving the back of her hand at him.

I was still on the phone. 'Yes, Laura. I'm here. Now call IT and tell them it's this Josie kid who's most likely trying to break into the database. They need to stop whatever else they're looking at and get on her computer. Find out what's on it and lock it down. Then call me back once you make contact. I'm on the judge's cell,' I said, asking Fleming for her number and repeating it to Laura.

'What's there to get from your files, Alex?' the judge asked.

I bit my lip. 'More than you need to know at this point.'

'Give it up. I'm not going to be able to try this case. Ex parte, ex schmarte. Whatever adjournment you get, this one is already too messy for me to handle. I'll be reassigning it today. Is it the women?'

'Yeah. And I'd have to say girls, not women. Estevez likes them young. Names, addresses, aliases. Every which way we have to find them.'

'Your victim?'

'Tiffany's safe. I spent most of yesterday with her and she was good when she went home. Mercer had officers pick her up this morning when we learned this attempt was being made to gain access to my files and they're babysitting her in a hotel.'

'So Estevez is smart enough, desperate enough, to actually plant a mole in your office?'

'Apparently so. That idea never occurred to me.'

'And Gino?' the judge asked. 'Do you think he's capable of — ?'

'No way,' I said, walking to the window to look down at the street behind the courthouse. 'I can't imagine he's involved.'

'Very gracious of you, Alex,' Fleming said sarcastically. 'I wouldn't be quite so certain. These other girls, are they in danger?'

'I suppose it depends on whether Josie was

successful in breaking and entering into my computer system. It's a big ring this guy runs. He's got a posse out there who stand to lose a lot of money if Estevez goes down.'

The first few distinctive notes of the theme song from *The Good, the Bad and the Ugly* played out on Fleming's phone. She looked at the incoming number and passed it to me.

'Two guys from the squad have been dispatched to look for Josie. Josie Aponte. She's a brand-new paralegal assigned to Child Abuse,' Laura said. 'And the IT crew is headed straight for her computer.'

'Make sure the techies hold back until the detectives are hands-on, so we don't tip off that we're onto her if she doesn't know yet. That should be done within five minutes, right?' The District Attorney's Office Squad, an elite branch of the NYPD with officers handpicked to work complex investigations, had its own version of a mini precinct just one flight upstairs from my wing. 'Keep me posted.'

Judge Fleming reached for her phone and started for the door. 'Let's move this to the courtroom. I want to put this whole thing on the record. The Bar Association can make Gino sweat out his role in this. Let's see if I can get Josie's prenup out of her. I haven't had my chance to do a tough cross since I graduated to my judicial robes.'

'I think we've met our match,' I said, following her out. 'Can you imagine what balls it takes to go through all the security clearance for this job, then walk in ready to commit a felony, smiling at me every time she passed me in the hallway? Josie's made of tough stuff.'

'Estevez says he's got a kid. It's hers?'

'I don't think so. There's a baby mama, but he keeps her away from all his business.'

The court officers and reporter were caught by surprise when Fleming and I walked back in. Moretti was on the phone but hung up when he saw us.

The judge stepped onto the bench and everyone resumed his or her position.

'You want Mr. Estevez in here?' the captain asked.

'No. Not now. Not ever again,' Fleming said. 'Tell him I hope his parole officer hasn't been born yet.'

Moretti was seething.

'I'm thinking of who the toughest judge on the block is, and that's where this case will be tried. I'll adjourn this for a month,' she said, tossing the case folder to the captain to hand to the clerk. 'Let Eddie Torres have a crack at Mr. Estevez.'

The Honorable Edwin Torres was as formidable as he was smart and solid. The fact that he packed heat was known to every inmate, and none had dared any tricks in his courtroom.

'Your call, Mr. Moretti. Do you want to testify before or after Ms. Aponte?'

'Testify about what, Your Honor?'

Fleming was trying to come up with a reason to get Gino on the witness stand. 'People's lives are at risk here, sir. Do you understand that? What did you know about this harebrained

35

scheme to get into Ms. Cooper's files?'

'Nothing. Absolutely nothing. Is Aponte Josie's surname? I didn't even know that.'

'You better hope she says the same thing. She'll be up here in — what?' Fleming asked, looking at me.

'Probably another few minutes.'

'Ladies first, Your Honor,' Moretti said.

'Cute, Moretti,' Fleming said. 'This just happens to be the wrong time and place for cute.'

'You want me to question her, Judge?' I asked.

'Not a chance. She's all mine.' The young woman had flaunted her relationship with Estevez in open court, and Fleming would try to hold her toes to the fire, on the record, before the police met with a refusal to answer questions. She opened her notebook and started to write in it. 'Just give me some background, Ms. Cooper. Was Josie Aponte one of the women in the defendant's stable? Did she work for him?'

'I don't believe so. I never heard her name before today.'

'What's his MO?'

I didn't answer.

'Stand up and start talking, Ms. Cooper.'

I didn't want to give away my whole case to Moretti, but I was getting the feeling that it wouldn't matter much at this point.

'On your feet. That's good. How did Estevez meet his girls?'

'He's got a couple of young men on the payroll who scout for him.'

'You know their names?'

36

'I do, but — '

'Don't worry. If I need them when I'm questioning Señora Estevez, you'll give them to me. Scouted where?'

'The usual places, Your Honor. One went inside the Port Authority terminal, trolling for runaways who get off the bus from some godforsaken town a thousand miles away, twenty-four/seven. No shortage of hungry young girls in that hellhole. The second guy waits outside, in the Slade.'

'Not so fast,' Fleming said, scribbling in her book. 'What's a Slade?'

'Sorry. Street name for a Cadillac Escalade. It's the Estevez pimpmobile of choice. The sweet-talker who was inside the terminal opens the back of the SUV. Shows off the goods — '

'Goods?'

'Whatever he's promised to the kid he's trying to hook. If she's seventeen and likes sequins and high-heel shoes, he's got some glitzy clothes to show her. If she's fourteen and wants designer makeup and bubble gum, there's plenty of that.'

'Then it's into the Slade and off to meet the wizard. That's how it goes?'

'On a good night, yes, Your Honor.'

'Pay close attention, Moretti. Pretend like you're hearing this for the first time. Where's the meet, Ms. Cooper?'

'Mr. Estevez keeps a separate apartment, just for the purpose of breaking in the young women. Not the address on the court papers, which is his home.'

'You've seen it?'

'Detectives executed the search warrant I drafted, Judge. Lots of photographs for the jury. Three bedrooms — one for him, another for a female assistant who hangs out there to chill with the girls and prep them for Estevez, and the third for his intended victim.'

'Judge, I don't even know how to begin to object to what's going on here,' Moretti said.

'It's easy. You say 'objection' and tell me it's meant to cover everything that's being asked and answered for the next hour or so, and I'll say 'overruled.' I'll say it just once, and you'll understand I mean it for every time you would have flapped your mouth or even rolled your eyes at me. You don't represent Josie Aponte, and this hearing is about *her* conduct. You're extraneous to this whole proceeding, Mr. Moretti. I'm just waiting to see whether your conscience makes an appearance today.'

'May I continue, Your Honor?'

'Yes, Ms. Cooper.'

'The apartment I'm referring to has been completely sound-proofed.'

'Loud music? Parties?'

'Not much of either, Judge. It's mostly to muffle the screaming.'

'That should have been obvious to me. I must be slipping. You've got a rape charge in here?' she said, referring to the indictment.

'In almost every instance, Estevez starts with a sexual assault on the victim. No grooming period, no adjustment. They're brought to the apartment one at a time, and he makes each one have sex with him.'

'What's the force? Or is that what you mentioned in the voir dire?'

'No, the trafficking aspect starts later. There are at least two rape charges per victim. One is statutory because they're all under the age of consent. The other is first-degree. Estevez uses physical force. Smacks them around when they resist, uses neckties and socks to secure them to the headboard, then has intercourse.'

'These girls have injuries? They've been examined — ?'

'No injuries,' Moretti said. 'Not a single one. Not a scratch.'

Fleming looked me. 'Is that true?'

'Estevez and his crew don't let the girls go, Judge. That's the whole point. First he takes a shot at them, one girl at a time. One sexual assault at a time. Then he and one of his alums from the program — an older woman, like, maybe nineteen — spend a few weeks softening the kid up. The vic's made to think she's Estevez's girlfriend. Clothes, video games, music, a gradual introduction to drugs and alcohol. But they never get to leave the apartment. Not once.'

'Stockholm syndrome,' Fleming said. 'The girls form a traumatic bond with the hostage taker. That's how they protect themselves emotionally.'

'Of course Ms. Cooper will have to prove that.'

'Apparently she thinks she can, Mr. Moretti. Go on.'

'That's why there's no medical evidence,' I said. 'Nothing contemporaneous to the initial assaults. The second series of events begins after the bonding. It's the period of coercing the young women to work for him. To be trafficked.'

'A machete and a full-face mask?'

'Accompanied by some powerful verbal threats, and the backup of the posse just waiting to have at them. Then Estevez has them branded and off they — '

'Branded?'

'The tattoo, Judge,' I said. 'When they're ready to turn tricks, he brings in a tattoo artist, to make sure they're each marked as his property.'

'Is that part of the torture?'

'Most of them view it that way.'

'Oh, please, Ms. Cooper,' Moretti said. 'These kids leave home with more tats and piercings than most carnies have by the time they're forty. What's one more?'

I reached into my file for some photographs. 'The Antonio Estevez logo, Judge.'

I handed one of them to the court officer to pass to Judge Fleming.

She turned it upside down. 'What am I looking at? What body part?'

'That's the inner thigh, about an inch below where Ms. Glover's left leg meets her torso.'

'And the image?' Fleming said, squinting at the inked area.

'It's supposed to be a woman in the center, with a man on each side of her.'

'The men are both aroused, it seems to me.'

'That's the plan.'

'And the words? Do I see lettering?' Fleming said, putting on her glasses.

'Yes, ma'am,' I said. 'It's all about power and control for Estevez. It spells out, I SHARE MY BITCH. They seem to be the words he lives by.'

'A sentiment that will serve him well in state prison, I'm sure,' the judge said, looking up when she heard the courtroom door open, 'where he's probably hoping that he's not the one who becomes the bitch.'

It was one of the detectives from the squad, Drew Poser, walking toward counsel table.

'Bring Ms. Aponte right in, Officer. She's not Ms. Cooper's witness; she's mine.'

'I don't have her, Judge,' Poser said, holding his arms out to his sides. 'That's what I'm here to tell you.'

'Did she give you a hard time, Detective?'

'I mean she's history. No hard time. No time at all.'

'But she works on the eighth floor,' I said. 'She whispered something to the defendant and then she went back downstairs to the office.'

'Maybe what she whispered was 'sayonara,' Alex, 'cause she never swiped her ID to get back into our offices from the elevator bank. And there's nothing personal at her work space. No pocket-book, no cell phone — nothing but an empty desk.'

'So Josie Aponte just quit?'

'I don't think she worried about giving the traditional two weeks' notice, Alex. Not once she got exactly what she apparently came here for.'

'I know,' I said, taking my seat at the table and massaging my aching head with both hands. 'The entire case file of Antonio Estevez.'

'I'd say she's got a copy of pretty much everything that's on your computer. Maybe that's what she wanted to communicate to your perp,' Poser said. 'All I can tell you, Alex, is you've got no secrets now.'

4

It was four fifteen when Drew Poser and three of the court officers from Part 53 walked me down the quiet corridor to the private elevator, tucked in the southeast corner of the courthouse and accessed by a key distributed only to judges, security staff, and the district attorney himself.

'I'll take her from here,' Poser said.

'What was the adjourned date?' I asked, unable to concentrate on anything but the information on my computer that now made so many people vulnerable to the Estevez crew.

'You got a month, Ms. Cooper,' one of the officers said. 'Judge Torres, November twentieth.'

'Can you believe this, Drew?' I said as the doors closed. 'You know how much work we've got in front of us now? Victims to call, detectives to warn. God knows what's on there.'

'Aponte won't get far. Special Victims is pulling all their guys off the street to concentrate on finding her before she can spread the word.'

The doors opened onto the anteroom at the rear of District Attorney Paul Battaglia's office. He had been the elected prosecutor of New York County for so many terms that the physical space had been overrun by awards from every civic group in the city, hanging on walls and leaning against bookcases. The strong odor of the Cohibas that he smoked from the crack of dawn till he closed his eyes at night infused every inch of territory he occupied.

'Laura said to tell you that Battaglia wants you,' Poser said, steering me away from the exit door to the hallway and toward the DA's inner sanctum. He knocked and I heard Battaglia call for me to come in. Drew Poser opened the door but backed off and was gone.

'You ought to be beaming about Raymond Tanner's arrest,' the DA said as I crossed the enormous room to get to his desk, 'but instead you look like the bottom fell out.'

'It did. We had to adjourn my trial just now. Antonio Estevez.'

'Damn. I've got that human-trafficking key-note for the White House conference in three weeks. I wanted to go in with a hot verdict. What did you do that for?' Battaglia's annoyance was palpable. He bit into the half-smoked cigar as he talked to me.

'It wasn't entirely my doing.'

Why wasn't I surprised that none of my colleagues had come in to the district attorney to tell him that there had been a serious breach of security? No one liked delivering bad news to him. He was the kind of recipient who delighted in shooting the messenger.

'What happened to Fleming?'

'Not her fault, either,' I said, telling him an abbreviated version of the story.

'Who's responsible for hiring the Aponte girl? How did she pass a background investigation?' He reached for his phone to ensure that heads would start to roll.

'The squad is on it, Paul. The story isn't even

44

an hour old. Let me get facts for you.'

'Get me names. That's the surest way to get facts.' Battaglia was a man who held a grudge. There were political enemies he was proud of telling me he had despised for decades, though he often couldn't recall what had occasioned the hatred.

'I've got to go see what else was cherry-picked off my computer,' I said.

'The Tanner arrest is good news, Alex. I had the local reporters in here a little while ago. They want a couple of lines from you, but I told them I'm not letting you talk. Any problem with that?'

'None, thanks. That's just the way it should be. And I'll give you all the news on Estevez as the cops work it through.'

'Your computer files — did she get every-thing?'

'I'm about to find out. I was under the impression that each case entered into my system has its own security code. I'm praying that she only got into Estevez's file. It's bad enough with the number of victims in his case — finding them, relocating them, making them safe,' I said. 'Keeping them under our wing so they'll show up for trial. If she got anything else off my machine, I might as well disappear for a month.'

Battaglia removed the cigar from his mouth and blew smoke rings in my direction. 'There have actually been times I'd have liked to make that happen to you. Right now isn't one of them.'

I made my way to the front door to let myself out.

'That memo I gave you during my last campaign, Alex,' Battaglia said, slowing me down.

'Which one?' I asked. The legal staff tried to keep a Chinese wall between the DA's politics and office business. I thought it safest to take the route of short-term memory loss. 'I don't know what you're talking about.'

'Reverend Hal. And you know exactly what I mean. Reverend Hal and his Church of the Perpetual Scam.'

The ill-tempered Harlem pastor had courted Battaglia and volunteered to support him in the most recent election, in exchange for this office looking the other way on a financial transaction with money stolen from tithed sums of parishioners.

I had been led to believe Battaglia had refused the offer, especially since it had been made shortly after an underage worshipper had come forward to my unit to report inappropriate sexual advances by Reverend Hal.

'I had no case against Shipley, Paul.' It was my practice to keep every file my unit had ever created, because of the recidivist nature of the crime. I'd even had victims who'd come back a second time. But I didn't want the wrath of Paul Battaglia on my back just yet. 'I'm sure Laura wiped the slate clean on your memo.'

I didn't have the slightest idea what the personal transaction between Shipley and Battaglia had actually been. I assumed, at worst, that the DA had planted his memo with me as a form of future insurance of his good intentions.

'Let me know what you find. You put me in any kind of embarrassing situation publicly, Alex, and you can be sure I'll hang you out to dry. You'll wish you had disappeared before I had the chance to get back to you.'

5

'Who died?' I asked, walking past Laura's empty desk into my office.

Three prosecutors were standing behind the chair in which the head of our Cybercrimes Division, Aaron Byrne was seated. Drew Poser and another detective were in front of the desk, stacking case folders in piles. They each looked like there was a corpse on display in the middle of the table.

'We're gathered here trying to save your ass,' Ryan Blackmer said. He was standing between Nan Toth and Catherine Dashfer, all three senior prosecutors from my unit. 'But if it takes mouth-to-mouth to get your career back on track, I've got other plans for the night.'

'The mere thought of that image inspires me to breathe deeply on my own, Ryan,' I said. 'How does it look?'

'Not as bad as I feared originally,' Aaron Byrne said. He was more skilled with computer navigation than any lawyer I knew.

'What did Aponte get?'

'First of all, her name isn't Josie Aponte, okay? A heavy dose of identity theft from a criminal justice student at John Jay College got her in the door of our hiring office.' Byrne was studying my computer screen and typing as fast as his fingers could go.

'So who is she?'

Catherine raised a finger to her lips. 'Shh. Let Aaron work.'

'Laura gave you my password?'

'A monkey could have gotten through that,' Aaron said. 'Nothing more creative than your law school initials and the year you graduated occurred to you?'

The University of Virginia — UVA — had been easy to remember after a dozen other changes over the years. I had gone through the initials of my fiance, Adam Nyman, who'd been killed in a car crash the night before our Vineyard wedding, and an assortment of significant dates in my life but had recently returned to the initials of my alma mater as the key to unlock my data.

'In fact, Alex has been looking for a monkey on Match.com,' Ryan said. 'Gave up her 'prosecutes perps' nickname for 'lonely lady lawyer.' Once she knocks off Estevez she can go with 'my pimp's a chimp.''

'Well, I've changed all the password info for you,' Aaron said, taking one hand off the keyboard to hand me a Post-it note with a series of hieroglyphics scribbled on it. 'Secure it. Learn it. Eyes only for you and Laura.'

'In fact, Chapman says Alex sometimes confuses that long prehensile monkey tail with another organ that — '

'Who cares what Chapman says, Ryan?' I snapped. 'What's Aponte's real name and how much of my case information is compromised?'

'We don't know who she is yet,' Drew said.

'She had to be fingerprinted to get this job,' I said.

49

'You don't think Estevez would try to embed a mole who'd be roadblocked before she got her toe in the door, do you? His mole has no criminal record. He's smart.'

'Smarter than I am; that's for sure.'

'Amen to that,' Ryan said. 'Your Wellesley degree with a major in English lit is taking a backseat to Antonio Estevez and his street cred.'

'So this girl — whoever she is,' I said, 'has no rap sheet, but she has the balls to take on this assignment. What'd she get?'

Aaron Byrne leaned into my screen. 'You're screwed on Estevez. She copied everything in that folder.'

'Damn. Damn it.' I was walking in circles, furious at myself for enabling this breach because of the obvious password I'd chosen. 'It's on my head now if anything happens to Tiffany and those other young women.'

Nan raised a hand at me. 'Calm down. Tiffany's under control and we'll find everyone else before his posse does. It's more important that you work with Aaron to identify the cases that might have been in the same portal.'

'Go through these folders with me, Alex,' Drew said, passing the top three to me.

'I thought the FBI claimed this setup was foolproof,' I said, taking them from him.

'Technically it is,' Catherine said. 'Except for human error.'

The feds' cyberteam had devised a special computer system for our office, in recognition of the fact that hundreds of thousands of case files had to be managed independently of one another. Too many people had access to computer stations — legal and support staff, civilian investigators and cops — that were spread out in both of the large city buildings we inhabited. The sheer volume of DANY employees put a lot of information at risk.

People of the State of New York v. Andrew Kreston.

I focused on the name on the manila folder, first in a tall stack of cases awaiting trial or reassignment to another unit member. Each of the files contained at least one count of sexual assault. Some had top charges of murder in the first degree, while others referenced surviving victims who had been subjected to just about every kind of abuse one might imagine.

'Kreston,' I said, trying to think of the way I had structured my virtual storage cabinet. 'Sodomy first degree. Male victim. Drugged and assaulted. No connection to Estevez.'

'Legal issues,' Aaron said. 'Any overlap?'

'None whatsoever.'

'Looks like you've got it firewalled. Should be fine.'

'Second one is Harry Wiggins. Serial rapist. Four victims, all strangers. Housing projects on the Lower East Side. Nothing to do with trafficking.'

I put that folder to the side and looked at the third one. 'Jamil Jenners. Attempted murder, attempted rape. Choked a woman till she lost consciousness. She was coming out of the restroom in a Chelsea club.'

'Clean and clear,' Aaron said.

I reached over for the Wiggins case.

'Go back a step,' I said, unhooking the red string from the back of the folder and pulling out the papers.

Aaron Byrne stopped typing and looked up at me. 'I thought you said not related.'

'The cases have nothing to do with each other. But both of them involved a motion to consolidate the counts in order to try the defendant for all his victims at once. Gino Moretti opposed it successfully, and the lawyer for Wiggins tried the same tactic, too, without a shot.'

'You mean you used the identical motion papers in both instances?'

'I'm trying to think,' I said, pulling on strands of my hair. 'It was three months ago.'

Everyone was staring at me.

'I'm just not sure, but it's possible.'

Catherine picked up my phone. 'Is there a speed dial to Special Victims?'

'The second button.'

'Is your travel agent on speed dial, too?' Ryan asked. 'One way to Afghanistan. Leaving tonight.'

'Take it.' I handed the folder to Ryan. 'You've always wanted this one. The *Post* will give you front-page ink if you nail this guy. I'm nauseous even thinking about the possibility that someone like Estevez knows where to find these good people.'

I could hear the clacking keys of the computer as Aaron Byrne tried to figure if the case had been stolen by the Aponte impostor.

'All good here, Alex,' Aaron said. 'You only used a blank template for your motion for joinder. You used language and names specific to each case, so there's no hole in the wall.'

Ryan pushed the folder back in my direction.

I shook my head. 'Keep it. Estevez has been put over for a month. Get Wiggins in front of a jury as soon as you can.'

Drew Poser kept passing folders to me while I racked my brain to think of common features between and among the cases.

When we finished scouring the two piles on the desktop, Catherine began to read through the index cards boxed on the far corner of my desk. They contained the hundreds of names of defendants indicted by other lawyers in the unit.

I perched myself on the arm of one of the chairs and rubbed my forehead. 'I approved all of these grand jury actions at the time they were submitted, but you'll have to refresh me on some of them. There are so many.'

'Okay,' she said when I gave her a blank look after the sixth or seventh name. 'Wanda Evins. You must know this. The mother who brought her fifteen-year-old daughter to New York from Kansas City to set her up for business during the Super Bowl last year.'

I closed my eyes. 'Check that one, Aaron.'

'She was pimping her kid?' he asked.

'I'm sure I cross-referenced this with Estevez. It actually fit the trafficking laws.'

'Yes,' Nan said, 'but mother and child are tucked away at home in Kansas. I'll get the screening sheet and call to check on them.'

'Go back to what you said to me in the courtroom, Drew.'

'About what?'

I stepped out of my heels and ran my stockinged feet across the ratty carpet. 'My secrets. You said that all my secrets are gone.'

'Well, I was just — '

'What did you mean?'

'Nothing, really.'

'He meant that a lot of your personal information wasn't well protected, Alex,' Aaron Byrne said. 'Yeah, Wanda Evins is a hit.'

'I'm on it,' Nan said. 'I'll cover them.'

'All the stuff in your Word files isn't secure, in the way most of the case folders seem to be. Like, here's a bunch of letters.'

'You keep personal correspondence on here?' Ryan asked.

'No. No, I don't.'

'Letters to the Bar Association, looks like some to a few of your victims, recommendations for a couple of guys who left the office this year. By the way, the one to the City Bar has got your home address on it, Alex.'

'That's where they bill me.'

'What's the difference?' Drew Poser asked. 'Everything anyone wants to know about people is on the web. I'm sure Alex's phone, her e-mail, her contacts, her shoe size — it's all out there.'

'Then why did you make the crack about my secrets? What do you think I've got to conceal?'

'Your thin skin, for one thing,' Ryan said. 'You want everybody to think you've got the hide of an elephant when you're soft as a marshmallow inside.'

'I'm just drained. It's been a lousy day.'

There was nothing personal on my office computer, I reassured myself. My texts and e-mails were a different thing. They wouldn't make good reading for strangers.

'What the hell is this?' Aaron said, throwing his hands up in the air like the keyboard was toxic. 'Why in God's name are you mentioned in a letter from the district attorney himself to Reverend Hal Shipley? It sounds like Battaglia took money from that Jhericurled dirtbag, and then you dropped a case against him?'

'I didn't have any case — and no, I wasn't aware I was cc'd on any correspondence,' I said, looking from one friend's face to another as I started to pace across the room. 'Are we going blood oath for a moment? Cone of silence? 'Cause the DA is going to have my head on this.'

'Have your head on what?' Nan asked. 'Or is this the cue for me to say I've got to be going?'

'Don't leave me now.'

'What's the story, Alex?' Aaron said. 'What's this about?'

'There should be a memo there from Battaglia to me. About the reverend.'

'Got it. There's the memo and then there's also this letter. Maybe Rose Malone,' Aaron said, talking about Battaglia's executive assistant, 'sent a copy to Laura, since it mentions you, and Laura downloaded it to your documents.'

'I swear I never saw any letter.'

'I'll print it. You'd better read it before it goes viral.'

'If any of this correspondence goes viral, I might as well be looking for work,' I said. My palms were breaking into a sweat. 'My piece of it was simple. We had a vic who claimed a statutory case against Shipley. Mercer worked it to the bone and couldn't get it to stick. Girl has a psych history and liked being around the celebrity — '

'*He* counts as a celebrity?' Ryan said.

'She's fifteen. Even you'd count as a celebrity to her with a triple-homicide jury verdict under your belt. Her mother dragged her to a few of Hal's rallies. Mercer thinks it was all an attempt at blackmailing him that backfired.'

'Do you know anything about a fraud investigation against Hal?' Aaron asked.

I put my head in my hand and exhaled. I couldn't tell them the little I knew about the tithing improprieties or Battaglia would kill me. That was still a confidential investigation. 'Nan,' I asked, 'would you do me a favor and call Rose? Ask whether Battaglia has left for the day? I might as well do something to earn the hangover I'm going to buy myself tonight.'

'If you do that, Nan,' Aaron said, 'you should also ask Rose if she's the one who copied Alex on this letter.'

'Please don't. Not yet,' I said. 'I promised the DA I wouldn't breathe a word of his contact from Shipley. Just see if he's still here.'

The printer powered up and churned out two pages, which I picked up from the tray.

I faced the wall as I skimmed them.

'Jesus,' I said, starting to read the document again. 'This letter thanks the reverend for his contribution, but Battaglia told me he didn't take any money from Shipley.'

56

'Could be a contribution of another kind,' Catherine said.

'Who would want anything of any kind from him?' I spoke the words and then stopped in my tracks. 'I don't understand Battaglia at all.'

'What is it?' Nan asked, walking back in from Laura's desk to tell us that Battaglia had left the office at five thirty, more than half an hour earlier.

'It's four paragraphs long. It's — it's dated about three weeks before I dismissed the statutory case against Shipley. Right after the DA thanks Hal, he tells him in this letter that 'my chief of the Special Victims Unit,'' I said, hanging imaginary quotation marks in the air, ''says you have nothing to worry about in regard to the malicious stories being circulated about you.''

'You must have known Battaglia traded on that kind of information,' Drew Poser said.

'No, I did not. Certainly not in a pending investigation. It's totally improper. Two weeks before the dismissal I still had no idea whether I had a real case or a psycho teen. This makes it look like the DA was in fact doing favors for Hal Shipley and dragging me into the deal.'

'What do you think this means?' Catherine said.

'Nothing good,' I said. 'At the very least, he was trying to curry favor with the devil.'

'But the boss never micromanages your cases.'

'Exactly. And, Aaron, what does it say in my files about a fraud investigation?' Now that I'd read the letter, I knew there was no point in

57

keeping the little I knew about Battaglia's dealings with Shipley a secret from them. These were my closest professional allies.

'Give me a minute. There's a link here,' he said to me. 'That doesn't ring any bells?'

'Yeah, there's a slight tinkling. Just tell us.'

'The letter in your documents folder kicks over to the white-collar division. Looks like there's a tax fraud allegation that's been opened into the reverend's nonprofit profit center.'

The tithing scam was about to come out in the open, way before Battaglia was ready for anyone to know-about it. It was as though someone was trying to plant the seed in that division that Shipley indeed had the protection of the district attorney.

'So that's my fault, too? I'm unleashing this monster and, on top of it, I'm going to take the fall for Battaglia's double-dealing?'

'Hold tight,' Aaron said. 'The fog is lifting.'

'What does that mean?'

'It means that the letter from District Attorney Paul Battaglia to the Reverend Hal Shipley was just dumped onto your computer today. Not months ago, at the time it was written.'

'What?' I said. 'Maybe I should ask Rose why she did that after all.'

'It wasn't Rose,' Aaron Byrne said.

'Who, then?'

'This letter was uploaded to you — and filed by Laura around noon, with your documents — by Josie Aponte. Or whoever it was who stole the Antonio Estevez file.'

We were all trying to connect the dots at once.

'What you're telling us,' I said, 'is that there is some kind of connection between Estevez, a world-class sex trafficker — '

Detective Drew Poser finished my sentence. 'And the Reverend Hal Shipley, who's a world-class pimp in every sense of the word.'

'Aaron,' I said, aware that more than half of what the white-collar lawyers dealt with was Internet crimes, 'you know everyone in the fraud division. Will you nail that piece of it for me as discreetly as you can? We need to know as much about this as possible or you'll be drawn into the quicksand with me.'

'Starting right now,' he said, pushing back from my desk. 'Be back to you by morning. All you have to do is figure out the link between Estevez and Shipley.'

'Well, if there is one,' I said, 'why would Estevez want to do anything to discredit Shipley? It might cause his flock to think twice about giving to him.'

'Nothing has ever made Shipley's people second-guess him, Alex. They seem to like the scoundrel side of the reverend.'

'Whatever the link,' Drew said, 'it's pretty obvious Estevez and Shipley have the same goal. Looks like they've got a plan to bring you down, Alexandra Cooper.'

6

'Let's knock off,' Aaron said. 'What's your day like tomorrow? That's Thursday, right?'

'Right. It's only six forty-five. Why don't we keep at it?' I asked.

'Your witnesses are all accounted for,' Drew said. 'And your trial is adjourned, so you're wide-open tomorrow, to answer Aaron's question.'

'What's your rush?'

'I've got a class to teach at NYU,' Aaron said, 'and if everyone is safely tucked in for the night, let's pickup first thing in the morning.'

'Hey, it's only *me* they're aiming at, guys. Take the rest of the day off, why don't you?'

'You've been telling us there's nothing personal in your files here,' Drew said. 'You can't go face-to-face with Battaglia till he shows up in the A.M., and we've got three teams looking for the Josie Aponte wannabe. Stay here late by yourself, but that's when the roaches come out of the woodwork to play. Get a life.'

'C'mon, Alex,' Catherine said. 'Time for a cocktail. There's a Dewar's with your name on it at Primola. Nan?'

'Have to help the girls with math homework. Have one for me.'

Catherine waited till I shut down my computer. I threw a trench coat over my suit against the cool fall air, and we walked down the dimly lit corridors to the elevator.

Centre Street was populated, as usual, by a mix of lawyers and perps — the former leaving work after a long day or pausing for a meal, the latter just released after an arraignment in night court. Too many of the arrestees were making their way to the Canal Street subway station. The last thing I needed was some frotteur — a subway rubber — celebrating his release from custody on our way uptown. Catherine was known to paralyze them with a single kick.

'I know you don't want to train it, but there are no cabs in sight,' Catherine said.

'I'll punch in Uber,' I said. The app for the service usually resulted in a black car arriving at the courthouse within five minutes. I tapped out our location and the address of the restaurant, one of my favorite Italian eateries, on Second Avenue in the Sixties.

'I spoke with Marissa. All good with Tanner. It's wise for her not to join us tonight, so she'll go home as soon as he's on his way down here to meet the judge.'

'So who's at Primola besides Mike?'

'Most of the guys from the task force that has been trying to hunt Tanner down,' she said. 'Mercer called Vickee in, too.'

'Sweet. I know she'd rather be home with her son at night.'

Vickee Eaton, Mercer's wife, was also a detective. She was assigned to the office of the deputy commissioner for public information and usually knew more about what was going on in headquarters than most of the chiefs. We were close friends, and I was godmother to their four-year-old, Logan. I'd spent many nights in their guest room while Tanner was on the loose.

'She and Mercer want to stay for dinner with us.'

'Guess that trumps my plans,' I said, glancing at my watch. 'I was supposed to meet an old friend who's just in town for a couple of days. I can always move that back to a nightcap.'

The car arrived seconds later and we settled in to the backseat.

'You want to tell me how it's going with Mike?' Catherine asked.

I was very comfortable confiding in the close circle of women with whom I'd worked for so long at the DA's office.

'Baby steps,' I said, leaning my head back against the seat cushion. 'We're taking it very slow. So far, so good.'

'Sorry, but that must have been a weird transition — the first time you took your clothes off — after working together for such a long time.'

'Weird but good. You know, even in bed — '

'TMI, Alex: Stop right there,' Catherine said, holding her hand between our faces. 'Way too much information.'

'I wasn't headed where you think,' I said, smiling at her. 'No inappropriate reveals here. I was just about to say that Mike's never going to cease taking shots at me. It's totally disarming. There's no angst, no pressure, no relationship psychobabble. We just make each other laugh. It's refreshing after some of the self-involved guys I've dated.'

'It's great to see you relaxed and happy. You know I told Mike if he ever made you cry, I'd break every bone in his body.'

'Catherine — it's been six weeks. That's all. Don't blow things out of proportion.'

'Just for the record, Grand Central Terminal's a pretty offbeat place to start an affair.'

'Foreplay only. It was that weekend in September that we went to the Vineyard.'

'Yeah, the one that was supposed to be ladies only. The one you canceled on me.'

My old farmhouse on a hilltop in Chilmark, overlooking Vineyard Sound, was the most romantic spot I'd ever known. It was a haven for me, a small piece of paradise where I was able to escape from the stress of a constantly challenging job. My colleagues and I held lives in our hands — our victims, the accused, those wrongly accused, and the cops who fought to keep our city safe — every day of the week.

'Pick a date. We can do it next month.'

I was the third child — two older brothers — of a marriage between a doctor and a nurse, an ordinary upbringing until my father and his partner revolutionized heart surgery with the invention of a small plastic device used in operating rooms worldwide. The Cooper-Hoffman valve had paid for our educations, and the trust fund established with its proceeds allowed me the luxury of a Vineyard vacation home that I couldn't have dreamed of on a public servant's salary.

'Yes. Let's go before it gets too cold,' Catherine said. 'You'll have to tell me how you managed to seduce a man in your country house when you can't even cook. You could store some of your shoes inside your oven, it gets so little use.'

'Can you believe that Mike cooks? Like, really well.'

'You're shattering my image. I know he loves chowing down fried clams at the Bite, and I can see him sitting at the bar at the Chilmark Tavern, chatting up the hostess. But cooking? He's such a tough guy. Just makes you think a woman would love to take care of him,' Catherine said, 'although you're really useless at that.'

I picked my head up. 'I beg your pardon. I've got certain charms. Limited in the kitchen, maybe, but talents that come in handy.'

'So what did he serve?'

'Oysters from one of the island ponds, which Mike shucked himself. And lobster. Two-and-a-half-pounders from Larsen's — which he cooked to perfection.'

Larsen's Fish Market, in the tiny fishing village of Menemsha, had the most amazing selection of fresh seafood, off-loaded from working boats that docked right at the back door in the small harbor.

'You melted the butter and poured the drinks. A match made in heaven.'

'Don't forget I'm in charge of the fireplace, too. I even remembered to open the flue.'

'Mid-September? Wasn't it a tad warm for a fire?'

'I opened all the windows. The fire helped with the atmosphere,' I said. 'You can't imagine how nervous I was.'

'Did you manage to get through the first night

without any shop talk?' Catherine asked. 'No double helixes or autopsy photos or dramatic readings from the penal law?'

'Totally social. I don't think Mike's ever gone that long without measuring someone for a body bag.'

Catherine was quiet for the next few blocks. 'I have to ask,' she said. 'Did any of your demons show up after dark?'

'You're a great friend,' I said. She had been witness to all of my darkest moments over the years. 'Thanks for asking. No, nothing at all. No nightmares, no one stalking me, no old lovers. The whole thing felt very safe, very normal.'

'For a change.'

'And the cat's out of the bag,' I said as we pulled up in front of the restaurant. 'That's kind of a relief, too.'

Giuliano, the owner of Primola, was seating people at a table by the window as we walked in. 'Signorina Cooper,' he said. '*Ciao*, ladies. Good to have you here. The guys are all waiting for you in the back.'

He pointed past the bar to the area in the rear of the crowded room. Several tables had been pushed together for the dozen or so men — and Vickee — who had worked relentlessly since summer to find the elusive Raymond Tanner.

I saw Mike's dark hair, his back to me, and we made our way through the hungry New Yorkers who were three deep the length of the room as they waited for turnover.

Mercer was the first to see us and raise a glass in our direction.

'I'd hardly call it waiting for us,' Catherine said. 'The team seems to be throwing back some celebratory drinks in anticipation of our arrival.'

'Hey, Coop,' Mike called out to me. 'Grab yourself something from the bar.'

I gave him a thumbs-up and we stopped at the end, next to the waiters' station. I ordered a Dewar's on the rocks and for Catherine a glass of pinot grigio. We mounted the two steps that separated the rear room from the main floor of the restaurant, and the detectives greeted us with whistles, cheers, and a toast to the young rookie — unknown to all of them — who was on his way down to the courthouse to take Tanner to his arraignment.

'Here's to you, Alex,' one of the men said. 'Bet you'll sleep like a baby tonight.'

'I've slept well every night, because you guys were on the job.' No need to tell them about the times I closed my eyes and still was sure I could see the image of the letters that spelled KILL COOP on Tanner's hand.

'They were all just a little slow on the draw, Coop,' Mike said.

'You leave my task force alone, Detective Chapman. They had a few things more urgent on their plates than my stalker,' I said. 'Now, why don't you sit and we'll get some dinner for you?'

Vickee came around from the far side of the table to give me a hug. 'Way to go, girl. Raymond Tanner was a great big accident waiting to happen, wasn't he?'

'To put it mildly.'

'All good?'

I smiled at Vickee. 'I guess stranger things have happened, but yes, all good.'

'Five more minutes till you take your seats, guys,' Mike said, motioning to me with his forefinger. 'C'mon, kid. Time for the final question.'

Mercer, Mike, and I had a long-standing habit of betting on the last *Jeopardy!* question whenever we were together on a weeknight evening. These detectives were two of the smartest men I knew, and our vastly different areas of interest made it fun to be challenged, whether at the morgue or my place, crime scenes or chic restaurants.

The small television was in the short corridor behind the dining room, hung out of sight but close enough so that diners could track sports scores or breaking news.

Mike followed me into the space, off to the side of the busy kitchen. 'You feeling okay?'

'About this news? I couldn't be happier,' I said, sipping my Scotch. 'The rest of my afternoon cratered, but that's not your problem.'

'You'd be wrong about that, Coop. Antonio Estevez and his crew?'

'Correct. Possibly related to the Reverend Hal Shipley. I'll tell you later.'

'Am I breaking something up?' Mercer asked.

'We were just waiting on you, Mr. Wallace,' Mike said. 'Time for the big question.'

Mercer clinked his glass of vodka against my drink, and Mike reached over my arm to hit us both. At the same time, Alex Trebek had come onto the screen after a commercial break and was about to reveal the final answer to the trio of contestants.

Mike Chapman was a graduate of Fordham University, where he had majored in military history. He'd been obsessed by that subject since childhood and knew as much about it as any scholar I'd ever encountered. Mercer Wallace was raised by his widowed father in Queens. The Delta mechanic had papered the walls of his son's bedroom with maps of the world, and there was barely a square foot of it with which Mercer wasn't familiar. Geography was where his depth of knowledge was concentrated.

Mike grabbed the clicker off the top of the monitor and un-muted the sound.

'All right, gentlemen,' Trebek said. 'You're each within a hundred dollars of the others, so I assume any one of you can win.'

I had majored in English literature before deciding that a career in public service would be my focus. Reading the Romantic poets and dense nineteenth-century British novels was my favorite way to escape from dry legal briefs. All three of us were on sound footing when the categories touched on Motown music or classic movies of the 1930s and 1940s.

'Tonight's Final Jeopardy category is 'The Wild Wild West,'' Trebek said as the words were revealed on the giant game board. 'What will each of you wager on the Wild Wild West? We'll see in just a minute.'

'I'm in for forty,' I said, doubling our usual bet of twenty dollars.

'Just because you grew up on reruns of

Bonanza?' Mike said.

'You obviously don't know that my childhood dream was to be Annie Oakley.'

'Hard to imagine since you're so skittish around guns. Double or nothing.'

'Don't you two go all sky-high on me,' Mercer said. 'I'm in at eighty bucks. I've got a little mouth to feed at home.'

Trebek's voice boomed from the speaker as he revealed the answer. 'He was the first man executed by the federal government in the Dakota Territory.'

'See that?' Mike said. The three contestants grimaced as they struggled — or appeared to be doing so — to write the proper question as the show's iconic 'Think' music played loudly. 'We're all on equal footing. It's about murder.'

His encyclopedic knowledge of all things homicidal took Mike back through generations of killers and their weapons of choice.

'You're up, Alex,' Mercer said as the music stopped and Trebek pointed at the first of the three men standing on the stage.

'Who was — ?' I couldn't pull up the name I wanted. 'Who was Billy the Kid?'

'So wrong in every direction that you ought to pay triple the ante,' Mike said, reaching out his hand for my money. 'Billy the Kid's real name was William Bonney. Killed so far south of Dakota that it was practically part of Mexico. New Mexico. And shot by Sheriff Pat Garrett, not hung by the feds.'

The first two contestants had drawn blanks also.

'You're next, Mercer,' Mike said.

'Who was Jack McCall?' Mercer asked, just as the contestant who had been in the lead revealed to Trebek that he had written, 'Who was the man who shot Bill Hickok?'

'That's almost the right question,' Trebek said, 'but we were looking for his actual name. And that's Jack McCall. Who was Jack McCall? I'm sorry, gentlemen. Let's see what you wagered.'

Mike slapped Mercer's hand in a high-five as he clicked off the TV. 'Broken Nose Jack, they called him. Shot Wild Bill in the back of the head during a poker game. A pair of aces and a pair of eights. That's why they call it the dead man's hand when you draw those cards. McCall was acquitted by the first jury and then retried . . . '

'Now, that's double jeopardy,' I said. 'You can't have a second trial after an acquittal.'

'First trial was in Deadwood,' Mercer said. 'When the feds heard about the acquittal, they said the trial hadn't been a formal legal procedure because Deadwood was an illegal town in Indian Territory, so double jeopardy didn't apply. No constitutional violation.'

'Yeah, they nailed McCall in Yankton, tried him again, and strung him up from the tallest tree,' Mike said. 'You gotta love a place where the prosecution gets two bites of the apple. It would have helped your batting average a whole lot, Coop.'

I smiled and took another sip of my drink. 'We don't keep scorecards, Detective. One and done works fine for me.'

Mike led us back to the tables where everyone in the group had seated him- or herself, counting the twenty-dollar bills to split with Mercer. Vickee motioned me to an empty chair beside her. One of my favorite SVU detectives, Alan Vandomir, was on my other side.

Mercer stayed on his feet to make the first toast. 'I've got a candidate for rookie of the year,' he said, naming the young officer who had collared Raymond Tanner. 'Puts all you gold-badged first and second graders to shame. You've been running around town for two months without a scintilla of perp progress and — '

'We were looking for love in all the wrong places,' one of the guys shouted out.

'And now some kid gets the job done in your stead. The commissioner asked me to send you his best and to announce that the Raymond Tanner Task Force is officially disbanded.'

'I'll drink to that,' Vandomir said.

'I just want to add,' I said, leaning on Vickee's shoulder as I got to my feet, 'that I am especially grateful to each one of you, personally, for making this work a priority.'

'We weren't worried much, Alex,' Pug McBride said, displaying his empty glass over his head to the waiter. 'Chapman had your back.'

'He's had her back for years,' the sergeant said, reaching for one of the bottles of wine on the table. 'Now he's got a hand on better body parts than that.'

Most of the guys laughed, so there was no point in protesting.

'It's all about Tanner tonight,' Mercer said, knowing the banter, the focus on my vulnerability, would make me uncomfortable.

'The kid cop sounds like a star,' Pug said. 'If that stunt don't buy him his gold shield, nothing will.'

'Goes to the head of the class for deceiving the devil,' Mike said. 'I told the lieutenant he ought to ask for an interview with him. Grab him now before any bad habits set in. He's my kind of cop, building the devil's bridge.'

7

'I'll bite,' Vickee said. 'What is it?'

'The bridge?' Mike asked.

'There's a Devil's Bridge off the tip of the Vineyard,' I said. I remembered it from the days when I fished with Adam Nyman at the crack of dawn. 'It's a treacherous archipelago of boulders that strings out below the Gay Head Cliffs toward Cuttyhunk Island, under the water where the ocean meets the sound.'

The deadliest marine accident in New England's history occurred in 1884, when a passenger steamer — the *City of Columbus* — ran aground on the shoals of Devil's Bridge, killing more than one hundred people. I had heard the story from descendants of the dead still on the island, haunted by the tragedy that had occurred within sight of the Gay Head Lighthouse.

'Brush up on your folklore, ladies.'

'We're about to get a touch of Brian Chapman, are we?' Pug McBride said, laying on his thickest brogue. 'I miss your father every day, Mikey.'

Mike's father, Brian, had a legendary career in the NYPD, much decorated for his heroism and his brilliant investigative work. It was his great pride that Mike pursued a college degree instead of following him onto the job, but when Brian dropped dead within forty-eight hours of turning in his gun and shield for retirement, Mike went directly from his Fordham commencement to sign up for entry in the Police Academy.

'There are devil's bridges all over Europe,' Mike said. 'Masonry arches from medieval times — in France and Spain and Italy, and of course throughout England and Ireland — each of which comes with its own version of a folktale.'

'What does it have to do with being a cop?' Vickee asked.

Mike was sitting directly across the table from Vickee. He placed his glass of vodka on the table and pointed at her with his forefinger, picking up the dialect of his County Cork roots. 'So my great-aunt Bronwen — she was from Wales, as you can tell by the name — she came from a town near the great Mynach Gorge.'

'You giving us blarney, Chapman?' Pug asked. 'I heard this one from your old man more times than I can count.'

'Roll with it, Pug. The ladies seem to be ignorant.'

'Welsh fairy tales?' I said. 'Guilty as charged.'

'Mynach's one of the most scenic places in the countryside, with dramatic waterfalls that drop nearly three hundred feet down the gorge. And the problem was, back in the day, there was no way to cross that gorge to get to the other side — to town, to the fields where the cows were grazing, to church — '

'We get your point.'

Mike took another slug of vodka. 'So Bronwen's great-great-great-granny made a pact with the devil. She got Satan himself to agree to

74

build a bridge for her,' Mike said, snapping his finger with a loud click, 'and to do it overnight. But he wanted something in return.'

'He always does,' Vickee said.

'Well, that time he wanted a promise that he could have the first living soul who crossed his bridge the next morning,' Mike said. 'Stayed up all night getting the bridge made — you can still see it spanning the gorge today — and then he hid himself right at the end of the rock pile. Just like a rapist hiding amid the boulders in Riverside Park. Waiting for the first living soul.'

Vickee waved the back of her hand at Mike. 'You forget, Detective, that the kids growing up in the projects don't exactly know the folktales you were brought up on. Might not be the same risk/reward ratio.'

'Don't distract me, Vickee. I'm on a high here. I've got everybody but Pug spellbound.'

'Heard it before, Chapman. The little old lady — aye, your auntie Bronwen herself — she deceives the devil. He builds her a beautiful bridge in the most unlikely of places — '

'And instead of giving him a living soul to ravish, the clever woman sends her dog on ahead of the beautiful young maiden,' Mike said, lifting his glass in the air. 'The first living thing, only it happens to have four legs.'

'So this smart cop used the dog to roust Raymond Tanner from his hiding place,' I said.

'And like the devil, who was so enraged by the old lady's trick that he leaped into the falls and was never seen in those parts again, the rookie has rid us of the evil Tanner.'

'Yeah, he built his own bridge to Rikers Island for the night,' Pug said as the waiter tried to get everyone's attention to announce the dinner specials. 'The devil played right into the kid's hands.'

For the next two hours, we did what cops and prosecutors do when thrown together with good food and an excess of alcohol. We told war stories. Pug on the homicidal maniac who had paralyzed the subway for half the summer; Alan on the child molester who dressed in his mother's clothes to lure kids into the apartment; Catherine on the guy who jumped bail fifteen years earlier only to be nabbed in Georgia by her cold case unit and charged with a dozen more rapes along 1–95.

When Vickee finished her chicken piccata, she left the table to go outside to call the public information office to see whether there was any word on the Tanner arraignment.

I was still working on my orecchiette con broccoli rabe, enjoying a cool glass of pinot grigio, when Mike walked around the table and took Vickee's seat next to me.

'You okay, Coop?'

'Yes,' I said, smiling back at Mike. 'This time I think it's just mind games, not physical threats. You've heard what Antonio Estevez pulled off?'

Mike nodded. 'Yeah, Drew called me about it. Really slick. And sticking stuff into your document files by uploading it from another DA's office computer? The dude's got game.'

'Next time I see him, I'll tell him you're a fan.'

'At least you get a reprieve from the trial.

Maybe we can figure something to do with the weekend.'

'A last Vineyard trip for the season? Give me something to look forward to.'

Mike and I were still trying to feel our way through the rhythms of a relationship. We each had apartments of our own and had spent few nights together since we'd starting dating. The irregular assignments of a homicide detective rarely synched with my litigation schedule.

'Sounds like you've got a full plate till then,' Mike said.

'Tomorrow I get to put my head on the block for Battaglia to chop away at.'

'Estevez?'

'You probably haven't heard the whole story about Reverend Hal yet. I may have lots of time on my hands once the DA finishes with me.'

'The reverend don't scare me. I got scores of snitches who'd drop a dime on him in a heartbeat. Federal tax fraud, which means city and state are bound to follow; kids out of wedlock that he supports with money from his phony church; ruining the life of an innocent prosecutor in the Twainey Bowler case ten years back, and still not paying his dues on that. Bring him on, babe, 'cause I'd like nothing better than to spit in his face.'

'Thanks. I hope whatever you spit is even half as toxic as Hal's own venom.'

'Keep drinking, kid. It's good for your attitude,' Mike said. 'I've got three more midnights to work and then off for two days. You want me to drop you at home when I leave?'

'I'll hang for a while.' I looked at my watch again. 'I'm good. It's nice to see everybody again.'

'I have to stop at the morgue to pick up the autopsy photos of yesterday's stabbing. Lieutenant Peterson and the ME don't see eye to eye on the nature of the wounds. I'm going to take off in a few minutes,' he said, patting my thigh under the table.

Mike was working a week of midnights. The lieutenant's to-do list usually added a few hours to the grueling tour of duty he and his colleagues liked so much.

While he was leaning in, talking to me, Mike's cell went off. He checked the phone number. 'Let me step out and talk to the office.'

'I'll get some fresh air with you,' I said.

Catherine looked up at me from her end of the table when she saw me stand. 'I'm coming right back in,' I said to her. 'Just walking Mike out to make a call.'

Vickee was a couple of feet away, coming back in our direction, hands raised over her head with double victory signs! 'Spoke to my boss, gentlemen and ladies. Raymond Tanner, aka Raimondo Santini, aka Ronald Tanney, has appeared before the court and has been remanded without the possibility of bail. He'll spend the night in leg irons and cuffs in the Men's House of Detention before being transported tomorrow to Rikers Island.'

'That calls for another round,' Pug said. 'I'm off for the next two days. Nothing would make me happier than a Tanner hangover.'

'I haven't felt this good since the beginning of the summer,' I said, shaking off the courtroom drama of the day. 'This arrest kind of puts Josie Aponte in perspective.'

'Good to hear. C'mon, Coop. I'm going out to use Vickee's phone booth,' Mike said, referring to the patch of sidewalk in front of Primola that was a quieter spot from which to make and receive calls.

It was close to ten P.M., and although Mike's tour didn't start till eleven thirty, he and his team were often called in early if a case was breaking.

He dialed the number and waited for Peterson to answer the phone. 'Hey, Loo. What's happening?'

Mike listened, and I just leaned against the door of the restaurant. 'Where?' he asked.

Murder investigations in Manhattan were split between two elite squads. Mike worked in North Homicide, which covered the island from the tip of Spuyten Duyvil, facing the Bronx, to 59th Street, the lower border of Central Park. The South squad handled everything down to the farthest end at Battery Park.

'Deep-six the morgue photos for now, right?' Mike asked, then waited again. 'Got that.'

'What is it?' I asked after he ended the call.

'Eight million stories in the naked city and none of them are pretty,' Mike said, holding the door open for me. 'Got a domestic in the two-eight.'

'The victim's dead?' I asked, turning sideways to get through the bar crowd.

79

'That's why they called the homicide squad and not auto theft, Coop.'

'How'd he kill her?'

'You keep making these sexist assumptions,' Mike said. '*She* offed her main man. Her boyfriend of two years. Shot him in the back of the head when he was sleeping. Wiped out the savings under his mattress, according to his daughter, who found the body.'

The Twenty-Eighth Precinct was a largely residential area of Harlem. The current policing tactics of the commissioner and a crime-prevention strategy by the DA had brought rates of violent attacks way down, and homicides in particular had plummeted.

'So she's waiting there to be cuffed?'

'Now, you know my job isn't that simple, Ms. Cooper,' Mike said, grabbing his glass from the table and taking a last swig of vodka. 'The vic's body was just found an hour ago, but this seemed to have happened late last night. No telling where the perp-lady is by now.'

'The girlfriend's your prime suspect?'

'Like I say, she's my perp till I learn otherwise.'

'Call me later, will you?'

'No, ma'am. You get a good night's sleep tonight. I'll give you a wake-up call instead. Get you ready to take on the district attorney. Feed you some breakfast of champions and all that.'

'Be caref — '

'I've already got a mother, Coop.'

Mike said his good nights around the table, kissed Vickee goodbye, and parted from me as though he was still just a professional colleague.

He was ten feet away before he turned and doubled back. 'If it helps you count sheep tonight, I've got a crumb for you to feed Battaglia when you see him.'

'Always useful,' I said.

Paul Battaglia kept ahead of the game by trading on inside information. Those most loyal to him dropped nuggets of facts — literally as valuable as pieces of gold — which gave him the power to strategize on policy and politics before leaks hit the tabloids or the street.

'The lieutenant says the deceased was a worshipper at the church of the Reverend Hal. Might even have been his bagman, which would account for the mattress money. Use the info with Battaglia if it helps distract him, keep you out of his sights. I'll be going into Holy Hal's sanctuary with a search warrant before too long.'

8

'Things going okay for you?' Vickee asked, moving her chair closer to mine. 'You've certainly got Mike in a good mood.'

'Can you remember what it's like at this stage of a relationship?' I asked.

'First time or second?' Vickee and Mercer had split years ago, before Logan was born, because she feared his devotion to the job led him to take risks with his life. 'It's always tricky at the outset.'

'Even trickier with our work situation.'

'C'mon, now. Mercer and I are both on the job. We used to have cases together all the time. That can't be the issue.'

'Totally different dynamic than yours, with one of us prosecuting and the other handling the investigations.'

'Why? You've always ridden these guys as hard as they're able to go. Like you're suddenly afraid Mike can't take direction from you?'

'Nothing new about that, Vickee,' I said with a smile. 'Mike and I will go right on doing what we've always done. He and Mercer are the best cops I've ever known, and that never changes. They do the heavy lifting and I get the evidence to hold up their collars in court.'

'So stop making a big deal about it.'

'I think the department bosses are watching us like hawks. Battaglia, too. I'm not exactly sleeping with the enemy, which is how they seem to be treating us, but it does make things very complicated sometimes. They figure I'm just playing with their ace detective. That once I toss him aside he'll be useless to them.'

'Well, are you?'

'Am I what?'

'Just playing with Mike's emotional well-being.'

'I'm out of here before I snap at you, okay?' I lifted my bag off the floor to pull out some cash and get ready to leave. 'Are you turning on me, too? Everybody is pushing this relationship along because we've been in each other's lives for so many years. We're not even living together yet or anything remotely close to that. Mike's a quirky guy, Vickee. You know that as well as I do.'

'And you're all sunshine and light? Give me a break, girl.'

'I have never in my life claimed I was easy. But this is a man who lives in a studio apartment so small and so dark that he nicknamed it 'the coffin.' This is a guy who is so used to his privacy and his man-cave ways, who keeps every ounce of his sensitivity bottled up inside him so far that even a suppository wouldn't unglue him, that there are times I — '

'Don't you even think about bad-mouthing Mike Chapman to me, Ms. Cooper,' Vickee said, wagging a finger at me.

I dug in my bag again to find my phone. 'Why are we having this conversation? I think it's a little too much Scotch on my part, for sure. I'd never bad-mouth him. I simply tried to give you an honest response when you asked me how things are going. And all I said is that some things are tricky with Mike and me. You want this transition to be a smooth one? Then give us some time and space.'

'Don't lay one of your high-profile, strung-out, going-to-pieces bits on him because of this Antonio Estevez dirtbag. He doesn't need it right now, okay?'

'Like I would do that?' I said, tapping the Uber car service app. 'What's got your nose so out of joint tonight? Mercer must be complaining about the fact that Mike and I have something going on.'

'Forget I said anything. And for God's sake, don't tell Mike. You texting him already? He's got a homicide to deal with.'

'This whole conversation is forgotten,' I said, pushing back from the table. 'And no, I don't text him while he's working a scene, Vickee. Something has you all gnarled up.'

'What's with Uber?' Alan Vandomir asked, catching the screen on my phone before I stood up. 'I'll drive you home.'

'No problem. I have no intention of breaking up this cozy gathering. You stay right here,' I said, punching in my destination on the app. 'I'm close enough to walk, but if I said I was going to do that, all you Cub Scouts would be on your feet to protect my honor.'

'Whatever's left of it,' Alan said.

'Giuliano is right at the front door. He'll see to it that I get in my chariot, and here's some dough for my share of the bill,' I said, plunking

84

down money, then reaching for a biscotto as I left the table. '*Ciao*, guys. See you tomorrow.'

I shimmied through the bar crowd again and looked down at my phone. An Uber driver had responded to my request and would be at the exact location I ordered, right around the corner from the restaurant on 65th Street, in two minutes.

I waited inside for a bit, to make sure the driver would be there. Giuliano held the door open for me. 'Thanks again, Alessandra. Everybody have enough to eat?'

'Perfect, Giuliano. See you in a few days.'

I stepped down onto the sidewalk and turned north on Second Avenue, in the direction of my apartment. Traffic was heavy, as it usually was, heading for the entrance to the 59th Street Bridge out of the city, just a few blocks the other way.

At the first corner, I crossed Second and made a left turn onto the quiet side street, looking over my shoulder to make sure Vickee hadn't followed me out. I couldn't figure out why she was so testy this evening, and I didn't want any more judgmental jabbering.

The black sedan I expected wasn't there yet, but it looked as though an SUV had pulled up to take the job.

I walked toward it, at the edge of the curb next to the fire hydrant. The windows were tinted, but I could see the driver motioning me to open the rear door.

I heard the click of the lock and I pulled on the handle. Just then, I picked my head up and could see the lights of a black sedan approaching the rear of the SUV.

I hesitated for a second as I opened the door, wondering if there was a mix-up in cars. But in that single moment, I felt a tug on my arm from a figure sitting in the backseat of the SUV. His hand was on my throat before I could open my mouth to scream. He covered my nose with a cloth that reeked of the powerful sweet smell of chloroform.

I tried to pull my head back and break away, but in that instant my entire world crashed to black.

CHAPMAN

9

'Nice, Sarge,' I said, pushing open the bedroom door inside the apartment of the late Wynan Wilson. I had put on my gloves and booties in the hallway. 'Nice that you two waited for me.'

'Dead men don't got anything better to do than wait, Chapman. There's too much lead between his ears for Mr. Wilson to be out and about causing trouble. Just figured I'd chill with him till you got here.'

'What's the word on the ME?'

'The doc's got a vehicular on FDR Drive. Highway Patrol tells me she just declared the driver dead at the scene. Should be here in fifteen or so.'

I took a couple of steps toward the bed. The belly flab of the large man cushioned his corpse against the paper-thin mattress. He was face-down on cheap linens that had a sheen to them — kind of like fake satin — except for the large patch below Wilson's head that had been soaked in a mixture of his blood and brains.

'You know him?' I asked the sergeant. 'Wynan Wilson?'

'Regular pain in the ass.'

'Felony pain in the ass? Bad rap sheet?'

'Nah. More like a nuisance than a terminal condition.'

I took my pen out of my pocket and lifted some strands of hair from around the entry wound, which was dead center at the indent in the rear of Wilson's skull.

'Crime Scene should get here before the doc. I asked them to rush it. She's got good aim, am I right, Chapman?'

'Hard to miss when you put the barrel of the gun against the flesh while your target is sound asleep.'

The entrance wound was small and symmetrical. There was the abrasion ring I expected to find on Wilson's skin — the residue of gunpowder and cordite — along with the clear imprint of the gun barrel.

'That's what you're assuming.'

'Gotta start somewhere, Sarge. Pretty tough for a big man to let someone get that close to him with a cold hard piece of metal and no sign of a struggle. Either he anesthetized himself with three-quarters of that bottle of Rémy or you've been nipping at it while you dialed me up.'

The cap was off the bottle on the nightstand. The pungent odor of the alcohol was almost enough to mask the familiar scent of death.

'The fave neighborhood brew. Me, I'd rather go lights-out with a six-pack of Bud.'

I squatted next to the bed. 'And I'm thinking she straddled him to get the best angle.'

'Whaddaya mean?'

'It's all in the details, Sarge. See those marks on his side? See where the fat flops over the waistband of his shorts?'

The sergeant leaned down and squinted. 'So?'

'They're not stretch marks from a pregnancy. You clear on that?' I said. 'Same thing on both sides, the left a bit higher on the torso than the right. Not enough to lacerate the body, but just to leave a scratch. I'm guessing the girlfriend had boots on when she mounted him with her gun. Zippers on the inner calf.'

'Whoa. Like S and M? Like this was a game and Wilson forgot the safe word?'

'Nope,' I said, straightening up. 'Like 'these boots were made for running out on you the minute I sink a slug in that pea-size nugget that some folks call a brain and run off with the right reverend's wrong money.' The shooter was perfectly positioned for the strike. Wilson's on his stomach, right side of his head on the mattress. No pillow. Shooter is right-handed. Mounts him 'cause she knows he's out cold and won't feel it. Positions the barrel right against the head, pointing up a bit, where it will do the most damage. Much more reliable than trying to direct it while standing beside him. What's her name, Sarge? The suspect's name.'

The sergeant looked at his steno pad. 'The daughter knows her as Keesh. Been with the old man for almost two years.'

'Is she known to the department?'

'Yeah, KTD as Takeesha Falls. Thirty-six. Born in — '

'Priors?'

'Only a shoplift in New York. But — '

'Gotta be half a hooker.'

'No half about it, Mike. Full-on pros in DC and the great commonwealth of Virginia. Like ten times over, in her younger days. And an arrest for armed robbery in Baltimore that was dropped because of her cooperation against her codefendant.'

'Got it. A woman of great principle and dignity. Another fit in Reverend Hal's fucked-up flock. You got an APB out on Keesh?'

I was face-to-face with the dead man, kneeling at the head of the bed. He didn't seem to notice my presence. His eyes were shut — as they had probably been at the time of his murder — and rigor still locked the muscles of his jaw. That fact confirmed that he had probably been dead less than thirty hours, but the medical examiner would ascertain that point with greater certainty.

'Yeah. We went with it about an hour ago.'

'She's had a full day's jump on us,' I said. 'That sucks. Either of them own a car?'

'Nope. Guys are checking Port Authority and the train stations, as well as all her local haunts. As soon as Lieutenant Peterson gives me backup from your team, we start hitting her friends and contacts here.'

'She works other than hustling?'

'Braids hair occasionally. Makes 'em into dreadlocks. That count as work?'

'It's a look, Sarge.'

'You see some of those pro ballplayers? You can bring them down by their dreads instead of a full-on tackle.'

I reached my right arm in under the mattress. I'd done it enough times that even the ME wouldn't have a clue I'd been there.

'Keesh got it all, Chapman. All the cash.'

'You know that how?'

'Well, I, uh, the first cops on the scene did

exactly what you're doing, and then I tried my own luck when I got here.'

'Damn it, Sarge.'

'You want me to turn my pockets inside out? You think I'd take — ?'

'Don't wet your pants, Sarge. It's not the money. I'm just worried about whether all your digging in the box springs rocked the body. This case looks pretty much straightforward. I don't want to screw it up with postmortem artifacts like bruises on Wilson's gut 'cause there was a treasure hunt going on beneath him. I don't want to set Keesh up with a self-defense argument by having her claim he was face-to-face with her, threatening her, so she had to shoot just as his back was turned.'

No one was supposed to touch the body until the medical examiner arrived. But the natural instinct of good cops to look for identification in the clothing of a deceased found in a park or deserted apartment, the curiosity to see whether there were bullet holes or stab wounds that caused the death, or the desire to be the first to find a clue that might solve the crime drove many investigators to break the most basic rules.

'You got a rock crusher here, Chapman. Don't look to blame me if you can't nail Keesh for murder. There'll be fingerprints and DNA of hers all over this pad.'

'She's been banging the guy for two years, Sarge. Of course Keesh has left junk all over the place. That won't be dispositive of anything. What's the daughter's name?'

'Wilson's daughter? Angela. Twenty-eight

years old. She's good people. Works as a home health-care aide for an old lady up the block.'

'Is that her wailing?'

'Yeah. I stashed her with the next-door neighbor so you could talk to her. I didn't want her to leave.'

'Thanks.'

'She's been howling on and off the whole time. I thought Pops here might actually open his eyes from the commotion. I'd get to her soon if I was you.'

'You would have told me if there was any sign of a gun.'

'None. And neither Keesh nor the deceased had permits.'

'You say Wilson was bagging money for Reverend Hal but he wasn't known for packing?'

'In this part of town, you couldn't have a safer job than working for Hal. He's got an army of ex-cons in his stable, doing all his dirty work, keeping the skeptics in line. Mess with his moneyman and you're not likely to make it out of church.'

'So Keesh has a history of partnering in at least one armed robbery. She's a girl who can find her way to an illegal gun,' I said, walking around to the far side of the bed and sliding my hand in again. 'And Wilson would have been stupid not to have one.'

'You're ignoring what I just said about the scuttlebutt on the street. No need.'

'I put it in the category of 'nice to know,' Sarge. Maybe he didn't carry,' I said, pulling open the drawer of his nightstand with a gloved finger, 'but my bet is when he was holed up in this dump, he had heat at the ready. Just a matter of finding it.'

'We didn't do a search.'

'Glad of that,' I said. 'We'll take care of it. Just thinking Keesh would have known where he kept it. Another arrow in her quiver to claim he pulled his own gun on her while he had a load on from the Rémy and she had no choice but to protect herself.'

'You work for the defense team these days?' the sergeant asked.

'Gotta think like the best lawyer money can buy. Best lawyer the Reverend Hal's missing money can buy, 'cause that's who Keesh will have.'

My father had taught me most of what I know about investigating a case. He knew — and I had learned firsthand from watching Coop in action — that the point wasn't just to make an arrest. It was to arrest the right guy and to make sure you got the evidence properly so it held up in the courtroom, no matter who the mouthpiece was for the accused.

'How old was Wilson?' I asked.

'Sixty-six.'

'So maybe she was cheating on him,' I said. 'A little more than half his age. Or he thought so and they fought over her possible infidelity.'

'I'm telling you he was sound asleep. What does it matter if they argued before that?'

'May not matter at all if the ME is sure Wilson died right where you found him.'

'You're just playing 'worst-case-scenario homicide dick,' right, Chapman?'

I went into the bathroom and opened the medicine cabinet. There were blood pressure pills and Tums — nothing stronger.

'Impressive, isn't it?' the sergeant asked, standing in the doorway. 'Gets to be a senior citizen with some dough to spend, enough to hook up with a broad in her thirties, and he don't even need Viagra. Wilson's the man.'

'So much for the idea that you didn't search the place.'

'Well, the medicine cabinet,' he stammered. 'Just wanted to see if he was on heart pills or had any complications like diabetes. The doc will want to know.'

'There's not a health condition known to medical science, Sarge, that complicates a hollow-point bullet through the cerebral cortex. Don't juice me.'

'Hey, I didn't disturb anything. It was a preliminary — '

'You must have thought there would be a few bills stuck to the denture cream,' I said, brushing past the uniformed sergeant to head to the kitchen. 'How about in the cookie jar? You stick your nose into that, too?'

'I opened the fridge. Only thing in it was a meal Wilson never got to eat that his daughter cooked for him. My mother had this habit, Chapman, of hiding her extra dough in the freezer when she went upstate on vacation. Figured burglars would never look there.'

'Wouldn't have worked at my house. The freezer was the most popular spot. Ice cubes never lived to be two days old, once Brian got home from the squad,' I said, pulling open drawers and looking on shelves between cans of soup and packages of ramen noodles.

'Brian was aces, Chapman. Nobody better.'

I played cool to the comment, but truth to tell was that I couldn't hear it enough. My father had been hero to more victims than I could count, but he was even larger than legend to me.

I crouched in front of the sink. 'Did you check the roach motels?'

'Are you crazy? This building is like a cockroach sanctuary. Like a homeless shelter for the little suckers. Wilson has traps under the sink and behind the toilet and in every crevice in the kitchen. I feel like I'm crawling with them already.'

I reached under the sink — the dark, damp environment that was so welcoming to these creatures — and pulled out one of the large boxes of Black Flag that was clustered in there.

'Your gloves are gonna need gloves if you touch that,' the sergeant said.

I opened the first box. 'No vacancy at this motel.'

'How many days' catch you figure that is?' the sergeant asked, leaning over my shoulder. 'Not such a good housekeeper, that Mr. Wilson. Guess the roaches are lured right in by the smell of those hormones.'

'Pheromones,' I said, reaching for the second box, a few inches behind the first one. 'Not hormones, Sarge. They're pheromones.'

'Must be another fifty in there. You got a thing for them, Chapman?'

'Nope. I've just got a hunch.'

The first three cardboard boxes of stiff roaches would be off-putting to most people. The fourth and fifth cartons were far more attractive.

Someone had removed the chemical compound that invited the hardy bugs inside to die, and lined the boxes with three layers of aluminum foil. Wrapped inside the foil were hundred-dollar bills, dozens and dozens of them. That seemed to be how Wilson had protected his money from all kinds of unwelcome visitors.

'Pain? What pain did he have before his head exploded?'

' 'Livin' la Vida Loca.' The crazy lover who takes away your pain, like a bullet to the brain. You know, Mike. Ricky Martin.'

'I get the crazy-lover bit. Seems to be the case here.'

'Ask Alex. She does a killer imitation of Ricky's dance moves. She loves that song.'

'She does?'

Amazing the things you learn about someone you think you know so well, when you hear about her from the perspective of others.

'Yeah. She rocks it. You must have been working the night of Nan's birthday party. A few too many Dewar's and Alex was putting on a show with Ryan Blackmer. The girl has moves,' Lee said. 'What other rooms we got?'

'Bathroom. Seems the sergeant and his rookies were eager to get in the game. He tells me nothing was touched, but I'm not betting on it. And a tiny kitchen. That's where I struck oil.'

I waited while Lee checked out the bathroom and then crossed back to the kitchen. I couldn't dance to save my life, yet I knew Coop liked it almost as much as she enjoyed cross-examining every lying scumbag she'd ever faced.

'Roach traps? You moved them to get to the oil?'

'Took them out from under the sink. You can still see the foot-prints of each of them from the liquid that leaked onto the cardboard and left a stain.'

We were both on our knees, my flashlight

beaming into the dark hole. 'I took these five boxes out and left the rest in place. The first three? Enough *cucarachas* to line up head to toe, string them to Jupiter and back.'

'No kidding? I've got to text Alex a picture of the roach mortuary.'

'She's sound asleep, Lee.'

'Tomorrow, then. That girl's lived a charmed life. I think she saw her first cockroach when she showed up at the scene of a homicide we had together in the projects ten years ago. Like they didn't migrate to the fancy part of Westchester where she grew up. Lucky thing.'

'Yeah.' Lee was right about Coop's charmed childhood. I had wasted way too many hours wondering how her background and mine could possibly find common social ground.

'How about the next two boxes, Mike?'

'Hundred-dollar bills, my man. Lots of them. Maybe more once we toss the place.'

'Bingo! I thought the broad killed him for his money.'

'Maybe so. But she didn't get all of it — that's for sure.'

'We'll start shutterbugging. Why don't you go to the wailing wall and calm Wilson's daughter down?'

'Have a heart, Lee. It's her pops lying here with a hole in his head.'

'You want me to snap the green before you go next door?'

'Keep it where it is for the moment. I want to see what the daughter knows. I want to see if she claims the missing loot was her father's or the property of the not-so-right reverend. Give me thirty minutes.'

Lee and his partner were setting up their equipment as I walked out the door of Wynan Wilson's small crib. His daughter, Angela, was in the adjacent apartment. I didn't need a floor plan. I just followed the sound of the sobs.

The door was unlocked. I knocked lightly and twisted the knob. She and the neighbor, a slight elderly woman in a blue chenille robe, were sitting on the sofa. There was a cup of tea on the table in front of Angela, but it was still full.

'Hello, ladies. I'm Mike Chapman,' I said, extending my hand with the gold and blue shield of the NYPD detective division to show my proper ID.

'We've been expecting you,' the older woman said.

'Thanks. And thanks for taking care of Ms. Wilson,' I said, before turning to the dead man's daughter. 'I'm so sorry for your loss. And for the fact that you had to see your father this way.'

Angela Wilson nodded, blowing her nose at the same time as she tried to get her emotions under control.

I had a habit of running my fingers through my hair, sort of subconsciously, so that I wasn't even aware I was doing it. Coop thought it was a nervous reaction, that it made witnesses think I was working my first homicide or something. I didn't know how to stop doing it, since most of the time I didn't know that I was. But now Angela Wilson was watching the top of my head instead of making eye contact.

'Tea, Detective?' the neighbor asked. 'Or something stronger?'

'No, ma'am. Nothing, thank you.'

'Then I'll excuse myself, Detective. It's Angela you want to see.'

The women hugged each other and the older one left the room. I pulled up a small armchair across the table from Angela and started to talk. I asked her how she was feeling now, and whether she'd taken any pills or had anything to drink. Neither, she told me.

Her eyes were red and the skin beneath them was puffy and tear streaked. I riffed for a while about how difficult her work must be, the fact that the sergeant had told me she was an only child, and my big lie to her that someday the image that had been created tonight — the sight of her father's head blown to bits in his own bed, the crimson fluid spattered around him — would fade to a distant memory. That would stay with her as long as she lived.

'May I ask you some questions, Angela?'

'Certainly, Detective. I'll do my best to answer.' She was wringing a handkerchief with both hands.

'Mike. Please call me Mike,' I said, with a glance at my watch. It was after midnight. 'Did you work yesterday?'

'I did. Yes, I did.'

Her shift was twelve hours, from eight A.M. to eight P.M., caring for a woman in her late nineties — who was in good health, she said, though too frail to manage at home by herself.

'Had you planned to visit your father after work?'

'No. I hadn't expected to do it. I was going to meet a friend of mine for a late supper, around ten o'clock, at a restaurant just two blocks from here.'

'The friend, may I ask his name?'

'A woman. We went to high school together. We have dinner once a month. She's a nurse at Columbia Presbyterian.'

'Sorry to interrupt you,' I said, after she spelled the friend's name for me.

'It's okay,' Angela said, sniffling into her handkerchief. 'I called my father, probably around four o'clock in the afternoon.'

'On his landline, or does he have a cell?'

'No landline anymore. He's got a cell phone.'

'What's the number?' I hadn't seen one anywhere in the apartment. I texted Lee to look for it immediately and when Angela gave me the number I texted the lieutenant to have TARU — the Technical Assistance Response Unit — start tracking it.

'Anyway, I hadn't seen him in almost a week. I called to ask if he needed anything, but he didn't answer.'

'What about Keesh? Wouldn't she get what he needed?'

'Keesh doesn't live here. Least not most of the time. And the reason it was so good for me to come by is that my father said that she was out of town for the week.'

'Out of town?' Not the three words I wanted to hear about my suspect.

'Don't get that worried look on your face, Mike,' Angela said. She was focused again on the top of my head. I must have had my hand in my hair. 'She never goes far.'

'Where to?'

'I didn't want to burst my father's bubble. Keesh would just move in with somebody else who fancied her, brief as that might be. Somebody with a fatter wallet than my daddy.'

'Didn't he know that?' I asked. 'Wasn't there a chance that he'd run into her on the street?'

'Daddy? I've got to back you up so you understand him. He only went two places when he left home — the community center and the liquor store. If Keesh stayed clear of both of those, she might as well be on Bourbon Street in New Orleans, 'cause Daddy wouldn't see her.'

'But — ?'

'I know. You're going to ask me about food. Doesn't he — didn't he — have to eat?' Angela said without my prompting. 'Yeah. Cans of soup, and mac and cheese for the microwave. Wash it all down with Rémy and my father had everything he needed. With Keesh? That's all he got. Which is why I liked to check up on him. I'd go home when I got off work and pick up some homemade food to bring him.'

'And you did?' I asked.

'Yeah. I made meat loaf the night before — two of them — and some black-eyed peas. Called Daddy again around nine o'clock to say I was on my way. I was gonna heat it up for him, sit and talk for a while — ' Angela said, choking up and covering her mouth with the handkerchief.

I waited while she composed herself.

'I called mostly to make sure that Keesh hadn't come home a couple of days earlier than Daddy expected. Hadn't come back to him, dragging her sorry tail between her legs.'

'Did he — ?'

'No. No, he still didn't answer. Went right to voice mail.'

'Did that worry you?'

'Not really. My father's healthy as a horse. Excuse me. My father *was* perfectly healthy. When he didn't answer it usually meant the TV was on and he couldn't hear the phone ring. I put the food in a shopping bag and started over here.'

'But Keesh,' I said. 'What if she had showed up?'

'Daddy would have called me. Right as rain. Two of us couldn't be in the same room,' Angela said, dabbing at her puffy eyelids.

'What's your beef with Keesh, Angela?'

She lowered both hands to her lap and looked at me like I was crazy. 'You kidding me or what?'

'I just walked into this story tonight. Blank slate. Help me here.'

Angela's expression turned to ice. 'You need a guide dog for this, Detective? You always so slow on the pickup?'

'Maybe so.'

'My daddy was carrying on with a ho. Plain and simple,' Angela Wilson said, spitting each word out with equal emphasis. 'Takeesha Falls is a full-on ho.'

'I'm — '

'She don't care who she rubs up against, as

long as there's a cash bonus for her lovin', using that word really loosely.'

'I'm confused a bit. I thought your father was a churchgoing man.'

'Church?' she said, waving the hand with the handkerchief over her shoulder. 'Last time Daddy went to church was for my mother's funeral, fifteen years ago.'

'Stay with me, Angela. This is helpful. All I know — all I was told by my boss — was that your father was a good man, a really decent guy, and that he worked — '

'Daddy hasn't worked in five years, Detective,' she said, her annoyance temporarily displacing her emotion. 'Lost his job driving a livery cab with a few too many arrests for being intox'd behind the wheel. And that was a good thing, getting him off the road.'

'Okay, but the information we had was that he worked at the church, for Reverend Shipley.'

'Ha!' Angela Wilson's laugh split the quiet of the small space like a roll of thunder. 'Don't make me sick, Detective. That man don't have no church. Some of you white boys are as dumb as you look. You, too, Detective? What church would that be?'

She stared at the top of my head while I tried to answer her.

'Well, he's a preacher, isn't he?'

'Without any brick-and-mortar place to preach. The man started life as a backup dancer for Little Richard, Detective. Put a collar on and made himself a minister, and nobody calls his bluff on that, ever. All he does is run some bullshit — excuse me, please, but I'm rather agitated — some bullshit organization that keeps his fat old face in the newspapers. Wants you to think he robs from the rich to give to the poor, when all he does is stuff his own pockets with his take.'

I didn't have to ask questions. I just let Angela run with it.

'Was Daddy there? I told you so. The community center is where Shipley ran the show from. You know that. He controls all those protests against you guys. Against the police.'

Cops hated Hal Shipley. I tried to keep that in the back of my mind so it didn't infect how I looked at Wynan Wilson's murder.

'Gotham City Humanity Activists, Detective. I know you know that operation. You know what smart folks in Harlem call it, or don't you? Every organization has an acronym these days, doesn't it?' Angela said. 'Use those first three letters of *Gotham*, put them together with the rest of the first letters of his *city humanity activists*. We call it *GOTCHA*!'

I smiled for the first time since meeting her. *GOTCHA*. The guys in the squad were going to love this one.

'I like your smile, Detective.'

'And I like your candor. Do you know Shipley?'

'Hate's a strong word, and I don't use it often. But I hate that man.'

'But it's fair to say, isn't it, that your father didn't feel the same?'

'Shipley paid the bills for Daddy, didn't he? I

109

mean, not literally. But he trusted my father to take home those bunches of little envelopes, the ones filled with cash. Those fools who'd send in money from direct-mail advertising. Fifty dollars from a widow in Pittsburgh or twenty from an ex-con in Memphis. For the reverend to carry on his noble work.'

'What did your father do with the money?'

'Sat in front of the TV at home, just opening those envelopes and stacking up the cash. Too many nosy people in the community center. Planted it under his mattress for safekeeping.'

'Then how did he get it back to Shipley?'

'You're gonna make yourself bald, you keep stroking your hair like that, Mike,' she said.

'How do you think he got it back?' I said again.

I wanted to hear it from Angela without suggesting an answer to her. I didn't expect what I got.

'Takeesha Falls is the Reverend Shipley's whore, Detective. You need a fancy gold shield to figure that one out?'

'I don't know the players, Angela.'

'Here's the scorecard, Mike. Nobody loves — loved — my daddy more than I did. Warts and all, he was a sweet man.'

'I hear that.'

'You think Keesh falls in love with an overweight, out-of-work alcoholic who lives in a fourth-floor walk-up? Don't give her no bling or take her out for cocktails more than once every two weeks? Hooker with a heart of gold? I sort of doubt it.'

'She's Shipley's — ?'

'I'm not sayin' she was ever in bed with him. Not necessarily speaking of that kind of whore. But she's on his payroll, too. Does all his bidding, sexual and otherwise. Shipley introduced her to Daddy, knowing my father's fondness for a particular type of woman. She encouraged his drinking habit to stop him from too many demands on her body. Most of all, Keesh was supposed to be the watchdog, keeping Daddy honest and delivering the cash to the reverend, at the time and place most appropriate for his receiving of it.'

What at first glance seemed to be a straightforward domestic homicide was sprouting wings that would carry it all the way to City Hall, where Shipley had unfettered access to the gangly new mayor, who didn't seem to take a step — or make a misstep — without the reverend. This unorthodox treatment of the cash proceeds of the Gotham activists' fund-raising went hand in glove with Shipley's personal history of tax fraud. Coop was going to love this twist.

'Let me ask you this, Angela,' I said, as too many random thoughts of how far up the ladder this killing would lead raced through my brain. 'Does your father have a gun?'

The handkerchief was in her lap. She played with its rolled edges.

'Did he. You mean did he have one?'

'Yes. Sorry for that.'

'Course he did. Small one,' Angela said. 'Don't know what you call them — pistol or

111

revolver — but a small black one. It's not there tonight. I looked for it.'

'Where did he keep it?' I had opened the night table drawers for the same reason.

'Right by the front door. On the stand under the TV. It was the best place to have it, so that nobody got in that he didn't know.'

'You — you didn't take anything out of there, did you, Angela?'

'Like the gun, Detective? Like I've been talking crazy enough so you think maybe I shot my daddy to put him out of his misery?'

She was all puffed up now, full of outrage at me.

'Not the gun. No, I wasn't thinking of the gun,' I said. I took the chance of smiling at her for a second time. 'In my book, everyone's a suspect till I put the cuffs on the killer. Can't ever rule out the first one who finds the body.'

'You think I hate Keesh enough to set her up, don't you?'

'I believe you loved your father. That's why it's also hard to ask you whether you think he ever helped himself to any of the reverend's money. But I've got to do it. I've been wondering, with all that cash, if you think he — '

'I hope to God he did, Detective. I hope he took fistfuls for himself,' Angela Wilson said. She was on fire now. The whites of her eyes, streaked with ruptured blood vessels from hours of crying, glistened as she talked to me. 'I hope Daddy had it hidden well enough that his bitch didn't find any of it.'

'Did you search for that, too, Angela?'

112

'You got a real mean streak, Detective. You know that? Start out nice and easy, but you got a streak.'

'I've been told. You haven't seen that side yet. I got no reason to show it. I'm asking you the same thing I'd ask anyone else in this position.'

'I didn't say I searched anywhere, did I?'

'You looked for the gun.'

'Damn right I did. I called 911 just as soon as my hand stopped shaking so bad I could actually dial the three numbers. Then I looked for the gun in case Shipley or any of those felons he collects showed up at Daddy's bedside before you gentlemen did.'

Angela Wilson was weeping again.

There was a soft knocking on the apartment door.

'Give me five more, Lee. We're almost done,' I said, without taking my eyes off Angela.

'Right now, Chapman,' he said, cracking the door to talk to me.

'Back off, will you? Five minutes.'

I was getting everything I wanted and more from Wilson's daughter. I didn't need Petrie to interrupt her mood swings or the flow of her information.

'Pretty urgent,' Lee Petrie said. 'The Most Reverend Hal Shipley is here to offer a moment of silent prayer over the body of Wynan Wilson.'

11

'Mike Chapman. Homicide.'

'Hal Shipley. The Reverend Hal Shipley. Pleased to meet you.'

I didn't want to remind him that we'd met before. The circumstances were never happy ones when a police officer crossed the path of a self-righteous charlatan. I almost put his lights out when he led a protest at the wake of a cop who'd been slain by a teenage psychopath. I'd wanted to collar him ten years back when he'd lied about a young woman who had fabricated a rape case and identified an innocent man as her assailant. He had sneered at me on the steps of City Hall and in the stairwell of a housing project where a parolee had ambushed a rookie cop.

'You mind stepping out of Mr. Wilson's apartment? It's a crime scene.'

'Wynan Wilson is a dear friend of mine, Detective. I'd like to see him, be alone with him for a moment. Pray for his soul.'

'Not possible. Just kindly back out into the hallway. You shouldn't have been allowed in, in the first place.'

'I'm his spiritual adviser,' Shipley said, putting the palm of his hand on my chest. 'You don't understand.'

'Get your paw off me, Hal.'

'Do we know each other?'

'Not really.' All cops looked alike to Hal Shipley. It wasn't a matter of race. We were Blue. NYPD Blue. 'Back it up.'

Shipley took a glance around the small room, then turned and went into the hallway. I had sent Petrie's partner in to sit with Angela Wilson. She wanted a go at the reverend, but I told her to save it for a day or two. She was whimpering now, and Shipley's ears picked up the sound.

'Is that Angela?' he asked.

'Let's take your business downstairs.'

'Who's your supervisor, Detective?'

'Someone who doesn't like you any better than I do. You lead down and I'll follow.'

Hal Shipley's laced shoes had a better shine than my loafers. The three-piece suit was an affectation he had sported for years, though its material showed it as clearly off the rack from some discount store.

When he reached the first floor he was ready with questions.

'You'll wake the neighbors, Hal. Try the vestibule.'

I joined him in the space that separated the building entrance from the locked door to the apartments above, and I leaned against the row of metal-fronted mailboxes. There was no room for him to posture for me or to squirm if he didn't like the direction of my questions.

'How'd you know Wilson was dead?' I asked.

'Friends, Mr. Chapman. We have many mutual friends.'

'Which one of them told you? And how? In person, by phone call?'

'I'm not here to answer questions. I'm here to ask them.'

Shipley swiveled toward the glass panes in the upper part of the front door and looked out.

'You got peeps with you, Rev? Leg breakers or what?'

I could see over Shipley's head. Two husky men in overcoats were standing guard beside his double-parked, dark-tinted-windows SUV.

'Pallbearers, Detective. Wynan's honorary pallbearers.'

'A little premature, don't you think?'

'My people have a tradition, Mr. Chapman. I'd like to say a prayer over Wynan.'

'What part of 'it's a crime scene' don't you understand? The medical examiner is having a look at the deceased right now.'

'Well, before they remove the body to the morgue.'

'Why don't you help us for a change, Rev? Tell me where the killer is.'

'If only I had the power to know,' Shipley said.

'Surely you've figured out who he is.'

Shipley's eyes narrowed and he stared into mine. 'Now, how would I — ?'

'Or she. Who she is.'

The reverend was a man who couldn't easily be baited. He fixed his gaze but never blinked.

'Wynan was shot,' Shipley said. 'That's what I've heard. Is that much the truth?'

'The gospel, Rev.'

I took a plastic case of Tic Tacs out of my pocket and popped two in my mouth.

'Was — was there a fight?' he asked.

116

'Now we're getting into need-to-know territory. I'm just not able to tell you.'

'Angela — she's the one who found Wynan?'

'Yes, she did.'

'I think I can offer her some measure of
comfort, if you'll let me see her.'

'I got the firm impression that she worships
somewhere else, Rev. She doesn't have quite as
much admiration for you as her old man did.'

'Time to mend fences, Detective. A time to
heal, a time to mend.'

'I know you think cops are heathens, but I've
spent plenty of time in church. To everything,
Rev, there is a season. A time to refrain from
embracing.'

'Ecclesiastes.'

'The Byrds. A time for dying, and this wasn't
meant to be Wynan Wilson's moment. So why don't
you tell me what kind of work he did for you?'

'Certainly. That's no mystery, Detective,'
Shipley said. 'Wynan was a helping hand at the
community center I run. He assisted me in
recruiting newcomers and did minor chores,
taking care of the mail and such.'

The reverend could bullshit with the best of
them.

'Where did he recruit, Rev? At AA meetings?'

'Are you implying that Wynan had a drinking
problem? I never saw the slightest evidence of
that,' Shipley said. 'What he did after hours was
quite his own business.'

'Looking around his apartment tonight, can't
say I saw a computer. How'd he handle that mail
for you?'

'He was responsible for recording the names and addresses of contributors, which he'd pass along to my secretary. Make a record of the checks and so on.'

'I don't think the man was a skilled banker, Rev. Kind, gentle, fond of the ladies, but I doubt he was the J. P. Morgan of your organization.'

'We'll have to ask my secretary just what his duties were. I've got a lot of responsibilities so I'm not exactly hands-on with everything,' he said, glancing out the window again.

'Word is you're hands-on with the cash. Word is — '

'You can stand in this — this half a hallway, Detective, and be as rude as you want, but it won't get you answers to — '

'For the moment, Rev, this vestibule is my office. That's as good as it gets in the NYPD. It's my office and you're my witness. There'll be a subpoena on your desk before noon asking for the name and address of every contributor, a copy of every letter that has come in during the last year. That is, if the IRS doesn't have that stuff already. Make sure nothing disappears between now and then.'

Hal Shipley laughed at me. In my face. Then he took his phone from his pocket and appeared to be texting someone.

'Wynan Wilson was your bagman. Excuse me. One of your bagmen. You can practice that asinine guffaw till it chokes you, Rev, but that's the worst-kept secret in the hood. Now, when's the last time Wilson brought money to you?'

Shipley ignored me and kept texting. When he

118

finished the message, he looked up and spoke to me. 'I have no idea what you're referring to, Detective.'

'You think I don't know why you showed up in the middle of the night, shot out of a rocket, to get here and be alone with Wilson? Alone in the apartment? He must have shorted you a few bucks.'

'You about done, Mr. Chapman? 'Cause I got places to go.'

'You going to pay a condolence call on Takeesha Falls?'

'Miss Takeesha will be mighty sad about Wynan,' Shipley said, shaking his head. 'You seen her yet?'

'Good try, boss. Mighty good try. Yeah, Keesh and I had a real come-to-Jesus moment. She was so broken up she almost regretted being such a straight shooter.'

Shipley snorted again. 'I'll call that bluff on you.'

'Course you will. No doubt you've got her hidden away, right where you want her.'

'What's up with your imagination, Mr. Chapman? It's running you wild. People know better than to talk to me this way.'

'I'm shaking in my boots, Rev. What are you going to do? Organize a protest?'

His iPhone buzzed and he unpocketed it again to look at the response to his text.

'I'm going to be all over you, like horseflies on a pig's ear, till I get to the bottom of this, Reverend Shipley. There's a man upstairs who met an untimely end — a good old guy — and he was all wrapped up in your business. And it stinks to high hell,' I said. 'I'm going to be — '

'You're gonna be sitting this one out, Detective,' Shipley said, holding up his phone to my face.

'I don't work for you, Rev. And unless you've got a pipeline to the police commissioner, I doubt that text you just sent has any relevance to this homicide.'

'I've got a better pipeline than that, Mr. Chapman. This here's a return text from the mayor's chief of staff. The police commissioner answers to City Hall.'

'Twelve noon, Reverend,' I said. I've had smackdowns from the top brass for better reasons than my interface with a total jackass.

Shipley walked out and started down the steps of the old brown-stone. One of his lackeys opened the rear passenger door of the Suburban. He looked back, cocked his thumb and forefinger as though firing a pistol, and called out a single word to me: 'Gotcha!'

12

I tried to get the plate number of the SUV as Shipley and his crew sped off. I couldn't see the first three figures, but I was pretty sure it ended in C78.

I checked my phone for messages but there were none, so I made my way back upstairs.

'Sorry to break away, Lee. Last thing we needed was Hal Shipley snooping around in here.'

The young medical examiner seemed to be wrapping up her work while Lee Petrie continued to take pictures of Wynan Wilson, who'd been turned onto his back.

'Amen to that,' Petrie said.

The exit wound was as large as I'd expected it to be, irregular in shape and bloody. In all likelihood, the bullet had exploded within the brain tissue and surrounding muscle as it passed through Wilson's head.

'What do you think, Doc?' I asked. 'The muzzle was directly against Wilson's skin, wouldn't you say? Jammed tight in there, wasn't it?'

I had never seen this pathologist before. She seemed tentative and nervous when she answered me. 'Probably so.'

There was no 'probably' about it. Last thing I needed on this case was a neophyte practicing her art on a high-profile murder.

'It's a hard-contact wound,' I said. 'Perforating. You saw the searing, the abrasion ring, didn't you? The autopsy's going to show soot particles and unburnt powder.'

'Lay off, Mike,' Lee said. 'The autopsy will tell her whatever it does.'

'You know anything about bullet size yet?' I asked, directing the question to the ME.

'Don't mind him, Doc. He's always impatient,' Lee said. 'I dug the bullet out of the wall, Mike. Show it to you when I'm done. Thirty-eight caliber. Nothing special. Check the crap all over that pillow in the corner.'

'Gray matter? Whatever Wilson had left for a brain?'

'Nah. Killer probably held it over the gun to try to muffle the sound. Residue and stuff. The lab will get it. The brains and bone are on that pillow on the left side,' Lee said, pointing it out to me. 'And all over the wall. The slug got glued to the plaster underneath some cranium fragments, that flap of skin you saw, and a lock of hair.'

'Lucky for the lady next door. Could have taken one behind the ear while she was heating up her teapot,' I said. 'You want to talk about angle of yaw?'

The medical examiner looked like I had impaled her foot on the carpet with a sharp question.

'He's testing you, Doc,' Lee said. 'Mike's not one of the world's great feminists.'

'Everybody's got to prove themselves, okay?'

'Angle of yaw, my ass. You're playing with her.'

'No offense taken. I think I'm done,' she said.

'I'm really interested in the angle, Doc. No kidding. I mean, the shooter was right-handed, don't you figure?'

'Probably so.'

'And the deceased was belly down, his head slightly to the side. So you'd have to be a contortionist to wedge the gun against the base of his skull just by — I don't know — just by kneeling alongside the bed. Couldn't do it and get this perfect result.'

'I can speculate all you'd like, Detective,' the pathologist said. 'But I'd much prefer to have this conversation after I've done the postmortem.'

'You made a record of those marks on both sides of the gut, didn't you?'

'Sure did,' she said, taking off her paper gown and vinyl gloves and closing her tool bag.

'Can we talk about them?'

'Day after tomorrow,' she said. 'My place. You'll be there for the autopsy?'

'Wouldn't miss it for the world,' I said. 'Have you got a car downstairs?'

'Yes.'

'My partner will walk you down,' Lee said, continuing to photograph Wynan Wilson from the least-flattering angles, his bottle of cheap liquor just out of reach when he needed it most.

'The van is outside,' she said. 'Okay if I tell the men they can remove the body?'

'Fine with me,' Lee said.

We said our good nights and she was on her way.

'You think I need to do anything else here?' Lee asked. 'Photos of the wall enough?'

'If I were you, I'd send some men back tomorrow to take down this four-foot square of plaster. We're going front-page *New York Post.*'

'Don't make me laugh,' Lee said. 'Poor old fool gets offed by a greedy hooker. It's nobody's news.'

'More like *Rubout for Randy Rev's Cash Stash* running on top of the fold. You watch. Mix Shipley into this and there's going to be double trouble. Maybe triple.'

'You want to count the cash here or at the property clerk's office?' Lee asked.

'Wait till your partner gets back. Safer with three of us, especially since he doesn't know me. I can count it again when I voucher it with the clerk.'

Lee was running through his mental checklist of tasks.

'You know what that asshole just did?' I said. 'Shipley. I mean Hal Shipley, not the doc.'

'What?'

'He didn't like being questioned about the murder, so he texted the mayor's chief of staff. Thinks he can throw me off the case.'

'Who's the chief of staff? You know the guy?'

'Nope. It's not a guy. It's that cop-hating broad who's a pal of the mayor's crackpot wife.'

The new mayor was despised by the rank and file of the department. He had campaigned with a priority plan to end the long-established stop-and-frisk policy that had saved countless lives and thwarted scores of violent crimes. And

124

his first official decision was to order his counsel to settle a civil lawsuit by four perps who had rampaged through Times Square a decade earlier, assaulting half a dozen citizens, their conviction vacated because of a jailhouse confession by a psychopath codefendant. The settlement came at an outrageous cost to voters, even though smart money still favored the group's guilt, and the mayor's own appointed city lawyer — a Hal Shipley disciple — had declared no signs of any law enforcement wrongdoing.

'I know who you mean. Shitslinger. Ronnie Shitslinger.'

'You're cracking me up, Lee. You'll have Wynan laughing in a minute,' I said, snapping my finger. 'Very close. It's a name like that. It's Ronnie Sonlinger.'

'Shitslinger is what she is, Mike. You know she lives with a convicted killer?'

'That's been all over the papers. That and the fact that he constantly tweets nasty anti-cop sentiments. The commissioner won't be backing this up. The broad should be fired.'

'Yeah, but then Mrs. Mayor won't have anybody compatible to pass her time with.'

I bit my lip to stop from laughing out loud.

'I'm truthing you, Mike. She and Sonlinger spend their time together ragging on the cops who keep them safe.'

We were both scouring Wilson's digs for any other signs of relevant evidence before closing off the apartment.

'He's a one-term mayor,' I said. 'Save your energy.'

'Clawed his way in this first time. Reporters said he won by a landslide, but the fact is nobody turned out to vote. Like, nobody at all. Sixty percent of twenty pathetic votes is still only, like, twelve votes. Nobody cared.'

'They seem to care now,' I said.

As unpopular as the mayor had been since taking office, his wife was viewed as an irrational nuisance.

'There'll be a ruckus if she tries to dump you, Mike.'

'Commissioner Scully won't have any of that, not that anybody would give a damn.'

Keith Scully and I had a long history together, most of it good.

'Shipley and this mayor go way back, don't they? Shipley got Harlem to turn out for him,' Lee said as he packed up his camera equipment. 'Alex hates him, too. The reverend, I mean.'

'She won't talk about it.'

'Yeah, but I was there, Mike. I heard him.'

I looked up. 'Shipley?'

'Yeah. It was her third big case. Third or fourth, in the courthouse across the street from her office.'

Paul Battaglia had assigned Coop to the pioneering Special Victims Unit of the DA's office at a surprisingly early point in her career. Her predecessor had resigned abruptly, and he had come to rely on that rare combination of skill and compassion that hall-marked her career.

'Came to be, Battaglia wouldn't let her walk through the crowd without a bodyguard,' Lee said. 'Boy, did she fight that.'

126

'But she needed it, didn't she?'

'Yeah, Alex needed it all right. Because Shipley brought himself — and probably bought himself, too — a whole posse of rabble-rousers. The perp on trial was one of his faithful, but he just happened to be a serial rapist. Best way to take the attention off the bad guy was to harass Alex Cooper. Day and night, on the street in front of the courthouse, even in the hallway of the building. It was just after Shipley's Twainey Bowler fiasco.'

'The false accusation a decade ago?' I said. 'I know he scorched Coop that time.'

'Scorched? He flat out tried to torpedo her. Made it personal, Mike. Real personal. Shouted "Jew bitch!" every time she passed through the crowd.'

I was pissed off. I had known Coop then, but not well. I was sorry I hadn't punched Shipley in the face fifteen minutes ago. Sorry I hadn't shoved his fat face through the panes of glass in the vestibule window.

'Nobody spoke out, did they?'

'The only one with the balls to take the reverend on was Alex herself,' Lee said. 'But Battaglia gagged her. Told her to take the high road.'

'Fuck the high road,' I said. 'It's usually a dead end.'

'So how come nobody takes Shipley on? Nobody ever calls him out?' Lee was marking each piece of evidence he had bagged so I could take it to the lab for analysis.

'They're all cowards. Gutless wonders.'

'He's on the steps of City Hall when the mayor gets sworn in. Think I'd be there if I hadn't paid taxes in a decade? Think you'd be invited if you had invented some fake crime ten years back and made some poor law enforcement guy lose his job? And never apologize for or explain it, even a decade later? You and me, we'd be walking a beat in Coney Island. News jocks even use him now as a talking head.'

'Last thing I'd ever want to be.'

'Chris Matthews? He plays hardball with everybody else but treats Shipley like he's the next pope. Joe Scarborough? Not shy about going after corrupt politicians, but Shipley's got a permanent pass. Imus? Yeah, Imus has no use for him. He's the only one.'

'When I walk into a room and hear Shipley's voice on the tube, pontificating about justice, I just want to throw a tire iron at the screen.'

'Hold the thought. Your day will come. Rumor has it he's getting his own TV show,' Lee said. 'Like on one of those cable channels that don't care if ratings are in the toilet.'

'He's had his own show for years, hasn't he?' I asked. '*The Price Is Right*. That's Hal Shipley's show. The price is always right for Hal to play.'

'Nobody takes him on, like I say.' Lee Petrie was just about ready to go.

'I think his luck is about to change, Lee. Coop has the fortitude to take him on. And it looks at the moment like all roads lead to Hal Shipley,' I said, thinking about the district attorney and his connections to the reverend. 'Coop'll thrive on this one. She'd like nothing better than to put his

128

guilty ass behind bars.'

'What did Angela Wilson tell you? What did Shipley say? You're gonna jail him for what?'

'Aiding and abetting a homicide, Lee. That's where I'm going with this, before the feds ever get out of the starting blocks on their tax case,' I said. 'We're going to nail the fat fuck for murder.'

13

It was just before seven A.M. when I reached the lab. The ME had taken samples of blood, skin, and hair along with her to the morgue, so the routine testing and any forensic work she might order would get under way immediately.

I had stopped at the property clerk's office to re-count the money that Lee Petrie, his partner, and I had been through once at Wilson's apartment. Twenty-seven thousand large, all under the roach-infested sink. I got permission to take the bills with me to the lab instead of vouchering them and letting them sit on a shelf collecting dust, in case we might be lucky enough to get touch DNA off any of them.

I had the bullet that killed Wynan Wilson for the ballistics examiners. No spent shell — the shooter had been cool enough to pick up her debris. No gun yet, but that could be just a matter of time. I had toiletries that either Wilson or Keesh might have used, and kitchen utensils that might yield results about the most recent visitors. Saliva from the highball glasses in the sink could tell us whether the deceased had a drinking partner.

Once I'd signed off on everything, I walked outside to my car. It was a nippy fall morning. I started the engine and then checked my phone for messages.

Nothing from Lieutenant Peterson, so nobody

at City Hall had dropped a dime on me. I was right about Shipley's bluff.

And nothing from Coop.

She didn't want to bother me at a crime scene and expose me to the ribbing of the other guys, who were comically ruthless at the news that Coop and I had hooked up. I didn't need to jack her up, either, before her meeting with Battaglia about the computer mess created by Antonio Estevez and his bride.

Garden-variety domestic, I wrote to her in an e-mail. She'd get the irony in that once I told her the full story. It's how law enforcement referred to O.J. Simpson's murder of Nicole, until an incompetent judge and an overhyped media frenzy screwed the case up. *Perp in flight, but you'll like my idea to smoke her out.*

I sent her a second e-mail. *Assign a star to handle this one, will you? Someone who can withstand a little heat from the New York Times.*

Coop would want this case for herself, but with Shipley tied up in the investigation — if not in the actual crime — she would recuse herself. I knew that. But I also knew that she would pull the strings from behind the scenes and that nothing would derail her from outing the truth about the reverend, even when political pressure fanned the flames.

The last e-mail was personal, to separate it from any discovery motions that would put our correspondence into play. Far-fetched, but after Estevez, worth doing.

Hey, Coop. Going home for a few hours' sleep. The weekend will feel really good. So will you.

131

14

'Mike? It's Catherine. Am I getting you at a bad time?'

I caught about three hours' sleep before my cell phone buzzed. I sat up on the side of the bed to sound alive for the conversation.

'Not a problem. Coop gave the Wilson case to you?' I asked. 'What does an adult say that sounds as good as 'awesome!'? You are so gonna love what I've got — '

'I don't know anything about the case. That's not why I'm calling.'

'What's up? What do you need?'

'I'm looking for Alex,' she said.

I checked my watch. It was almost noon. 'She's with big, bad Battaglia. Taking the weight for the Estevez leak. She wasn't looking forward to the meet, but that's what was looming when I left the shindig.'

'The DA didn't get in until almost eleven. He called over for her to come see him right away,' Catherine said. 'Laura hasn't heard from her yet and the boss is steaming.'

I laughed. 'You must be low broad on the totem pole. You've been assigned to ask me to look under the covers and see if she's hiding in bed with me? Doing the deed with — ?'

'I'm sorry, Mike. The last thing I want to do is intrude on your personal life. She's not answering her phone, her texts, her e-mails. I figured you might be at her place and — '

'I'm home. Which is where I live, in case anybody in your public information office needs to know. The high-rent district gives me agita. Grown men walking their Yorkies and cockapoos look at me like Stanley Kowalski just moved into the building.'

'You've got a mighty inferiority complex, Detective Chapman. I'll have you over to our digs. We've got lots of manlier dogs there. You'd be the George Clooney of the black Lab-walking set,' Catherine said. 'Now, would you mind trying to raise her up for me?'

'Sure. Sure thing, Catherine.'

I popped open my in-box to look for return messages from Coop. There were none. I pressed the button to dial her cell, which went straight to voice mail.

'Stop pouting, blondie. I don't want to have to send out the Mounties for you. Call me.'

My apartment — the coffin, as I liked to call it — was smaller than Wynan Wilson's. I walked past three days of dirty clothes hanging from the back of a chair into the bathroom.

I turned on the shower and stepped in. I like cool water — Coop calls it cold. It's bracing and better for me than the tons of caffeine I ingest every day to restart my engines. Besides, I don't have the patience to wait for it to get to its maximum lukewarm high temperature.

I wrapped a clean towel around my waist, grabbed my razor to go over my face, and picked up the phone. Nothing back from Coop.

I hit Catherine's number and she answered

instantly. 'No sign of life,' I said. 'We'll just have to wait her out. What time did your party break up?'

'She didn't leave the restaurant all that long after you did. And she was testy.'

'Welcome to *my* world,' I said. 'I get testy from her in spades. What do you mean?'

'She was all excited about Tanner's arrest. Like one of the guys said when she walked into Primola, first time she'd be able to sleep like a baby.'

'Could be that. Could be she got wrecked and just turned off her phone, let herself relax with Tanner in custody.'

'She didn't drink all that much. She wasn't wrecked.'

'You're not telling me you're worried, are you?' I asked.

'Not about Alex,' Catherine said. 'I'm actually worried *for* her, Mike. Afraid her temper has gotten the better of her this time.'

Alex Cooper could be cooler than a glacier in the courtroom. We had all seen her take on cold-blooded killers and hotheaded adversaries. She was amazing grace under pressure and indefatigable in standing tall for the vulnerable, for the victims without voices.

But Coop had a hair-trigger temper that she managed to keep in check in professional settings. Up close and personal she lost her shit way too often.

'Pat McKinney?' I asked. He was the immediate supervisor who had tried to wreck Coop's career several times. 'Or Battaglia himself?'

'The district attorney. I don't know whether Alex had time to tell you last night,' Catherine said, 'but he totally laced into her about the Estevez business. He actually told her that if anything that came out of it embarrassed him, she might as well make herself disappear. I'm worried that maybe she took him literally and is playing hard to get.'

'I clocked out at eight A.M. I should have called her then like I told her I would, but it got kind of busy at the Wilson apartment,' I said. 'Haven't seen the morning news. Anything there to suggest trouble for Coop?'

'Not in print. The radio reports claim Hal Shipley showed up at the scene of a homicide last night,' Catherine said. 'Is that the domestic you went out on?'

'Yeah, but it has nothing to do with Estevez. Nobody's talking. There's only a daughter and she's helping us. Maybe neighbors saw Shipley pull up and go inside, but we threw him out pretty quick.'

'Well, Alex didn't assign it to anyone, either.'

'Could be my fault,' I said. 'Didn't see the need to wake her up for no good reason. We didn't make an arrest. And I didn't want her to go in to talk to the DA with information about Shipley that could only have come from me. He wouldn't have liked that.'

'Good plan.'

'While I got you, can you draft me a search warrant for Shipley's office? I told him I'd be there today, looking for records that might relate to the murder. Follow-the-money kind of stuff.'

'Wait for Alex. I don't know who she'll assign to this.'

'Suit yourself. Let me look for her, Catherine. I'll call you later.'

'I'll let you know if she graces us with an appearance.'

I dressed quickly and grabbed two cups of black coffee at the corner deli before I walked the block to my car. Coop's apartment wasn't very far from mine, but the few avenues to the west of me represented miles between the style of my old tenement building and her fancy co-op.

I was sipping the first cup when my phone buzzed. I stopped and put the paper bag on the roof of my car. 'Hello?'

'Chapman? Peterson here. You don't sound like yourself.'

'Hey, Loo. I just burned my tongue on some java.'

'You need to get up to the squad and fill me in on the new case.'

'I can talk to you about it now. I'm working midnights this week.' Peterson knew my schedule. He was never difficult about this kind of thing. 'I wasn't planning to come by the office till then.'

'I asked you to get up here. Now.'

'What for?'

'Do you look for trouble, Chapman, or does it just attach itself to you like a remora to a shark? All natural and such?'

'Wait, Loo. Give me a break,' I said. 'The mayor's chief of staff got to Scully? That's sick. You know that?'

136

'Not that nitwit. The mayor's wife herself.'

'Oh, *that* nitwit.'

'Yeah, well she's working her voodoo on the commissioner. He wants me to get your side of the story — eyeball-to-eyeball, face-to-face, chapter and verse.'

'Voodoo, too? I didn't know that was part of her skill set,' I said. 'Can't say I'm surprised.'

'Scully called me at home. I'm on my way in to the city,' Lieutenant Peterson said. 'How fast can you be at the office?'

'An hour. Sorry to break up your day, Loo. Give me an hour.'

'Make it faster than that, Chapman.'

'I'll be there as soon as I can. I've got one stop to make on the way.'

15

'What's up, Vinny?' I asked the doorman standing at the front desk of Coop's building.

'Everything's calm, Mike. The way I like it.'

I stopped and leaned an elbow on the desktop. 'You might as well go into hibernation with the Yankees done for the season.'

'You're telling me.'

'You see Ms. Cooper this morning?'

Vinny thought for two seconds, then shook his head.

'Not going out?' I asked, then thought — unhappily — that maybe she had come in early this morning if she had spent the night somewhere else. 'Or in?'

'Nope. I've been on the door since seven thirty. The guys relieved me a couple of times for my breaks, so could be I just didn't see her. But I didn't.'

'And who was working last night?'

'Oscar was here till one a.m. Then Patrick, till I came on.'

'Thanks, man. I'll just take a run up,' I said, slapping the marble top and walking to the elevator to press the button for the twentieth floor.

The doormen in Coop's well-run building had known me for years. The shift from being her professional colleague to something more personal must have thrown them off, too.

I stood in front of her door and rang the bell, but there was no response and no noise coming from within. The daily papers, which she still preferred to read in hard copy rather than online, were on the hallway floor. I picked them up to take inside.

Coop had installed an electronic keypad a few months back, after the last time she had left her keys in the office. I knew the code and tapped out the four numbers that unlocked the door.

'Yo! Alexandra Cooper,' I said, stepping into the foyer.

Silence.

'Coop?' I didn't think about it often, but I was the only person in her world who called her Coop. To everyone else she was Alex or Alexandra, the formal name she liked best.

The master bedroom was off to the left. I walked in and glanced around. The king-size bed was made up with the Porthault sheets that she loved — a trust-fund luxury, not affordable on a DA's salary. It was as neat as a pin.

That didn't tell me anything. Coop was religious about making her bed. She did it as soon as she — as soon as we — were out of it, even before she showered. She liked the feeling, she'd told me not long ago, of getting into the crisp, cool, high-thread-count cotton percale sheets at the end of a difficult day.

I walked to the bed and stroked the pillow on her side. I leaned over and sniffed the case for the scent of her Chanel perfume but couldn't make it out.

She wouldn't like me snooping around her

apartment without reason, and I wasn't sure that I had a good one. I was still conflicted about the change in our relationship — not because I didn't love Coop, but because I worried that the gap in our backgrounds was too enormous to overcome.

I looked on the night table for messages or notes. She was an inveterate scribbler — a compulsive list maker, a hoarder of paper with sentimental expressions of affection, a woman with a deadly memory for detail who nevertheless left reminders to herself for every chore that needed tackling. There were no notes or lists needing action today.

There was a postcard from her best friend from college, Nina Baum, on top of the dresser. The two corresponded that way every day of the week.

Taped to the mirror was a photograph of Coop and me ripped from one of the tabloids. It was taken after the confrontation at Grand Central Terminal, when I escorted her off a railroad car that had stopped for us on 125th Street. I had covered her shoulders with a blanket and held her close to me with an arm around her. It was a night that had broken down the barriers between us, and Coop liked the photo — despite the terror in the hours before it was taken — because she said she liked what my embrace represented.

There was a white wicker hamper in the dressing room between the bed and bath. Coop's loyal housekeeper would be here on Friday.

I lifted the lid and looked in. There was

140

underwear and lingerie and a pale pink cotton shirt, but none of the clothing she had been wearing when I left her at Primola.

Her shoe fetish was a bit ridiculous. She rarely wore the same ones two days in a row. I looked at the lineup of heels but didn't have the faintest recollection of which ones she had been wearing the night before.

I passed the guest room on my way back to the foyer, and that was undisturbed. I swept through the living and dining rooms, but nothing was out of place or suggested a visitor. The den was neat, too, and in the kitchen there was not even an empty cocktail glass in the sink.

My last thought was the hall closet, to see if any outerwear was gone. The weather reports last night suggested a drop in temperature. But the camel-hair coat was hanging in place.

I dialed Catherine's number and she picked up after two rings. 'You got anything?' I asked, trying to sound neither annoyed nor anxious.

'Battaglia backed off, so I let it drop,' Catherine said. 'He's got a meeting with the governor about decriminalizing marijuana. Alex caught a break.'

'But you still haven't heard from her.'

Catherine hesitated briefly before answering, but I caught the hitch in her voice. 'No.'

'You cool with that?'

'Yes, actually. I am.'

'Okay,' I said. 'Okay.'

I turned to look around once more before leaving the apartment.

'I mean, after you and I talked, I called Vickee.

They were sitting together before Alex left the restaurant,' Catherine said.

'What am I doing here, playing twenty questions?' I asked. 'This conversation is like pulling teeth.'

'Maybe you should talk to Vickee.'

'I'm talking to *you* now, Catherine. Is there something you want to tell me?' I had the sense, actually, that there was something she *didn't* want to tell me.

'Vickee thinks Alex was really peeved. That Vickee set her off, without meaning to.'

'Who walked Coop out? Last to see her? Was it Vickee?'

'No,' Catherine said. 'She wouldn't let anyone walk her out.'

'Figures. Stubborn to a fault.'

'She said Giuliano would put her in a cab.'

'Got it.' I could talk to him if I couldn't get straight answers from Coop's team. 'I'm at her apartment now. I don't think she ever came home last night.'

A bit too much hesitation, again, before Catherine spoke. 'You might want to talk to Vickee before you get yourself more wound up, Mike. I think Alex had a plan to hang out with some friends.'

16

'You want me to give Ms. Cooper a message when I see her?' Vinny asked.

'No, thanks, pal,' I said, walking out of the lobby. 'See you.'

Coop didn't owe me explanations for any of her behavior at this point in our relationship, and I shouldn't have been disappointed that she didn't let me in on her social plans. I had more important business waiting for me at the squad office. My job had always been my first priority. I needed to keep it that way.

Lieutenant Peterson had made it into his Manhattan North command from Rockland County before I had motored uptown from my pad with a slight detour to Coop's apartment.

He was a chain-smoker, and grandfathered into the department by such long service — or so he thought — that he gave no mind to nonsmoking rules inside police buildings.

His ashtray already had four butts in it by the time I went into his office. 'Sorry you had to come in, Loo. Wish you had been there with me so you could have seen this for yourself.'

Peterson was old-school. He hated it when I put my feet up on his desk, but that was the kind of mood I was in. He had no use for foul language either, so I opted for my physical comfort.

'What do I look like to you, Chapman?'

'Excuse me?'

'Do I look like a clown?'

'No, sir.' I took my feet down immediately. Peterson was one of the men in the department for whom I had total respect.

'I'm not talking about your feet. I'm talking about your work, Chapman,' the lieutenant said, pulling on another cigarette. 'I'm talking about your mouth. I get the feeling you just think I'm your rodeo clown.'

'What — ?'

'You think my job is to keep the men in headquarters at bay every time you get thrown off a bucking bull. I ought to just run around with a clown suit on, making sure you get yourself out of the arena before you get gored to death.'

'You know that's not so, Loo. You know I think the world of — '

'Keith Scully's getting fed up with you, too. What's the story on the Wilson scene?'

'Sure. Nine-one-one call comes in. Vic's daughter, totally legit, finds her father's — '

'Fast-forward.'

'You want details, I thought.'

'Scully trusts you to get the investigation right, Chapman. It's the human intercourse you screw up to a fare-thee-well.'

More than you have any idea, Loo.

'Tell me about Shipley,' Peterson said. 'How and when he got there. Every word he said, and more important what you said to him.'

I spent the next fifteen minutes reconstructing what I could of the conversation.

'That's all there is? You square with me?' the lieutenant asked.

'Totally.'

'He's claiming you insulted him, Chapman. That you were too rude to a well-respected ally of the mayor to represent the NYPD.'

'Rude would have been telling him what I really thought of him. I held back, Loo, out of respect for you,' I said, smiling at Peterson, who didn't find any humor in the situation.

'The cash you found — twenty-seven thousand — did you tell Shipley about that?'

'No way. But I'm sure he was there looking for dough.'

'Why?'

'I assume Wilson was skimming some off the top. Keesh had to have a sense of Wilson's weekly draw and how much he spent on her to keep her around. No real way for anyone at the center to know how much money people were mailing in or offering the reverend under the table, and that's just the way Shipley liked it. Long as he could trust Wynan Wilson . . . '

'The minute you find out anything from the lab, you let me know. Got that, Chapman?'

'So I'm on the case, right?'

'Yeah. Shipley had no business being at the apartment while you were working it, and the mayor's wife certainly doesn't get to call the shots in my squad.' The ashes on the tip of Peterson's cigarette were about to singe his lips. He removed the stub and used it to light the next one.

'Then I'm back in business,' I said. 'Thanks, Loo. I'll head down to the DA's office and get a search warrant.'

'Pug McBride does the warrant. Talk him

through it. Sending you into Shipley's place today would be like sticking the reverend with a red-hot poker.'

'Pug? Give me a break, will you? He won't have a clue what he's looking for. And I can't tell him. It's like porn, boss. I'll just know it when I see it.'

'What kind of search warrant would that be, Chapman? A little too loosey-goosey to pass muster in a court of law,' Peterson said. 'We go in tight and clean on this operation.'

'Let me pick who searches with Pug?'

'Shoot.'

'Jimmy. Jimmy North.'

Peterson tilted his head and took another drag. 'Good choice. Smart kid.'

Jimmy North had been third grade for a couple of years. He was new to homicide, but he was a really fine detective. He was a third-generation cop, with two younger brothers in uniform. North was that rare combination I sort of identified with my own policing skills — his college education hadn't fucked up his street instincts. We all liked teaching him and he soaked up the knowledge like a sponge.

'Alexandra isn't handling this one with you, is she?'

'She took the day off, Loo. I haven't talked to her.'

He seemed not to trust my answer. 'Well, best if she stays on the sidelines. She and Shipley have a history.'

'That's where she'll be,' I said. 'You keeping me on a leash, too?'

'Now that I dragged you in, why don't you work this shift, Chapman? Get your case loaded up in the system. Stay close in the event Commissioner Scully gets pushback.'

'Where's Jimmy?'

'In the field. Who do I send him to at the DA's office?'

'Talk to Coop's secretary. Someone in the white-collar division has Shipley on a fraud watch. But this homicide has all the signs of domestic violence. The DV assistant who's catching today should work on the warrant together with him.'

I closed Peterson's door behind me and walked through the grim squad room to my desk.

I settled in with my steno pad to do my case reports. I punched in the UF 61 number for the homicide of Wynan Wilson — the Uniformed Force document that had been filled out by the first cop on the scene — and the file came right up on my screen.

The NYPD was probably the last institution to join the computer age. Until very recently, I had done all my reports on a typewriter. Now every crime was entered into the Enterprise Case Management system, and every person working on the matter could access it and contribute as evidence developed. Officers in patrol cars had iPads that gave them rap sheets of suspects and case dispositions in real time, and could even provide information on the number of gun arrests at a building location when they responded to a robbery in progress.

147

Not only was the Wilson 61 already uploaded, but so were Lee Petrie's digital photographs of the crime scene and evidence.

I closed the screen without starting my report. I pulled up the motor vehicle bureau site and searched for cars registered to Hal Shipley and the Gotham City Humanity Activists' center.

Shipley owned two cars — a silver Mercedes sedan and a light-blue BMW two-seater convertible. I guess activists like their money going to well-wheeled leaders.

Three of the machines registered to the Gotham center were SUVs, and the fourth was a minivan. Shipley could man a small protest anywhere in the city just by filling up his own fleet.

I checked the plates, but none of them ended in C78. I'd do that search later to find who had been chauffeuring Hal to the Wilson apartment. The plate number might not matter at all.

It was almost five o'clock when I finished entering all my case reports into the computer program. I spent another twenty minutes on the phone talking Jimmy North through the search of Shipley's office and what to look for.

Nan Toth, one of Coop's closest friends, would handle the warrant but couldn't go before a judge to get it signed till tomorrow morning. The tricky part she had to navigate was to make it all about Wynan Wilson but allow us to get our mitts on Shipley's paper trail.

The ME called to confirm that I would be present for the autopsy, also in the morning, at nine o'clock.

I turned my attention back to the information I had about Takeesha Falls. I left a message for Angela Wilson, asking how she was doing and whether she could give me names of friends of her father's who might tell me more about Keesh. I still had a few hours in which I could try to do some interviews.

Guys were in and out of the squad at the four o'clock shift change. You never just worked a solid eight hours in homicide. Witnesses were hard to find and interviews ran over, so the day detectives were only now signing out.

I didn't look up at the footsteps behind me, though they were lighter than most of the guys'.

'Heard you got a live one.' Vickee Eaton kissed me on top of my head. 'Don't you go making work for us at public info, Mike.'

'Detective Eaton, since when did you start making house calls?'

She shrugged. 'I'm on my way home. Mercer's working late, so it's just me and Logan, and he's happy hanging out with my sister, getting his sugar high from the candy she feeds him.'

'Manhattan North isn't remotely on your path to Queens, and I just had the pleasure of your company last night, so this must be an emergency stop for — '

'No emergency. Just — '

'For advice to the lovelorn. Is that it, Vickee?'

'I don't have any advice, Mike. You know that.'

'Then what?'

'Two things. I know you spoke to Catherine today. She really doesn't want to be caught up in the middle of anything between you and Alex.

149

It's one of the reasons I'm here, 'cause she got what she knows from me. The second thing is that I'm getting nervous. I mean, I wasn't until a little bit ago.'

'Why now?' I said, pretending to lose myself in a photograph of Wynan Wilson's head.

'I was tough on Alex last night, okay? I thought she'd be happy about Tanner, but I didn't know much about what had gone on with Estevez until Catherine told me today. I pushed some mean buttons — even about you.'

'So?'

'Well, yes, Alex has got a terrible temper. When I heard she was playing hooky, I felt like I was part of the cause. But she'd never disappear without telling Laura to cover for her. She's never left Laura hanging, even if she planted a white lie to take a day off.'

I hadn't thought of that, but it was probably true.

'Mike, I couldn't do this to you on the phone. Tell you — '

'Let's have it, Vickee. This must be my eyeball-to-eyeball day. First Peterson, now you.'

She waited till I looked at her. 'Alex wasn't on her way home last night when she walked out of Primola. You need to know that.'

'What's that old saying? Free, white, and twenty-one.' I had a knot in the pit of my stomach. 'Excuse my political incorrectness, Vickee. Back in the day — '

'You need to take this more seriously, Mike.'

'I'll bite. That's what I'm supposed to say, right? Where was she going?'

'I got a phone call last week from Jake.'

'Jake Tyler?' The knot felt more like the ache from a sucker punch. He was one of Coop's ex-lovers, a news jock who fancied himself in the line of succession for a Lester Holt anchor job at NBC.

'Yes,' Vickee said. 'He told me he was coming back to town for two weeks and wanted to know if I thought Alex would see him.'

Selfishly, I'd been happy when Jake was stationed in London after he and Coop broke up a few years back. I wasn't about to get in the game and try to match wits with the Yale grad/Rhodes scholar who had snake-charmed his way into her bed.

I rolled my chair toward the computer. 'Thanks for having my back, Vick.'

'I did, Mike,' she said. 'Don't get snide with me. I told Jake she was in love with you. And very happy about it. I told the man to leave it be.'

'Obviously, Coop still carries a torch, don't you think? For him, or for the NBC peacock.'

'I was so annoyed at her last night I was seeing red. I was sure he'd called her, but she didn't want me to know. Then today, Catherine said to me Alex told her, on the way to Primola, that she couldn't stay because she was supposed to meet a friend for a drink. That has to be Jake.'

I threw a balled-up sheet of paper at the wastebasket and missed by a foot. 'What am I supposed to do about it, Vickee? Get real.'

'Find her, Mike. Find out what this is all about before she gets hurt. And before she hurts you any more than she's already done.'

151

17

'What'd you get?' I was outside the station house on the street, leaning against Vickee's car.

'The intern who answered at the news desk didn't have cell phones for any of the reporters,' Vickee said. 'I used my NYPD public info credentials to find which hotel he's at, and lucky to have gotten that. Jake is staying at the London.'

'West 54th Street. Convenient to Rock Center and the NBC studios. Coop loves herself a fine hotel. Somebody else to make the bed.'

'Give it a try, Mike.'

'I'm not sure what you want me to do, girl.'

'Worst-case scenario? Alex didn't keep her assignation with Jake and we've got real trouble on our hands.'

'Even worse than that case scenario? I get to the London and find a love nest, but a menage is not what they had in mind,' I said. 'Giuliano put her in a cab when she left the restaurant. She's just embarrassed to see you or me.'

'Turns out he didn't walk her out,' Vickee said. 'Al Vandomir told Catherine he saw her using her Uber app to order a car.'

'To go five blocks? That's not her style. She always walks home from Primola.'

'Exactly. That's my point.'

'So what do you propose? Dumping her phone, checking her credit card to see if there's an Uber receipt with her destination?' I asked. 'I'd be treating her like she's a perp — or like I'm a stalker. She'd have my head for that.'

'I want to know where she is, Mike. Just like you do.'

I wasn't sure I needed to know the truth. After ten years of verbal foreplay, I didn't fancy rejection quite this way.

'Maybe she flew off the handle, me pressing her about playing with your emotions. Maybe she just, I don't know, disappeared, like Battaglia suggested — like to the Vineyard. We can talk sense to her.'

'She's not there.'

'At her house?' Vickee asked. 'How do you know?'

' 'Cause I called the Chilmark police when you went to freshen up. They rode up and checked the house,' I said. 'All locked up and nobody home. Got the call back while you were on the phone with the intern.'

I was pacing the sidewalk now. I was somewhere between jealousy and concern, but not even twenty-four hours had elapsed since we'd all been together. Coop often let her team take what she called 'mental health days' — just a break from the stress of a very difficult job.

A trial had blown up in her face, an impostor hired by the DA's people had hacked into her computer and stolen an unknown measure of professional and personal information, and she was obviously in some kind of turmoil — maybe regret — about our affair.

'I know you've got a conscience, Mike,' Vickee

153

said, pulling open her car door. 'So it's on your head, okay? Whatever is going on with Alex.'

'Hold on,' I said, grabbing the door before she slammed it shut. 'Because you've decided to put the weight all on me? That's why it's there?'

Vickee nodded. 'May not be fair, but you've got to do it.'

'Okay. It'll give me something to occupy myself with for the rest of my tour. I guess murder doesn't trump your pal, even if she's just livin' *la vida loca*, huh?'

'Bring her back in, Mike. And you'll stay in touch with — ?'

'I've made a fool of myself for less important reasons. Sure, I'll call.'

When Vickee reached for her belt I closed the door. It was time for my meal break anyway. I went inside, told Peterson that I'd grab a bite and then canvass some of Wynan Wilson's neighbors to see what they'd heard the night of the murder, and went back out to my own car.

It was the height of rush hour, so it took me almost an hour to crawl down Broadway to get to 54th Street. I parked the car, went to the front desk of the London — making my way past all the Eurotrash clientele clogging the lobby bar — and asked for Jake.

'Certainly, sir,' the receptionist said, the French accent coating her words like a treacly sweet syrup. 'I'll ring his room for you.'

She looked me up and down with a keen sense of disapproval while the rings went unanswered. 'I'm sorry, sir. Mr. Tyler is not in at the moment.'

'What's his room number?'

154

'I'm sorry again, sir. But I can't give you that information.'

'I bet you can,' I said, putting my badge on the countertop. 'Homicide.'

I didn't exactly whisper the word. The receptionist's eyes opened wide, and the woman beside me inquiring about a driver for the next day placed the forefinger of her gloved hand next to the badge.

'Did I hear you say 'homicide'?' she asked, while the receptionist scurried off to get her supervisor. 'Is everything all right here?'

I gave the bejeweled older woman my best grin. 'Except for the dead man, it's fine.'

'Here? A murder?'

'No, ma'am. Not here. You're perfectly safe, if all that glitz in the lobby isn't lethal.'

She turned her head to look at the other guests just as the senior desk clerk arrived. 'Do you have a problem, Detective? May we take it into my office?'

'No problem at all. If you'll have security accompany me up to Mr. Tyler's room, I just need to look around for a few minutes.'

I had the woman's attention again. 'Jake Tyler? The NBC reporter? I just saw his on-air segment fifteen minutes ago,' she said. 'Surely he's not hurt?'

'No, ma'am.'

'Don't tell me,' she said, her gloved hand to her throat. 'He's not a suspect in a murder case? That's not possible.'

I put my finger up to my lips, hinting that I was telling her something in confidence. 'Just a

155

person of interest at this point,' I said, using the bullshit term that had become so popular on television news. 'No charges yet.'

Fuck Jake and the horse he rode in on.

'Would you please step into my office?' the clerk asked, repeating his request. He was anxious to get me out of the way of his guests. 'It's Mr. — ?'

'I won't, actually. It's Detective,' I said. 'Mike Chapman. Homicide.'

'Let's avoid a scene, shall we?'

'Happy to. Get the head of security to take me up to Jake Tyler's room and open the door. All I need is a quick look around and I'm gone.'

'I can't do that, Mr. Chapman. Our guests are entitled to their privacy.'

'Fair enough. I can have Emergency Services here with a battering ram in no time.'

'He's bluffing,' the young Frenchwoman muttered to her boss. 'I didn't even tell him the room number.'

'No,' I said, hitting the keypad on my phone. 'But NBC will and then you'll have a real mess to clean up.'

I dialed Vickee's number and got her voice mail. She was probably giving Logan his evening bath. 'Detective Eaton? Call NBC again — the guy who told you Jake was here at the London — and get his room number. I'm bringing ESU in to break down the door.'

'In that case, Detective,' the supervisor said, 'let me get security to take you upstairs. Two minutes is all you need?'

'For starters.'

156

I didn't have to wait long for security. Two men in suits huffed and puffed their way to the front desk in short order. They introduced themselves and took me to the elevator, to a suite on the sixth floor. One of them knocked but got no response.

The taller man of the two was holding a key card. He inserted it in the lock and the door opened.

The room was empty.

Jake's suitcase was on a luggage rack in the living room area of the suite, open, with sweaters visible on top. His laptop was on the desk, with papers scattered around it.

I walked into the bedroom and the security guys followed. The bed was made. I looked in the closet and saw only men's suits and shirts hung neatly there.

I checked out the bathroom. His toiletries lined the side of one of the two sinks, and a small plastic cosmetics bag, covered in a pink azalea pattern, was next to the other sink. I picked it up and noted the toothbrush and lipstick case inside. I tensed up.

'What are you looking for?' the shorter guard asked.

'What's it your business?'

'I thought maybe if I could help, it would go faster.'

'Did you hear me say I was in any kind of a hurry?'

I glanced at the towel rack opposite the sink. There was a bra and a pair of panties hanging over a plush towel.

I picked up the lacy lingerie. The bra was a C cup — way too big for Coop to wear. The underwear covered a much broader ass. I liked those facts.

'Somebody pays the rates to get a suite at this joint, and they're taking in laundry up here on the side?' I said.

'You gotta be kidding,' the taller man said. 'The room rate is nothing. They charge twelve bucks to wash a brassiere. Twenty to clean and iron a man's shorts.'

'How many key cards did Jake ask for when he signed in?'

The same guy checked his iPad. 'Just one.'

'He registered alone?'

'Yeah.'

'You've got cameras everywhere?' I asked.

'Lobby, elevators, corridors.'

'Good. If it comes to that, I may need to see last night's film.' I reentered the bedroom, pulling open a dresser drawer, with my back to the living room. 'You got someone who can keep an eye out tonight? See when Mr. Tyler comes home for the evening, whether there's a dame with him to claim her clean underwear?'

'Sure.'

'That won't be necessary, Mike,' Jake Tyler said, stepping into the room. 'She's on her way here right now.'

18

'What in God's name are you doing here, Mike?' Jake asked.

'Looking for Alexandra Cooper.'

'You got the hotel to let you break into my room?' he said, striding to the desk to pick up the telephone. 'You gone crazy or what?'

I grabbed the receiver from his hand and waved off the security team. 'Why don't you guys go on downstairs? Tell the boss the two of us are going to have a cocktail together.'

'I want your names,' Jake said, pointing a finger at them as they walked out.

'Forget them,' I said. 'It's my doing. And it's not what it looks like, Jake. I know Coop met you for a drink last night, but we're all — '

'She never met me, Mike. She stood me up.'

'Whaddaya mean?' My concern immediately ratcheted up a dozen notches. 'I know you called her a week ago. I understand I wasn't supposed to know about it.'

'But obviously you do.'

'Vickee just told me an hour ago. Coop never said a word.'

Jake was at the minibar. He helped himself to a small bottle of single-malt Scotch and handed me the vodka. 'There's no ice till they do turndown service later tonight. Best I can offer.'

I put the bottle to my mouth and threw back my head.

'When did you speak to her?'

'Like you said, a week ago.'

'And not since?'

'Sure. I thought you meant — '

'Most recently, Jake. If you don't know where she is, then we've got a problem.'

'Then we've got a problem,' he said, pouring his Scotch into a glass from the tray above the minibar. 'Or you do.'

'When, then?'

'Yesterday. We spoke twice. First time was in the morning, when I called her at the office. I confirmed that she would meet me for a drink at seven o'clock. At Patroon. You know, it's her favorite — '

'I do know. I do happen to know that.' Nothing like getting cuckolded at the best bar in town, in front of the owner and the staff who had followed the progress of my courtship of Coop. I swallowed the rest of the bottle and let it burn its way to my gut while Jake spoke.

'You know, this wasn't about trying to horn in on your relationship, Mike.' Jake had one hand in his pants pocket and the other arm leaning on the mantel over the gas fireplace, like a good ole boy hoping to soft-pedal bad news.

I was angry and in pain, and beginning to get scared for Coop. 'I didn't think — '

'It's long over between Alexandra and me. Long over.' He lifted his glass in my direction. 'I'm rooting for — '

'I knew it was long over, once I saw the panties of the big-assed girl you got draped over the towel rack. You just called Coop because — ?'

160

'I called her because I'm doing a big series — a five-parter, national news — on the backlog of rape evidence collection kits, Mike. She's the expert. I checked with prosecutors and forensic experts all over the country before I rang her up. Nobody knows this stuff better than she does,' Jake said. 'And if you don't have the courtesy to leave here before my friend arrives, I hope you'll be able to suppress your usual display of sophomoric humor and not focus on her tits and ass.'

'You said you spoke to Coop twice.' I found myself frantically looking around the room for something to hang on to, something that would have been a physical link to Coop. Now I hated the piece of me that was full of green envy. I wanted her in reach.

'Yes. Alex texted me from Primola.'

I hadn't been close enough to her during most of the evening to notice whether she'd been sending messages or not. It wouldn't have struck me as unusual if she had.

'She told me about the man who was arrested yesterday and about the impromptu celebration with the cops and with Catherine.'

'She broke the date?' I asked.

'It wasn't a date, to begin with.'

'Excuse me, Jake. A business meeting, in the evening, at a big-ticket restaurant like Patroon. Stupid of me to confuse it with a date.'

'Alex told me about how things had changed with you the first time I called her. So did Vickee, before I even got through to Alex. Vickee didn't want me to upset what you've got going.

Alex is in love with you, Mike. The spirit in her voice was infectious. You know what I think? I think she wanted to see me in person to make it clear to me that she was glad we split. That she actually came out where she wanted to be.'

'So that text from the restaurant is when she told you she wasn't coming, right?' I said. 'But did she give you any idea of what she was going to do after the dinner with the guys?'

Jake shook his head from side to side. 'She didn't break it off, Mike. That second call just pushed the time back. Alex said she probably wouldn't get to Patroon until after nine o'clock.'

The girl was sending me mixed signals. It wasn't like Coop to be all business after dinner and drinks at Primola. She must have really wanted to see Jake, despite the way he was downplaying it. She obviously had no intention of making the short walk home when she left the others. She had ordered a car service to bring her to meet Jake.

'She actually called Stephan herself,' Jake said, referring to the maître d'. 'She suggested to him that he put a drink or two for me on her tab — which was really sweet, I thought.'

I never thought of describing Coop as sweet. Kind and thoughtful and warm — except when she wore the armor, the tough veneer she thought conformed to the image of her held by her adversaries.

'But then the owner himself came along. Do you know Ken?'

'Yeah, I do,' I said.

'I hadn't seen Ken in a year or more. So we

had dinner together — time kind of flew by while we talked. Cuban cigars, now that the embargo is lifting, fly-fishing — '

Like I had a life share in a river in Scotland to catch salmon with my fly rod. *Not my style, newsboy.*

'And I kept on waiting for Alex after Ken left.'

'Did you hear from her again?'

'Nothing. No call, no text, no e-mail. It got to be after ten and I just figured she was — well, that she was with you.'

'Look, Jake,' I said, growing more worried and agitated by the minute. 'I've got no idea where Coop is. None of us do. No one at the office heard from her all day and the ladies politely assumed she was holed up here with you. Didn't you think to reach out to Vickee or to Catherine when — ?'

Jake held out his arm toward me when the phone rang. 'Yes, yes, I'm here in my room,' he said, presumably to someone at the front desk. 'Yes, you can send her right up.'

'If you don't mind, Mike, I'm expecting a guest now,' he said, walking to the door of the suite and holding it open.

'You didn't wait long to make a backup plan, did you?' I said.

'Looks as though we both got stiffed last night. And like I said to you earlier, Mike, now Alexandra Cooper is *your* problem.'

19

'You look like shit, man,' Mercer said to me when I opened the door of Coop's apartment to let him in.

It was about an hour after I left Jake at his hotel. Mercer had been working an evening tour but took off early when I told him Coop was gone.

'That's better than how I feel. I didn't take this seriously till — '

'Nobody did. Vickee's been tearing her hair out,' he said, tossing his iPad on the sofa. 'Where do we start?'

'Call in every chit we've got,' I said. 'Get TARU working on her phone and e-mail. Use a contact at the Taxi and Limo Commission to track the car services to see if anyone picked her up. Check whether traffic has video cameras on Second Avenue that might have caught her leaving Primola.'

'We do all those things ourselves starting right now,' Mercer said. 'But who do we tell?'

I looked at him like he was crazy. 'Tell? How do you mean? There's nobody to tell till we figure out what's going on.'

'Wait a minute, Mike. Let's get on the same page here. Alex walks out of a restaurant to meet a guy for a drink and she gets, what, vaporized?'

'You said it right. She gets *what*? Where'd she go? We're all starting from the idea that she's in the wind 'cause she wants to be. There's no suggestion of any kind of foul play. We're not even twenty-four hours out yet.'

'It's not aliens that swept her away from here, okay?' Mercer said. 'That's the only thing I'll give you.'

'Good. One group of suspects eliminated,' I said, pacing back and forth. The bright city lights from the living room windows illuminated the dark night sky like search beacons, but we had no ideas about where to look.

Mercer sat down, opening his device to start his compulsive list making. 'You know Alex better than anybody.'

'Don't make that assumption. She doesn't let people in. Not the parts of her she doesn't want to expose. Not even to me.' ,

'Yeah, well, maybe you waited too long to try.'

'Take your best shot, pal.' I turned my back to Mercer and stared out at the slice of Central Park visible between the tall buildings.

'You've got to tell someone, Mike.'

'I called you, didn't I?'

'I mean her parents, for example.'

Coop's mother and father had retired to the Caribbean. 'They're not in the country. And what do I tell them that doesn't have them going berserk before we know anything's wrong?'

'I'd want to know. I'd want to know the second there was a suspicion that something was off-kilter,' Mercer said. 'And now there is.'

'Then you call them. I've got better things to do.' I flipped my steno pad onto the dining room table and started dialing my phone.

165

'Battaglia will go ballistic if you leave him out of this.'

'I don't work for him.'

'How about the lieutenant? You've got no secrets from him,' Mercer asked. 'And the commissioner? Scully's been great to you.'

'When's the last time you looked at the patrol guide?'

Mercer grumbled. He went to the refrigerator, pulled out two cans of Diet Coke, and handed me one. I snapped the ring and took a drink.

'What's that got to do with anything?' he asked.

'Okay, Detective Wallace. What's the crime we're reporting, exactly?'

'I'm hoping to God there isn't one.'

'Good. What do you expect the police commissioner to do, in that case?'

'We sure as hell have a missing person.'

'Not according to the NYPD patrol guide,' I said. 'A missing person can be a lot of things. She can be under the age of eighteen or over the age of sixty-five. Not Coop. She can be mentally or physically impaired. Not the broad I saw yesterday. Possible victim of drowning. Not on the sidewalk on Second Avenue on a clear night in October. A person who indicated an intention of committing suicide. Not one of Coop's problems. She just invited me to slip away to the Vineyard with her this weekend. Broiled lobster, chilled wine, warm fire, and hot lips, if I can make light of this. Last category in the guide is absent under circumstances indicating involuntary disappearance. Maybe we'll develop that

166

— you and I. But as of this moment, we don't have a single one of the categories for the commissioner himself to declare Alexandra Cooper a missing person.'

Mercer picked up a silver-framed photograph of Coop from the sideboard in the dining room. It was taken at Logan's christening, and she was holding the baby in her arms.

'You're not wrong,' he said. 'We'll get pushback from the top.'

'Damn right we will. That last category — involuntary disappearance? If you remember this crap half as well as I do, that little group of complaints gets lodged in the local precinct. They don't go to Major Case; they don't go to some elite unit. They just sit and rot for an entire week on some squad commander's desk in the Nineteenth because there isn't a damn thing to investigate. It's not even twenty-four hours since one of us has heard from the diva of the DA's office, Mercer. We'd be laughed out of the station house.'

'Major exception here, Mike,' he said.

'What's that?'

'It's hard for a human being to have more enemies than a career prosecutor,' Mercer said, taking his time to speak. 'Alex has to be up top on a lot of hit lists.'

'She knows that. Knows that her specialty attracts some mean motherfuckers. Rapists, child molesters, wife-beaters.'

'She's been threatened before. Big-time.'

'Comes with the territory. Most of her colleagues have also.'

167

'She's in the middle of a huge screw-up right now,' Mercer said. 'Antonio Estevez. And what did Drew Poser tell Alex when they discovered the computer hacking? That somebody was trying to bring her down.'

I kicked the base of a huge terra-cotta planter that held some kind of tall, exotic plant. 'Makes no sense, Mercer. If they were out to kill her,' I said, not meaning the words to be as cold as they sounded, 'she'd have been dead on the street. And if it was a kidnapping, there would already be signs of it — someone claiming credit or demanding ransom.'

Mercer took a minute to think about those points. I had gone from unconcerned throughout the day, to pissed off when I learned about her date with Jake, to beginning to lose my mind at the thought of Coop in the hands of the bad guys.

'Unless,' Mercer said, 'it was a kidnapping gone wrong.'

I lowered myself onto a chair, put my elbows on the table and my head in my hands.

'Look at the time I've wasted, Mercer.'

'We've got to stay cool, Mike. Not going to help her if we don't think it through. I was just throwing out a far-fetched idea, a reason why no one has claimed to have her yet.'

I picked up my phone again and continued dialing.

'TARU,' the voice on the other end said after three rings. 'Detective Bowman.'

'Bowman? It's Mike Chapman here,' I said, giving Mercer a thumbs-up. 'I need a favor.'

168

'Again? Dude, you are like deep into me over here. We're swamped this week. Haven't you honchos at homicide ever heard of terrorists?'

'Can't stand those guys. Wish they'd just stick to blowing each other to bits,' I said. 'But I've got something more urgent. I need you to find a cell phone for me. Stat.'

'Like a where's Waldo situation?' Bowman said. 'Who's Waldo and where's his phone, right? Like, whatever happened to good old pounding-the-pavement detective work?'

'Love to chew the fat with you, Bowman, but this time Waldo's a prosecutor who hasn't been heard from in almost twenty-four.'

'Didn't hear it on the nightly news.'

'Still under wraps.'

'Like he's pranking you, maybe?' Bowman asked. 'A pranking situation?'

'Like she's taking a breather.'

He whistled into the phone. 'She? Is it your main squeeze, buddy?'

'Good news travels fast,' I said.

'I just did a ton of work on that today for Drew Poser. DA's squad. Alex Cooper's computer. You know it got hacked?'

'Yeah. Heard that. I want to talk to you about what's on it — at least, I'm sure she'll want to — but she took the day off and we can't raise her now.'

'Difficult broad, Chapman. Always has been,' Bowman said. 'Hope nobody snatches her, because he'll live to regret it. 'Ransom of Red Chief' situation. They'll be wanting to give her back to you faster than you can say Alex Rodriguez.'

169

'Here's the phone number,' I said, reciting the ten digits of Coop's phone. 'How fast can you get me a location?'

'Depends. The DA puts all kinds of blocks on their phones. And it depends how far she's traveled. These e-mails I downloaded today from her account talk about her place on Martha's Vineyard, and that can take longer because it's out of range, so — '

'Forget about reading those personal e-mails, Bowman,' I said.

'How's life in the fast lane, Chapman? Didn't know you could write poetry like Shakespeare.'

'Lose it, man. I don't send her e-mails. Just lose your plan to play with me,' I said. 'When will you have an answer?'

'Consider it done. Cover me with a subpoena tomorrow, okay?' Bowman said. 'I'll call you back.'

I hung up and waited until Mercer finished his conversation.

'I got Bowman at TARU. He'll do a GPS search on Coop's phone,' I said. 'What did you get?'

'That was the main business office at Uber — the night manager,' Mercer said. 'I gave Alex's name and the fact it was charged to her American Express account. Date, time, location of pickup, and supposed drop at 46th Street at Patroon.'

'He'll do a search for you?'

'Yeah. He may or may not give me the info depending on whether I can back it up with a subpoena.'

'Of course we can. Call Catherine. She'll cut them tonight.'

'Look, Mike,' Mercer said. 'I'll stick with you until midnight. I'll give you four more hours before we make this an official report. I'll call anyone you say and poke my nose in any place you tell me if you think it will lead us to Alex. But don't go dragging anyone else into this phony operation and put their jobs at risk.'

I looked at the time on my phone. 'Fair enough,' I said. 'Four hours it is.'

I searched for the number of the Midtown Manhattan Security Initiative and hit CALL when I found it. The networked surveillance project — a joint venture of private businesses and public agencies — was staffed by NYPD officers 24/7.

I didn't know the guy who answered the phone. 'I'm Mike Chapman. Manhattan North Homicide.'

'How can I help you?'

Teams of these cops sat in front of banks of monitors that streamed video of streets and avenues all throughout the day and night. It seemed like a thankless job to me, but it had become a popular counterterrorism tool and in the meantime captured crimes in progress and countless traffic violations.

'I'd like you to check video for a particular location last night.'

'Okay. If we've got it covered on camera, I can get a guy to do it. You say it's about a homicide?'

I was chewing on the inside of my cheek. 'A possible lead. Just that.'

'What location?'

'Second Avenue. Start at 63rd and go up to about 68th. I know you've got Second 'cause of the bridge. Seven P.M. till midnight.'

There was nothing out of the ordinary about this request. And since bridges and tunnels were such vulnerable locations for terrorist activity, I knew there would be cameras all along the busy avenue leading downtown to the 59th Street entrance.

'What am I looking for?'

'Anything unusual. A car parked too long, with someone waiting in it. Thugs on the sidewalk, maybe with weapons they draw on a pedestrian. Scene that looks like an abduction,' I said. 'Person being yanked off the street.'

'Man? Woman? Kid?'

'Woman,' I said, pausing for a deep breath. 'Tall blonde in her late thirties, maybe in a trench coat. Possibly on the east side of Second, heading north.'

'Alone?'

'You tell me,' I said, giving the cop my name and number. 'How about those side streets? Have you got cameras on them?'

'Mostly no. Sixty-Sixth and 67th are the streets with crosstown buses. They're covered, but the others aren't.'

'Okay,' I said. I didn't like the answer. 'I need this as fast as you can do it.'

'On it, Detective Chapman. Call you back.'

I turned to Mercer. 'You've got to be patient,' he said. 'Now you've set some things in motion, we wait for the responses.'

'We wait for nothing,' I said, grabbing my steno pad. 'Let's hoof it down to the restaurant. Retrace Coop's steps. Maybe we can scare up a witness or two.'

20

A light drizzle had begun to fall. Mercer and I were on Second Avenue, just outside of Primola restaurant.

Giuliano told us Coop had slipped out after saying good night. He hadn't seen which way she went.

'Home is to the north,' I said. 'That's the logical direction.'

'She wasn't going home, Mike. Get that through your brain,' Mercer said. His phone rang as he was talking to me. 'Wallace here.'

Coop hates teeming rain in the dark of night, I thought while Mercer fielded the call. I couldn't think of where she might be and how she would feel if the weather continued to grow more foul.

Mercer listened to the caller and then spoke, leaning against a lamppost to write something down. 'I understand. Give me his name and phone number, please.'

'What is it?' I asked.

'That was the night manager from Uber. Everything's computerized and since it's charged to the customer's account immediately, the information is easy to retrieve.'

'Shoot.'

'Alexandra Cooper ordered the car. Pickup in front of 240 East 65th Street.' Mercer pointed across the avenue, into the block that ran between Second and Third. The destination she

174

punched in was 160 East 46th Street.'

We both knew that was Ken Aretsky's Patroon. We both knew she'd intended to keep her date with Jake.

'The job got entered into the system as incomplete,' Mercer said.

'Meaning what?'

'Alex got charged for the ride she never took. She didn't cancel the car, and the driver waited ten minutes at the site before the base cleared him to leave. Incomplete.'

'Call the guy,' I said.

Mercer glanced at his pad and dialed. His message went to voice mail.

'Sixty-Fifth Street doesn't have NYPD surveillance cameras,' I said. 'Let's cross to the north and see if we get lucky.'

We walked past a bagel joint, a dry cleaner, and the old-fashioned diner on the corner. I jogged across the street.

'Bingo!' I turned to wave Mercer on. 'Just what we needed. Sunshine Deli.'

Korean delis were consistently the site of more armed robberies than any other kind of business in the city. Almost every one of them had installed security cameras over the register and outside the entrance to the store. I looked above the door, at a corner of the awning, and saw the small black device.

'Police,' I said to the young woman behind the counter. She looked terrified, even after she saw the gold shield. 'The video camera — how much tape is on it?'

'What?'

'The camera? How many hours at a time does it record?'

Her English was lousy. I understood it, though, when she said, 'Twenty-four.'

'We need to look at it,' I said. 'Right now.'

A customer came in for juice and a quart of ice cream. The woman made his change and then looked back at me.

'My boss not here. Come back tomorrow.'

'No way, lady,' I said, hoisting myself up onto the counter and reaching for the camera, which was mounted on the wall. If I didn't look now, there would be little chance of getting what I needed tomorrow morning. 'You know how this works, Mercer?'

'Is it digital or is there tape in there?'

I was pulling at the camera and its small black case. 'Looks like tape.'

The woman had picked up the landline and was jabbering into the phone in Korean.

'Then it will just loop over itself,' Mercer said. 'It will rerecord every twenty-four hours, replacing the old images.'

I pulled the entire unit out of the wall while the woman let out a yelp. I handed it to Mercer, who took the case apart.

'An empty spool,' he said. 'Just meant so that if anyone thinks about doing a stickup in here, there appears to be a video.'

'Nothing there,' the woman said. She had started to cry.

'Cheaper this way,' I said, telling her to stay calm. 'How about the one on the outside of the building? Any film in that?'

'No, sir. We never been robbed. Very safe neighborhood,' she said. 'Not like last place in Queens. Many robberies.'

I threw the useless camera on the counter after I jumped down, handing her a twenty-dollar bill. 'Sorry for the trouble, ma'am.'

We walked out and I followed Mercer up and down the block on both sides of the avenue. We didn't see any cameras and most of the businesses were shut down for the night.

Mercer's phone rang again. 'Wallace here.'

He turned his back to me.

'Southwest corner of 65th and Second,' he said. 'There's two of us. I'm a really tall black guy, and my partner is about six foot one, dark hair. Seven minutes? Thanks very much.'

I put my face up into the falling rain, then lowered my head and shook it off. 'Who's coming?'

'That was my Uber friend. The driver who was supposed to pick Alex up is working again tonight. He just dropped a passenger off at New York University Medical Center. He'll come up First and be here as fast as he can.'

We ducked into the diner to get out of the rain while we waited. I called the cop at the Midtown Security Initiative.

'I know you've got a lot of images to go through. We can narrow it down for you,' I said. I gave him the time of the incomplete Uber pickup. 'Fast-forward to the top of that hour. The woman will be coming out of a restaurant midblock on the east side of Second, walking north. She should cross at the first light. Get as

177

much of 65th Street as you can capture. There's a black sedan — an Uber, if you can make out the sign in the driver's side window — that pulls into the block either shortly before or after the woman does. I'll have more for you in fifteen minutes.'

Five minutes later, a black Mercedes E500 came across 65th Street from First Avenue and stopped in front of the fire hydrant near the entrance to 230 East 65th.

'C'mon,' Mercer said, pushing open the door and crossing the avenue. I was just a few steps behind him.

We introduced ourselves to the nervous man who had stepped out of his car.

'I'm Sadiq,' he said. 'My boss says there's a problem.'

'No problem,' Mercer said, holding his arm out to keep me back. 'We need your help, okay? It's about last night.'

'I didn't do nothing. Nothing at all,' he said, talking with his hands, which were trembling as he made circles in the air. 'The lady didn't wait for me.'

'What lady?'

'Miss Alexandra. That was the name on the order.'

Since Uber drivers didn't know their fares personally — as many car service regular accounts do — it was common for them to ask for the passenger by first name when they pulled up to a location.

'Were you late?' Mercer asked.

'The request came in,' Sadiq said. 'I was only

about twenty blocks away. I gave a response time of six minutes.'

'Did you make your estimate?'

'I ran into a Con Edison crew, which slowed me down,' he said, rain dripping off the folds of his turban and streaking his face like tears. 'Maybe one minute late. Maybe two.'

'Did you actually see the lady when you reached here?' Mercer asked.

'Well, how do I know? How do I know her?' Sadiq asked. 'Very impatient lady.'

'What do you mean impatient?' I asked. 'How do you know that?'

'He's mine, Mike, okay?' Mercer didn't want me flipping out on Sadiq.

How would this driver have known about Coop's quick temper unless he'd had her in his car and she snapped at him?

'Slow it down,' Mercer said. 'No need for you to be shaking, my friend. Just tell us what you saw when you pulled up last night.'

Sadiq shook his head up and down. 'Well, I knew I was running a bit late. I was at the light on the far corner. It turned red just when I reached it.'

The driver pointed across the avenue.

'It wasn't very cold. There were people — many people — crossing the street in front of my car. I couldn't really see into the block ahead, where I was supposed to make the pickup,' he said. 'But I was trying to look for Miss Alexandra.'

I hated that he called her by name. It sounded more like they had actually met.

'When the light changed, I started to drive. I

179

pulled up a little beyond where we are right now,' Sadiq said, gesturing with his left hand. 'I saw a lady. I saw Miss Alexandra and I began to honk my — '

'How did you know it was her?' I asked. 'Did she speak — ?'

'Yo, Mike,' Mercer said, pushing me back with his outstretched arm. 'I can handle this.'

'Well, I don't actually know,' Sadiq said. 'She seemed to look up like she was expecting me, but then she got into another car. A car parked a few feet in front of me.'

'You called her 'impatient,'' Mercer said. 'Why's that?'

'Because I was only a minute or so late, and she wasn't polite enough to cancel the job. So I had to charge her for it. That's the only reason I said it.'

'Could you see if there was anyone in the vehicle ahead of you?' Mercer asked.

'Not really, Mr. Detective. Not at all. The windows were tinted, actually.'

'This woman you saw, Sadiq,' Mercer said. 'Can you describe her?'

'Not really.'

'Anything. Anything at all?'

Sadiq looked from Mercer's face to mine. 'You talk to me like I did something bad.'

'Not yet, you didn't,' Mercer said. 'What did she look like?'

The driver seemed almost fearful to admit that he could give a description of Coop, like that would implicate him in some inappropriate conduct.

'Even your turban is sweating, Sadiq,' I said, watching the rain fall from it. 'What do you know? What are you so worried about?'

The young man looked as shocked as Mercer.

'Excuse my partner, sir,' Mercer said. 'You haven't met the real incarnation of 'impatience' till he chimes in. And on top of that he's just rude.'

'I believe the woman I saw had light-colored hair. Blond. And she was wearing a raincoat, even though it was dry.'

'Young? Old?'

'About my own age, sir,' Sadiq said. 'I'm thirty-four.'

'What did you do when she got in the other car?'

'I waited in this very spot. I actually waited ten minutes, perhaps twelve, just to be sure that my passenger wasn't someone else. Someone who'd been delayed.'

'Did you try to contact her?' Mercer asked.

'I did. I texted two more times that I was on location before I canceled the job. That was when I left.'

'Where did you go next?' Mercer asked.

Sadiq's hands were going in circles again. 'Nowhere.'

'What does that mean? How could you go nowhere?'

'I stayed right here, Mr. Detective. There's usually a lot of business on the Upper East Side in the late evening. People coming out of bars, movies, going home late.'

'What was your next job?' Mercer asked.

'I — uh — I didn't have a next job, sir,' Sadiq said, staring at a crack in the pavement. 'I had only planned to work until midnight. The next order that came in from an address on 79th Street had a destination in New Jersey.'

Mercer didn't seem to like the fact that Sadiq had shut his operation down shortly after the time Coop disappeared. 'What don't you like about Jersey?'

'Nothing in particular, Mr. Detective. It's just that I live on Long Island, and if I had accepted the job, I wouldn't have gotten home till after two A.M.,' Sadiq said. 'My wife wouldn't have been pleased.'

'Was your wife awake when you got home?' Mercer asked.

'Not exactly. I mean, she never is when I work that late.'

I liked that Mercer was putting the screws to the nervous cabbie, who'd been the last person we knew to see Coop.

'Did you see anyone between the time you arrived at this corner and the time your wife — well, woke up?'

Sadiq clasped his hands together and thought. 'No, sir. Not that I remember.'

'Think hard, Sadiq,' Mercer said. 'You want to tell me anything else you can think of about the woman you saw? Anyone else you can describe on the street?'

I couldn't help myself from butting in. 'You didn't happen to get a plate number of the car that took your fare away from you? Even a partial plate? Some letters or numbers?'

182

'Excuse me for correcting you, sir.' The young man couldn't even look at me when he spoke to me. 'You are mistaken.'

'What about?'

'I wasn't mad at the lady or at the other driver. I still charged my fare,' he said. 'And it wasn't a car she got into. You're wrong about that. I didn't look at the license plate so I cannot tell you that. But it wasn't a car. It was an SUV.'

Mercer jumped in over me. 'What kind of SUV? You know the make, Sadiq? Do you know what an Escalade is?'

Mercer was on high alert. He was thinking of Antonio Estevez and his Slade.

'I don't know all the models. But it for sure wasn't an Escalade,' Sadiq said. 'All I know is definitely it was an SUV.'

Mercer was ready to go after Estevez — the man who wanted to bring Coop down.

I was hell-bent on pinning the Reverend Hal Shipley against a wall to get the whereabouts of his SUV fleet and posse of pallbearers.

21

'We got a mess on our hands,' Lieutenant Peterson said to the captain in charge of the Nineteenth Precinct, sitting in the squad room on the second floor.

It was eleven o'clock at night and guys were getting ready for the shift change. The midnight tour would be understaffed, like it was all over the city. Those who were ready to knock off were looking at us like we'd walked into their offices with the Ebola virus, staying far enough away to avoid contagion but curious about what we'd brought into their tight little village.

'And you've decided now was the right time to lay it on me?' Captain Abruzzi said. He looked like a man who had someplace to go. Well-cut double-breasted suit, designer tie too expensive for a cop's salary, carefully styled comb-over — he should have learned to cope with the bald bit years ago — and way too much cologne at this hour. 'The commissioner knows?'

'Scully wants Mike, Mercer, and me at One PP at seven hundred. The district attorney, too,' Ray Peterson said. 'He's expecting a call from you tonight. He insisted that we make a formal report so you can have one of your men get started on the basics.'

Peterson had a slender, bony frame — like a skeleton with some clothes thrown over it. He was tall, and he leaned his elbow on top of a file

184

cabinet while he ran down the story for Abruzzi. 'Why'd you sit on this, Chapman?' the captain asked. 'Too busy with your *Jeopardy!* bullshit to know you had a 'gone girl' on your hands?'

'I didn't — '

'He didn't sit on it,' Peterson said. 'The people in the DA's office as well as the guys in the department — and Vickee Eaton from DCPI — thought they knew what they were dealing with.'

I probably hadn't missed a Final Jeopardy question in a few months. I couldn't focus on anything after Vickee put this in my lap.

'Scully knows I'm using a Jane Doe to take the report?' Abruzzi asked. 'Not Alex Cooper's name anywhere on paper?'

'That's his decision,' Peterson said. 'The media would be all over the fact that a prosecutor has disappeared, and it's not what any of us want until we make a plan tomorrow morning.'

'I got only two men working.'

'That's all you need,' I said. 'Mercer and I will fill them in. TARU's trying to pull up her phone now. We got some ideas already that he and I are going to follow up on.'

I didn't need any hairbag detective with good manners supervising my late-night interface with Hal Shipley.

Peterson pointed the two fingers holding his cigarette at me. 'Forget your ideas, Chapman. The captain's gonna run this tonight.'

'Yeah,' Abruzzi said, not seeming to be very interested in Coop's status. 'We've had lots of

185

security details on her apartment over the years. Dances to her own drummer, that one. Jet-sets around. Wouldn't surprise me if she's on a jaunt somewhere.'

'She's not on a jaunt, Captain,' I said. 'Trust me on that one.'

'You the one filing the report, Ray?' Abruzzi said to Peterson. 'I need a name.'

'It's me,' I said, trying to get the captain's attention.

'I need a next of kin. Does she have family or — ?'

'Her family doesn't know yet,' I said.

'You better check with them before you put me through hoops, gentlemen.' Abruzzi shook his head. 'Maybe there's a reunion you don't know about.'

'You want me to help with a list for tonight?' Peterson asked.

'I know where her crib is. Start there, I guess.'

'Mercer and I have been to the apartment. Everything's in order,' I said. 'Nothing from the doormen, either.'

Abruzzi squinted and stared at me. 'You been inside or you just asked them?'

'In case you don't know it, Captain,' Peterson said, 'Chapman's been dating Alex. That'll be a factor in how this whole thing goes forward.'

He tilted his head and looked at me again. 'Hats off to you, Chapman. You the latest in a long line of unsatisfied customers?'

There was no point in wasting my energy by belting the man temporarily in charge of Coop's well-being.

'You got an alibi?' he said, jamming a stick of chewing gum in his mouth as he smiled at me, happy to work his way under my skin.

'Dead man with a hole in his head where his brains used to be,' I said. 'It's worked for me before.'

'Maybe she just wanted a night off,' Abruzzi said. 'Everyone except the lieutenant knows you'd be hard to take on a regular basis.'

'True enough, Captain. I'm no prize. Good thing whoever's waiting up for you isn't allergic to that musk crap you've poured all over yourself. She might gag on it while she's chowing down on your — '

'Cut it out, Chapman,' Peterson said.

'Did you know, Cap, that *musk* comes from the Sanskrit word for *testicle?*' I said. 'And I didn't even have to learn that on *Jeopardy!* One whiff of the stuff and it was pretty obvious.'

'I got all the plate numbers,' Mercer said. He had planted himself at an empty desk and done something constructive while I churned about Abruzzi's reaction. 'That's a way to get started. Three SUVs registered to Shipley's Gotham Center and one to Antonio Estevez.'

'I read about this Estevez character in this morning's paper,' Abruzzi said, directing his comments to Peterson. 'What does Shipley have to do with Alex Cooper?'

'Nothing,' I said. Nobody was going to get in the way of my tryst with the reverend. 'Mercer pulled it up for me 'cause it has to do with my homicide.'

'I think the most important thing at this point

187

is Antonio Estevez,' Peterson said. 'He pulled some very sophisticated stunts to get out of his trial, and they involved hacking into the computer files in Alex's office.'

'What about this Tanner mope?' Abruzzi asked.

'Street bum. Crazy like a fox, but I don't think he has the connections from inside the can, just hours after his arrest, to have someone lined up to do harm to the DA,' Peterson said. 'Down the road it might be a different thing with him. No question he'd like to see Alex dead.'

It had been one thing to hear threats from time to time about cops or prosecutors when they were sitting in your presence, but really different when the subject of the conversation was out of range, presumably in danger.

'I'm taking Estevez,' Mercer said. 'That's an evil dude. I wouldn't put anything past him.'

'Have you got a command log that goes back a few years?' Peterson asked Abruzzi. 'Get one of your two guys to hammer it out tonight. Check whether anyone who's been trouble before is in or out of jail.'

'Sure. One of them can run things from here. The other is good to go with Mercer.'

I knew they'd try to shut me out of this investigation. I wasn't surprised. But I could still get Jimmy North to come out with me and take a stab at Shipley after Peterson signed off. There was still a legit connection to Wynan Wilson's homicide that had to be explored.

My phone rang and I practically slid off the desk to get it out of my pocket and answer it.

'Chapman.'

'Listen, Mike, it's Bowman.' The detective from TARU who'd been looking for Coop's cell phone.

'Whaddaya got?'

'Nothing good. Looks like her last communication was a text around ten something last night. She called for an Uber car service, and a driver responded. His name is — '

'Sadiq. Yeah, we got that.'

'Well, you ought to look for him. There's no receipt, no end-of-job survey.'

'We're past that point, Bowman. Where is she?'

'I got no idea, Mike. It's that kind of situation. She's not talking to anybody. Nobody at all.'

'Pings, Bowman. You got any pings? Everything with you is a situation,' I said, ranting into the phone. 'What's Coop's situation? You tracking the GPS on the phone? You must know where it is.'

'I can't tell you where it is. Last trace of the phone, best I can make it out, was just north of the 85th Street Transverse, in the middle of Central Park.'

22

'You know what you're doing is going to bring out all the rug rats you're trying to keep from knowing about Alex, from finding out she's lost in space?' Mercer said. He had rolled over the curb and parked the car on the sidewalk of Fifth Avenue, just to the north of the Metropolitan Museum of Art.

I got out and slammed the door. 'I can't tell if you're just playing devil's advocate or if you've forgotten you're my best pal. You're saying no to every idea I come up with.'

'I'm trying to focus you on getting the right kind of help for her,' Mercer said, 'and doing that without getting yourself a paid vacation in a nuthouse.'

I crossed the transverse entrance and started into Central Park. It was twelve thirty in the morning. When I lost the light of a streetlamp, it was as though I was off to trek in the woods.

'You're either with me or not,' I said.

Casual park regulars were home and tucked tight in bed. There would be a couple of dog walkers, some afraid-of-nothing runners, scores of homeless people, and an occasional stray. The roadways were closed to vehicular traffic.

'I'm always with you, Mike. Even when you go off the charts.'

'I'll start searching,' I said, turning on the compact high-beam flashlight that Abruzzi had given me before we left the station house. 'You wait on Fifth for Emergency Services.'

'You know what you're looking for?'

'Everything.'

'I don't have to remind you how many cases Alex has prosecuted that took place in — '

'In this park? No, you don't,' I snapped. She had sent countless sex offenders to jail for attacking nannies pushing strollers and environmentalists in the Ramble, and dragging joggers off the reservoir path as well as the paved walkways. Two homicides — one in the Ravine and one linked to the Indian Cave — had been headline cases for months at a time.

'The lieutenant is calling in a team right now to work with Alex's crew from the office to pull every perp she's put away and check their parole status,' Mercer said.

'I heard him. I'm not one to sit in front of a computer screen if I can do something more useful. Neither are you.'

'Tanner's stalking ground was this park.'

'I'm telling you Tanner's not in my scopes at the moment,' I said. 'This would take a perp with the means to launch a major operation.'

'Estevez could do that. So could Shipley. But neither one has a link to this location.'

'So it's a scam to throw us off track for a while,' I said. 'Maybe we're being gamed. That's what the judge accused Estevez and his lawyer of doing. Gaming her. Tell the guys from ESU to use their floods to light up the area north of the transverse like a Christmas tree. No piece of paper, no kind of debris, is unimportant. Tell them to bag it all.'

'Leave some bread crumbs so I can follow your trail.'

'You'll hear me loud and clear.'

I left the search of the pathways for the guys who would follow shortly. There had been twenty-four hours during which passersby might have picked up items of significance — pieces of Coop's jewelry if it had been discarded, her iPad and phone, any files she might have been carrying. By now, if not kept by the finders, the items would have worked their way to the Central Park Precinct station house, and the lieutenant had promised to follow up on that idea.

I ducked behind a thicket of bushes, hunched over, and used my beam to scan every inch of the ground.

There were piles of leaves almost everywhere. It was October and the trees were shedding.

I got on my knees and tamped them down. Most of the leaves were scattered into small groupings. Other piles were large enough to conceal a body.

I didn't make much progress in the first fifteen minutes. I was zigzagging from the south end of the grid — the transverse wall — going north for twenty feet, and then reversing my direction. Trees got in my way, and boulders, too. Coop would have been cursing the brilliant landscapers who had put every one of these in place to create what she called this great man-made playground.

The first thing I found was a pair of men's sneakers. I didn't know whether they'd have any significance, so I tossed them ten feet over to the paved walkway for Emergency Services to voucher. There was a bong that I slipped into a plastic baggie in case we needed DNA from the saliva on it. I didn't put gloves on until I clamped my hand onto a dead squirrel.

'Hey, Chapman,' I heard a familiar voice calling. 'Get your ass out of the bushes. It's time for the bright lights.'

I stood up. It was one of the senior Emergency Services detectives. I raised my hands and smiled at him. 'Don't shoot.'

'Got my orders from Abruzzi and Peterson,' he said. 'Don't ask any questions about who you're looking for, relieve you of this particular assignment, put on my biggest spots, and go over every square foot of — '

'Correction. Square inch. And no relieving me.'

'The CO of the park precinct is sending his anti-crime squad to do the grid with me. Whatever kind of case you got, try and make yourself useful somewhere else.'

He turned his back on me and gave his men the order to set up the floodlights and get to work.

Mercer was on the path. 'Why don't we leave this to ESU and go for a ride?'

'Don't humor me.'

I was snapping at my best friend. The fear that was gnawing at my gut was disrupting a normal interaction with the cop I trusted most in all the world. I should be making professional decisions, but I had a horse in this race and I was losing my focus.

193

'Mike,' Mercer said. 'Let's go look for Shipley's SUVs. See if we can find them. You got a legit reason to be snooping around him. You're still looking for Keesh as Wilson's likely killer.'

I didn't answer.

'For a murderer,' he said. 'Let these guys get on the ground. Odds are they won't find anything here, Mike. You know that as well as I do.'

I wanted to say that they didn't know what they were looking for. But truth was, neither did I.

'You ought to go home and get a few hours' sleep,' I said.

'When you do, man.'

'It's different with me,' I said, pulling off my gloves and tossing them in a garbage pail as we walked toward Fifth Avenue. 'It's Coop. I got my heart in this now.'

'Course you do,' Mercer said, almost in a whisper. 'That's good to hear.'

I stood on the sidewalk and watched as the lights perched atop the giant tripods burst on.

'You Chapman?' a young detective asked.

'Yeah.'

'My boss gave us the instructions,' he said. 'I'm watching the perimeter while the others search. If paparazzi start showing up because of the activity here, we tell them nothing, right?'

'Why, what do you know?'

'Nothing. I don't know nothing. Missing girl, is all.'

'Then you know too much already,' I said. 'Tell them it's a practice run. Like for a potential terrorist threat. Nothing about a girl.'

'Good idea. They all buy into that terrorist shit.'

Mercer was about to cross the street to get to his car. The senior detective was walking toward us, holding out a clump of plastic bags. 'Help me here, Chapman, will you?' he said.

'Sure. What you got?'

'This one has cigarette butts with lipstick on them. Your victim, does she smoke?'

The inside of my cheek was already raw when I bit down on it again. I couldn't think of Coop and the word *victim* in the same sentence.

'Not a smoker,' I said. 'But keep the butts for possible DNA. We don't know who she's with.'

He held up a second bag. 'Expired Metro-Card.'

'Good. We can track the purchase. Make sure Peterson gets that ASAP.'

'Ten-four,' he said. 'And I know this park is like a regular lover's lane. This here's a thong. A bright-red lacy thong. Like the last lap dancer who parked herself on me.'

Not a pretty picture.

'I figure we gotta grab all the underwear we come across.' The detective was laughing as he held the thong up in my face. 'Any chance this belongs to your missing broad?'

'No way,' I said, turning my back on him. Nausea swept over me as I thought of Coop without clothes, without underwear, in the hands of a psychopath.

'Can't ever be sure, Chapman. She's not a nun, is she? Give us a clue.'

I knew her lingerie as well as I knew my own shorts. I just couldn't say that out loud.

'Trust me on this one,' Mercer said to the detective, slapping me on the back to get me moving toward his car. 'We know our vic, dude. Somewhere between a lap dancer and a nun, but it's definitely not her thong.'

23

'You know he doesn't park these expensive pimped-up wheels on the street in the middle of Harlem,' I said.

'Why not? Can you think of anybody who messes with the reverend?' Mercer answered. It was close to two thirty in the morning and we were cruising the streets in the area between the Gotham center and Shipley's apartment. 'Probably the safest cars in the hood.'

'We've been around three times,' I said, holding a printout of the cars and plate numbers. 'Nada. Absolutely nada. Let's check out the parking garages.'

The car stopped at a light and I opened the door. Mercer pulled over and parked in front of a fire hydrant.

The first two garages we walked by had closed at one A.M.

Teenagers we passed on a street corner started taunting Mercer with chants of, 'Five-oh. We know you five-oh.'

The old TV show — *Hawaii Five-O* — had long ago provided the nickname for cops on ghetto streets. Even with the stunning gentrification of parts of Harlem, I gave away Mercer's presence as surely as if I had worn my police badge around my neck.

Three blocks from our car, and half a block from Shipley's home address, the mouth of a

197

large garage yawned at us. Open twenty-four hours.

I followed Mercer down the ramp. The old black man behind the bulletproof window in what served as an office had fallen asleep. Mercer rapped on the glass.

The startled attendant sat up straight. 'What you want?'

'These three cars. Let's take a look at them,' Mercer said, passing him the plate numbers.

'I can't help you.'

'Does that mean they're not here or they're here?'

'Means just what I say. I can't help you.'

'Fat Hal got your tongue, Pops?' I asked.

'Don't sass me, boy. I just park cars.'

There was no need for Mercer to show his ID. We were the man, and this guy didn't like it any more than the kids selling weed on the street corner.

'Someone was murdered not far from here,' Mercer said. 'A nice man.'

'Wynan Wilson,' he said. 'Knowed him for a long time.'

I let Mercer worm his way back into the man's good graces while I continued on down the ramp and around the corner. He was trying to cajole the attendant into talking to him by using Wilson's daughter's name and describing her despair.

There were about a hundred cars parked below. Most were Hondas and Toyotas and Fords. The three SUVs were easy to spot, lined up in a ready-to-go-at-a-moment's-notice position against the right wall.

198

I walked over to the first one and opened the door. The good thing about the cars being in an attended garage was that most probably they would be unlocked.

The interior was as clean as though the SUV were brand-new. I sat in the driver's seat and opened the glove compartment. Nothing was inside. I pulled the lever to raise the rear door, got out, and walked around. The back was empty as well. Someone took very good care of the vehicle, or had gone to great lengths to purge it of any signs of a disturbance.

I closed the doors and swiveled to the second car. Mercer was coming toward me and the old man was limping along behind him.

'Stay out, boy!' he yelled to me.

'Just having a look.'

'You'll cost me my job.'

The second car was as well tended as the first. Not the first crumb on the floor or seat, not a single slip of paper stowed in the side pocket.

'I promise we'll watch out for you,' Mercer said.

The wide-awake attendant was in a frenzy. 'Don't be doing that.'

I pulled on the handle of the third SUV and the door opened. I sat in the driver's seat and again reached across to the glove compartment.

Mercer had the door behind me. 'Hold up, Mike. You've got to see this.'

I stood and pushed the old man out of the way. There was a stain on the camel-colored seat leather. A small one, but it looked like blood.

I couldn't move. The rear seat, behind the

199

driver's position, was, according to Sadiq the Uber driver, where Coop had gotten into a black SUV.

'Lean in, man,' Mercer said, getting out of my way. 'Take a look. It's probably blood.'

'I get it,' I said.

I didn't want to see Alex Cooper's blood. I couldn't tell the blood type of the spot I was looking at and I couldn't know what its DNA fingerprint was — I just had it in my head that it was Coop's and I needed to shake that thought.

'Your skin is completely ashen. You've gone gray, Mike.'

'No, I haven't. Let's call the precinct and get this mother impounded. Get it out of here before Shipley can spirit it away.'

'You're thinking about Alex. That's why you look so bad.'

'I'm not — I'm — '

'Meanwhile, I'm assuming the blood has something to do with Takeesha Falls — something bloody she carried out of Wynan Wilson's apartment. Not Alex. Let the lieutenant stay on top of the search team.'

'I'm trying to do that, Mercer. It's not going to work.'

The old man was on his way back to his little office.

I heard someone running and looked back at the ramp, knowing it could not have been his footsteps.

A tall African-American man, both hands tucked in the pockets of his black overcoat, was coming toward us. 'Hands off, gentlemen. Hands off that machine.'

I threw a glance at Mercer.

'Pops pressed a button in his office. Must go straight to Shipley's bodyguards,' he said.

My fingers were firmly wrapped around the handle as I dialed 911 with my free hand.

'I said don't touch.'

'Can't hear you, dude. I'm talking to the police,' I said.

Mercer identified himself and told the tall man to slowly bring his mitts out of his pockets.

'Mike Chapman. Homicide. Put me through to the two-eight, stat,' I said, holding until she got me connected to the desk officer. I explained the situation and asked for two cops to come to the garage to secure the car until it could be towed to the pound for evidence collection. I could always deal with warrants before the actual search got started.

The tall man turned around and started to walk away.

'Hold it right there,' Mercer said. 'Right there.'

The man stopped but kept his back to us.

'Are you the driver of one of these machines?'

'From time to time.'

'You work for Shipley?' Mercer went on.

'Time to time.'

'Look at me when I'm talking to you.'

'Do I have to look at that prick you got with you? My boss really don't like him.'

Mercer waved at me to step away. 'Just talk to me.'

The tall man pivoted around.

'Do you have the names of the men who drive these cars? All the names?'

The man shook his head from side to side. 'I'm not good with names. You'll have to check with the office.'

'Is one of these cars assigned to you?'

'I just stick close with the reverend. That's all I'm supposed to do.'

'The night before last — Wednesday evening — where were you?' I broke in.

The tall man glared at Mercer instead of responding to me.

'I'm just going to ask you the very same things he is,' Mercer said. 'You might as well answer one of us.'

'Wednesday night,' I said, 'did you go into Central Park?'

I could feel myself lurching out of control. There was an art to questioning people, a skill I had learned first from my father, and right now I wasn't capable of exercising the patience and control it required.

'My mother always cautioned me to stay out of the park at night, you know? It kind of creeps me out to go there.'

'So tell me what you did on Wednesday,' Mercer said. 'Start around five o'clock in the afternoon.'

'I'm being square with you. I just don't recall.'

'Try harder,' Mercer said.

'I was with Reverend Shipley. I know that for sure. You ask him and I'm certain he'll remember.'

'Where's Keesh?' I blurted out. 'Takeesha Falls. Where is she?'

The tall man looked at me and laughed. 'Now,

202

there's a mystery for you, isn't it? The reverend's looking high and low for that girl. We think she's in mourning. Gone into seclusion and all that.'

If Shipley wasn't hiding the woman, then he was certainly looking for her. He must have figured she made off with some of the Wynan Wilson cash that belonged to Shipley himself.

More footsteps. Two uniformed cops showed themselves on the ramp, with the wide-eyed attendant at their heels.

'Good timing,' Mercer said. 'These three cars — that third one in particular — we're going to get them taken out of here. You'll have to — '

'One thing before that,' I said. 'This gentleman works for Hal Shipley. He needs a lift over to the North Homicide office. He's ready to spill the beans on Takeesha Falls.'

The man laughed at me again, but not before the attendant scurried back up in the direction of his office. He was about to drop a dime on the tall man. It was never good form to snitch on the Reverend Shipley's friends.

'No such thing, Detective.' He cocked his head and grinned at me. 'You trying to get me hurt?'

'I'm afraid word is out on the street already. That old guy has a pipeline to important people, right from his little bulletproof cage,' I said. 'Once he squeals on you, you'll be safer in the homicide squad than on Adam Clayton Powell Boulevard.'

His jaw locked in place.

One of the two cops radioed in for backup to take an informant to the squad. 'We can stay with the car. Another team will be here in four minutes to transport Mr. — '

'Mr. Who?' I asked.

The tall man wasn't talking.

I walked toward him to pat him down before I left him with the cops. He flinched when I made him raise his hands over his head, but he complied. He leaned against the hood of an Acura while I searched him.

'No hardware,' I said. 'Give these guys your ID.'

He removed his wallet from his pocket. I looked at the name on the license — Ebon Gander, which meant nothing to me — and handed it to one of the uniformed men. Then I took hold of the wallet.

'Well, well. You are just awash in hundred-dollar bills, dude. Four or five thousand of them.'

I handed him back the money. 'Let's be sure to tell the detectives to look over the Franklins for possible blood, in case these bills just tiptoed out of Wilson's apartment along with Keesh.'

Ebon Gander twitched.

'Let's go, Detective Wallace,' I said. I had just diverted enough of my mental energy to keep Coop out of this narrative — to form the thought that maybe this man had been Keesh's getaway driver, which would account for the bloodstain in the car and the big bills in his wallet.

'We got a condolence call to pay.'

Mercer hesitated, like he didn't quite know what to do about me.

'Don't you want to know where?' I asked.

'It's three o'clock in the morning,' Mercer said to me softly, pleading for some kind of rational thought on my part.

'Time to pay a visit to Fat Hal, pardner. Once we tell him Mr. Gander's been talking to us — '

'I'm not saying a word to you or anyone else.'

'I don't see it that way, Mr. Gander. The way I figure, you might as well be talking. I'm pretty certain once the reverend learns you're up at the homicide squad and the cars are impounded and your wallet has grown pretty damn wide, I'm quite certain your goose will be cooked.'

24

'I'm going to save you from yourself,' Mercer said.

'I want to see Shipley. I want to do it now.'

We were in the car and Mercer was headed south, away from Shipley's home.

'I had a call from the police commissioner's office as I walked out of the garage.'

'They've got news?'

'No news, Mike. No news. But Scully wants you down there at headquarters.'

'The meeting's at seven A.M. We got time for — '

'You got no more time to make a fool of yourself, man. Scully wants you in early because he's also called for someone he wants us to talk to,' Mercer said. 'About Alex.'

It was probably just a ploy to distract me.

'You are in no shape to rip Shipley into bite-size pieces at the moment,' Mercer said. 'Your head's somewhere else. You were asking questions like a third grader back there.'

'Did you call Vickee, too?'

'Yeah. All quiet. She's been sleeping with the phone at her ear. Checks it regularly for e-mails and texts, but nothing's come in.'

'So who does Scully want us to talk to?' I asked

'Don't know. The commish tells you to be somewhere and you show up. Probably the guys from Major Case, don't you think?'

'I'd like to handpick the players. Put together the best of the best. For Coop, I mean.'

'That could happen,' Mercer said, merging onto the drive to go downtown. 'She means a lot to a lot of guys in the department. And to Scully.'

I was quiet for most of the drive. So was he.

We parked in the garage at One Police Plaza and took the elevator up to the fourteenth floor, where all the brass were assigned.

The executive officer of the chief of detectives was expecting us. 'The chief wants you to go into his office and stretch out for a while. I'll let you know when he comes in.'

The office had a striking view over New York Harbor, with the bridge lights glittering across to Brooklyn and then over to Staten Island. The chief had a massive desk and a conference table with a dozen chairs. There were also two leather couches against the walls.

'Get yourself half an hour,' Mercer said. 'You'll be no good without it.'

'I'm not much good as it is. I got bad things running through my brain.'

'Your head has to be clear, Mike. You can't go there,' Mercer said. 'Alex is a strong woman. She's a fighter.'

He sat down and made himself comfortable, his head on the armrest and his feet hanging off the end of the six-foot-long couch.

'In a fair fight, my money's on her. But what was that with the SUV? An abduction? She doesn't stand a chance with some animal who means to tear her limb from limb.'

Mercer pretended to be sleeping. I took his lead and laid myself down on the other couch.

My eyes closed and immediately I felt guilty. I opened them wide and rubbed them with my fists. How could I be still for even a minute with so many unknowns to be resolved?

I must have dozed for a couple of hours. Fitfully, I knew, because I had been checking my phone and my e-mails from time to time.

The XO — executive officer — knocked on the door and stuck his head in at 6:25. 'Rise and shine, Chapman,' he said. 'The doctor's making a house call for you.'

Mercer was upright before I was. A fiftyish-year-old woman in a dark gray suit came into the room. 'Are you Mike Chapman?' she asked.

'Yeah,' I said, my fingers instantly combing through my hair. Mercer's head was down as he walked to the door to leave the room.

'I'm Dr. Friedman. Ricky Friedman. I'm a psychiatrist, and I sometimes work with — '

'Whoa, Mercer,' I called out. 'You knew about this? You brought me down here so some shrink could try to get inside my brain? You — '

'Scully and Battaglia will be in the big office in half an hour, Mike. Listen up, will you?' Mercer said. 'Somebody a helluva lot smarter than you is working on a plan here.'

'It's not about you,' Friedman said. 'It's about Alex Cooper. Do you understand that?'

'Of course I do,' I said, flailing my arms as I looked out the window at the commuters starting to fill the Brooklyn Bridge roadway. 'You going to use a Ouija board, Doc, or a Freudian dream analysis to find her?'

'What I'd like to — '

'You want to know what I was just dreaming? That some sexual predator — some miserable fuck that Coop put away for brutalizing young girls — is holding her hostage, forcing himself on her repeatedly. Will that really be helpful to — '

'That's quite possible, Detective Chapman. It's certainly one of the most likely scenarios, just like you say, isn't it?'

I stopped in my tracks and turned around to look at the doctor. She was carefully coiffed and well dressed — a full-figured woman with an intelligent face, if there is such a thing, who was clearly a straight shooter — willing to confirm that my worst nightmare might be true.

'As long as you don't tell me I'm nuts,' I said.

'No guarantees, Mike,' she said, seating herself at the conference table. 'I'm calling you Mike, okay? I know a lot about you already.'

'From?' I asked, as I pulled out a chair opposite her.

'Lieutenant Peterson. The commissioner directed him to give me a thumbnail sketch a few hours ago.'

'What about you? What do I need to know before I open my mouth?'

'Med school at Columbia. A healthy private practice for twenty-five years,' she said. 'I like what I do. I like helping people in desperate situations. The department brings me in from time to time to work with the profilers.'

'That's utter bullshit, Dr. Friedman. No

disrespect, but profilers aren't detectives,' I said, starting to mimic a typical profiling discussion. ' "The deceased was bound by an electrical cord so you guys should be looking for a killer who has one ear and plays Mahler symphonies on his piano. The petechial hemorrhages in the eye-balls of the corpse suggest a Rorschach pattern, which means the perp is an artist who fancies himself a Jackson Pollock type.' You think that kind of psychodrivel is going to find Alexandra Cooper?'

'Stop wasting my time, Mike,' Friedman said. 'Tell me about her.'

'What for?'

'Because the more we know, the greater the likelihood we can get a handle on this.'

'Because nothing else has worked, right?'

'Where's the Chapman humor I've heard so much about?' she asked.

'No place for it in this.'

'Don't lose it, Mike, whatever you do. She's going to need that when we get her home,' Friedman said. 'You want coffee?'

'Red Bull. Two of them.'

'I have coffee and an egg sandwich on the way. It's better for you than an energy drink,' she said. 'Eat a real meal every few hours, get your caffeine from coffee like you usually do, take cat naps several times throughout the day, and rely on the professionals that Scully is pulling together. Your adrenaline is only going to carry you for so long before it fizzles out.'

I liked that she was forthright.

'Tell me about Alexandra. Tell me why you love her.'

I stared at the diamond pin on the lapel of Dr. Friedman's suit. I had barely been able to communicate those thoughts to Coop. I couldn't speak them out loud to a stranger.

'Look, Mike. Lieutenant Peterson told me you're lovers. Ten years of a very close friendship before that, is what Vickee Eaton says. I get that Alex is smart and has lots of backbone, and that she has far more compassion than you're able to summon in any circumstance. I know from the work she does that she's tough.'

'Not tough enough to stand up to something like this.'

'Take me inside her head, Mike. Let me get a feel for how she thinks and acts,' Friedman said. 'It will help me understand how she's dealing with her captors, if we've got a kidnapping here.'

My head snapped up. 'Is that what Scully says?'

'Nobody knows. There's no body, so that gives us hope.'

'There's no ransom demand, either.'

'That could come at any time,' she said. 'Or not at all. In some instances, the victim is held for days or even months — '

'Don't tell me my business, Doc.'

'Then talk to me about the Alexandra Cooper who's not in the newspaper headlines.'

I clasped my hands under the table, wringing them as I thought about Coop. Fatigue had overwhelmed me. Fatigue and a great deal of fear. 'The part of her I like most — the part that scares me for her right now — is how soft she is.'

I didn't just mean the touch of her skin, which

211

was smoother than I'd imagined it to be for all those years I'd fantasized about taking her lady-lawyer clothes off and getting her in bed.

'Good start, Mike.'

'What you don't see when you watch her rip apart a defense witness in the courtroom, or when she's standing beside Paul Battaglia at a bank of microphones talking about some scumbag who sodomized a bunch of kids, is that she's completely soft on the inside. She's completely mush beneath that bruiser exterior.'

Dr. Friedman nodded her head.

'Scully, even Peterson, might think she can cope with one of these monsters, but I'm telling you that Coop can't.'

'I understand you. We'll come back to that,' Dr. Friedman said. 'Why do you call her 'Coop'? So far as I can tell, you're the only person who does.'

'Just a nickname,' I said. 'Don't know, actually. I've been doing it since we first started working together, ten or twelve years ago.'

'It's cold, Mike. She's got a beautiful name. It's an odd way to address your lover, by her surname.'

I brought my hand up and pointed it straight at the woman's face. 'If I wanted to talk to Dr. Ruth, I'd have asked Scully to call her in.'

Friedman worked around me, never breaking the calm demeanor of a shrink sent from central casting.

'How does Alex handle personal problems, Mike?' she asked. 'I know that she tackles professional ones directly and with absolute

212

resolve. When she's confronted with a personal crisis, what does she tend to do?'

'This is no-win for me, Doc,' I said. 'She'll kill me for telling you.'

'I like your smile. You ought to use it more,' Friedman says. 'What does Alex do?'

'She cries. She actually cries a lot, like, at the drop of a hat.'

'Really? That surprises me. No one else has mentioned it.'

'Not professionally. Man, you'd never see that at the office. It's just — I don't know.'

'Do you think you do things that make her cry?'

'No, ma'am,' I said, sitting upright. 'Last thing I'd want to do.'

'So what is it?'

'Wait, go back a bit. I'd say the temper flares first. Yeah, usually the wild temper before the tears. This guy — these guys — they press the wrong button, and no telling how Coop will react. If she shows a flash of her temper, they could come down on her hard, couldn't they?' I took a deep breath and blew it out. 'She'd better hold on to those tantrums.'

'What do you do, Mike? I mean, when she flares up? Do you fight with her?'

'No percentage in that, Doc. I just let it pass.'

'Really? You've got a strong personality yourself. You don't take her on?'

'You never win. That's the thing with her. At least I never win.'

'And what does that do to you, Mike? How do you react?'

213

'I turn on a classic movie, pour a strong drink, read an old Chandler or a new Connelly or Coben. Just give it up till it blows over.'

'Well, that's unlikely to happen,' the doctor said, 'if she's being held by thugs. Just giving it up to her, I mean.'

'Then, tears,' I said, with a sober nod to reality. 'Coop's got this really tough hide — that's what she wants the world to see. She took on this job when women weren't always recognized for aggressive prosecutorial skills. She stood up when few others did. Built this team of Amazon warriors around her — they're amazing women, and so are the guys who work with them. Talk to Ryan and Evan — two of her favorites in the unit. They know what makes her tick as well as I do. Get her home? Surround her with all the silks and satins that she was accustomed to, growing up in a privileged household? It's a totally unfamiliar world to me. But I'll tell you Coop melts. She goes to pieces at the first sign of a conflict.'

'Temper tantrums and emotional meltdowns,' Dr. Friedman thought out loud. 'Those would present very different reactions to her captors, if indeed she's in trouble. It would mean opposing ways to handle Alexandra.'

It was chilling to think of anyone 'handling' Alexandra. Handling my Coop.

'Who would you say is the person — the people — who mean the most to Alex?' Friedman asked. 'After you, of course.'

'By no means am I in first place, Doc. No way,' I said. 'She's got amazing parents. Both have worked hard, raised three nice kids, made some real money, and use it to do good for other people. A lot of good. They're her first concern, if someone is, well, like, leaning on her to — whatever.'

'I understand.'

'Two brothers — I'd say their kids are pretty important to Coop,' I said, putting my elbows on the table so I could rest my head in my hands. 'It would be pure torture for her to think of anyone going after her family.'

'Thank you. I know how hard this is, but we need to figure the pressure points. As many of them as we can.'

'Yeah. You better count in her friends next — all the people in her unit. They go to the mats for each other. Her best friends outside the office, too — Nina Baum and Joan Stafford, from way back in her life . . . '

We spent the next fifteen minutes going through my personal index of things that meant something to Coop — people, principles, ideas, even material things. Friedman was good. She knew how to draw things out of me that I hadn't even thought were there.

'How about the district attorney himself?'

'Battaglia? Better think again, Doc. Coop idolized him when she was a kid. Came to know that after thirty years in office he's a politician — what a surprise — just worried about covering his own ass. Uses her and all his staff to take care of those needs. It's amazing justice gets done as often as it does.'

'Good to know. I can take him off the list.'

'I hope somebody's told you that Reverend Shipley may be mixed up in one of Coop's big cases. This guy Antonio Estevez — the one who had her so upset this week — is probably linked to Shipley.'

'I hadn't known that. The lieutenant did mention that you have Shipley in your sights. He and the mayor — you've got a thing about them.'

'Is that the medical term for it, Doc? A 'thing'?' I pushed back from the table and started pacing up and down the room. 'Shipley's lower than dirt and the mayor's an asshole. What's his biggest accomplishment of the year, do you know?'

'Well, I — '

'He passed legislation that allows New Yorkers to keep ferrets as pets. Got that? And what was my first homicide after the law passed, Dr. Friedman? Death by ferret. Did you read about that one? A pet ferret bit the nose off a two-month-old baby. The nose first, and then the lips. The ferret-fucking mayor ought to be in jail, where he belongs, for causing the death of that child.' Dr. Ricky Friedman let me vent. She watched me as I walked back and forth, ranting about the politicians when all I really wanted to do was get back on the street and find Coop.

'Are you done?' she asked me.

I had taken an apple off the chief's desk and was tossing it in the air.

'You're a very angry man, Detective.' Dr. Friedman was frowning at me.

'Tell me something I don't already know.'

'Are you often this way?'

'Ask the lieutenant.'

'I'm asking you, Mike. Peterson said nothing about this.'

'So you're worried that this is what Coop has to put up with on a regular basis, huh?'

She forced a smile. 'Inappropriate aggression, foulmouthed, violent — '

'I'm not violent, Doc. Not violent,' I said, trying to modulate my voice so I didn't sound like a madman. 'And what's inappropriate here? The woman I love has gone missing. You haven't seen what you think is aggression yet.'

'There could actually be good news in your behavior, Mike,' Friedman said. 'Maybe this soft-as-a-marshmallow, sweet Alexandra — '

'I never said 'sweet,' did I? Don't ever mistake Coop for sweet.' Jake Tyler had called her that, but it was too washed-out a word to describe her.

'What I'm trying to say is that maybe there's a chance she decided you weren't the right man for her after all. Perhaps she's embarrassed and needs to step down for a while, or then again — '

'You're not the first genius to think of that since the other night, Doc. Don't pat yourself on the back quite yet,' I said. 'What's the other possibility?'

'Not a brilliant observation on my part, either, Detective. But if I wanted to get at *you*,' Friedman said, 'if I wanted to cause you more pain than you've ever experienced in your lifetime, the way I might go about it — the way you weren't vulnerable even two months ago — is by targeting Alexandra Cooper.'

217

'That's crazy, Doc. You've got to be crazy to think that,' I said.

'You've probably made more enemies than she has, Mike. Maybe we ought to be looking for someone who's got a grudge against you.'

25

'What press inquiries have you had?' Commissioner Keith Scully took his place at the head of the table in his office at One Police Plaza at exactly 7:02 A.M. Behind him was his desk, the same one used by Teddy Roosevelt when he was appointed NYPD's commissioner in 1895.

The deputy commissioner in charge of public information answered the question as others filled in around the conference table. 'A few calls a couple of hours ago asking why there were floodlights in Central Park, but I put out the fire with one of those looking-for-an-alligator-out-of-the-sewer scares. Nobody seems to know about Alex Cooper.'

Scully motioned me to take a seat on the side of the long table, next to the end, where Lieutenant Peterson was positioned. The district attorney was on one side of Scully — shuffling in his seat to get a more commanding view of the group, clearly not used to being anything but the lead dog.

Mercer Wallace sat next to me, as though he could protect me from myself if I got out of control. Vickee Eaton sat opposite me. Captain Abruzzi didn't seem particularly pleased to be in the mix, but the chief of detectives, beside him, had insisted on his presence. The young detective I'd asked Peterson to throw in — Jimmy North — was next to Vickee,

219

introducing himself to her.

There were four men from Major Case, a sergeant from TARU, and another lieutenant from Aviation. I guess Scully was ready to pull out all the stops.

Dr. Ricky Friedman, my new keeper, took a backseat behind Vickee, so she could keep an eye on me and monitor all signs of my psycho-unsuitability.

'Thanks for coming,' Scully said. All his marine bearing was on display. He wouldn't waste a minute on niceties. 'The last contact any colleague or friend had from Alex Cooper was between ten and eleven P.M. on Wednesday. There's a driver who claims to have seen her get into an SUV on East 65th Street at the end of that period. We're checking him out, but we have no reason to think he's not legit, and he has no criminal history. It's now seven hundred, Friday morning, and we haven't had the first sign or suggestion of her whereabouts.'

Everyone in the group looked grim. I half expected that *Perry Mason* moment when Coop walked in the commissioner's door and the show ended.

'Where is she?' Scully asked. 'And if someone has her — or had her — where and why?'

The district attorney started to speak. 'I think — '

'I'm not looking for answers, Paul. I'm going to lay out the issues and then we can all address them,' Scully said, brushing the DA off with the back of his hand. 'What do we tell the media, and when do we do that? Feed them a

220

missing-prosecutor story before we have all our ducks in a row and the story — the search for Alex — takes on a life of its own.'

Some of the folks were jotting down notes, even though we were still dealing with the obvious before getting down into the weeds.

'How do we handle her family — her parents and brothers — and who is going to be the liaison for that task?'

'Her folks don't know yet,' I said.

'Yes, they do, Mike,' Vickee said. 'The commissioner asked me to call them late last night. They're flying in today.'

'You should have told me,' I whispered to Mercer, but he was in Scully's corner on this. He kept his back to me and signaled his disregard.

I didn't think I could be more nervous than I was, but the idea of a face-off with the Coopers was daunting — even though my rapport with them throughout the years when I was just their daughter's good friend had been great.

'The chief of detectives will be in charge of consolidating all the efforts that the department is undertaking, and this will be massive. Nobody flying solo, am I understood?'

We all nodded.

'Peterson already has men working with Battaglia's Special Victims Unit and IT team. They're running every perp Alex has prosecuted, starting with the most recent and going back in time. The ones in state prison — Correction is working with their visitors' logs and phone records. Parole is giving him every sex offender who's been released, in the same order. Who they're living with and whether they're reporting to SOMU.'

The Sex Offender Monitoring Unit had post-parole oversight of the alumni association of Coop's bad boys. Some of the perps were loners, but most had tentacles to other criminal agents.

'They're going to go into overload pretty quickly. It's a long list, between Alex's investigations and the hundreds that have gone through the unit under her watch. I assume, Paul, that you can give us all the backup we need on tracking down connections?'

'Certainly.'

'Great. It all feeds up to the chief of detectives. Every bit of it. I've got to have one go-to man who knows everything,' Scully said. 'TARU is in charge of all tech equipment. Phones, laptops, social media. They're surfing twenty-four/seven for posts and tweets and anything related to the stuff that just got hacked on Wednesday. Drew Poser said it best the other day — Alex Cooper has no more secrets. Not professional, not personal.'

My cheek was so raw from biting that it had started to bleed. I could taste the blood when I swallowed hard.

'That brings us to Detective Chapman.' Commissioner Scully fixed his eyes on me and everyone followed suit, except Mercer, who still had his back in my face. 'Nobody knows Alex Cooper better than Mike Chapman.'

Battaglia couldn't conceal his scowl.

'I don't have ten detectives as good as Chapman,' Scully said. 'But the tabloids are

222

going to have a field day with this angle.'

'Don't tell them,' Battaglia said.

'It's out there, Paul,' Scully answered. 'It's all over the courthouse.'

'It's got nothing to do with this investigation,' Ray Peterson said. His e-cigarette was a poor excuse for the real nicotine he craved. 'They're both single adults. You know I don't like scandal, but that's not what this is.'

'I'm with you, Ray. I just haven't figured out whether to be up front with the reporters or let them think they're surprising me and go with it a few days down the road, when they're looking for a piece to give the story legs.'

'Do I get to be heard on this, Commissioner?' I asked, trying to keep my voice level. 'I don't know what's worse. That you've got an attitude that we won't have Coop back for days, or that my only use is to be 'legs' to titillate the public when the *Post* is out of red meat.'

'Bottle it, Chapman,' Scully said. 'I'm getting to you.'

I didn't move a muscle. I didn't want to give Dr. Friedman the satisfaction of reacting.

'Antonio Estevez,' Scully said. 'I'm putting Major Case in charge of this one. Not the trafficking part. Finding that Aponte girl, checking out the guys who work for him, locating any vehicles, and making whatever the connection is to Hal Shipley.'

'My people started that on Wednesday afternoon, when the case blew up in Alex's face,' Battaglia said.

'Your people don't seem to get the urgency of

223

all this, Paul. They knock off at cocktail hour most of the time. We'll run it from headquarters, and you,' Scully said, pointing at one of the Major Case men, 'you're the man in charge.'

The detective acknowledged the assignment.

'What about Shipley himself?' Lieutenant Peterson asked.

Scully turned to Paul Battaglia first. 'When this session breaks up, you and I need a private sidebar about the reverend, okay? I'm hearing things I don't quite understand.'

The district attorney said, 'Certainly,' but he was clearly unhappy to do it.

'Chapman's got the Wynan Wilson homicide to wrap up — and he's got to be interviewed for that — and then there's this possible link to Estevez, too. Reassign Wilson to anyone in your office, Ray,' the commissioner said. 'You've got a prime suspect in the girlfriend — what's her name?'

'Takeesha Falls,' I said, pissed that Scully was taking the case away from me.

'I'm not doing this — I'm not superseding you — because of the mayor's chief of staff and Shipley's complaint,' Scully said, turning from the lieutenant to me. 'I promise you that, Chapman. The lieutenant can stick anyone out there to find Ms. Falls. The case seems pretty open-and-shut. But I'll need you available for every question that comes up on Alex. We'll need you to think for us the way she does.'

'You taking me off the street, too?' I asked, pressing my forefinger against my lip to make sure no blood was visible. I didn't want it to show any more than I wanted to reveal my inappropriate aggression.

'No. Not if you follow commands. You and Mercer and Jimmy North — you three can take orders as well as use your best instincts. You'll be part of the task force, okay? As long as you can compartmentalize your very short emotional fuse.'

I looked at Scully and nodded in the affirmative.

'Bottom line, Alex Cooper is AWOL, and we're going all-out to get her, am I clear?' Scully said. 'First time it's happened, and — '

'Actually, Commissioner, Alex did something like this once before,' Vickee said.

All eyes turned to her, except for Scully, who slapped the table in front of the district attorney. 'Nobody told me that.'

'I didn't know,' Battaglia said.

'It wasn't nearly for this many hours,' Vickee said. 'I didn't remember it until I got home last night. I called her secretary, Laura Wilkie, on my way down here and she confirmed what I thought. It was a Friday and Alex just skipped out for the day with no notice to anyone. So there could be precedent for this, although way too much time has gone by now.'

That would explain why Vickee hadn't mentioned it when she drove off after stopping to see me last night. It didn't explain why she hadn't brought it up until right now.

'It was just a single day, two years ago, the only time Alex went off the radar screen without alerting Laura,' Vickee said. 'By the point I had started to worry about her, late that night at the beginning of a weekend, she checked in with me.'

'What was that about?' Scully said. 'I mean, before I send out all the troops, do you happen to know?'

'I don't have a really vivid recollection of the cause of the whole thing,' Vickee said, trying to do a lateral to me. 'Mike probably does.'

'Me? First I'm hearing of it.' I flattened both hands on the table and lobbed the ball back at her. 'Thanks, Vick, for the vote of confidence.'

'Do you remember, Detective Eaton,' Friedman asked, 'whether it was an argument between Alex and Mike, if she reported it to you then, or something else he had done?'

I was as curious about Vickee's response as the doctor.

'They'd just worked a big case together. Mercer was involved, too,' Vickee said. 'It all ended on Governors Island, with a serial killer — and a particularly savage scene, even for those of us who deal with this kind of brutality on a regular basis.'

'And Mike?' Friedman asked. 'Did he — ?'

'I didn't do anything to her, Doc.' I could see Friedman twisting thoughts of extreme violence around in her brain. 'I swear on her life.'

'I think, Mike, that the fact that you didn't do anything was the problem,' Vickee said, addressing me directly while everyone around the table looked and listened. 'Alex was devastated by that — by the scene she had witnessed with Abreu's victims, by the fact that Mercer was injured by a sting grenade, remember?'

'All too well,' I said. Mercer had been knocked unconscious — and temporarily blinded — when a military grenade was detonated just feet from him by the murderer.

'And then her own close call with the killer, inside the fortress,' Vickee said, lowering her voice. 'Alex wanted — well, intimacy and . . . '

'Intimacy? Look me straight in the eye, girl, and tell me that again. There was a little something between me and Coop at that point, Vickee,' I said. 'It's called the Atlantic Ocean. She had all the intimacy she wanted with a certain Frenchman at that particular moment.'

'That was an escape for Alex. Not the real deal, Mike. If it wasn't affection she craved from you, it was certainly empathy.'

'I'm not long on empathy, Vick,' I said, keeping a grip on my emotions. 'Coop's been aware of that as long as she's known me, and it's never going to change.'

Dr. Friedman was waiting for me to crack open in front of her eyes, a pleasure I was determined to deny her.

'Mercer and Coop — they deal in the living,' I said. 'They hold hands with survivors, they offer compassion, they coax them back to life and get them beyond their ordeals. Me? I like working homicide exactly because that kind of shit isn't for me. I could stroke Wynan Wilson till I'm blue in the face, Detective Eaton, and at the end of the day he's still dead. I don't do empathy, okay?'

'Alex had been close to coming unglued that

night, during that deadly storm,' Vickee said. 'Even if you didn't mean to disappoint her, Mike, that's how she felt. She wanted to get away from you for a while to clear out her head. She wanted to get as far away from you as she could.'

26

'We didn't disagree about anything,' I said to Scully. 'She was clear as a bell when I left her. We were supposed to spend this weekend together on Martha's Vineyard. We're good on all fronts, if anybody's interested.'

He had called a short break and took me into the hallway when the coffee and sandwiches were delivered to pin me down on what my last exchanges with Coop had been.

'She can make a fool of you, Chapman, if that's her goal — but not the rest of us,' he said as we reentered the room. 'You think of anything else, let me be the first to know.'

I made sure Dr. Friedman saw me pick up two egg sandwiches and a large black cup of joe. I lifted the hot cardboard cup in her direction and mouthed, *Cheers*.

The commissioner was ready to open the plan up for discussion.

'I say we hold the disappearance back at least one more day — maybe two — before we put it on the news,' the district attorney said. 'Let her family absorb it tonight, when they get to town.'

'You've got to weigh that,' Abruzzi said, 'against the likelihood of getting useful tips from the public if we give the information out. See something, say something. People love to call in all kinds of sightings.'

'Total waste of time,' one of the Major Case

229

guys said. 'No disrespect, Captain, but you end up chasing down a whole bunch of bullshit. Someone saw a tall skinny blonde in a Costco in Queens; someone watched one shooting up at Hunts Point; someone tailed a brunette who looks an awful lot like the missing lady except for her height and hair color. We're more likely to find Judge Crater with those call-ins than Alex Cooper. Let's leave it to the pros for forty-eight hours.'

Most of us were in agreement about that.

'Who's meeting her parents at the airport?' Battaglia asked.

'I can do that,' I said.

'I told them I would,' Vickee said. 'You want to come — ?'

'All yours.'

This experience was the kind of explosive event that could rip friendships apart. I had seen it happen over and over again as people subconsciously ascribed blame to others. Most of the time, when the dust cleared, it was impossible to put Humpty Dumpty together again.

'Okay,' the commissioner said, 'where were we? Tell me about the SUVs in Shipley's fleet, Mercer. What's happening there?'

'Three of them have been impounded, sir. Just waiting on manpower to drive them in,' Mercer said. 'I called the lab a minute ago. Got a confirm that the stain on the seat is human blood.'

'My lawyers don't even have the search warrant signed yet,' Battaglia said. 'How'd you get to the stain?'

'I cut a piece of the seat leather before Mercer

and I left the garage,' I said.

'Without a warrant?' Battaglia asked.

'Exigent circumstances.'

Keith Scully grinned. He liked the boldness of my move and the fact that I could meet Battaglia's incredulous smirk with a legal term of art.

'Wilson's murder? Exigent? I wouldn't think so.'

'The blood is either Wilson's,' Mercer said, stepping in because he sensed I would choke on the thought he was about to express, 'or it's Alex Cooper's.'

Battaglia closed his mouth.

'She was seen getting into an SUV, if the Uber driver is to be credited. The lab will have a blood type any minute, which will eliminate one of the two — they have different types. And DNA,' Mercer said, 'by noon.'

'I had Shipley's man — Ebon Gander — being questioned in the squad at four A.M.,' Peterson said to Scully. 'He had thirty-seven hundred in big bills. Talked pretty good until my guys took that away from him to voucher. Then he ponied up with a lawyer.'

'He's under arrest?' the commissioner asked.

'Waiting on the blood results. If it's Wilson's blood, we'll hold Gander as an accessory. He admits to being the driver of the car. One of the drivers, anyway.'

Scully's orders were clipped and comprehensive. Everyone in the room was assigned a list of things to do or to oversee. Aviation was ready for choppers to go airborne if leads took us over

231

bridges and through tunnels. Contacts with other agencies were to be cleared through the chief of Ds on a need-to-know basis.

'So this task force is official as of 8:37 A.M.,' Scully said.

He'd give it a name. He always did.

'I'm calling it Operation Portia.'

'That sucks, Commissioner,' I said.

'Watch your mouth, Chapman,' Peterson said.

'Sorry, Loo,' I said. 'I apologize, Commissioner. It's just that you told me to think like Coop. That's what I'm doing.'

'Portia's a Shakespearean character in *The Merchant of Venice*,' Battaglia said, giving new meaning to the word *pompous*. 'She's a lawyer — a smart and beautiful lady lawyer, and — '

'She's a cross-dressing heiress who pretends to be a lawyer,' I said. I had the advantage of having seen the play with Coop and knew her feelings about the character. 'A rich girl who was anti-Semitic and a bit of a racist, and all the guys in town are after her for her money. Don't do it to Coop.'

'Operation Portia.' Scully stood up and pushed back his chair. 'No detail is too unimportant to pass along to me. Nothing.'

He paused to get everyone's commitment on that.

'A communication goes out to every command and patrol car in the force at nine hundred hours. 'Operation looking for unnamed woman of Alex Cooper's physical description, last seen on Wednesday evening in a black SUV going westbound on East 65th Street. Possibly across

85th Street Transverse road in Central Park. Anything else?'

'You want to mention chance of injury or may not be conscious?' Abruzzi asked.

'Not on this first salvo,' Scully said. 'I just want every man and woman looking for her, and if anyone saw anything suspicious on Wednesday evening, maybe this will wake them up.'

No one disagreed.

'The chief of detectives will be coordinating everything from right here in One PP. Questions? Or are you ready to — ?'

My phone began to vibrate on top of the conference table.

'I hope it's important, Chapman,' the commissioner said to me, annoyed by the interruption. He turned back to the team. 'So are all you guys ready to go ahead and find Alexandra Cooper?'

'It's a text,' I said, my hand trembling as I picked it up and saw it was coming from Coop's phone. 'From her.'

'Real time? She just wrote it now?' Mercer pushed back from the table and got on his phone as he leaned in toward me.

Everyone in the room started buzzing about the text. I hoped they were all so stunned they wouldn't notice I had the shakes.

I opened the message and stared at the two words before I said them out loud. I was trying to make sense of them, trying to be the hero — Coop's hero — and cut the operation short. But it was just two ordinary words.

'*Bar*, it says. And then there's a space, and it says, *Bed.*'

Mercer was talking to someone, one finger plugged in his ear to keep out the noise in the room. When he hung up the phone after ninety seconds he looked dejected.

'One of the rookies found the phone fifteen minutes ago, caught in the branches of a bush in Central Park, just west of the roadway overpass,' he said. 'The team bagged it and took it into the station house. Alex must have typed the message Wednesday night but apparently didn't have the opportunity to hit SEND.'

'Then how — ?' I asked. I had set my phone down on the long table and planted my hands firmly on either side of it.

'The cops immediately charged it up to see if anything that might help us had come in or out, before they sent it downtown,' Mercer said. 'One of them noticed the draft on the screen and tapped SEND.'

'She must have written the words Wednesday night,' I mumbled. 'Maybe she got caught doing it and her abductor tossed the phone into the park.'

Keith Scully slammed his hand on the table to restore order. 'Give me the text again, Chapman. What does it say?'

The two words that Coop had texted to me before her phone was discarded gave no clue to her location. I spoke them aloud three times for the commissioner and his task force, and then read them silently again. *Bar . . . Bed.*

She hadn't told me anything at all.

27

'So this text addressed to Mike,' Commissioner Scully said, 'is the last thing Alex tried to get off from her phone Wednesday night.'

I looked across at Dr. Friedman and just stared her down. I was the person Coop reached out for — not rejected — when something went bad.

'Where's the phone now?' Scully said.

The text had succeeded in keeping everyone in the room.

'Crime Scene's going over it for touch DNA and prints,' Mercer said. 'Then they'll rush it down to TARU.'

The tech guys would work their magic. If it were possible to pinpoint the exact time and location that the phone landed in the park, it could be a help. And they would dump her device for any incoming calls — something that might have diverted her Wednesday night — as well as outgoing messages Coop may have sent.

There would certainly be some of her DNA on the phone, and perhaps partial prints of someone else. If she had in fact been abducted, there was the chance that her captor's DNA was in the data bank and his prints in the system.

I tore two sheets of paper out of my memo book. On one of them I printed the word *BAR* in all caps. On the other I wrote *BED*.

Peterson saw me do it, then walked to the commissioner's desk. He grabbed a stack of

235

paper and passed it around so everyone could follow suit. Ricky Friedman just watched.

'Does any of this speak to any of you?' Scully asked.

Captain Abruzzi wasn't writing. 'Yeah, she was on her way to a bar — which we already knew — and then she was going to bed with whoever she was off to meet at the bar. If it looks like a duck and quacks like a duck, what are you jumping through hoops for?'

'I doubt she'd be texting me about the going-to-bed part, Cap. Not with another guy,' I said. 'Unless it was you.'

'Maybe she was trying to tell you it was over, Chapman,' Scully said. 'Meant to be cryptic till she could get the entire message to you.'

'She's not a cryptic woman,' I said. 'The English lit major in her, Commissioner. She writes — she overwrites every thought she's ever had. Two-word texts? That's not the way she communicates.'

'What are the options?' Lieutenant Peterson asked. 'First call is whether Alex got into the SUV voluntarily. What's his name — Sadiq? He didn't see any signs of force, did he?'

'Coop knows the first rule of kidnapping. Never get into the car. Never. Once you do it's too late.' I had heard her give that lecture dozens of times, backed up by every FBI statistic in the country. Kick, scream, bite, fight. Just don't get into the car or your chances of being found alive ever again are significantly diminished. 'Sadiq wasn't in a position to see into the SUV — tinted windows and all.'

'But he doesn't describe a struggle?'

'No.'

'So did Alex get in because someone she knew pulled up and offered her a ride?' Peterson asked. 'What do you think?'

I reversed the order of the words by shifting the papers in front of me. BED and BAR. It didn't matter. Maybe they were meant to be as obvious as Abruzzi thought.

'You can't rule it out,' Vickee said. 'But who? And that would be just way too coincidental to be credible. There'd be something on her phone to confirm it, don't you think? A communication with somebody, even it if wasn't Mike.'

'You can say it out loud,' I said. 'If Coop was in a friendly situation — if she had been secure, in the company of a person she knew, she probably would have texted Jake Tyler to apologize for being late and to ask if he was still waiting for her.'

'If she did,' the TARU sergeant said, 'it will all be on her phone when we get it. Are they rushing it downtown to Bobby Bowman?'

'On the way,' Mercer said.

Lieutenant Peterson was back to how Coop got into the car. 'So let's assume it wasn't a friendly encounter, okay? Assume the worst. How'd they get her off the street? And I'm saying 'they' because there was a driver, and Sadiq says she got into the side of the SUV behind the driver, so if there was force used, it's coming from at least one more person in the backseat.'

'Could have been she was smacked on the head with a billy club or a jack,' one of the Major

237

Case guys offered. 'Sorry, Mike. I'm just being real. I don't mean like gray matter all over the interior of the SUV — I mean just stunned is all. Stunned enough to pull her into the car.'

'Look, Chapman,' the commissioner said, 'if this is too raw for you to listen to, we can pull back and you can work with Peterson out of the squad office. It's understandable. In fact, it's probably the smartest way to go.'

'Did I say anything? I'm thinking just the way the rest of you are.'

Except that every now and then the idea of a physical blow to Coop hit me like a tire iron in my chest.

'I wouldn't imagine it was anything that split her skull in pieces like a cracked egg,' another detective said. 'This text was written — what — maybe ten minutes to half an hour after she was grabbed, right? TARU will nail that timeline down, but it had to be written after she got into the vehicle.'

'I just said 'stunned,' didn't I? We're not talking permanent brain injury,' his colleague responded. 'Still together enough to write the words. *Bar* — that's Patroon. *Bed* — it's whoever she was cheating with.'

'What else would just temporarily knock her out?' Peterson asked.

'A knife to her throat or a gun to her temple would keep her quiet,' Abruzzi said. 'Might gain her compliance without leaving a mark.'

'I'd be in at the show of a weapon,' Peterson said. 'Nothing more than that necessary to get me into a car.'

'How about something toxic over her face?' the TARU sergeant added. 'What are the current drugs of choice?'

'I doubt anything was delivered by syringe,' Mercer said. 'She'd have to have been pretty still already, with a vein exposed, to ensure a hit. Discard that idea.'

'No, I meant the old-fashioned way. A rag over her nose. Chloroform.'

'You've seen too many bad movies,' I said. 'Chloroform isn't any kind of guarantee. You'd have to get it smack over the vic's nose and hold it there. You picturing a tough guy in the back of an SUV coming on to Coop with an 'Excuse me, miss, would you stick your head into this rag and tell me if you think it's chloroform?' Nah, not happening.'

'Take a step back,' Mercer said. 'I've had three, maybe four cases with it, and Alex worked on one of them with me.'

'So?'

'It's easy to get. My perp bought it online from a chemical supply company in Canada. In fact, Vickee, call Catherine and tell her to pull the Juarez case from 2009,' Mercer said. 'See if that fool is still locked up.'

Mercer went on. 'Suppose there's someone strong enough to grab Alex by the arm when he opens the car door and calls her name. She leans over and he's got a grip on her, and before she can open her mouth to scream, the soaked rag has her nose covered.'

'What's the point?' I asked.

He practically put his face up against mine.

239

'Maybe the point is that it's good news, if you think about it.'

'You and I must have very different definitions of *good*.'

'Listen up, Mike. If somebody wanted to kill Alex Cooper — and those threats have been real from time to time — he apparently had the opportunity to do that on Wednesday night,' Mercer said. 'She could have been taken out by a bullet walking alone on a side street. She could have been stabbed and left for dead. I'm looking at the fact that she may have been abducted as opposed to killed as a good thing.'

'On East 65th Street? Have you got it confused with the South Side of Chicago? Anacostia or Watts? We don't get so many drive-bys in the silk-stocking district, do we, dude?' I said, getting up to pace the perimeter of the room. 'Now, we get to talking about dump jobs, you'll have to admit this is prime real estate for that.'

Dr. Friedman inched forward and asked Vickee what kind of job I was talking about.

'That's what we call it, Doc, when the bad guys pick a vic off the street, drive off to some remote place to do whatever piece of the nasty it is that they want to do, and then dump the body in another location altogether,' I said. 'What's to say Coop hasn't been killed? What's to say she's not — ?'

I couldn't finish the sentence

'Sleeping with the fishes?' Abruzzi said. 'Curled up in the weeds alongside the Belt Parkway? Use your head, Chapman. If someone was looking to snuff a prosecutor, he'd want it to be a very public dump. She'd be lying at the feet of the Angel of the Waters in Central Park. She'd be splayed across the information booth in Grand Central. He'd want the city to know she was offed. That's not what we've got.'

'Then, what?'

'The alternative may be almost worse.'

I didn't think Abruzzi was wrong. The thoughts I couldn't deal with involved Coop in the hands of a sexual predator.

I needed to get out of headquarters and continue looking for the monster who had her, so I could rip his throat out. The air in the commissioner's office was stifling.

'Could we get back to chloroform for a minute?' Mercer asked. 'It makes sense as a weapon if you're telling me that Alex was alert and able to send — to try to send — Mike a text *after* she was forced in the car.'

Several heads around the table were nodding.

'I mean, all it does is provide a short-term knockout, if it works right. Five to ten minutes at best, unless it's applied to her nose and mouth continuously,' Mercer said. 'Suppose Alex was overcome by the chloroform, let's say. Not hurt. The drug was just used to overwhelm her and get her off the street as quietly as possible.'

Lieutenant Peterson was the first to agree. 'Go with it.'

'The driver takes off and Alex is in the backseat with another guy.'

Mercer's words had me squirming. I must have looked like I was going to fling myself

241

through one of the commissioner's windows.

'Sit down, Chapman,' Scully said.

'She comes around at some point, not long after the cloth comes off her face.' Mercer turned to me to deliver what he figured was the good news. 'That wouldn't have happened if they wanted her dead, Mike.'

'Unless they were ISIS,' Abruzzi said. 'Then they want her wide-awake so they can torture her. You know how they treat their prisoners, don't you? Burn them to a crisp, behead them — all kinds of medieval torture tactics. I bet they got sex crimes that would make your guts explode. Did she ever prosecute a terrorist? Man, those beasts would have a party with Alexandra Cooper.'

'What is it with you?' Scully asked the captain.

'He's a dick, boss,' I said. 'Always was, always will be.'

'Chapman shouldn't be in the room,' Abruzzi said. 'He doesn't belong on this task force. He's thinking with his private parts and not his head.'

'It's below the belt for both of you,' Peterson said. 'Cut it out. Chapman's in this until he wants off the case. Go on, Mercer.'

'We can get a pretty close guess on the time from the point Alex gets into the SUV till the phone is — what would you say? — tossed? Tossed into the park.'

'So she's come around,' the district attorney said. 'Maybe she had her phone in her hand — '

'No, no,' Mercer said. 'She'd have dropped it once she went limp if she'd been holding it.'

I had been party to this kind of brainstorming

session dissecting crime strategies more times than I could count. I had offered ideas about the manner of death or the disposal of bodies — ideas that would have distressed the next of kin in any given case if they'd been party to the conversation. I was sick to my stomach with Coop at the center of these hypotheticals.

'She keeps it in her pocket,' I said. 'If she was wearing her trench coat, she'd have had the phone in her pocket at some point. Or sticking out of the top of her bag. Not in her hand.'

'So Alex comes around,' Mercer said. 'We know that. Obviously, she had the opportunity to get the phone in her hands to write two words — words that make sense — so she was pretty alert. Maybe she was trying to say more than she got off. But she must have been caught in the act and whoever was next to her in the seat grabbed the phone and threw it away.'

'Everybody okay with that as a jumping-off point?' Scully said.

The people at the table looked at one another and murmured assent.

'It's more complicated than that,' I said.

'What is?'

'If she's alert enough to be trying to signal me, then she's too smart to be sending me words that the bad guys would make sense of if they caught her. Too obvious, these words. They don't mean what they say.'

I pushed the two pieces of paper away from me.

'Each of you,' Scully said, 'needs to have someone in your respective offices start playing with *bar* and *bed*. Use the dictionary, use restaurant guides, use every letter of the alphabet.'

'Mike's right, Commissioner,' Vickee said, pinning the papers with the two words on them to the table with her forefingers. 'Alex is a puzzler. Does the Saturday *Times* crossword faster than Bill Clinton, and he's supposed to do it lightning quick. These are clues to something, but you're wasting your time if you think these six letters are literal.'

'Now we've got a regular Bletchley Park going on, don't we? All these smart broads who are better than computers at figuring things out. Too bad I've never met one of them,' Abruzzi said. 'Myself, I'm lousy at word games. And the guys in the Nineteenth squad? Could be a few of them can play bingo, but that's as far as they go. Might save us all some effort if we bring a psychic into the conversation next. Does Ms. Cooper communicate with the spirit world, too?'

'You can lead this part of it, Mike,' the lieutenant said to me, ignoring the captain. 'Get a quiet place to work and puzzle out the clue.'

'*Barbed*,' one of the Major Case guys said, sliding the two pieces of paper together. 'Maybe she just meant *barbed*? Like a place with barbed wire around it.'

'That's a big help. Narrows the search down to about a million locations citywide,' his partner piped up next. 'Maybe it's a pirate who has her. I look at these and I see *blue beard*.'

'What?' Peterson asked.

'Scramble the letters and I get the word *beard*,

244

with an extra *B*. So it's Bluebeard or Blackbeard.' The old-timer threw his hands up in exasperation. 'Let me know, Chapman, when you come up with what was going on in Ms. Cooper's personal think tank.'

'We ready to get to work?' Peterson asked Scully.

'I got some snitches who might be helpful with the Estevez angle of this. I'll get right on it,' the Bluebeard aficionado said to the commissioner. 'If you can take a little more heat, Chapman, I gotta say I never worked a case with Ms. Cooper, but I think you're giving more credit than she's due with this breaking-the-code crap.'

'Why's — ?'

'She always seemed like an Afghan to me — the dog, not the tribesmen. Long and lean, a fine, shiny coat of hair. Nice to walk out with, show dog and all that, but not so much brainpower as she's cracked up to have. I'm with the captain on the *bar* and *bed* thing. I'll buy the first few rounds if I come up wrong on this.'

'Start saving your dimes,' Mercer said. 'I'll be drinking big.'

The group began to break up as the executive officer on the desk outside came into the room and took the commissioner aside.

'Get me out of here, Detective Wallace,' I said. 'You and I need a plan.'

The commissioner held up his hand and we all stood still. He finished his conversation with the XO and turned back to us.

'I'd like to have some volunteers, gentlemen,' Scully said. 'The commanding officer of the

245

Central Park Precinct just called in. One of his men who worked midnights just told him about some unusual activity he saw near the park on his way in on Wednesday.'

'A damsel in distress?' the old-timer asked. 'The iPhone toss? Something real, or just make-believe?'

'Everything's real until proven otherwise, okay? It's nothing as dramatic as the sighting of a kidnap victim or as specific as a cell phone coming from an identified vehicle. But it's an SUV incident worth a follow-up, so they tell us. You want this one, Mike?' the commissioner asked.

'I'll pass.' Homicides spoiled you for working the grunt jobs and minor incidents.

'What else you got?' the lieutenant asked.

'Hal Shipley's on his way to the pound to try to liberate his three vehicles.'

'That's rich,' I said. 'Yeah, Mercer and Jimmy and I would much rather go to Queens and do a face-off with the reverend.'

'Exactly the scene we don't want, Commissioner,' Lieutenant Peterson said. 'I'll get a man on that immediately. What else?'

'What is this? You gonna transfer me to the rubber-gun squad before this operation even gets started?' I asked, eager to have a confrontation with almost anyone who crossed my path. 'Take my weapon away 'cause you think I'm a danger to myself?'

'Or others,' Dr. Friedman said. 'Yourself or others. That would be my standard.'

'Nobody's taking your gun, Chapman. Just keep quiet,' the commissioner said. 'The third

246

call probably has nothing to do with this matter, but the notification just came in and we have to think of every possibility.'

'What is it?' Battaglia asked.

Keith Scully grimaced and looked away from me. 'There was a jumper on the George Washington Bridge this morning. Roughly four A.M. A woman who climbed over the railing from the walkway, poised to go into the river, but thought better of it and went on her way before the cops could get to her.'

'Mary, Mother of God. I'm taking that one. We'll go to the bridge, the Port Authority Police,' I said. 'No way that was Coop.'

The GW Bridge was one of the most popular sites in the metro area for suicides. Fifty million dollars had been set aside by the legislature to build a nine-foot fence above the walkway to prevent the jumps, which averaged almost twenty a year, but construction hadn't even started.

'There are surveillance cameras twenty-four/ seven that sweep the bridge,' Scully said. 'I'm told there are grainy images of the woman. Not great close-ups but should be good enough to ID.'

'What makes you so damn sure it wasn't Alex?' Peterson said.

I was walking to the door of Scully's office. 'Because she's terrified of heights, Loo. Because she's so damn scared of heights I doubt you could get her to walk over the Hudson River if I tethered her to my waist, much less climb on a railing and look down.'

'So you're not saying she wouldn't have

247

reached that point,' Dr. Friedman said, 'because she wasn't so depressed, are you? The woman on that bridge — who might just be Alex, if she had made the decision to end her life — has apparently reached the depths of her despair. You're not addressing the issue of Ms. Cooper's possible depression.'

'I'd address your front teeth with my right fist, if you were a guy.'

'Chapman!' Peterson roared at me.

'The woman is not depressed, Loo. She had nothing to be depressed about.'

'C'mon, Chapman,' Battaglia said. 'She had the rug pulled out from underneath her in the courtroom and — '

'That's happened to her before. She fights back from it every time, with the best team in the world to back her up.'

'And someone hacked into all her secrets. Who knows what the hell is going to hit Page Six, and when?'

'If I'm the biggest secret you thought she has, Mr. Battaglia, then the gossip columnists are in for a major disappointment. There's no other personal dirt on Coop's hard drive,' I said. 'You, on the other hand, sir — you've been playing pin the tail on the reverend with Hal Shipley and some of your other constituents for years, rumors have it. It seems to me that it's your secret deals that are about to unravel.'

I opened the door and motioned to Mercer and Jimmy to follow me.

'Don't go anywhere, Chapman,' Peterson cautioned me.

'Holding tight, Loo.' Although my left leg was jiggling like I'd been bitten by a tarantula. 'But I think we need to get a move on.'

Commissioner Scully told one of the Major Case guys to deal with the Central Park debrief, agreed to let Peterson intercept Shipley at the auto pound, and confirmed that I should look at the GW Bridge video to prove — or disprove — that the distraught woman was Coop.

'And, Doc,' I said, halfway through the door, reminded of the language in the campaign poster that was framed and hung behind Battaglia's desk, 'if you're worried about anyone jumping, keep your eye on the district attorney. It's not nice to play politics with people's lives.'

28

'This is a fool's errand,' I said to Mercer and Jimmy as the three of us took the elevator up to the Port Authority Police office on the Manhattan end of the spectacular double-decked suspension bridge that had spanned the Hudson River since 1931.

'Then I'm happy to be one of the fools,' Mercer said. 'We can make quick work of this.'

'Scully's trying to keep me at arm's length from this investigation.'

'He hasn't put you in a straitjacket yet, Mike. Let's keep on.'

We were met at the top by one of the patrol officers from the PAPD's Emergency Services Unit, who led us into a small room, like a watchtower, perched above the great river that separated New York State from New Jersey at this point.

It was ten thirty on a brilliantly clear fall day. I could see north to the Tappan Zee Bridge and south past the new Freedom Tower and beyond the majestic Statue of Liberty, which stood at the mouth of the Hudson in New York Harbor.

'Are you the man with the video?' I asked after our introductions were complete.

'Yes, sir.'

'Were you actually working at four A.M.?'

'Yeah.'

'Emergency Services — you've got the

250

toughest assignment in the book,' Mercer said, 'and on a bridge hung hundreds of feet over the water.'

In all police departments, these were the cops who handled every imaginable hazardous task, from structural collapses to car and rail accidents to victim rescue from every kind of life-threatening situation. The GW was the world's busiest motor vehicle bridge, and I had seen Emergency Services officers climbing towering cables to rescue workmen whose gear had broken, truck drivers whose trailers had jackknifed perilously close to the edge of the span, and dying patients stuck in ambulances when a political stunt resulted in the intentional jamming of the bridge during rush hour not long ago.

'Hey, I asked for this work,' the officer responded. 'It's pretty exhilarating.'

'The woman last night,' I said, as he went about turning the monitor around to show us the footage, 'did you actually get to see her? I mean, close up? In person?'

'Nah. The bridge is more than half a mile across. Almost forty-eight hundred feet to be exact. By the time we got the call and I was dispatched — I was handling a car accident on the far side of the river, where the Palisades Parkway merges with the bridge entrance — she was already hoofing it back to this side.'

'You followed?'

'Yes, but she disappeared into thin air,' he said. 'That's pretty common, once these suicides change their minds. I've talked my share of

251

jumpers down off the ledge when they're right at the tipping point, but if they've backed off before we get to them, they don't stick around for me to give them a parking ticket or a recommendation for counseling.'

'How about rolling the tape?' I asked.

Mercer and I sat in front of the large screen, with Jimmy North behind me. The officer stood beside Mercer so he could point out the figures.

'There was a lot of fog at that hour of the morning, so you won't see much at first,' he said. 'I'll freeze-frame it when she comes into view.'

The screen lit up when the video started to run. Between the blackness of the water and the hazy sky, all I could see were the endless vertical cables and the striking gray aluminum color of the steel tower on the Jersey side, obscured in places by the wisps of fog.

'Four A.M. and there's all that traffic?' Mercer said.

'There's always traffic, man,' the officer said. 'This is when the early-morning commute begins. Firemen, cops, nurses — all the essentials whose tours start in an hour or so. They get into town to avoid traffic, park, eat breakfast, and go to work.'

I was focused on the walkway on the south side of the bridge, but the fast-moving cars created a blur. 'Hard to see,' I said.

'Fourteen lanes of traffic. Over a hundred million vehicles a year. You can understand why we don't get to everyone in time.'

'Now that I watch this, sure.'

'You'll see a guy going westbound on a bicycle

on the upper level. Then she comes out of the night murk.'

I adjusted my seating and stared at the walkway. The cyclist lit up the path with his neon-yellow windbreaker, reflectors on his sneakers and the rear of the bike, and a bright-white helmet.

It wasn't quite the final airport scene in *Casablanca*, but a woman emerged from the fog just seconds later.

'It's not Coop,' I said. Then I watched her walk, holding my breath as I did, and looked again. 'Maybe. Maybe so. Freeze it right there. How high is that railing?'

'Just three feet above the concrete,' the officer said. 'No barriers, no nets. It's why we're such a magnet for jumpers.'

'I didn't mean that,' I said. 'I'm trying to figure out her height against a known marker.'

All we could see at this point was the back of the woman's head. She was tall and thin, and her hair was medium length and blond, like Coop's.

'Let it run, Mike,' Mercer said. 'Run it through once before you keep stopping it. I don't think this one moves — you know — like Alex.'

The officer hit the PLAY button and the woman continued walking, briskly, away from us. She was dressed in a short jacket and dark slacks. I cursed the slacks. If I could have seen the shape of her legs — the slender calves down to perfect ankles — I'd have known Coop anywhere.

She took ten or twelve steps and I knew Mercer was right. 'Not Coop,' I said. 'The walk

253

is off. I was looking at the height and general build, but you nailed it.'

'How do you mean?' Jimmy asked.

'She's bouncing on the balls of her feet,' Mercer said. 'It's a little thing, but it's just not the way Alex carries herself.'

The fog had cut into our line of sight. Then the woman reemerged, stopping abruptly just past a phone mounted on the railing with a sign that read LIFE IS WORTH LIVING: CALL LIFE-NET and an 800 number.

She grabbed the railing, looked down at the water, and swung her leg over the side. 'So not Coop.' I was practically shouting. 'What was I thinking, for even a minute?'

The woman's profile was all wrong. Her nose was prominent and hooked, not straight and patrician. She had bangs on her forehead that reached her eyebrows, and a double chin, not Coop's chiseled bones and angular lines.

'Definitely not.' Mercer let out a sigh, too. Relief, I assumed. 'Definitely not Alex. And Alex could never swing her leg out over that iron rail after looking straight down from that height — she would have passed right out.'

'Big-time,' I said, pushing back to stand up and look down at the land below us.

Mercer hit the PLAY button again and leaned in to watch, two or three more times. He was careful that way. I didn't need any more convincing.

'What do you guys want me to do about this person?' the officer asked. 'She'll be back, sooner or later.'

254

'Your usual follow-up,' Mercer said.

My moment of euphoria had passed. The woman who'd been ready to jump just hours earlier was, to the best of our knowledge, still alive. I didn't have the emotional energy to worry about her. Coop's fate was still a mystery, which I seemed powerless to solve.

29

'Here's the elevator, Mike,' Mercer said.

'I'm walking down.'

'It's like nine hundred steps, twenty flights of stairs or more.'

'C'mon, Jimmy. Let the old dude with the football player's knees ride to the bottom,' I said. 'I'm taking the scenic route. What do you know about Fort Washington?'

'This neighborhood? Washington Heights? I hear it's coming back.'

'The hood was lost to Dominican drug gangs in the 1980s. The Red Top Gang, the Wild Cowboys — real urban marauders,' I said, slowly starting down the staircase, which was enclosed in steel mesh, offering the same great views as the walkway above. 'It's back all right. But I'm talking about the fort itself.'

'I'm not as good on my military history as you, Mike.'

I stopped on the first landing and looked to the north, pointing out the spot to Jimmy. 'Not even fifty yards from here is where the remains of the walls of the fort are, inside Bennett Park. I used to come here to play as a kid.'

'I've never even heard of Bennett Park.'

We wound down to the next level. I kept taking deep breaths of the morning air, happy for the brief distraction. 'Well, the fort was built in 1776 so that George Washington could defend

New York during the Revolution.'

I pressed against the steel caging and looked across the Hudson. 'Fort Lee was built on the other side, to prevent the British from going upriver and to provide the troops with an escape route to the west — to Jersey and Pennsylvania — in case they did.'

'So Fort Lee is named for an actual fort?' Jimmy laughed. 'I thought it was just a bunch of condo livers hanging off the Palisades, waiting for Governor Christie to screw up the traffic patterns in some kind of political vendetta.'

'You wouldn't be entirely wrong,' I said, grabbing the banister for the next flight down and allowing myself to laugh at the Bridge-gate memory. 'Nope. Not only was Fort Lee the birthplace of the motion picture industry — '

'For real?'

'Yup. Thomas Edison's film studio, Black Maria, was built here, and dozens of others followed. Long before there was a Hollywood. And more than a century earlier than that, General Charles Lee of the Continental army held down this escarpment for old GW himself.'

'Was there a battle here?' Jimmy asked.

'Yeah,' I said, looking down. 'This point is the highest piece of land in all of Manhattan. Pure schist. Washington decided that twin forts here could stop the British warships.'

I had never brought Coop to this point. She would have loved it for the spectacle of the river view, if I kept her away from the edge and the open heights, and she would have listened to my history with her usual keen interest. I leaned on

257

the banister for fear my own knees would go weak on me each time I envisioned her with captors.

'I guess they didn't,' Jimmy said.

I shook my head. 'Did you ever hear of chevaux-de-frise, kid?'

'Never took French.'

'I wish the same were true of Coop.'

Jimmy grabbed both my shoulders from behind me, a step above, and rocked me a bit. 'She's going to be okay, Mike. With the info going out to the entire patrol force this morning, we're going to get lucky today. I'm sure of it.'

I was babbling to keep my mind from wandering back to visions of Coop's condition. I was staying in my comfort zone, in the history that was my escape from death and darkness.

'Chevaux-de-frise were a medieval form of battle defense,' I said. 'I clearly have a lot of educating to do with you. They were portable frames, Jimmy, usually made from logs. Anyway, Washington had them constructed to be sunk here into the river — right at the bottom of this staircase and all the way across to the Jersey side. They were loaded with boulders from the heights, where the fort was, sunk to the bottom, and chained into place with giant hooks on both sides of the river in order to paralyze ship movement on the Hudson.'

I put my hands in my pockets and kept spiraling down. 'Can you see all the way to the ground?' I asked. 'Washington had batteries directly beneath us — where this bridge foundation stands today. It's called Jeffrey's

Hook, a piece of land that juts out into the water. And batteries on Spuyten Duyvil Creek, and on the King's Bridge, crossing the Harlem River. The fort itself was shaped like a five-pointed star. Five bastions that — '

'Like Fort Jay?' Jimmy asked. 'That's a coastal star-shaped fort on Governors Island.'

He had probably been reminded of the fort by Vickee's comments this morning — a scene that was apparently the genesis of Coop's unhappiness with me.

'Fort Jay is four points. Fort Wood — that's the one on Liberty Island, at the base of the statue — that one's an eleven-point star. Fort Washington here was built like a pentagon, with five bastions.'

A sharp whistle screeched from below. It was Mercer trying to get my attention. Jimmy and I were about halfway down the tower.

'Yo!'

'Let's move it, Mike,' Mercer yelled.

I picked up the pace and started trotting down the stairs. 'You ought to read about the battle of Fort Washington,' I said. 'Great story, bad ending. Three thousand troops in this very fort, with General Washington himself watching from across the river. The British had four thousand Hessian troops backing them up. Wiped this place out at the end of '76, and Washington retreated to the west.'

'Will do,' Jimmy said. 'Maybe I'll come back with you and get the whole picture. Tour all the forts, okay?'

'You're likely sucking up to me or you're a

259

good man,' I said, calling out over my shoulder. 'Either way works fine for me.'

Mercer was waiting for us in the small enclosure at the foot of the giant tower.

'You got my girl?' I asked. 'Or are you just whistling 'cause you're lonely down here?'

'We got places to go, Mike,' Mercer said. 'Peterson just called me. There's some junk starting to float in from all over the city because of the alert that went out to every cop on the job when we left Scully's office. Blondes in Brighton Beach, trench coats abandoned on the subway, an unidentified young woman who overdosed on Metro-North last night. But — '

'So he's going to send me out on some wild-goose chase so I don't — ?'

'Suit yourself, Mike,' Mercer said, turning his back on me. 'Just suit yourself.'

'What's the 'but' about, man?'

'I was about to say to you that Major Case may have something to look at, is all. You're either with me or — '

'I'm with you.'

'The cop in Central Park who saw something on his way into work?' Mercer said, reminding me of one of the items on this morning's checklist. 'Seems there's a second piece to his encounter. Worth a shot, if you'll come with me to see if it takes us anywhere. To see if it gives you any ideas.'

'Of course I will,' I said, tailing behind Mercer with Jimmy North. 'Where to?'

'The boat basin. The 79th Street Boat Basin.'

The Upper West Side marina was in the

Hudson River, about five miles in a straight shot downriver from the GW Bridge.

'A sighting?' I asked, closing my eyes to squeeze out a thought of any possible connection between Coop and a boat parked in a marina.

'Not that,' Mercer said. 'But at two o'clock in the morning, in the off-season, it's a weird time and place for a guy to be swapping out license plates on his SUV.'

30

I stood under the vaulted Guastavino tile ceiling of the giant rotunda, marked by the same classic arches and design as the Oyster Bar in Grand Central Terminal, and sipped another cup of black coffee from the Boat Basin Café.

The vista was unique. Right off 79th Street, built in 1937 as part of a project to cover the New York Central's West Side railroad tracks, the marina was still the only place in Manhattan that offered year-round residency on boats. The rotunda was below street level, underneath the circular road that held the heavily trafficked entrance and exit to the West Side Highway.

'Low rent, river view,' Mercer said, joining me to look out at the Hudson. The tidal currents were so strong in this riverway that very few boats dared make it a permanent home.

'This place is in bad need of repair,' I said. The slats in the wooden dock were broken and splintered. 'I think I'll keep my coffin, even without the scenery. How many slips are there?'

'One hundred sixteen. Peterson's ordered the names of all the owners.'

'And the guy who's working in the office?'

'He came on at eight this morning,' Mercer said. 'The office is closed overnight this time of year. Just a security guy who swings by — when he's not asleep at the switch. Peterson's waiting on him now, but on the phone he claims he didn't see anybody around.'

'Nothing missing? No boats?'

'Not even an oar, Mike.'

'Stealth operation, then, if it happened here.'

'Or they greased the hand of the security guard.'

We stepped out into the sunlight and headed toward one of the wooden docks, to the right of the café exit. We were waiting for the lieutenant to appear with the two witnesses we needed to download.

Mercer followed me onto the dock. The first few vessels were houseboats that looked like they'd been berthed at the marina since it opened. They didn't appear to be seaworthy or comfortable but seemed attached to the wooden piers like barnacles to the bottom of a skiff.

'That's a pretty nice sport fish,' Mercer said, pointing at the fourth boat in front of me. It was a forty-three-foot Egg Harbor Express, with a large fighting chair positioned in its stern.

I kept on walking, out to the end of the dock.

'Anything speaking to you here, Mike?' Mercer asked.

'No. Nothing at all.' I glanced around at the different boats — small Grady-Whites and Boston Whalers to a few larger, classier numbers tied up at the end of the largest dock. 'Not like the days when Aristotle Onassis and Malcolm Forbes parked their yachts here, I'm afraid.'

'I mean, about Alex. I know how much she loves the water,' he said. 'I know you were boating together on the Vineyard last month.'

Coop had been a competitive swimmer in high

school and college. She loved the ocean, she enjoyed doing endless laps of crawl in a warm pool, and she treasured day sails and cruises with friends who kept their boats in Menemsha. I didn't picture her diving into the swirling current of the polluted Hudson River.

'See that beauty?' I said, pointing at a sleek blue-hulled motor sail called the *Leda*, docked behind the last small powerboat. 'That fifty-foot Schulte Mariner?'

'Yeah.'

'One of Coop's friends has that same model. We spent an afternoon sailing with him over to Cuttyhunk and back. He even let me drive it for a while. Pretty special toys, these things.'

The sunlight was stronger that day in September than it was now. It had danced off Coop's hair, and she had snuggled down on the backseat, her head on my lap, to get out of the wind.

'Has Alex ever mentioned this boat basin to you? Ever mentioned coming here to visit friends?'

'Never. She knows some folks who pass through town on large boats, but they stop at the Chelsea Piers or across the river in the fancier marinas.'

'I never had a case with her here,' Mercer said. I knew he was going through his mental lists of perps who might have come back for revenge of some sort. 'Plenty of crimes in Riverside Park — nothing special about Tanner going to that spot — but never at this place. Did you?'

'Nope. We scooped a DOA out of the water three years ago. Pug and me. A drunk who fell in about twenty blocks north of here but got hooked on the tip of a kayak over there, which kept him from getting washed out to sea. Nothing else.'

I looked to my left, at the mighty torch of Lady Liberty, raised high over her head, above the seven points of her crown, and then to my right, back up at the GW Bridge, where the world's largest free-flying American flag was catching the wind.

'No reason to link this place to Alex, then, is there?' Mercer turned and headed back toward the café.

He knew the answer. I followed him. It was unseasonably warm. I felt clammy and in need of a shower. Every part of me was beginning to ache.

Peterson had the first cop waiting for us at one of the large round tables, inside the café — out of the bright daylight. 'This is Officer Stern,' the lieutenant said. 'Central Park.'

We greeted each other and sat down. A few preliminaries and he cut to the chase.

'I was coming in for a midnight on Wednesday, running a little late, heading for the station house to sign in.'

Built in the nineteenth century as a row of horse stables and gardening sheds, the rambling series of Gothic cottages on the 86th Street Transverse had been restored and reopened as a high-tech police operation in 2013.

'I was on my Harley, heading uptown on Third Avenue. There was some Con Ed construction jamming up the flow, so I cut over, aiming to go uptown on Park or Madison. I was on East 73rd, just off Lexington.'

'What time was it?' I asked.

'It was after eleven fifteen, I know. I was gunning it so I wouldn't be late for roll call,' Stern said. 'Turned out I was. Especially because I stopped.'

'Stopped for what?'

'There was a vehicle — a black SUV, actually — parked on the right side of 73rd Street. The driver opened the door kind of suddenly and I had to swerve to avoid hitting him when he got out of the car.'

So far the time of night was right and the location was between the spot on East 65th Street where Sadiq saw a woman get into a black SUV and the place in the park where Coop's phone was picked up by the search team.

'I pulled the bike over and looked back to make sure I hadn't rattled the guy or knocked him over,' Stern said, his tone measured and calm. 'That's when I saw there was no plate on the front of the car.'

'No license plate?'

'Nope. So I parked the Harley and took out my shield, since I didn't look much like a cop, and started to approach him.'

Laconic worked well as a delivery style for Gary Cooper, but Stern was making me crazy.

'The guy was already on his knees in front of the SUV, screwing on the plate.'

'Did you talk to him?' I said. 'What about the rear plate?'

'Yeah. I asked if he was all right. I asked if he needed any help.'

'You didn't get his ID or the tag number?'

'I got everything I was supposed to, man.'

'Was he alone?'

Ray Peterson held up his hand and signaled me to back down.

'So he stood up. I could see the second plate on the ground next to him. I asked for his driver's license and — '

Ray Peterson cut in. 'This is Officer Stern's memo book, okay? The driver was Harold Harrison. DOB makes him forty-four. Ran him. No criminal history.'

'Harrison told me he'd just bought the car from a friend in the city. They all had dinner together and he should have put the plates on outside the man's apartment as soon as he left, but he forgot to do it till he started on his way across town,' Stern said. 'But he knew he couldn't chance driving home to New Jersey without the plates, so he stopped to put them on. That's right where I came along.'

'Anything else?' Mercer asked.

'Well, not at the time,' Stern said. 'I called the info in to the desk sergeant 'cause I obviously didn't have access to a police computer on my personal bike, like I told the lieutenant.'

'You got a call back?'

The officer nodded at Mercer. 'All clean. The driver as well as his plates,' Stern said. 'But it bothered me. Three guys, the woman asleep in the — '

'What woman?' I broke in. 'Tell me about the woman.'

'Just weird how she slept through the whole thing, me talking to the men in the car and all.'

'She was sleeping? I mean, you're sure she was alive?'

'Don't go jumping to conclusions that it's Alex,' Mercer said. 'Let's get the whole story.'

'That or she was drunk,' Stern said. 'Passed out, maybe. I didn't stop to take her pulse.'

He seemed bothered when I pressed him. I had to hold my tongue.

'So at the end of my tour Thursday morning I ran the plate again, 'cause I just didn't like the way the whole thing went down, you know? This time it came up stolen, reported about an hour after I first called it in. There I was, standing in the street, worrying about the guy because I thought I clipped him with my bike, and he's a total scumbag after all,' Stern said. 'Stolen driver's license that he picked right out of the vic's pocket and stolen tags from the schmuck's car.'

31

'Start with the girl,' I said.

I was on my feet. Peterson had turned the questioning over to me while he lit up another cigarette, leaning against the edge of one of the vaulted arches open to the river.

'She was the least of it, man,' Stern said. 'She never opened her mouth.'

The officer was regretting the collar for larceny that he had missed. I was hell-bent on finding Coop.

'What did she look like?'

He twisted his mouth to the side. 'Caucasian,' he said. 'They were all white guys. I'd say she was my age. Early thirties. Light-colored hair. That's all I could see.'

'Did you ever make an arrest for a sex crime?' I asked. 'Take a perp down to the DA's office?'

'Lots of felonies, but never rape.'

'Ever meet an assistant district attorney named Alex Cooper?'

Officer Stern shook his head in the negative.

'Were you talking to the men in the car? Is that what you said?'

'Yeah. The one in the passenger seat got out to help his buddy when I walked back to my bike to call the sergeant. By hindsight, he may have been getting ready to take me out if I'd come back with bad news,' Stern said. 'I told him to get in the car.'

'Did you get his ID?'

'No reason to, Detective.'

'I guess.' I was short on understanding and long on Monday morning quarterbacking.

'When he opened the car door to get in, that's when the lights went on and I could see another guy in the backseat.'

'Awake or asleep like the girl?' I asked.

'Totally awake. He asked me how long they'd be held up.'

'Anything distinctive about the men? About their looks? Scars, marks, tats — anything at all?'

'Not that I can think of. The driver and his pal, they both had real dark hair,' Stern said to me. 'Kind of black, like yours. The guy in the backseat was sort of red. He may have had a slight brogue, too.'

'May have? Or did he?'

'He said all of one sentence to me, Detective. Maybe he did.'

Irish? I'm sure in Coop's rows of file cabinets there were mutts she'd prosecuted who were as Irish as me and my ancestors, but I couldn't pull any up in the moment.

'Anything else about her? About any of them?'

'Yeah,' Stern said. 'She smelled something awful.'

'Smelled?'

'Too much perfume, I figure. Just when the door was opened I got a touch of it. Sickly sweet.'

Mercer and I exchanged glances.

Peterson had let the cigarette burn down to his lips. He heard Stern's comment and walked over to continue giving us the details.

270

Harold Harrison was an investment banker from Connecticut, in the city drinking with friends to celebrate his recent divorce. They were in a crowded sports bar in the East Eighties, sometime after nine P.M. on Wednesday, and he didn't know that his pocket had been picked until he went to pay the tab. His friends covered the bill, but when Harrison went outside to see whether he'd left his wallet in his car, the vehicle was still parked there but the license plates were gone.

'Professionals,' Mercer said. 'Total pros. They undoubtedly scouted their mark — or they had a couple of potential marks — going into the bar, already a bit tipsy. One of them stayed with Harrison's car. The minute his wallet was pinched, off with the plates.'

'Maybe it took longer than they thought,' Peterson said. 'So they scoop Alex up, then pull over to put the clean plates on in case they're stopped, in case one of her friends had happened to follow and got a partial.'

'Damn it,' I said, turning to the unhappy young police officer. 'Didn't you get the VIN off the SUV?'

'What for? The plates, the license — they checked out clean.'

'We'd know who owns the car, now, wouldn't we?'

'Lay off him, Chapman,' Peterson said, thanking Stern for his follow-up and asking him to wait on a bench outside the café till he was cleared to go. 'There's another piece of the puzzle to give you.'

He walked out the other side of the café — toward the paths to the east, which led into Riverside Park or up the enormous winding staircases to the asphalt roadway — and returned with a middle-aged cop in uniform.

'Hey,' he said, taking his hand off his frayed belt and extending it to Mercer first. 'Seen you around. I'm Jaworski.'

'Mercer Wallace. And this here is Mike Chapman.'

'Jaworski does steady midnights in the two-four,' Peterson says. 'He was working Thursday morning.'

'Tell me,' I said.

The Twenty-Fourth Precinct included the boat basin, a lot of Riverside Park, and the Upper West Side.

'I didn't think much of it until my boss called me about the blast from the commissioner's office this morning, with the alert about a missing woman in a black SUV,' Jaworski said. 'My partner and I were patrolling in an RMP early Thursday morning, not that we ever saw a woman in the vehicle.'

'What vehicle?' Radio motor patrol cars were the familiar blue-and-whites of the NYPD. What the hell did he think was so important if he never had his eyes on Coop?

'It was just coming up on two A.M.,' Jaworski said. 'We've got Sector Charlie, which includes the marina, so we usually swing by a few times during the night. There's not very much action on the water this time of year, but we always check it out in case someone goes all Natalie

272

Wood on us. The sergeant had us patrolling the park extra heavy this week because of the big arrest Wednesday morning. You know about that?'

'Yeah,' Mercer said. 'Raymond Tanner.'

'Okay. So it's one of those make-the-public-feel-safe programs,' Jaworski said, resting both hands on his paunch, which hung out over the belt. 'Lots of visibility and police presence. Step up the patrols.'

'Got it.'

'My partner was the driver. We just finished checking out the park. Decided to take the underpass and come out on the round-about up above here,' he said, pointing up and circling his arm to indicate the road overhead. 'I spotted an SUV, a black one, pulled over out of the traffic flow, like at the very top of the staircase down to the marina. The driver was on his knees behind the car, so I thought maybe he had a flat or something.'

'You stopped,' I said.

'Sure. Got out and walked over to him. He was working in the dark, so I beamed my flashlight at him to give him a hand.'

'Was it the tire?'

'Nope. He had a screwdriver,' Jaworski said. 'Told me one of the bolts had come out of his rear plate and it was flapping like crazy when he drove.'

'Connecticut plates,' I said matter-of-factly.

'No. New Jersey, actually. I gave your lieutenant the plate number.'

'Did you call it in?'

'What for?' Jaworski said. 'The tag on the front of the car was fastened on tight. The man's story made sense. He didn't do nothing.'

'And in the car?'

'Nobody there. I shined my light in before I left, when he got back in the driver's seat. Then he thanked me and took off.'

'You know who Alex Cooper is?' I leaned in and asked.

'Should I?'

'She's a prosecutor. DA's office. You ever take a sexual assault arrest down to Centre Street?'

'I don't do arrests,' Jaworski said, smiling at me. 'The city don't pay me enough.'

There were plenty of guys in the department who thought like he did, especially as the time to collect a pension grew closer. They didn't want to mess up their steady tours, risk injury, deal with erratic court appearance dates, and be required to testify under oath to anything.

'Why are you here?' I asked, throwing up my hands in Peterson's direction.

'My sergeant called me at home this morning, after that message from the commissioner was sent out. I guess 'cause we're not that far from the transverse crossing, and me and my partner saw this SUV with a guy screwing on a plate in the middle of the night.'

'It gets better,' Peterson said.

'Yeah, he brought me in for a day tour. Overtime,' Jaworski said. 'The guys in the squad ran the Jersey plate this morning, just 'cause it's a black SUV in the general location from late Wednesday night, Thursday morning.'

274

'They were stolen,' I said. 'Right? Like it's a big surprise at this point, Loo, right?'

'MD plates,' Peterson said. 'Taken from a doc's car while he was supposedly paying a house call to a lady friend on West 80th Street, sometime after he parked at midnight and before Jaworski spotted them at two A.M. Pretty bold to lift them — two separate times and places — from a city street.'

'Mercer's right. We're clearly dealing with professionals. Three of them, at least.' I was trying to think like the bad guys. 'Two sets of plates if not more. Fresh. A well-conceived plan to keep the common-looking black SUV moving to their destination, maybe stopping to kidnap someone along the way. Even if the license number is captured on a traffic video or made by a cop on the beat, we'd never be able to prove after the fact that it was the same car.'

'Exactly,' Peterson said.

'You start checking all the TWOCed tags?' Plates that were taken without the owner's consent were TWOCed.

'Of course.'

'Any ideas to find the SUV? Anything about it that was distinctive?'

'We've got the car, Chapman,' the lieutenant said. 'Abandoned sometime in the last twenty-four hours. Right outside a chop shop in Queens.'

'VIN?'

'Completely disfigured. It will take a day or two to run all the possible configurations of the digits to see if we can pull up an owner.'

'Prints? DNA? There must be some way to tell if Coop was in that car,' I said, sailing my empty coffee cup across the room, missing the garbage pail by several feet. 'How about that sickly sweet odor? Maybe there's still a rag on the floor of the car?'

'There's a familiar odor all right,' Peterson said. 'That car's been wiped so clean you could perform heart surgery on the backseat with no risk of infection. The whole thing reeks of Clorox.'

32

'Are you following me because you don't trust me or because you want to talk?'

'What do you think, dude?' Mercer said.

'You like it, these two sightings?'

'It's all we've got. Work with these facts till something better comes along.'

I was already racing ahead of the facts. Bad images of this trio and their captive were forming in my mind's eye like clouds colliding in a thunderstorm.

'Sadiq puts Coop on East 65th Street between Second and Third, getting into an SUV, behind the driver, no ruckus. I'm figuring that's at something like ten fifteen, ten thirty,' I said, shading my eyes from the bright sunlight to look at Mercer. 'Officer Stern gets off his bike on East 73rd Street, maybe forty-five minutes later.'

'How about all the time in between?' Mercer asked.

'Maybe they were driving around, looking for a quiet side street to make the switch. Think how smart it is, really. There are surveillance cameras on all the main avenues and intersections that are capable of capturing plate numbers twenty-four/seven to give speeding tickets and violations. So these guys are savvy enough to think of plate changes. Maybe just pause for a while out of sight — make sure their captive is subdued — and that way there's no straight line of travel if we set out to examine the video footage.'

'Glad you can think like the bad guys, Mike,' Mercer said. 'So figure they've killed an hour doing like you just hypothesized. Now they pull over. One of them is putting new tags on the car — that would throw off the scent of anyone who saw the abduction and reported the old license numbers.'

'Script matches Coop's disappearance so far as it goes.'

'But she's still out cold,' Mercer said.

'You can keep reapplying something like chloroform anytime your vie comes around, long as it doesn't kill her by causing cardiac arrhythmia.'

'So after Officer Stern heads off to work, maybe Alex comes around.'

'Maybe.'

'At some point,' Mercer said, as we walked away from the massive granite rotunda and turned south, out toward the main dock of the marina, 'she hears the three talking about where they're taking her. That's when she slips the phone out of her pocket and tries to text you.'

Bar, I thought. The words *Bar* and *Bed*.

'The car goes from 73rd Street off Lex to 85th Street, to the transverse that cuts through to the West Side,' he went on. 'We know that because Alex's phone was thrown into Central Park and landed there. She'd composed a text to you by then — '

'Or part of one,' I said. The two words simply made no sense.

'The perps toss the phone and keep on going. Driving west.'

'And TARU owes us a time for the toss, but it's got to be between eleven twenty and twelve fifteen.'

'That puts the group on the West Side, in time to steal another set of license plates.'

'And by two A.M.,' I said, 'the only one left in the SUV is the driver.'

Lieutenant Peterson hadn't wanted officers Stern and Jaworski talking to each other, comparing notes and observations, until he had gotten all the information from each of them. Now he would be trying to confirm that the man each described as the driver was the same individual.

'So why the 79th Street Boat Basin exit?' Mercer asked.

I turned around to look back at the West Side Highway. 'It's a pretty central point of contact,' I said. 'You can go either south or north on the highway from right here. South shoots you straight down to the Battery, so you're on the way to Queens or Brooklyn in a flash. Even Staten Island. You pass the Lincoln and Holland Tunnel entrances to get to New Jersey.'

'Wrap under the overpass to go north,' Mercer said. 'Gives you the George Washington Bridge, the Henry Hudson Parkway north to the Saw Mill, to Westchester and Connecticut.'

'So the vic could have been transferred to another car right there. Another make, another model, another color vehicle, to further complicate things for us,' I said, pointing up at the asphalt roundabout where Jaworski had witnessed the second plate change. 'She could be in

Georgia by now. And we've got an entire department looking for her in a black SUV that's already been trashed. She could be in North Dakota or Arizona or — or in a landfill on Staten Island.'

'Now, that's fucked-up, Mike,' Mercer said, gripping my arm at the elbow. 'Hold yourself together, man.'

I swiveled around again, breaking loose and heading for the end of the dock.

'Why here?' I said out loud, rolling the two texted words over and over again. 'Why are we standing right here, at the boat basin?'

The gray-green water was calm now. Two men were loading live eels into a pail on their Boston Whaler to serve as bait, heading out for an afternoon on the river.

There seemed to be an unusual amount of activity on the Hudson, maybe because of the warm, sunny day. Or maybe it just seemed that way to me, because I had been overcome by inertia and the futility of my efforts to find Coop.

Bar and *bed* were simply two common syllables, and I was pushing them to give me a meaning they didn't have.

The Circle Line tour boat was full of passengers taking in the scenic shoreline. Water taxis crisscrossed from New Jersey towns to lower Manhattan, optimistic fishermen were motoring south to Sandy Hook to look for the ever-elusive October stripers, and athletic young men and women were paddling kayaks and canoes against the current.

I walked to the farthest point on the dock,

enjoying the breeze that came up from the water.

The quiet — the distance from all the chatter that had surrounded me since before dawn — was also a relief.

Mercer gave me some time alone. He leaned against one of the wooden piers and let me try to clear my head.

I did a complete three-hundred-and-sixty-degree revolution, fixing on the highway entrance to the boat basin on the land to the east above me, and once again due north to the mammoth engineering feat that was the GW Bridge. I scanned the Jersey coastline to see if it might hold a clue to Coop's whereabouts, and then stretched out over the end of the dock to look for the colossal arm and torch of the great lady, *The Statue of Liberty Enlightening the World* — as her creator had named her — standing tall on Liberty Island.

Why the boat basin? I asked myself. If not just a traffic stop for the perps to change cars and move their passenger, then there had to be a boat involved. And if a boat was involved, then where was it headed?

I squatted on the broken boards and drew imaginary letters with my finger. What had Coop heard the men in the car say to make her write *Bar* and *Bed?*

I looked up again and scanned the Hudson River one more time, as though searching out its source in the little town of Lake Tear in the Cloud and sailing away past its mouth at the head of Upper New York Bay.

What I needed now was an epiphany, a

281

lightning strike to my brain that would make things as clear to me as Coop thought she had done.

I played with proper names like Barton and Barstow and Barbara. I thought of crazy things like bedlam and bedbugs and bargains. I conjured objects that would be on this river, like barges and barrels and bedrock.

I must have spent ten or fifteen minutes fighting with the alphabet, pacing the dock and then squatting down to focus myself.

Coop had meant to send these words to me because she trusted that I would be able to make sense of them. But I was trying to force the six letters to talk to me, and they wouldn't comply.

I thought it through again. She must have heard the men say they were taking her to an exact location. She must have known by the time she wrote the two words, before they drove through Central Park to the West Side, that their next stop was the boat basin. And then someplace jumping off from right here, maybe someplace we had both been together.

Bar and *Bed*. I started over again. I babbled all the words that came to me from a mental scan of dictionary and encyclopedia *B*s.

I looked upriver and downriver and tried to recover factoids about every landmark on this vast waterfront.

Slowly, I pushed up from the dock. I stretched my legs and nodded.

Bar was short for the name of Frédéric Auguste Bartholdi, the French sculptor who conceived and designed the Statue of Liberty.

My wordsmith had given me the help I needed with the shorthand text she never got to send. *Bed* must have meant Bedloe Island, where the great statue had originally been sited.

I fist-pumped the air over and over again.

'What is it, Mike?' Mercer called out to me.

'I have it, man!' I shouted back at him. 'Go get Jimmy North. It's time for a sea cruise.'

33

'Slow it down, Mike,' Mercer said. 'Talk me through it.'

We stood on the end of the dock and looked downriver.

'It makes sense from every angle. Who knows how many clues Coop would have tried to give me if she'd had time. The words she wrote were never going to be obvious as place names,' I said. 'These clues wouldn't have been clear to her kidnappers unless they knew as much about New York City history as she does.'

'And you do,' Mercer says. 'So what makes those two ordinary words so highly charged, in your view?'

'First of all, it's a place Coop and I have been to together — with you, too — so of course she knows the names.'

'Of course. The night she wound up on Shooter's Island. The Kills. You took her inside Fort Wood till the chopper came to get us.'

'One of the shorter visits, but she knows everything about Lady Liberty that I do.'

'Go on, Mike.'

'We're looking for a location, right, where kidnappers might keep a prize prisoner. Liberty Island could be the place, don't you think? I mean, I'm not saying the worst is over or that's where Coop is now, but it's worth a look.'

'Give me more.'

'Start with the fact that it's an island,' I said. 'That makes it hard to reach, hard for people to get to. Nobody's just going to drop in on the group, are they?'

'You'd be wrong about that, man. You know it's a draw for tourists.'

'Pay attention to your local news, Mercer. The island was closed to visitors as of Labor Day, for the next six months. They're replacing all the rivets in the statue — like, twelve thousand of them, repairing the Lady's nostril and some of her missing hair curls, and pressure washing the whole damn thing to get rid of ten years of bird droppings.'

'And you think they'd be hiding, like, what, inside the torch?'

'Don't blow me off, okay? When's the last time you were out there?'

'Like most New Yorkers, never, except that night on business.'

'Then hear me out, Mercer. She's massive, the statue. Yeah, you could get lost inside her. Hitchcock did it. Robert Cummings. *Saboteur*,' I said. I was jumpy and agitated, talking at a staccato clip, like a hyperactive kid. 'But she stands on top of an old army fort.'

I had just pointed out the eleven-point star-shaped structure to Jimmy North an hour earlier.

'Fort Wood was built for the War of 1812 and eventually used as a garrison after the Civil War. It actually forms the foundation of the statue, the base of it.'

'So there are still military structures on the

island?' Mercer asked.

'I don't know what's inside the pedestal of the statue or the remains of the fort itself, but it's one of the great restored ruins of the city. The island is twelve acres, so there's also a small park and a bunch of outbuildings, even a caretaker's home,' I said. 'And it's one of the few places around Manhattan that you can only reach by boat. Only by boat.'

'And the trail of bread crumbs brought us right here to a boat basin. That's useful.'

'Coop likes all things French, and I'm into military history. That's why the clues work.'

'Tell me that again,' Mercer said.

'All right. The sculptor who had the idea to build this great statue is a Frenchman. His name is Frédéric Auguste Bartholdi.'

'How are you even sure that Alex knows his name?'

'Coop's been there plenty of times, by ferry. It's one of the first places she takes out-of-town guests. She thinks the Lady is a glorious creature.'

'Why does she figure *you* know the Frenchman's name, well enough for her to have you catch on to the word *Bar* in her text?'

'The whole point of the statue, Mercer, is to commemorate the Declaration of Independence and French aid to the Revolutionary War,' I said. 'It was a gift from the French Republic because of the longtime alliance of the two nations in achieving America's freedom. That's why Liberty is holding a tablet inscribed with the year 1776.'

'Of course. There's a military aspect to the island.'

'Who do you think picked the site for the statue? Who took Bartholdi to the little island in the bay?'

'I've got no idea.'

'Ever hear of a dude named William Tecumseh Sherman, the Civil War general?'

'Sure. Scorched earth,' Mercer said. 'Man refused to employ black troops in his army.'

'One and the same. He was considered to be the first modern general — well, except for his views on race. I've read his memoirs, so that's how come I know about Bartholdi,' I said. 'When Bartholdi came to this country for the second time, President Rutherford Hayes assigned General Sherman to meet him in order to choose the location for the statue.'

Mercer pursed his lips. He was thinking about it all.

'So you want any more on Bartholdi? That he fought in the Franco-Prussian War? That he first wanted to build this statue for Ismail the Magnificent, the pasha of Egypt, to mark the opening of the Suez Canal? Give me a war zone and I'll give you the answers.'

'I'm just trying to be your devil's advocate, Mike.'

'I got Captain Abruzzi, Dr. Friedman, and half the Major Case squad playing that role. Save your energy.' I was walking along the dock, inspecting the small motor launches that were tucked into their moorings.

'So what is Bedloe? *Bed*. How did that one hit you?'

'It wouldn't have leaped out at me without

Bartholdi, but the combination did it. The island wasn't renamed Liberty until the 1950s,' I said. 'Isaac Bedloe was a Dutch colonist. He actually owned the entire little island. Named for him. Bedloe Island, it was, for more than a hundred years.'

'Owned it? Why is that?'

'A few of the islands in New York Harbor, including Ellis and Liberty, were called the Oyster Islands by the Dutch, because they were so rich in oyster beds. Bedloe was a well-to-do merchant in the seventeenth century who bought the place. He imported tobacco from Virginia and exported pickled oysters.'

I saw the boat I wanted to use to motor down to Liberty Island. It was fairly new and appeared to be in great condition, with a pair of three-hundred-horsepower Mercury Verado outboard engines strapped on the stern.

'It's because of Fort Wood that I know about Bedloe,' I said. 'I've always been fascinated by the forts that were built to guard New York. Wood had eleven bastions and thirty guns protecting the western entrance to the harbor. I doubt they were ever used.'

I picked up the pace and started walking to the marina office, back at the entrance to the dock area. Jimmy North was standing under the first arch, watching Mercer and me. I waved at him to come out on the pier.

'You're serious about taking a look around the island?' Mercer asked.

Jimmy approached and I asked him what Peterson was doing. 'Wrapping up with the two officers. I think he's about to go uptown to his office.'

'Dead serious, Mercer,' I said, turning to look at him but walking backward toward the rotunda. Then I whipped around and talked to Jimmy. 'You stay here. Let me tell Peterson we'll do some more snooping around the marina. No need for full disclosure quite yet.'

'Sometimes, Mike, I really wonder about you,' Mercer said.

I backed him off with my hand.

'I was just coming out to get you,' Peterson said.

'Tell you what, Loo,' I said. 'The three of us will check out the boat basin parking garage for missing plates and stuff. I'm about to go talk to the marina manager to see whether he can suggest some locals to interview. Why don't you call me when you get a list of names of all the owners, and Mercer, Jimmy, and I can put our heads together? We'll see if any of this relates to Coop.'

Peterson reached out and put his hand on my shoulder. 'I like how you've pulled yourself together, son. Back there in Scully's office I was afraid you'd get all hotheaded and go off script.'

'You know I'm a team player. But I gotta tell you, Loo, it's the hardest thing I've ever done. You've got to give me some space.'

'We'll pull out all the stops, Chapman,' he said, the cigarette dangling from his lips as he moved them. 'I'll call you as soon as we get the list of boat owner names from the real estate office that controls the rentals.'

I thanked him for everything he was doing to find Coop.

Then, when Peterson disappeared into the shadows under the roadway, I hustled back to the dock. Mercer and Jimmy were on their phones, checking for updates and messages.

'Excuse me,' I said to the crusty old guy who was sitting in the tiny marina office. His radio was tuned to the VHF emergency channel and his TV muted, but with the local all-news channel playing. 'I'm Detective Chapman. Mike Chapman.'

I showed him the blue and gold. He wasn't impressed.

'I'd like to rent a small boat for a couple of hours this afternoon.'

'We don't usually rent boats. We rent slips. Gotta have your own boat.' He didn't look up from his copy of the *New York Post*, which featured a cover shot of the mayor tripping and falling on top of a protestor on the steps of City Hall. He had landed upside down, looking cockeyed and disoriented. The DAZED AND CONFUSED headline made me smile.

'I'm not interested in what you usually do. I'm interested in what I need right now.'

'You got a captain's license?'

'It expired.'

'Which boat are you looking at?'

'There's a thirty-two-foot Intrepid out on the first dock.'

'You got good taste.' The man looked up at me for the first time.

'Three hours, maybe four,' I said, reaching

290

into my wallet. 'In exchange for my driver's license.'.

He stood up and walked over to a long metal box, unlocked it, and lifted one of the keys. 'Have it back by April 1, Mr. Chapman. No nicks, no scratches. I assume this is official police business?'

'It is.'

'Then no nicks, no scratches, and no blood. The owner don't even fish with this gem. She can't stand the sight of blood.'

34

'Where'd you learn to drive a boat?' the man said, stripping off the seat covers and rolling down the isinglass cover that kept the cockpit dry.

'Martha's Vineyard. Out of Menemsha,' I said. 'Mostly fish off Devil's Bridge in Aquinnah.'

'If you can navigate those waters without breaking up, you'll be fine in the Hudson,' he said, stepping back onto the dock and handing me the keys. 'That's your chart-plotter screen on the left. Tells you where you are and operates the radar.'

'Check.'

Mercer and Jimmy were scoping the river as they settled in, one on the white leather seats in the bow and the other in the stern.

'Your depth finder there, and this here's the VHF radio. Keep it on channel sixteen unless the coast guard tells you otherwise.'

'Check, boss. What does she draw?'

'Three feet, no more than that. Keep her off the shoals.'

'Won't be a problem.' The Liberty Island perimeter had been dredged to receive ferries and large boats. This little speedster wouldn't present an issue getting right up to a dockage.

'Don't forget this baby has all the latest Furuno navigational systems. All you have to do is steer it,' he said. 'It's even got AIS.'

'What's that?' Mercer asked.

'Automatic identification system,' I said. 'We pop up on the radar screen of other boats in our range. It tells them who we are. It names our vessel.'

'What *is* the name of this boat?' Mercer said.

I hadn't even paid attention to what was painted on the hull.

'She's the *Dolly Mama.*'

I leaned over and looked at the stern, where the name was painted in bold gold letters. 'Not named for a monk, is it?'

'Nope. Owned by a woman named Dolly Dan, with eight grandkids,' he said. 'She winters in Palm Beach. Good people. Keep it clean and she'll never know.'

I walked to the console and put the key in to turn on the engines.

'Keep in mind, Mr. Chapman, there are no channel markers in this part of the Hudson.'

'Check.'

'As you pull out and enter the channel, give it one long blast of your horn,' he said.

'Aye, aye.'

He had untied the ropes from the cleats that held the boat against the dock and I was more than ready to kick off.

'Nice and slow in the river, okay?' he said, calling out his final instructions. 'No need to rough it up by making a big wake. Everybody's polite.'

'Thanks for the loaner. See you later.'

I put my hand on the throttle to get the boat in gear, honked the horn, and moved out onto the river, plowing straight across to the Jersey side to then turn left and head downriver with the flow of the traffic.

'Here's a pair of binoculars,' I said to Jimmy, removing them from beneath the driver's seat. 'You scan the shoreline.'

'Looking for — ?'

'You'll know it when you see it, pal. Best I can do.'

'Do you really know how to drive this thing?' Mercer asked, coming around behind the windshield to stand beside me.

'We'll soon find out,' I said. 'Kind of think it's like riding a bike. It'll come back to me.'

'Why didn't you tell Peterson the truth?'

'About our outing?'

The wind picked up once I powered the engines to fifteen knots. My hair was blowing and the cool air lifted my wilting shirt, which had felt as though it was glued to my body.

'Yeah.'

'Then he'd feel obliged to take it up the chain of command and we'd be called down to Scully's office and I'd be trying to make sense to those guys about the way these clues and the geography of the boat basin and Liberty Island feel right in my solar plexus,' I said. 'And by then it'd be close to midnight and we'd have lost the whole day to bureaucratic bullshit. You worried about hanging with me? You want me out here alone?'

'I have one worry, Mike. Just like you,' Mercer said. 'I want to find Alex.'

The channel was full of activity — everyone

taking advantage of being out on the Hudson on this spectacular day. I pulled back a bit on the throttle, happy to let others maneuver around me.

The buildings on the New Jersey side of the riverbank were a mix of new condos, old warehouses, and a variety of large and small boat moorings.

We went past West New York and Union City off to my right, slowing even more so that Mercer could scour the shoreline action. Jimmy had his binoculars focused on the Manhattan side of the water as we passed through the West Sixties and Fifties.

There was a large marina above Weehawken Cove, just opposite the Hudson Rail Yards in Chelsea. 'It's bustling in there,' Mercer said, asking for Jimmy to hand him the binoculars. 'Can you do a slow turnaround?'

'Fingers crossed,' I said, waiting for a water taxi to pass before I veered left and made a lazy circle with the boat.

'You know the ways those guys — if those are the guys,' Jimmy said, pointing at the crowded marina, 'you know the way they passed off license plates and then one of them ditched the SUV in Queens and the others probably got on some small boat, I'm guessing? Could be these guys had another boat waiting, right? Could have off-loaded their cargo anywhere along here, couldn't they?'

'Everything's possible,' Mercer said. 'Let's take each opportunity as she comes.'

'On our way?' I asked.

'Yeah. We can check out Chelsea Piers on the return, if we come up empty.'

'Okay.'

I was familiar with all the landmarks on the Manhattan side, but it was fascinating to see them from an entirely different perspective. There were new parks between the highway and the river just south of the Meatpacking District, which had once been such a rough part of town. The growth of tall buildings in Tribeca was a dramatic change, and the spectacular design of Battery Park City — ninety-three acres of land reclaimed from the Hudson River when the original World Trade Center was constructed for a mix of residential homes, commercial use, and parkland — never ceased to overwhelm me. That was especially true, I think, because it was the brainchild of Coop's brilliant uncle, a renowned architect and city planner — the Alexander Cooper for whom she was named.

All roads led me back to Alexandra Cooper.

We were closing in on the southern tip of Manhattan Island, where the original colonial settlement had given way to the financial center surrounding Wall Street.

Off to the right was the enormous Colgate Clock, first erected in 1906 and now refurbished — fifty feet tall. The factory it had been built to advertise was long gone, but the bright, bold face of the timepiece reminded me that it was two fifteen in the afternoon.

An armada of container ships seemed to be navigating the harbor in the Upper Bay. Some would make their way past us toward Albany, others were headed to the East River, and still more were on their way to the ocean and points all around the world.

How easy it was to hide a body in a container bound for a third world country. I had seen that movie dozens of times.

I steadied my hand on the throttle, steering the sturdy Intrepid closer to Ellis Island, my back to the sweeping vista of Governors Island, which had so haunted Coop after our encounter there with a crazed killer.

We didn't have far to go now.

We were off the tip of Ellis Island when I noticed a roadway. There was actually a paved bridge connecting Ellis, through which twelve million immigrants had come to this country, to the New Jersey mainland. Cars and trucks could access the island, which wasn't the case with Liberty.

'Can you see anything over there with the binoculars, Jimmy?' I asked.

'I don't remember knowing about any bridge to these islands,' Mercer said.

'Only Ellis.'

'A few cars and some delivery vans crossing back to Jersey,' Jimmy said. 'And it looks like there's a bunch more cars parked at the rear of the island.'

'We ought to put that on our list for the way back, too,' I said.

'Yeah,' Mercer said. 'Much easier access with a car.'

'The SUV was abandoned, guys,' I said. 'And it appears that three of the four people that were in it when Officer Stern saw it got out of it at or near the boat basin. I'm betting they used a boat to leave Manhattan, and I'm feeling lucky.'

'It's the great green Lady,' Mercer said, staring up at the gigantic monument as I eased up even more on the throttle and motored into the shadow of Liberty.

'I'm going to circle the island once,' I said, 'to see if there are any small craft tied up.'

'Why is she green, anyway?' Jimmy asked.

'When she was set here on Bedloe Island in 1886,' I said, 'Lady Liberty was the color of a copper penny.'

'You're kidding me.'

'No joke. But green film verdigris forms naturally on copper from long exposure. It took about twenty years to turn her this color, but that's what protects her from corrosion.'

I was practically next to the dock that extended out into the Upper Bay to receive tourist ferries. I was crawling along on top of the water, surprised to see that there were no boats anywhere on its long arm.

I picked up speed and stayed close to the shoreline. The magnificent statue towered directly above us, the tip of the torch reaching more than three hundred feet overhead.

'Can you see any workmen?' I asked.

'Negative,' Jimmy said.

I had made it past five of the points of Fort Wood that faced the waterfront and was circling to the south. There was an area of greenery, like a small park, directly behind Fort Wood and the pedestal of Liberty.

Then came a house, a two-story redbrick building, adjacent to a row of smaller units that looked like work sheds. Next there was the only other dockage, a long one that appeared to be commercial.

There were two gray-hulled boats tied up at the commercial dock. Fewer than I had expected. I ignored them for the moment and continued around the rear of the island, where there were several more work sheds and parkland. Then the remaining stars of the fort, the rear side, came into view.

'How about I try to dock this thing and we go ashore?' I asked.

'Sure,' Jimmy said. 'There must be somebody who patrols this place, right?'

'Rangers,' I said. 'National park rangers.'

'Federal jurisdiction?' he asked.

'Yeah. Feds.'

'How are you going to get past those guys?'

'Surely you've witnessed the Chapman charm,' Mercer said.

Jimmy laughed. 'Not so much,' he said. 'Not lately.'

'Mike's got blarney for every occasion.'

'Each of you guys, pay attention,' I said. 'Grab one of those bumpers — those navy-blue rubber things — and throw them over the side.'

I watched as they did as I asked.

'Now grab the ropes — you in front, Mercer, and Jimmy in the back. I'm gonna try to slide up nice and easy and one of you can climb onto the dock and tie us up to the cleats.'

I bounced the boat off the end of the dock like

a pool ball whacking against the walls of a table. Dolly Dan wouldn't approve of my parallel-parking technique.

Jimmy was more agile than Mercer. He jumped up on the dock and fastened the ropes to the metal cleats.

I hoisted myself up and put the key in my pocket.

We didn't get halfway down the dock before a man started coming toward us from land. He wasn't a ranger. He was dressed in civvies — khaki slacks and a blue sweatshirt.

'Hold it right there,' he called out to us. 'Who are you with?'

'NYPD,' I said.

'Show me.'

We each took our shields from our pockets to display them.

'What's the deal?' he said after looking at them.

'Official business.'

'Funny I didn't get a call about it.'

'Who are you?' I asked.

'I'm in charge of the work crew.'

'If I'd have known that, or your number, I would have called you,' I said. 'Instead, my boss called the park service. Head ranger. Bullwinkle or whatever his name is. Wears a big brown hat like Pharrell Williams.'

'Didn't he tell you the island's closed?'

'Knew that. But we're not tourists.'

'It's even been closed to my workmen the last two days. There's a private event tomorrow night,' he said. 'I just have a skeleton crew cleaning up for it. Then they're pitching a tent back there for the party.'

'That's why we're here. I mean, the private event,' I said. 'We're doing a security sweep.'

'Really?' he said, growing more obviously annoyed. 'A rap label pays three and a half million to rent this island for the night to debut a new album by Kanye and you clowns are doing a security sweep the day before? Don't waste my time.'

'What do you mean, waste it?'

'Their security men have been all over this island. You're a day late and a dollar short,' he said.

'Did you hear me say we're an NYPD detail?' I said. 'Do you understand that the mayor of the city of New York sent us to do this?'

'The mayor's coming to this shindig? You serious?'

'Where there's weed, there's our top dog,' I said. 'Go on, make his day. Call his office, do what you gotta do. But if there's a leak to the press that he's going to be here — maybe even with the governor of New Jersey, like a little political love-in — then I will turn the spotlight right back on you.'

I turned as though I was going to lead Mercer and Jimmy back to the boat.

'Hold up,' he said. 'And you want to do what?'

'A quick walk-through,' I said. 'Just need an hour or two. I'm not inspecting your rivets, if that's what you're afraid of.'

'If I catch hell from the ranger in charge — '

'Not to worry. It's all cleared through

301

headquarters,' I said. 'If you need us to score a few tickets for your kids for the party . . . '

'You can do that?' he asked, lightening up for the first time since our arrival.

'Mercer Wallace can get you whatever you need. He used to bodyguard Kanye when he moonlighted, back in the day.'

'Now we're talking, Detective,' the man said, wrapping an arm around Mercer and shaking his hand. 'Welcome to Liberty Island.'

35

'Where are the rangers?' Mercer asked as we walked toward land.

'With the island shut down to tourists, there's only one on duty in the daytime through this fall and winter,' the man said. 'He actually took a boat into Newark to help the group get a permit for fireworks tomorrow night. You'll probably meet him later.'

'So who guards the place at night?'

'Nobody lives here, if that's what you mean. The coasties watch over the island from the water. Otherwise it's all fenced off, as you can see, and pretty hard to get here or get onto.'

'I saw a small building — looked sort of residential — when we rode around the place,' I said. 'Right next to the commercial loading dock.'

'Used to be,' the man said, 'that Lady Liberty was a lighthouse. In the early 1900s, she was electrified. There were actually nine lamps in her torch, supposedly to guide boats into the harbor. So the house was built for the lighthouse keeper.'

'I never thought of that beacon as a lighthouse,' I said.

'Well, she wasn't much good at it. She's actually too tall to be useful to ships trying to navigate the details of the harbor. The Lady is prettier than she is practical.'

'And that house? Is it occupied?'

'Not now,' he said, shaking his head. 'There was a caretaker who lived in it for decades with his family, but it got too expensive for the government to keep up. Just last year they moved him out and shut the place down.'

We were off the dock and passed through the entrance in the heavy wire gate that encircled the island.

'I'll get one of my men over to — '

'Don't bother with that,' I said. 'We're totally low maintenance. Just got to stick our heads into enough nooks and crannies to satisfy the mayor. Hey, and how do we get those tickets back to you?'

The man shrugged and smiled. 'Whatever's easiest,' he said. 'I'll be here till late tonight and all day tomorrow. Just ask for Walter.'

'You got it, Walter. Four tickets, compliments of the mayor.'

Walter was whistling as he walked away. He turned around and waved at us. 'Take a look inside,' he said. 'The Lady's wide-open.'

I gave Walter an enthusiastic thumbs-up.

'Where are you going to get four tickets to Kanye's show?' Jimmy asked. 'Are you hallucinating?'

'You ought to be more worried about where Walter will be working next week unless we get this done quickly.'

'What first?' Mercer asked.

'The Lady herself.'

'Stay together or split up?'

'Start together. She's huge,' I said. 'Once we sweep through her we can make a plan to split

304

the rest of the island into three parts.'

The pedestal itself was enormous. Like the statue, the proportions of her elaborate base were gigantic. Set within the walls of old Fort Wood, the granite-stepped pyramid was a formidable foundation for the iconic lady.

I picked up speed as I went up the steps to the entrance, both men at my heels. I pushed against the huge, heavy door and it opened for us.

The ground floor of the pedestal was where tourists lined up — one thousand a day — for the elevator to take them to the foot of the statue.

'You good on the stairs, Jimmy?' I asked. 'It's about twenty stories to the top of the pedestal.'

He looked at Mercer and me and laughed. 'You guys aren't that old yet, are you?'

'Start climbing.'

'What exactly am I looking for?' he said, taking in the floor around us. 'Looks like it's been swept clean for the VIPs coming tomorrow.'

'Anything. Anything and nothing,' I said.

'And he means nothing,' Mercer said. 'If Alex has any way to communicate with us, she'd be trying. Could be she'd break off a fingernail or . . .'

'Manicured. Really pale pink.'

'Or pull out a few strands of hair. A piece of jewelry.'

'Look for writing on the wall,' I said.

'Graffiti?'

'Not that. But maybe something drawn in the dust with her fingers. Even just her initials.'

The elevator door opened. 'See you on top.'

I was examining the interior of the elevator cab for the same kinds of things, or even scuff marks that might suggest a struggle.

I took out my phone.

'Checking in with the lieutenant?' Mercer asked.

'Not quite yet. He's not looking for me and I'm not looking for him,' I said. 'I just thought I'd Google the number of steps up to the crown.'

I entered the search.

'You think I'm entirely off track, don't you?' I kept my eyes on my phone.

'Not a far-fetched theory, actually. And it's not a lot of territory for us to cover quickly,' Mercer said. 'What I like about it is that this place has been shut down since the end of the workday on Wednesday.'

'That, and getting here at two in the morning, there wouldn't be a soul to interfere.'

'We just have to find a link, if there is one.'

'Walter has to give us a list of the workers,' I said. 'Run that against parolees and perps.'

'Who's going to run all these lists for us? If you're doing nothing else, you're generating lists.'

'Coop's team at the office. They'll do whatever it takes. One name is all we need,' I said. 'I'm thinking Shipley.'

The elevator doors opened and we stepped out onto the landing.

'Shipley and this place?'

'No, no. Somebody in Community Affairs in the Twenty-Eighth Precinct must be all up into being liaison to Fat Hal,' I said. 'Much as he hates cops, Community Affairs can tell his peeps that some local orphans should be comped to see Kanye. You know who the liaison is?'

'I can find out.'

'Make a call. You know the reverend can get tickets for this concert. If we make that deal for Walter, we'll have a list of workmen's names before we leave the island.'

'You're right. I'll call Vickee. She'll have a department contact who can suss it out without dropping your name.'

I put my hand on his arm. 'Do not be calling your wife, Detective Wallace. Do not be telling her what we are up to, okay? She's sitting three offices away from Keith Scully and she's very vulnerable emotionally right now. Get this done another way.'

Jimmy wasn't even breathing hard when he emerged from the staircase. He shook his head at me. 'Not so much as a chewing gum wrapper or a cigarette butt.'

'So maybe I'm wrong,' I said. 'This whole trip won't take long. Mercer, why don't you make some calls and find out what's going on while Jimmy and I climb up to the crown. Your feet won't even fit on the steps.'

I leaned back and looked up, through the glass ceiling that had been installed at the very top of the pedestal, at the massive interior of the statue.

Inside her hollow body was a maze of armature, as far up as I could see. It was a vast honeycomb of steel bars, molded to fit the contours of the copper plates, which expanded and contracted with the weather. They ran

307

horizontally and vertically, joined by steel brackets best known as saddles. In here — no place to hide anything or anyone — were many of the thousands of rivets that had to be resecured.

'You ready, Jimmy?'

He was mesmerized by the intricacy of the statue's interior, the folds of her long copper robe — Coop said it was a stola, copied from the dresses of Roman deities — that rippled down from her shoulders to the very top of her sandaled feet.

'No elevator to the crown?' he asked.

'I just cheated and looked it up. Three hundred and ninety-three steps — almost thirty stories. And they're narrow and slippery from wear, so hang on.'

I led the way, winding upward in the staircase, determined to get to the top, which I remembered as having enough space to hold a cocktail party, if not a hostage.

The higher we went, the more claustrophobic the feeling. As hot as the afternoon sun had felt, it was about twenty degrees warmer in the body of the statue. There was no air-conditioning and she was airless inside.

When I reached the top, I was disappointed again. The space was remarkably clean, with three large speakers, the latest in hightech sound systems that looked as though they had just been installed for tomorrow's concert.

I walked to one of the windows, leaned my back against it, wiped the sweat off my forehead, and tried to catch my breath.

Jimmy was right behind me. I envied the effects of his daily gym routine.

'This is amazing,' he said. 'I've never been up here. It ought to be a required visit for every American.'

'Damn right.'

The view of the harbor, of the city, of the piece of the Atlantic Ocean that rubbed up against New York, was the most dazzling sight imaginable.

'Seven rays in Liberty's crown,' I said. 'For the seven continents and seven seas. And twenty-five windows right here.'

I moved along from one side of her head to the other, and then crossed back, looking at every frame as a separate photograph of the city.

Each vista offered so many possibilities for kidnappers to hide out. Our task seemed absolutely hopeless from this vantage point.

'Keep your spirits up, Mike,' Jimmy said. 'This was such a long shot.'

'Yeah, but if these guys knew Coop — I mean, if they were really out to torture her — here would be the right place to do it.'

'Her vertigo, you mean?'

'Dead-on. She'd still be waiting for me at the foot of the pedestal,' I said. 'Dangle her out one of these windows and she'd give up her own mother.'

'So be glad there's no sign of her here,' Jimmy said, hesitating for a few seconds. 'How about the torch? That's much higher still.'

'Yeah. Yeah, it's another forty feet or so. And the only way up there is a ladder.'

'I'll do it for you. I know you're not going to quit till you've seen this whole place.'

'The torch was replaced thirty years ago. Other than that, it's been shut down for one hundred years,' I said. 'I mean, totally shut down.'

'Accidents on the ladder?'

'Much worse than that.'

'How?'

'Ever hear of the Black Tom explosion? In 1916?'

'Can't say as I have, Mike.'

I looked out to our right and pointed off to a spot in the harbor, almost adjacent to Liberty Island. 'There used to be a spit of land out there called Black Tom. Not much bigger than a sandbar.'

'I don't see it.'

'Nothing to see now, Jimmy. But back then, the government covered the whole little island with munitions, meant to eventually help the Allies in World War I. In the middle of one hot night in July that year, some saboteurs set fire to the stash, causing a deadly explosion and an inferno that consumed all the ammo as well as the island itself.'

'And hit the statue?'

'Struck right on the torch. It's never been open to the public since then.'

'How do I get there?'

'I'm going myself. Let's walk back downstairs a bit. You'll see a door off to the side, to the left, when we get to the statue's neck.'

'This Black Tom thing,' Jimmy said, 'did they ever catch the guys responsible?'

310

'You're a lot like me, always looking for the police angle, aren't you?'

'You could say worse things.'

'They rounded up some Germans, if I remember right. They were the ones who had the most to gain for the munitions not getting to Europe, but the thinking was that our boys had something to do with it.'

'No kidding. The Irish?'

'In 1916 we were a bit wound up in our own fight for independence,' I said. 'Would be just like some thickheaded relative of mine to want to keep the goods out of British hands. You know Clan na Gael?'

'Heard of it, but I don't know much about it.'

'A powerful group fighting for Irish independence, and their greatest ally during World War I was the Germans. Anything to defeat the Brits. Took hold big-time in America, the clan did. So they were believed to be the driving force behind Black Tom. Besides, there was no question that the Irish controlled the waterfront. Ran the longshoremen's union. Very little happened in this harbor that wasn't under their watch.'

I reached the unmarked door first. I turned the knob, but it was locked. I turned the knob again, both ways, and added the weight of my shoulder against it, but it didn't budge.

'Locked,' I said. 'We may need Walter after all.'

'Let me try it,' Jimmy said.

But his effort was no better than mine.

'Let's go,' I said, and continued on down to the pedestal landing, where Mercer was waiting for us.

'Ready to call it a day?' Mercer asked.

'Why?'

'It's written all over your face. There's no trace of Alex here.'

'Who'd you talk to?' I said. 'What do you know?'

'Nobody back in command central is doing any better than we are, Mike.'

'No leads? No legit tips? No ransom demands?'

'Nothing,' Mercer said. 'Way too quiet for my taste. And yes, the ask is in for tickets for Walter. Why don't you tell him — somebody will have to pick them up in Manhattan since nobody knows we're here — and then we'll go back to 79th Street and you can power down for a few hours.'

I didn't want to argue with Mercer. We were both running on fumes. 'I want to see the inside of that caretaker's old house before we go. And I need some water or something. I'm really parched.'

I pressed the elevator button and we rode to the pedestal base.

We walked back out into the sunlight and down the steps. We circled the great monument in silence and started walking along the path that cut through the very center of the small island, making our way to the center of the workmen's sheds.

Halfway there, as we refreshed ourselves by the shade of the trees that lined the path, two young men, not much more than twenty-five years old, passed us going in the other direction. They were headed toward the statue.

'Hey,' Jimmy said to them. 'What's happening?'

312

They walked on past us without answering. One looked up and acknowledged us with a nod while the other just kept going.

'You want me to check them out, Mike?' he asked.

I took a glance over my shoulder at the two young men, both dressed in work clothes: white T-shirts, jeans, and boots. 'No reason to,' I said.

One of them, the taller one — well muscled and tattooed on both arms with colorful art stretching from his shirtsleeves to his wrists — had stopped in his tracks to stare back at us.

I was getting more and more agitated, and paranoid, too, but I forced myself to think rationally. 'Nobody likes having a cop appear on his doorstep, Jimmy,' I said. 'Can't say as I blame 'em.'

36

I was inhaling a bologna sandwich like it was an aged New York strip steak.

Walter was on the phone with his son, telling him he'd be able to pick up concert tickets sometime tomorrow morning from the desk at the Twenty-Eighth Precinct. He had generously parted with the stale leftovers in the office refrigerator so the three of us could eat.

'Your men did a great job cleaning up after themselves,' I said.

'We've got a red-carpet list coming. The National Park Service didn't give us much choice.'

'I'd like to see the names of your work crew.'

'Why's that?' Walter asked. 'You think we've got a security risk on board?'

'Just routine.'

He walked to an old file cabinet and riffled through some folders until he found the one he wanted. 'Local 46,' he said. 'Metallic Reinforcing and Lathers Union. A bunch of really good guys we got here.'

'That local is harder to get into than Yale Law School,' Mercer said.

The union had been around for a long time, and jobs in this hardworking brotherhood of construction workers were more likely to come by inheritance rather than application.

Mercer and I ran through the names together

314

before xeroxing the pages. It looked like my class list from parochial school. Rourkes, O'Connells, Boyles, Doyles, Cavanaughs, Dolans, Lanigans, Cooneys, Coonans, Fitzsimmonses, Kilduffs, Hallorans, and more Macs than I could count.

There was an occasional Finelli or Fernandez, but most of the men who did this dangerous work found the courage to walk on those steel beams in their bloodlines going back for generations.

'Got any slackers?' I asked, shaking the papers at Walter.

'Not a one. I've seen most of them climb up inside the body of the statue on those horizontal bars, three hundred feet high without a safety net, or shimmy up the ladder to the torch to change out a floodlight for the electricians,' he said. 'Like a buddy of mine remarked, once you've stood on the ground below and watched a man flapping around out in the wind high up on the nose of Lady Liberty, trying to patch a hole in her skin, you know there's no dress rehearsal for it. You've either got the nerve or you don't.'

'Amen to that.'

'How about ex-cons?' Mercer asked.

'Not very likely. At least not that I know of,' Walter said. 'I've been told the rangers have to do a thorough background check on everyone because it's federal property.'

'I'd like a shot at climbing that ladder up to the torch,' Jimmy said.

'Now, that's really out-of-bounds,' Walter said.

'Did you have anybody up there this week?' I asked with heightened interest. I was looking for

315

places that were totally out-of-bounds.

'Oh, sure. I'm just not looking for a lawsuit. That's why I left it locked up. Somebody misses their footing on that ladder and they're toast. But we cleaned it up in there for sure.'

'Then, can you let us see it?' I asked.

'I'll take you wherever you want to go.'

'The caretaker's house, too?'

'Let's get a move on, then.'

Walter led us out of his makeshift office and started to walk toward the redbrick residence.

'I don't blame you for looking in the house, Mike, now that we're here,' Mercer said, folding the list and putting it in his pocket. 'But the torch? Let's get home before sunset, man. Nobody took Alex single file up a ladder to — well, there'd be no purpose to it. You're clutching at straws.'

Everything we were doing was an act of desperation. I knew that.

Mercer's phone signaled the arrival of a text.

'What's that?' I asked.

'Vickee. She's telling me that the Coopers won't be flying in till tomorrow,' he said. 'Dr. Cooper had some significant — well, Vickee's calling it palpitations. He's hospitalized over-night and they'll evaluate him for travel in the morning.'

'So she thinks I've dodged another bullet, doesn't she? Vickee thinks I'm avoiding them.'

'Give your friends the benefit of the doubt, okay? All she wants to do is let us know what's going on,' Mercer said. 'You'd be mighty peeved if she didn't.'

Walter had walked ahead with Jimmy North while Mercer let me vent.

I heard footsteps on the gravel path behind me. The same two workmen who had passed us on our way from the statue to Walter's office were headed back this way, coming from the pedestal.

One of them, the tall one with tats, was carrying something rolled up under one arm. It looked like a sheet or thin blanket.

'Yo!' I shouted to them. 'Hold up there.'

They both ignored me.

'What's he carrying?' I asked Walter as I took off in their direction.

'A tarp. It looks like a tarp to me,' Walter said. 'They're all over the place.'

'I want to talk to those guys,' I said, breaking into a trot. 'We just went up and down the whole statue and I didn't see a single tarp.'

'Mike,' Mercer called after me, 'you're chasing shadows now. C'mon.'

'They're probably not coming from the statue, anyway,' Walter said. 'That kid likes to wander off by himself from time to time. Quiet type.'

'Still waters run deep,' I said. 'And sometimes foul.'

37

I followed the workers to the trailer at the edge of the easternmost point on the island. I tried the door but it was locked, so I knocked.

'Yeah?'

'NYPD. Mayor's security detail.'

'Yeah?'

'Come on out. I'd like to talk to you.'

'We're getting dressed,' one of them said. 'We'll be out in a few.'

I kicked the dirt around until the door opened. Neither one of the guys seemed to have changed clothes. They'd just put jackets on over their T-shirts.

'You are — ?' I asked.

'I'm Pete Fitzgerald,' the short redhead said. 'This here's Cormac Lonigan.'

'You got an uncle on the job?' I asked Lonigan. 'Queens Robbery Squad?'

'Not so's I know,' he said, swinging his backpack over his shoulder. 'Lots of Lonigans out there. Construction, bartending, firemen. None that I know of on the force.'

'What were you guys doing today?'

'Same as the others. Finishing the cleanup for the concert.'

There were a handful of construction workers in and around the sheds, closing up — it seemed to me — and getting ready to get on the ferry that was docking for the ride back to Manhattan.

'Where were you two coming from?'

'Over by the statue,' Fitzgerald said. 'Picking up our things.'

'We were just over there ourselves. I didn't see any blankets or tarps. Where's the one you were carrying, Cormac?'

'That? It's tucked in the trailer till Monday. Where they all are.'

'Show me.'

Cormac Lonigan stood in front of the trailer door like a hawk on top of his nest. 'We got a ferry to catch.'

'I'll see that it waits for you,' I said. 'Did Walter tell you we were on the island?'

'He didn't have to,' Lonigan said. 'Some of the men seen the three of you walking off your boat, talking to him. Then he started bragging about you getting tickets from the mayor and all that. Security detail.'

'Would you lighten up if I got you some tickets, too?'

'Not my kind of music, Detective.'

'Maybe Bono will do the warm-up for Kanye,' I said. 'Now, open the door.'

I was certain that Lonigan and Fitzgerald had gone back to the statue — to the fort, in fact — because they heard there were three cops on the island. Maybe that was true. Or maybe I just wanted to beat up on somebody.

Lonigan pushed open the door and stepped out of the way.

'Mercer,' I said, 'Jimmy. Why don't you walk these gentlemen back to the statue to let them show you exactly where they picked up the tarp?

I'll join you in a minute.'

'You don't have to get all bossy,' Fitzgerald said. 'We didn't do nothing. I'll take you back.'

I walked inside the trailer and scanned the room. It made my apartment look like a centerfold in *House and Garden*.

There was a row of lockers, mostly open, with jackets and overalls and baseball caps hanging from every hook. There were three cots without bedding, with clothing strewn about on top of them, a couple of small refrigerators, a space heater, and a bathroom at the far end.

A pile of tarps was stacked between two of the cots. I walked over and pulled at the edge of the one on top, but it was much heavier and a darker shade of taupe than the material Lonigan had been carrying.

I took a photo of the pile with my phone, and a video as I turned around the room once before going outside.

I jogged down the steps of the trailer to catch up with the group.

'Find what you needed, Detective?' Walter asked.

'Yeah. Exactly.' Cormac Lonigan wouldn't look up from the path, but I could see him smirking.

'I promised these officers that everything would be shipshape for the dignitaries, boys,' Walter said. 'They want to see where you were working.'

Pete Fitzgerald was looking to Lonigan to take the lead.

'My fault,' Lonigan said. 'I was coming down

from the crown early this morning after taking up the speaker system for its installation. The piece I was carrying was wrapped in a tarp. I dropped off the speaker, and when I was ready to leave, the elevator was full of more equipment being unloaded. So I took the stairs down.'

'He dropped one,' Fitzgerald said. The loyal friend backing up the lie, figuring that if we had gone into the statue, we must have taken the elevator. 'One of the tarps, I mean. I went back with him to fetch it.'

Jimmy North was champing at the bit to jump in but didn't want to step on my toes. I nodded at him to go ahead.

'That's so weird,' he said, ' 'cause just before we saw you this afternoon, I walked up every one of those three hundred and ninety-three steps. There wasn't even a dust bunny on the staircase, much less a tarp.'

Lonigan didn't flinch.

'Could be the boys are mistaken, Detective,' Walter said. 'Like I said to you, Cormac here likes his privacy.'

I doubted they were mistaken about something that had happened twenty minutes ago. But Walter's heart wasn't in his mouth, like mine was.

'Why don't you show these gents around the old fort, Cormac? More likely than not it's where you left your stuff.'

38

Cormac Lonigan trudged along ahead of me like he was on a forced march to a death camp. I told the others to wait outside for us while he led me into the fort.

'What's your problem, Lonigan?'

'I got no problem.'

'What is it you like about the fort?' I asked.

I knew it had been garrisoned and abandoned several times from when it was constructed until after the Civil War. At least nine of the wings of the original structure that had formed the eleven-point star had been cemented shut in the last restoration of the statue. Engineers had deemed it too dangerous — and too expensive — to try to maintain the granite and concrete that made up the once-armed and important coastal defense station.

'It's quiet in there,' he said. 'The walls are so thick it keeps the place quiet from all the banging when the men are at work. Sometimes I take my lunch break here. The granite makes it cooler inside, too.'

The only way into the fort itself, even though it was actually beneath the level of the huge pedestal, was to climb the steps of the pyramid-shaped base and then go down a staircase, where there was a small office and a gift shop. That was the part I had visited before with Coop, quite unexpectedly one night.

After we reached the pedestal plaza, Lonigan went down into the dark stairwell that was the entrance to the fort.

'Here's what you wanted to see, Detective.'

'It's pitch-black down here,' I said. 'Where are the lights?'

'I wouldn't know that.'

'What do you mean? Why not?'

'When I come down here the office is usually open, even when the statue is closed to visitors. There's someone answering phones and giving information,' he said. 'And I've usually got on a head-lamp from working up inside the Lady.'

'That's not — '

'It doesn't take me much light to eat a sandwich and hear myself think.'

'Show me around, Cormac.' Walter had given me a flashlight in case I couldn't find the light switches.

'Nothing to show. This is it.'

'What's through that doorway?' I asked, pointing the flashlight. There was an archway made of bricks, opening to the next dark area.

'I don't think anything at all.'

'Why don't we look?' I said.

'Go right ahead,' he said, fidgeting with his backpack.

'The operative word there is *we*, dude.'

He slipped the backpack off his shoulders and rested it on the stone floor.

There was a room beyond the area of the office where we had first entered. It held a few wooden chairs, which looked neither comfortable nor inviting. On the walls were several old prints of nineteenth-century soldiers on guard duty at the fort, and others depicting the battery of Rodman guns, especially built for seacoast fortifications that were mounted along the bastions of the eleven stars.

'Who was your ticket to the union?' I asked.

'Why? Is that against the law?'

'No, Cormac. It's a lucky thing. That gene pool of men who founded Local 46 is worth a lot of money, bought with a great deal of sweat.'

There was another archway and I tapped him on the shoulder to follow me through it. My flashlight revealed a long empty hallway ahead. The structure was finally beginning to resemble the interior of an enormous star. This was the side of one of its points.

'My great-grandfather was the first one in the family, on my father's side. Then so on down the line to me.'

The deeper into the old fort we went, the cooler and darker it seemed to be. There were holes in the wall that offered a bit of fresh air, as warm as it was, but mostly the dankness of the place dominated my senses.

'Any brothers work with you?'

'I got three older sisters. Only one brother. He's a priest, Detective. Had to happen to one of us in the family sooner or later.'

I laughed with him. Maybe he was just a nervous kid, I thought. Sullen and nervous. Maybe he'd had a bad encounter or two with the NYPD.

'I know the feeling. Would have been me,' I said, 'but the nuns figured I'd sprouted an

324

unfortunate mouth and good right hook way too young.'

At the end of the hallway — the tip of one of the star's points — the archway was completely boarded up. A large red sign that said CAUTION was affixed to the wooden crossbars.

'Seen enough, Detective?' Cormac asked.

He leaned against the brick wall and lit up a cigarette. He blew out the match and put it in his pocket.

'Probably so,' I said.

I ran my flashlight over the two-by-fours that blocked farther access to the fort's other starred points. At the bottom of the left corner, opposite Cormac Lonigan, were ashes. Anthill size but undisturbed, as though recently deposited. There were three or four spent matches around them.

'Is this your place, Cormac?' I asked.

'Nah. Like I said, I just come down near the office, the room behind it.'

'By yourself?'

'Usually so.'

He started to walk back in the direction from which we'd come.

I pressed my right hand against the wooden boards directly above the ashes. He heard the boards shift and turned to look at me.

'Don't lean on that, Detective.'

'Who put this up, Cormac?'

'I wouldn't know. I don't come back here.'

But somebody else did. Somebody who wasn't careful enough to pick up his matches or grind the ashes into the stone floor.

I examined the boards with the flashlight. The

nails on the left side of the CAUTION sign looked shiny and new. The ones to the right, where Lonigan had been standing, had already begun to rust from the dampness.

I banged on one of the long pieces of wood, about chest-high, with the heel of my hand. It cracked in dead center.

Cormac Lonigan shouted at me to stop.

I pulled at the wood and the end of it snapped out of the board behind, three shiny nails coming with it.

'Why stop?' I asked.

'Because that part of the fort's been blocked off for years,' he said. 'There's fallen granite inside and the ceiling's unstable. A man could get hurt in there.'

'I'm a sucker for two things, Cormac. One is exploring old forts,' I said, ripping at the other end of the board, oblivious to the splinters and nails, 'and the other is getting hurt.'

I lifted the flashlight from my belt, where I had tucked it when I started to pull at the jerry-rigged wall. I shined it into the space behind the separated boards.

'Give me a hand here, kid,' I said.

I couldn't see anything in the blackness beyond, but Cormac didn't wait to hear that. He threw his cigarette to the ground and bolted away from me.

The flashlight dropped from my hand as I turned to give chase.

The kid was faster than I was, but the second's hesitation when he stooped to pick up his backpack cost him the lead.

He was halfway up the thick stone steps to the pedestal base when I grabbed both ankles and brought him down.

He slid back toward me on his belly. I took a handful of hair at the nape of his neck to lift his head up a couple of inches and turn it to the side, slamming his right cheek against the solid granite slab. I expected the ringing in his ear would last for a month.

39

'Cat's got his tongue,' I said to Mercer, who had rushed to the bottom of the staircase when he heard me shout his name.

There was a three-inch-long scrape on Cormac Lonigan's cheek, and blood on his upper lip where there had previously been a smirk.

Mercer pulled him to his feet by the collar of his denim jacket.

'Who are you, kid, and what's behind that wall?' I asked.

'You know as much as I do,' he said.

'Where's the lady?'

'I don't know anything about a lady.'

'Where were you Wednesday night?'

He didn't answer me.

'Wednesday night, Cormac, where were you?'

'Left here on the last ferry. Went drinking with Pete. Ask him.'

'I don't want to ask him. I'm asking you.'

'I don't remember.'

'It's true,' Fitzgerald said. 'I live in Queens and we — '

'Shut up,' I said. 'Hand me your phones, both of you.'

They each removed their Android phones from their pants pockets. I told Jimmy to take them and start dealing with the information on them — last numbers called, texts sent, contacts listed — as soon as we got upstairs.

'You two want to help yourselves — you want to do anything that would save you from having me throw you out a window of the green lady's crown — you start talking.'

'I just work with the guy,' Fitzgerald said. 'We didn't do nothing.'

Cormac Lonigan didn't speak.

We would separate the two of them as soon as we emerged from this black hole and answers might come faster. I just wanted five minutes to look behind the boards.

'Walk him back inside the fort, Mercer. I dropped my flashlight there.'

We made our way through the dark passage, past the office and sitting area. Jimmy and Walter brought up the rear, with Pete Fitzgerald in tow.

'Look, Detective,' Walter said. 'This is going too far. I've got no business in here. We'll have to wait till the ranger gets back to enter this part of the property. That's the rules.'

'If you've got no business being here, Walter, then Cormac has even less,' Mercer said. 'You got anything to say, anything to explain his actions, be sure and tell us. If not, you're just along for the exercise.'

We reached the end of the long corridor with the boarded-up wall. I bent down for my flashlight and shined it on the broken barrier.

Mercer braced himself against the left side of the archway — his foot on the brick wall — and pulled on the board below the one I had broken. Three more planks, from waist-high to the floor, came loose, and the dark hole expanded.

'You got the kid, Jimmy?' I asked, before ducking inside.

'He's going nowhere.'

'You got no right to hold me,' Lonigan said.

'I'll think of one before it's time for a cocktail,' I called back at him. 'I promise you that.'

I stood up straight and pushed a few pieces of wood aside so that Mercer didn't cut himself. I shined the light ahead and could see that this side of the star's interior was badly deteriorated. Large chunks of the cement ceiling had fallen to the floor and been crushed on hitting the uneven stones. The wall was crumbling in places, allowing for some daylight to filter in.

'Watch your step, Mercer. It's like a minefield in here.'

We went eight or ten steps forward, taking care not to trip over the bricks and granite pieces that made movement difficult.

In another twenty feet, the area looked as though it had been swept clean of debris. I crossed the smooth stone floor and then, a few yards later, right before the corridor seemed to end, the minefield started as abruptly as it had ended. The granite was piled higher than what we had just walked through.

I placed one hand on the wall to secure myself and climbed along the stones to get to the very end. Here, beneath the archway, there was another barrier, but this one was more permanent. Instead of wooden boards, this hole had been bricked in ages ago.

I turned back to Mercer and crept along on

the rubble until I reached the area that had been cleared.

'Dead end?'

'Totally.'

Mercer crouched down and asked me to focus the beam of light in front of him. He ran his forefinger over the rough stones and back again. 'You could sweep all day, but the dust just keeps on coming. It seeps down from the ceiling and blows in through the cracks.'

'I hear you.'

I was studying every inch of the space.

'See this?' he asked me. 'Let me hold the flashlight.'

When he angled the light, I could almost make out footprints in the gray sand that had once been a concrete block.

'And there,' he said, pointing to the far wall. 'It looks like the outline of a — well, like a sleeping bag.'

'No need for us to guess,' I said, 'when somebody right here knows more than we do.'

I wanted to get my hands on Cormac Lonigan. I balanced myself on the uneven debris on the flooring and lowered my head to get back to the others. Mercer followed.

'We're out of here,' I said to Jimmy and Walter. 'Mercer, why don't you throw some cuffs on Mr. Fitzgerald?'

'I didn't do nothing. I don't know what's going on.'

Pete Fitzgerald was the weaker link. I was pretty sure of that. I'd always found there was a direct correlation between notching the cuffs a little tighter on the dumb accomplice — the guy along for the free drinks and the ride — and successfully squeezing some nuggets of information out of him.

'Jimmy,' I said. 'You go back to Walter's office and take Fitzgerald with you. Get whatever you can from him, and then I'll give you a plan for their phones.'

'Done.'

'Walter, if you even think of opening your mouth to anyone about what we got going on here, there'll be nothing I can do to save your sorry ass,' I said. 'You can read about it in tomorrow's news if you want to keep your job.'

'Whatever you say, Detective,' Walter said as he started up the steps after Jimmy.

Cormac Lonigan, alone with us, was looking to Mercer Wallace for protection. 'What about me?'

'Mercer's not about to help you, kid,' I said. 'Forget about him. After all, you and I haven't finished our conversation.'

I pushed Lonigan backward until he fell against the staircase and righted himself, sitting on the third step from the bottom.

'Let's begin with what you dragged your friend back over here to get — or do — about an hour ago.'

He didn't answer.

Mercer reached for the backpack and Cormac Lonigan groaned. He started to pull items out of it. First was a long-sleeved shirt and after that a pair of clean underpants. Then, rolled up in a ball, was a single bedsheet.

'I don't have any gloves, Mike,' Mercer said. 'Just open it up.'

There was a sharp pain in my gut. I needed to see if there was any blood on the sheet.

Mercer laid the fabric on the stone floor and opened it up slowly. A white strip of plastic fell out of the ball and landed a few feet away from me.

Lonigan had his elbows on his knees and his head in his hands.

The sheet was faded beige cotton, sized for a twin bed. I didn't see anything resembling a bloodstain as I glanced at it. There were other body fluids I was worried about, but they wouldn't be visible to me anyway.

'You weren't carrying a tarp,' I said to Lonigan. 'There's no tarp in the shed that you came back to pick up. It was this sheet.'

I wanted to grab him by the throat and choke him till he spit out the truth about Coop, but that would reduce me to the level of the beasts who had her.

I took a step toward him. He recoiled at my approach. I stopped to pick up the plastic strip by its tip.

'You are in one shitload of trouble, Lonigan,' I said. I was trying to control my voice so he couldn't hear the quiver in it. 'Chicago Single Loop Riot Cuffs. Available online for what? Like three dollars a pop.'

The half-inch-wide disposable strips of choice for temporary restraints. They were favored by police who had to arrest protestors or nonviolent criminals and by amateurs for more shades of gray than I could count.

If this sheet had been used to conceal or cover Coop, then this strip had been on her wrists, in all likelihood. I passed it to Mercer and watched him pocket it. The lab could provide the answer to that question.

I wanted my hands to be free.

'You better talk now,' Mercer said. 'My partner is not a patient man.'

'Take off your jacket and hand it to Detective Wallace,' I said.

He slowly removed the denim garment and passed it over to Mercer.

'Check the pockets,' I said. 'Then we're going to help you put on your clean shirt and shorts so we can keep the ones you've got on. Sorry I can't help you with a pair of pants, but you won't feel a chill till the sun goes down.'

I wanted the lab to have everything.

'This is crazy,' Lonigan said, closer to tears than I seemed to be. 'I didn't do nothing. I don't even know what was supposed to go on.'

'Pockets are empty,' Mercer said.

But I wasn't paying attention to him. I was totally absorbed by the body art that covered the kid's arms from the shirtsleeves to his wrists.

These were not tattoos. They were full-on tableaux of vibrant designs, chilling in their imagery of weapons and blood. But that was only Lonigan's left arm.

'Every picture tells a story,' I said to Mercer.

From just beneath the short sleeve of Lonigan's T-shirt on his right arm was a soft, wispy pattern that grew larger in size as it wound

334

around and around his arm. Black and white tufts of hair, it looked like, with a dark tubular center.

It was a feather.

And when the feather came to a tapered end on Lonigan's forearm, its point rested on a huge gray boulder.

A stone.

And just below that was the striking design of a compass, with each direction inked in a red color as bold as blood.

The arrow in the center of the compass pointed due west.

'That damn psychiatrist was right,' I said to Mercer. 'This has nothing to do with Alexandra Cooper.'

'What are you talking about?' he asked.

'Featherstone. Due west,' I said, reading Lonigan's art aloud to Mercer. 'The Westies. Mickey Featherstone and the fucking Westies.'

Cormac Lonigan glared at me.

'Then this is about your father,' Mercer said to me. 'About your father and about revenge. It's not about Alex and some demented rapist.'

'A little too early to celebrate, Mercer. The Westies aren't sexual predators,' I said. 'All the Westies like to do is kill.'

40

'Do you know who I am?' I asked Cormac Lonigan.

'You're a cop, is all I know.'

'What was your mother's name? Before she married.'

'Shauna. Same as it is now.' He was back to smirking at me.

'I'm Chapman. Mike Chapman. My father was Brian,' I said. 'Does that mean anything to you?'

He looked me in the eye and spat, intentionally missing me by less than an inch.

We were standing where the end of the dock met Liberty Island. He had removed his jeans and underwear — torn boxer shorts — when Mercer had pointed a gun at him. Now he was dressed only in the long-sleeved shirt and jockeys that had been in his backpack.

'You put the bracelets on,' I said to Mercer. 'I'm afraid I might pinch him.'

'What's the order of play?' Mercer asked me as I heard his metal cuffs click into place.

'There's a head on that boat.'

'You serious?'

'Lift up the cushion on the bench in front of the cockpit,' I said. 'Three steps down and there's a toilet. Put Mr. Lonigan down there on the seat, close the bench back up, and I'll tell you what's next.'

'Who's calling Peterson? You or me?'

'We'll flip a coin for it, Mercer. Now, hurry up.'

The Westies had been put out of business, I thought, almost two decades ago.

They were a notorious Irish-American gang that came to power in Hell's Kitchen in the 1960s, when much of the area on the far west side of Manhattan, from 40th to 59th Street, was a dangerous slum. Founded by two sadistic mobsters, Mickey Featherstone and Jimmy Coonan, the small band of twenty or so members took racketeering to a new level of violence.

I didn't know what to do first. I couldn't imagine Coop in the hands of any of these men, or their descendants. But I couldn't think straight.

My father had killed someone. He'd shot someone in self-defense. It was a story I'd heard over and over again in my childhood. I'd been eight when it happened, on the night of the birthday of one of my older sisters.

Mercer climbed out of the small head after securing Cormac Lonigan inside and stepped on the bench to get backup on the dock.

'We've got to let Scully know what's going on,' he said.

'I feel like I'm paralyzed, Mercer. I can't move.'

'What do we have?'

I was trying to put the facts together. 'That's just it. You tell Scully and this gets ratcheted up to a level that lets the bad guys know we're after them, without the first clue about how to find them.'

'He'll flood Hell's Kitchen,' Mercer said.

'The Irish mob's been out of there since before you and I came on the job. It's so expensive there now, so gentrified, you probably couldn't find an Irishman within ten miles of Hell's Kitchen.'

'Where did they go when they broke up?'

'Woodside,' I said. 'Mickey Spillane took them to Woodside.'

'Spillane?'

'Not the writer, dude. The gangster.'

'So, Queens,' Mercer said. 'Where Cormac Lonigan and Pete Fitzgerald live.'

'Yeah. And call Jimmy. He's got to keep Fitzgerald isolated and get the tech guys downloading the phone information.'

There were four long wooden crates on the dock. I sat on the first one, leaned forward, and held the top of my head with both hands. It felt like it was going to explode.

Mercer phoned Jimmy North and told him to keep Fitzgerald in lockdown and call TARU about the two confiscated devices.

'It's almost four thirty, Mike. I've got to check in.'

'Give me fifteen minutes. Think it through with me. If I do anything to make Coop's situation worse than it is, I won't be able to live with myself.'

'Fifteen and out, Mike. This is bigger than you,' Mercer said. 'If it does have anything to do with the Westies, then I'm pretty useless. You know how they operate and I don't.'

'That's what I can't get past.'

'Why would they have brought Alex here?' he asked. 'And why only for one night, or for two?'

'Because this is just a staging area, I guess. Someone on the work crew is involved. Maybe a relative of Lonigan's, maybe just someone who knew the island was pretty much off-limits these days, with no one to guard it at night.'

'They would have to know about the fort,' Mercer said.

'Apparently lots of people do. Especially the guys who work here. Go on downstairs, create a makeshift holding pen — '

'For Alex?'

'For Alex,' I said, speaking her given name, which sounded so much softer and more vulnerable than *Coop*.

'Then they find out there's going to be a huge media event,' Mercer said, 'and they have to get her off the island.'

'Maybe the endgame was always meant to be somewhere else,' I said, sweeping the air with my hand. 'Could be this was just a diversion. Maybe that's why they've moved her.'

'Don't go dark on me, Mike.'

'Maybe the endgame is in play.'

41

'You think this has something to do with Brian?' Mercer asked me. 'Your father?'

'I do.'

'I know there was a shooting, Mike. I know someone died. If you tell me who it was, maybe we can figure a connection to Lonigan,' Mercer said. 'We can get Peterson on the hunt to see if there's a link.'

'Thirty years is a long time to wait for revenge.'

'Give me a lead.'

'Mickey Spillane stepped into the mobster role in the late sixties, when there was a power vacuum in Hell's Kitchen. Sort of a gentleman gangster — bookmaking, policy — and then a slow buildup to loan-sharking. Bought turkeys for the needy on Thanksgiving,' I said, shaking my head at the idea, 'but began to break legs as he gained control.

'Spillane made a big mistake when he pistol-whipped a local accountant named Coonan for not paying his dues. The guy had an eighteen-year-old son known in the hood as Jimmy C — the kind of kid your mother was always praying you didn't grow up to be.'

'Yeah.'

'Jimmy C went up to the rooftop of a tenement on West 48th Street with an automatic rifle and just began to fire down at the street, fire at everyone he saw.'

'Not at Spillane?'

'Spillane was nowhere around. Jimmy C just did it to show he was mad about the whipping his old man took, and that he was moving into the turf. The rise of the Westies.'

'Where did Mickey Featherstone come in?' Mercer asked.

'Up from the streets of Hell's Kitchen, just like Jimmy C. Got noticed because he had a thing for killing people. He liked his hardware.'

'Jail time?'

'A few short stints. Then the army. Then psycho'd out of there. Back to the hood. Featherstone was Jimmy C's right-hand man for years,' I said. 'But their major falling-out happened when Coonan decided to go big-time and join forces with the Gambino family.'

'Featherstone got ruffled because that wasn't loyal to the Irish?'

'You nailed it,' I said. 'Coonan became John Gotti's guy. He put the Westies to work as contract killers for the Gambinos.'

'Now, that's a high-stakes business.'

'The highest. Ironically, Featherstone's the one who got convicted for murder — for one of the few murders he didn't commit.'

'Served time?'

'Not before he turned snitch, Mercer.'

'Featherstone was actually a rat? A big mobster like him?'

'Mickey Featherstone and his wife both agreed to be wired in order to get evidence against Coonan — that's how bitter the internal Westies feud had become. Rudy Giuliani indicted Coonan with Featherstone's information — one of the first big RICO cases. Racketeering going back two decades.'

'So one Westie boss winds up in jail,' Mercer said, 'and one in Witness Protection.'

'Giuliani declared the Westies dead, but that's just when all the wannabes began to crawl out of the woodwork,' I said. 'There were Shannons and Kellys and McGraths and Cains looking to lead the parade by then, get a piece of the action. It's like someone had lifted names off headstones in a Dublin cemetery.'

'Didn't Coonan have an heir apparent?'

'An unlikely one. He wanted the Yugo to step in for him, over all his Irish boys.'

'The Yugo?'

'Bosko 'the Yugo' Radonjic,' I said. 'He was a Serbian nationalist and for some reason Coonan took a liking to him. Started as a low-level associate — a parking lot attendant in a local garage turned gangster — but he was rewarded early for his efforts. That's when the next turf war for Hell's Kitchen began, in the late eighties.'

I swallowed hard and started biting the inside of my cheek again. It was an event that had ripped my family apart, the night I questioned whether my father was really the hero I'd thought him to be.

'My father was working homicide then. Hated the Westies for what they'd done, as Irish, to the Irish.'

'Had he known Featherstone and Coonan?'

'Sure he did. Not drinking buddies, but we all had relatives in Hell's Kitchen. Ate in the same pubs, went to the same churches, worked in the same unions and shops,' I said. 'Just earlier today I was telling Jimmy about playing as a kid in Bennett Park, about exploring Fort Washington just a stone's throw from the George Washington Bridge.'

'Yeah.'

'Half the kids I hung out with had fathers who were cops and firemen,' I said. 'The other half came from the wrong side of the proverbial tracks. Westies and thugs of all varieties. I wasn't choosy when I was out on the street.'

'The shooting?'

'Sure. The shooting,' I said. 'So the Yugo thinks he can dance into the Irish mafia, the Irish Sopranos, without a struggle. But the next generation of hoodlums thought otherwise. The demographics were changing and so were the profits, because drugs had come into the mix. Every tough guy seemed to be hungry for drug money.'

'Understood.'

'It was most often a family affair at this point. When Mugsy Renner was running drugs, he put the rest of his relatives into the action. Same for all the guys. Narcotics was following a big shipment of cocaine that was coming in through a mule from South America, bound for a safe house in Hell's Kitchen. It was Renner's crew against some of the Shannons — at least the ones who weren't behind bars.'

'Why was homicide involved?'

343

'Because the coke had been flown in through JFK. Three airline employees, cargo traffic agents, were supposedly in on the deal and let Renner's gang and their truck into the hangar for the pickup. The agents were tied up and executed, mob-style — single bullet to the back of the head. Not exactly the cut of the profits they had expected. So narcotics called in homicide for backup when they rushed in to raid Renner's headquarters on West 51st Street.'

It still made my blood boil to think of Renner setting up my father and his team.

'The cops walked into a trap, of course. The drugs were worth too many millions to sit in a tenement in Hell's Kitchen,' I said. 'There had actually been two dump trucks involved in the sting, and the one with the drugs got away clean. Never been found to this day. Renner parked a truck full of garbage in front of his house. When the narcs burst in on them in the middle of the night with a warrant, there was nothing to be found.'

'No drugs? No money?'

'Nothing. Nothing except Renner's crazy kid. His oldest son, Emmet, was up on the roof with an automatic rifle. Twenty-two-year-old with a history of mental illness.'

'Against a narcotics squad and homicide?'

'I'm talking certifiably crazy,' I said. 'He thought it wasn't against the law to possess a weapon in his own home, so as the cops were leaving, tempers flaring, Renner starts shooting off rounds, hailing bullets down on the street.'

I paused. I had been back to stare at that

building so many times as a young boy that I could see it in front of me today.

'Shooting *at* people?' Mercer asked. 'At the cops?'

'Nope. He was imitating Jimmy C. He was figuring his father could win control of the Westies just the way Coonan had done it when he was eighteen — with a great show of force from the roof of a Hell's Kitchen tenement.'

'It worked the first time, I guess.'

'Only now it was a street full of cops.'

'And they returned fire,' Mercer said.

'Just some warning shots, to show Renner they were serious,' I said. 'But then he shot a cop. Right in the head. The guy bled out on the street before anyone could help him.'

'So Emmet Renner was a dead man.'

'Not exactly. That would have been one thing. But what nobody knew was that his brother was up on the roof with him.'

I gnawed on my cheek again.

'By that time, Emergency Services had burst into the house on their way to the roof. Renner ducked down and the cops thought he was reloading,' I said. 'What they couldn't see was that the crazy bastard thought he'd initiate his brother into the Westies. Handed him the rifle and told him to take his best shot.'

I put myself in my father's shoes, as I had done thousands of times since that night.

'The gun barrel comes back over the side of the building, only this time Renner stands up. He fires the rifle and wings the guy right next to my father. Got his shoulder, and the blood splashed all over my dad's face.'

'So he fired back.'

'Damn right, he did. My father shot Renner in the head. One round, direct hit. Of course everyone on the street figured it was Emmet, the crazy one, who'd been shot. They had no reason to think he'd turned the weapon over to his brother. His brother, Charlie.'

'But it was actually Charlie who shot one of the cops, wasn't it?' Mercer asked. 'He shot the guy standing right next to your father.'

'Yeah, that was Charlie Renner all right.'

'And that's the man your father killed? Charlie Renner?'

'He wasn't a man, Mercer. He was five years older than I was then. He used to play stickball with me in Hell's Kitchen. He was an altar boy at St. Ignatius before I was,' I said. 'Charlie Renner was thirteen years old the night he died. That's the stuff that doesn't quite fit into the Brian Chapman legend, Mercer. My father killed a kid.'

346

42

'This has to stay between us for the time being, Loo,' I heard Mercer say. 'I need your word on that.'

Apparently, the short pause in the conversation meant he got Peterson's word.

'Mike's got an idea that this whole thing could have something to do with him and that Alex is just the pawn in all this,' Mercer said. 'What we need you to do is use your juice to find out where Emmet Renner is.'

Ray Peterson knew Emmet Renner's name well. All the old-timers did. He was a cop killer who'd skated because he, too, had turned snitch and testified against other mobsters for the feds.

'Last Mike knew, he was in Arizona in the Witness Protection Program. New name, plastic surgery, the whole nine yards. You'll have to cut through all the red tape with the feds to get that information.'

Mercer looked at me while Peterson asked him a question.

'He'll have to tell you himself,' he said, shrugging as he handed me his phone.

'Where the hell are you two?' Peterson asked.

'On our way back to the marina, Loo. I got sidetracked.'

'You don't even want the good news?'

'Is there any?' I asked.

'Yeah,' Peterson said. 'The blood in the

Shipley SUV is Wynan Wilson's.'

I breathed a sigh of relief that it wasn't Coop's. But I had already made the connection to the Westies that this just seemed to confirm.

'You hear me, Chapman?'

'I got it, Loo,' I said. 'Thanks.'

'Now, what is this with Renner, Mike? Your old man did the right thing at the right time. Twenty other cops were aiming at the shooter. Just nobody was as good as Brian, and none of them knew he was a — a kid.'

'There were threats back then, Loo. Don't you remember that?' I asked. 'How my mother had to leave town for a month. Take my sisters and me to my aunt's house in the Poconos.'

'Sure, but that was thirty years ago. Things change.'

'Things change if you've got all your marbles. I don't know what happens if you only started out with half a load.'

'Have you heard from Emmet Renner in all this time?' Peterson asked.

'Veiled threats. Bullshit from wiseguys I've locked up over the years,' I said. 'But he never came back to the city, so far as I know. It was part of his deal for turning state's evidence. That, and the desire to live a long life.'

'How about his father?'

'Mugsy?'

'Yeah.'

'He must be dead by now, don't you think? Didn't he get, like, six life sentences for all the rubouts he did?' I said.

'I'll check that, too,' Peterson said. 'What's got

you thinking about the Renners?'

'The shrink. That genius Scully sat me down with this morning.'

'Dr. Friedman? What does she have to do with it?'

'I blew her off when she said it, Loo, but I'm in a different place now,' I said. 'Friedman asked me all kinds of things about Coop, to see who'd be interested in kidnapping her and also to try to predict how she might respond. But then Friedman made the point that if there was someone who wanted to get to *me*, someone who wanted to cause me more pain than I'd known in a lifetime, they'd do it by targeting Coop.'

Peterson must have taken a drag on his cigarette to consider the point.

'You hear me?' I asked.

'Yeah.'

'Like the doc said, even two months ago there were no chinks in my armor. Now, because of the way I feel about Coop . . . '

'Yeah,' Peterson said again. 'And the word about you two is out.'

'I mean, it's not exactly headlining the society page, Loo. But most guys in the courthouse seem to know.'

'Perps, too, you think? Snitches?'

'Some.'

'Tell me about the threats, back in the day,' Peterson said.

I could call up the weeks after my father shot Charlie Renner as easily as I could walk someone through every hour of last night.

'Mugsy was heartless,' I said. 'Look at him cross-eyed and he'd have you knocked off. Emmet inherited that trait in spades, along with a heavy touch of insanity. There were a couple of sisters in between, and then came Charlie. And Charlie was the light of everyone's life. If anyone in that family was going to get out of Hell's Kitchen and make a life for himself, it was the kid. Mugsy and his wife — well, she was inconsolable. My mother tried to get the priest to set up a meeting with her, but there was no use.'

'Why not be mad at Emmet instead of your father?' Peterson asked.

'He had it in for both of them, but it was my dad who pulled the trigger,' I said. 'Rita, Jude, Gregory, Philomena.'

Mercer looked at me like I was nuts, but Peterson was a devout Catholic, and he spoke. 'Patron saints of hopeless causes.'

'My mother prayed to all of them.'

'I'll bet.'

'Anyway, word on the street was that the Renners were going to kill my father,' I said. 'Not while he was on the job. They didn't want to get tagged for another cop killing. But after he quit the force.'

'Only his ticker did it for him,' Peterson said.

My father had dropped dead less than forty-eight hours after turning in his badge and gun.

'Let me get on this, Mike. Let me find out about the Renners. Where did you say you were?'

'Close to the marina, Loo. You get any info,

350

Mercer and I are good to go.' I thanked him and ended the call.

'You're not even letting Peterson know where we are?' Mercer asked.

'To what end? If anyone's keeping an eye on this place and suddenly the Harbor Link shows up and tramps around the island, what happens to Coop?' I said. 'What we need to know, before we involve anyone else who might have some harebrained scheme to get to her, is where she is, and why.'

'Emmet could have come after you before now,' Mercer said.

'Sure. But this isn't a job he'd contract out,' I said, walking to the end of the dock and staring down at the water that ran past me. 'The pleasure of killing me is something Emmet Renner would keep for himself.'

'And Alex?'

'I've never been in love with anyone like I am with her.' I spoke softly. I wasn't used to saying that out loud.

'Emmet Renner wouldn't know that.'

'Sometimes I think everyone around me knew it long before I did. It shows, Mercer,' I said. 'Sometimes I think it's got me so lit up inside I must glow in the dark.'

He reached out an arm and grasped me by the shoulder.

'How does word get around?' I asked. 'My mother tells the priest that her son's a changed man now that he's got a woman he loves? Then the whole parish knows. My cousin who tends bar in Queens gossips to an old Westie? The

351

word's out in Woodside. Somebody sees the Page Six photo of me in a rented tux holding Coop's hand at the Safe Horizon charity gala two weeks ago? My cover's blown for anyone who reads that rag. The only thing new in my life is a love affair, and maybe that's reached the ex-con's retirement home in Arizona. Could be a dozen grapevines he heard it through. How the fuck would I know?'

'You were engaged before,' Mercer said. 'To Valerie.'

'Yeah,' I said, turning my back to him. 'Because I didn't think I'd ever have a chance with Coop. That's why I was ready to marry Valerie. Now maybe Dr. Friedman is right after all. Maybe people realize the best way to rip my heart in half would be to hurt Coop.'

'I hear you, Mike,' Mercer said, stepping up beside me and putting his arm on my shoulder.

We both snapped our heads at the sound of voices coming down to the dock from the island. It was Jimmy North and his prisoner, along with a park ranger.

'You guys need help?' the ranger asked, after Jimmy introduced us.

'We're good for the moment,' I said. Jimmy took Pete Fitzgerald back up to the wire fencing that ran around the island's perimeter and handcuffed him through the open metalwork so he'd be out of earshot.

'I told Jimmy,' the ranger said, 'that I can run him back to Manhattan anytime he'd like to go. The Fitzgerald kid, too. What'd he do exactly?'

'We're grateful for your offer,' Mercer said as I

parked myself on one of the crates. 'We're not able to tell you what happened till the police commissioner signs off on everything in the next few hours. Nothing violent. No felonies. But still kind of top secret, if that isn't being too rude to you on your own property.'

'I understand completely. I'm just here to give you what you need,' the ranger said. Then he pointed at the sturdy wooden box beneath me. 'If you're trying to keep things quiet over here, don't kick on that package. It's got some of the Roman candles for tomorrow's celebration.'

'Thanks for the warning.'

As soon as he walked away, Jimmy started talking. 'The guys at TARU will give you everything you want on the phones as soon as I get them over there.'

'How about contacts?' I asked. 'Did you run through all of the names on Lonigan's phone?'

'See for yourself. There aren't many,' Jimmy said. 'A lot of Lonigans, a girlfriend, some of the guys from the union, the main number in the office here.'

'Renner. You see anything listed for a Renner? Maybe Emmet?'

'No luck, Mike.'

Mercer folded his arms and looked back at the Fitzgerald kid, locked in place to the fence.

'Did he say anything to you once he and Lonigan were separated?'

'He's whining a lot about what he doesn't know. Doesn't seem too interested in giving up any dirt on Lonigan, if there's any to be had.'

'Let me see how I do,' I said.

Mercer's long arm reached out, his palm touching the center of my chest. 'Stay away from the kid, Mike. You've been spinning out of control.'

'I've got no reason to hurt him. I just want to talk to — '

'And I think we ought to get going before it gets dark,' Mercer said. 'I promised you fifteen minutes and your time is up.'

I walked back to the river's edge. The sun was behind me now, playing what was left of its light off the glass towers in the canyons of lower Manhattan.

'And get that Lonigan kid out of the head, will you?'

'When I'm good and ready, Mercer.'

I had no intention of letting Cormac Lonigan go until the lab did a thorough examination of the backpack, the sheet, and the plastic handcuffs. He could spend the night in the homicide squad if that's how long it took.

'What is it about the river for you?' Mercer asked.

'You don't want to know.'

'Is it Renner? Something to do with him or the Westies?'

'Renner just picked up where Coonan and Featherstone left off,' I said. 'Their whole thing was kidnapping.'

'Kidnapping?' Mercer asked. 'I thought the rackets was it.'

'Yeah, but when their vics didn't pay up, they got their revenge by kidnapping,' I said. 'They took relatives, they took local businessmen and their families — it was known as the snatch — and held them for ransom.'

Mercer was quiet for a minute. 'But there's no ransom here.'

'Not yet,' I said. 'Coonan had a guy who worked for him. A butcher. The neighborhood butcher. His name was Eddie Cummiskey. Eddie the Butcher they called him.'

'So?'

'Coonan used Eddie to kill his victims if nobody paid up. Dismember them.'

'You serious?'

Mercer came up beside me on the end of the dock.

'Stop asking me that. Of course I'm serious. I used to have nightmares, after my dad shot Charlie, that Eddie would take him apart one day, piece by piece.'

'That must have been jive, man. Not for real.'

'You think so? Check the Westies' files, Mercer. Coonan used to keep some of the dismembered fingers from the victims' bodies in a freezer in his office, so he could use them to plant fingerprints on guns his crew used in hits.'

'No wonder you had nightmares,' Mercer said. 'What did they do with the other body parts?'

'Coonan made Eddie the Butcher take them down to the Hudson,' I said, staring out at the darkening ripples in the water. 'Throw them in the water. Right there in Midtown, the West Forties and Fifties. One time Eddie forgot to puncture the lungs in a guy's torso and it bobbed to the surface a week later. Floated right into a sail-boat out for a ride off the Battery, or he'd never have been found. But usually the fish got the flesh and bones that sunk to the bottom.'

'I can't begin to imagine what those men were like,' Mercer said.

'The Westies made me ashamed to be Irish,' I said, looking from the Verrazano Bridge to my right back up to the GW on my left. 'They were murderous thugs, Mercer. And they used the Hudson River as their personal morgue.'

43

Mercer's phone rang. 'Wallace,' he said, then walked ten feet away from me to take the call.

'Who's that?' I asked.

'Catherine Dashfer,' he said to me. 'You want it?'

We met halfway and I grabbed his phone.

'You got something good?'

'This call didn't happen, Mike.'

'Shoot.'

'Battaglia's playing games with the police commissioner,' Catherine said. 'I'm not quite sure why.'

'I'll give you that piece of it. Scully thinks the district attorney is beholden to the Reverend Hal Shipley. It's been going on for a while, but it came to a boil this morning during our meeting,' I said. 'You have something about Coop?'

'I wish I did.'

'What, then?'

'Keep this to yourself, Mike, okay? Just you and Mercer.'

'To the grave.'

'Battaglia took the DA's squad off the search for Josie Aponte,' Catherine said. 'He put his civilian investigators on it instead of detectives and they found her around noon today.'

'That's great!' I shouted.

'Nobody knows. They're still questioning her pretty hard.'

357

'Where is she?'

'With family. It's pretty clear that she went from the courthouse to Penn Station and jumped on a train, down to South Philly where her sister lives. Josie's real name is Rosita Quinones. They picked her up at her sister's apartment.'

'What's she got to say?'

'Not exactly all you're hoping for, Mike,' Catherine said. 'Rosita's not talking yet. We've got all the senior people in the unit working on this, believe me. Once she realizes Estevez is unlikely to step forward to bail her out, we're hoping she rolls over on him. But there's no sign of any connection between Alex and the newlyweds — Rosita Quinones and Antonio Estevez — after the moment that she got out of the criminal court building.'

'But you're still digging? You're not giving up?'

'We'll keep digging, of course. It's just that a first dump of her cell phone and texts doesn't suggest anything going on that remotely involves a kidnapping.'

I hadn't thought for long that Estevez was behind Coop's disappearance. I didn't believe he could have orchestrated an abduction as sophisticated and clean as this one seemed to be. Rosita's skill was in tech work, and she had done all that was expected of her by breaking into the DA's office computer system.

'What was it Drew Poser said on Wednesday afternoon?' I asked. 'That Estevez was trying to bring Coop down, right?'

'Yes.'

'Seems to me he was on the way to getting that done by causing her enough embarrassment that all of us thought she might actually take some time off to chill,' I said. 'Nobody thought he was out to — to hurt her.'

'Battaglia's clearly aiming to undermine the commissioner by taking over the Rosita Quinones matter. He's hoping to see egg on Scully's face because the NYPD didn't make the arrest before she skipped town,' Catherine said. 'That's why you've got to protect me on this. I just wanted you to know that Quinones and Estevez are unlikely suspects in Alex's disappearance.'

'I get it, and I appreciate it. One suggestion for you?'

'Okay.'

'Keep your team as far away from this one as possible,' I said. 'There's some kind of link between Reverend Hal and Estevez, and the DA's a fool to try to take control of anything that involves Shipley. It will come back to bite him in the ass by the time all of this unravels.'

'Point well taken, Mike. I'm just a foot soldier here. I like to stay out of the line of fire,' Catherine said. 'But I was with Alex on Wednesday afternoon just after she left Battaglia's office. I got my first hint of how deep this trouble may go.'

I didn't offer anything I knew. I didn't want to compromise Catherine's position on Battaglia's staff. But it was beginning to dawn on a few of us that the DA's behind-the-scenes manipulations to retain political power might become transparent in the weeks ahead.

'You mean with Shipley?' I asked.

'Yes,' Catherine said. 'I hadn't known what a tough spot Battaglia put Alex in during her investigation of the complaint against Shipley, but then he tried to cover his tail with a file memo. And there is also the letter Estevez made Rosita upload on the computer. It's a real hornet's nest.'

'I hear you.'

'More importantly, Mike, how are you holding up?'

I didn't have an answer that made sense.

'Is there anything we can do to help you? We're all itching to be more useful,' Catherine said. 'Alex will be furious with us when she finds out we've left you hanging out in the cold.'

'Mercer's with me. We're . . . working through — ' I couldn't finish the sentence. I couldn't hold a thought for more than a few seconds.

I passed the phone back to Mercer. I had never felt as lost as I did now.

'Keep the faith, Catherine,' he said, ending the call.

Then Mercer turned to me. 'Now I have a better understanding of why you want to stay near this river, Mike, after what you said about the Westies. But we're taking this boat back right now.'

He stalked off the dock with Jimmy North, toward Pete Fitzgerald. I stepped on the gunwale of the Intrepid and lowered myself down. I lifted the bench and took a look at Cormac Lonigan. His discomfort level was high — bent over the toilet in the cramped, foul-smelling space with

360

his hands cuffed behind him — but he wouldn't give me the satisfaction of looking at me or asking for mercy.

'I'm riding with you on the boat,' Mercer called out. 'Why don't you let Jimmy go back with the two kids on the ranger's vessel? We can have Major Case meet them at the Chelsea Piers docks and take them for questioning, if that's what you want. Jimmy can get work started on the cell phones and take the backpack and sheet to the lab. Figure out whether this is all a Chapman red herring or actual evidence of a crime.'

I didn't want to let Lonigan out of my hands, but I didn't have much reason to keep him.

I shut the lid on the head again. 'That would mean too many cooks in the kitchen. Telling Major Case means Scully will find out before too long.'

'Look, Mike,' Mercer said. 'Ray Peterson can't run this whole thing himself.'

'He's with me so far.'

'Get Lonigan off that boat and let's head for the other dock.'

I was about to swing myself up on the gunwale again when the phone in my pocket rang.

'Mike,' the lieutenant said. 'Are you sitting down?'

'Ready for whatever you've got.'

'The old man, Mugsy Renner, he's still alive.'

'What?' I said. I could feel fire rising inside my gut. 'He must be eighty-six.'

'Eighty-eight and dying of lung cancer,' Peterson said.

'What prison?' I asked. 'We can race someone up there to talk to him.'

'That's just it. Six life sentences with no chance of parole, but two weeks ago Renner was granted a release.'

'A *what*?' I screamed into the phone. 'You run a mob of hoodlums, kill a few dozen people yourself, get nailed rock solid for six homicides, and some parole board decides twenty years later to override the trial judge who heard the grisly details and go lenient?'

'Calm down, Mike,' Peterson said. 'They call it — '

'I don't give a damn what they call it.'

'They call it a compassionate discharge. Truth is, the warden told me, the state can't afford the medical treatment for the aging prison population.'

I was off the boat and headed toward Mercer. I couldn't control my rage.

'Then let out the old men with terminal toe fungus who stole cars or robbed banks. Let out the thieves and the con men with psoriasis, not the murderers. Who cares if that bastard died in a jail cell?'

Mercer was jogging toward me.

'Where is he?' I asked Peterson. The wind had picked up as the sun lowered itself to the west. It carried my voice downriver with it.

'That's the thing, Mike. He's back in the city.'

'Woodside, Queens, no doubt. Where all the old Westies go to die.'

'You don't have to know where he is, okay? I'll handle that conversation myself, I promise you that.'

'I need to know, Loo. The last thing you can do is hold out on me.'

'You've got to keep your head together, Mike,' Peterson said. 'I got through to the feds, too. About Emmet Renner.'

'What did you find out? They've got a new leniency program in Witness Protection, too?'

'He's got a two-week pass from the program. They let him come home from Arizona to say good-bye to his old man.'

'One more Westie and I win the trifecta,' I said. 'Where are they, Loo?'

'Be sensible, Mike. That's not a job for you. You're not even going to recognize Emmet Renner, thirty years after the fact and enough plastic surgery so nobody who ever knew him can make him,' Peterson said. 'You see him on the street today? You'd walk right past him.'

'I'll figure this out without you, understand? There was Emmet, the oldest son, and Charlie,' I said, thinking of the kid my father shot, 'and then there were three girls in between. One of them must have taken the father in when Correction let him go. If you don't tell me the names, I'm sure my mother will remember.'

'I'm done with your threats, Mike. I'm taking two men from the squad and going out to Queens myself.'

'I'm sorry for breaking balls, Loo. And yours, most of all. But Parole must have given you an address, right? They couldn't let him out without accounting for his whereabouts.'

'I know his whereabouts better than I know yours,' Peterson said. 'Enough playing games

363

with me, Mike. You're officially off this investigation as of right now. I should have done this hours ago. Give the phone to Wallace.'

'You have an address, right? You're not driving blind, are you?'

'The man's in a hospital, okay? He's on life support. Yeah, he was released to his daughter's home,' Peterson said. 'But he's in a hospital now. He's in a hospital and his daughter's got the healthcare proxy. Shauna Renner decides when to pull the plug.'

'Shauna what?'

'Shauna Renner,' he said. 'The oldest sister.'

'Do what you gotta do, Loo. I'm off duty,' I said, ending the call.

I jumped on the gunwale of the Intrepid and kicked the side of the bench where I had stowed my prisoner away.

'She's Shauna Lonigan now,' I yelled to no one in particular. 'And the snatch of Alex Cooper is about Renner's revenge.'

44

'Coop's life is on the line because of me,' I said.

'And you expect me to believe you're going off duty?'

'Peterson swears he's taking Renner down himself. What choice does it leave me?'

'Let's give it a rest and we can come back fresh tomorrow.'

'Totally,' I said.

It was hard to look Mercer in the eye and lie to him, but going rogue was not in his playbook.

'Let's just talk to these two jerks again, before we go back,' I said.

'What did Peterson give you?' Mercer asked.

'Cormac Lonigan's uncle is Emmet Renner, and he's somewhere in the middle of a two-week pass to pray at his father's bedside,' I said. 'Praying hard to find out where Mugsy buried all the money he stole before he got sent away.'

Mercer held up his hand to Jimmy to signal an ask for five minutes more. He stepped onto the boat with me and lifted the lid of the bench.

Cormac Lonigan picked up his head.

'Time to catch up on family ties, Cormac,' I said. 'Sorry to hear about your grandfather.'

'Fuck you, Chapman. He'd say the same thing if he was here.'

'I know where he is, kid,' I said, pulling him to his feet. 'Only I don't think he's going to be there much longer, so we have to step up planning for the reunion.'

'My witness,' Mercer said to me, pushing me out of the way. I climbed back onto the deck of the boat.

The kid's eyes widened and he came close to freaking out just looking at the size of Mercer's hands. He had no way to know how much gentler the man was than I.

'Where's Alex Cooper?'

'Who?'

He was thin and wiry, but I was certain that belied the toughness of his Renner roots.

'The woman,' Mercer said. 'The woman your uncle Emmet is holding.'

Lonigan's lips were as thin as his long fingers. They were locked together in silence.

'You've got a chance to help yourself here,' Mercer said. 'Where's Emmet Renner?'

'Why don't you ask your partner where Charlie Renner is?' Lonigan said. 'He'd be alive if it wasn't for a cop named Chapman.'

I held my tongue.

'Talk to me,' Mercer said. 'Talk to me if you want to go home tonight.'

'You ain't got shit.'

'Maybe you don't watch enough cop shows, Cormac,' Mercer said. 'Trace evidence, it's called. That sheet you went back into the fort to get? There'll be DNA in the sweat that's on it, and skin cells that come off just from rubbing against it. The plastic handcuff, too.'

'Come back when you can prove it.'

Mercer asked him four more questions, but he refused to answer any of them.

'Let's talk to Fitzgerald again,' Mercer said, stepping onto the dock. 'I don't think he's going to take a fall for his buddy.'

I waited until Mercer's back was to me, then I bent down and removed one of my socks. I pushed Cormac Lonigan down onto the toilet seat, shoved the sock in his mouth, and secured it by tying my handkerchief around his face. Then I slammed the cover of the bench.

Mercer was already face-to-face with Pete Fitzgerald and asking questions by the time I came up behind him.

'Three years, maybe four,' Fitzgerald said. 'I haven't known him more than that.'

'Been to his house?' Mercer asked. 'Know his parents or any of his family?'

'Never been there, no. We've been on jobs together like this from time to time. And we have some beers after work. That's all.'

I was hanging back but ready to jump in and make answers happen.

'What does the name Renner mean to you?' Mercer asked with a steadiness in his voice that I envied.

'Relatives of Cormac's on his mother's side. I don't know them.'

Fitzgerald was obviously used to talking with his hands, but one was firmly tethered to the metal fence and the other seemed tongue-tied without its mate.

'Ever heard of them?' Mercer asked.

'Seems everybody has. My family's out of Hell's Kitchen, too.'

367

'Any relatives of yours ever call themselves Westies?'

'Went out of their way not to do, Detective. Good people, my folks. Hardworking people.'

'You ever been locked up?'

'No way.'

The onset of the dusk of evening helped the interrogation. Manhattan Island looked a million miles away.

'Accessory to murder,' Mercer said, 'is a very rough way to start.'

I don't know who was rocked more by the sound of the word *murder* — the kid or me. It took me a few seconds to realize it was Mercer's bluff to move Pete Fitzgerald in the right direction.

'I don't know anything about a murder, Detective,' Fitzgerald said, tugging at the fencing as he tried to plead with Mercer.

'He claims you do,' I said, interrupting Mercer when he least needed me to do it. 'Cormac Lonigan says you do.'

'I don't believe he's talking,' Fitzgerald said, shaking his head from side to side. 'He wouldn't talk to me; he sure ain't talking to you.'

'I know his uncle,' I said, lowering my voice. 'I know his uncle Emmet.'

Fitzgerald was breathing heavily, obviously confused about whom to trust.

'And I know his uncle Emmet is back in town.'

His eyes were jumping back and forth between Mercer and me like Mexican beans.

'You met Emmet yet?'

'No,' he said, his head still shaking.

'So what do you have now?' I asked. 'Ten toes? Ten fingers? Count 'em good, kid, 'cause we let you go back on the ferry but we hold on to Cormac, and then I put the word out in the hood that we've been talking to you, you might be a few digits short come Sunday.'

'I never met Emmet. I swear to you.'

I backed off and turned to Jimmy. 'We'll hold on to Lonigan,' I said. 'You get a head start out to Woodside right now. Pick a bar. Find Donahue's.'

There was a Donahue's in every Irish neighborhood. There must be one in Woodside.

'Have a few drinks on me. Throw Emmet Renner's name around,' I said. 'Then ask for Pete Fitzgerald. Tell them last time you saw him he was at the ferry pier downtown, talking to a bunch of cops. Then about eleven P.M., I'll come in with him, and by then — '

'Why would you do this to me? I don't know about any murder.'

I moved in on Fitzgerald again. He smelled of fear.

'You might as well talk to me.'

'I'll be a dead man anyway,' he said. 'Why should I talk?'

'Because if you tell us how to find Renner — and his victim — we can pick him up before you get home. If he's not hiding out on this island, then there's no reason for anyone to connect his problems to you.'

Fitzgerald rubbed his handcuffed wrist and stared at the ground.

'Has he killed that woman?' he asked.

'Which one, now?' I said. 'The one you don't know anything about?'

'Cormac's not one for talking much.'

'He told me he was drinking with you last night,' I said to Fitzgerald. 'Was that a lie?'

'It's true.'

'What bar?'

'Molly McGuire's,' he said, probably thinking he was confirming some kind of alibi for Lonigan.

I pointed at Jimmy. 'That's where you're hanging out, Detective. Molly McGuire's. You let everyone in the joint know that Pete Fitzgerald's squealing like a stuck pig.'

Fitzgerald swung around to try to grab the back of Jimmy's windbreaker to stop him from leaving, but all he did was wrench his arm. 'Wait! Don't be saying that, please.'

'What, then?' I asked. 'You know Cormac helped his uncle get onto the island late Wednesday night, into Thursday?'

'Let me loose from here,' Fitzgerald said. 'Everything aches, okay? My wrist, my legs, my back. You've gotta let me loose.'

'In time, man. Speak up.'

He turned his head toward the boat to see if there was any sign of Cormac Lonigan.

'No way his uncle came here,' he said. 'I don't know anything about his uncle, except Cormac's deathly afraid of him. Never met him till a week or so ago, but scared of him, just like his own mother is.'

'Well, that's in the category of 'nice to know,'

but it's not helpful to what I need to do.'

'Cormac left the island when I did on Wednesday,' Fitzgerald said, calmly and without emotion. 'Normal time, on the late afternoon ferry.'

'When did you come back?'

'Seven thirty Thursday morning. First ferry. And Cormac was on it with me.'

Fitzgerald was beginning to respond to my questions but directed his answers toward Mercer. I stepped back to let my old friend take the lead.

Mercer took the kid through Wednesday on the island in detail, and then Thursday, too.

'What about Thursday night?' Mercer asked.

'Cormac seemed jumpy, is all. I can't describe it, really, but he wasn't quite himself,' Fitzgerald said. 'I asked him if he wanted to have a drink or two. He didn't seem to want to go home, so he said 'yeah,' and off we were to McGuire's.'

'What were you drinking?' Mercer asked.

'Usually beer, like I did that night. But Cormac surprised me. He ordered vodka. Tito's,' Fitzgerald said. 'A double Tito's.'

The handmade Texas vodka had become popular in the city, but it was pricey for a construction worker in Queens.

'Two of those,' he went on, 'and he was toasted pretty quick. Asked me if he could borrow some money to buy a burger and another drink. No problem with that, but I told him he'd better slow it down. No point getting hammered having to work the next day.'

'Did he want to talk?' Mercer said.

'Not really. Just jumpy, like I told you. I thought it was to do with his grandfather dying and his uncle coming back.'

'He told you about that?'

'Not a word. But news about the Renners was all over the neighborhood, people wanting to stay out of their way and all.'

That was a fact I understood.

'Cormac had half a load on before he told me he had done something stupid. Something at work,' Fitzgerald said.

Mercer's style was as smooth as silk. You'd think he attached no importance to the questions he was asking.

'Like what?'

Fitzgerald rolled his head around and rubbed his neck with his free hand.

'C'mon, kid. You're almost there,' Mercer said.

'This will come back to me and then there'll be nowhere to hide,' Fitzgerald said, tears forming in his eyes.

'We know what Cormac did already, Pete,' Mercer said. 'We've got the evidence in his backpack. We don't need you to prove it.'

Fitzgerald looked at Mercer straight on. 'Then what am I doing? Then what is this about?'

'You need to save your own ass,' Mercer said. 'You want to separate yourself out so you're not charged as an accessory to kidnapping and murder? Then you'd best tell us exactly what you knew and when you knew it.'

Answers came faster now.

'So we're at the bar, and Cormac's drinking like a fish,' Fitzgerald said. 'Told me that a friend of his needed to spend a night on the island. Maybe two. Liberty Island. That he saw the big story in the newspaper last year about the caretaker being retired and the island without any security at night.'

'Yeah?'

'The friend seemed to know about Fort Wood already, about the way it was boarded up inside the old building.'

'You think Cormac told him?' Mercer asked.

'Could be. He likes to go down there on his break. Just hang out solo in a quiet place,' Fitzgerald said. 'He's pretty familiar with it.'

'And you?'

'I was curious about it, yeah. I went downstairs with him a few weeks back, in early September, I guess it was. I didn't think there was anything wrong with that.'

'Lunch break?'

'Exactly.'

'Popped a cold beer or two?' Mercer asked.

'It was a hot day. Yeah, we've done that.'

'So what about his friend who wanted to spend the night? How was he planning to get here?'

'Same way anyone else would, I guess. It's a two-minute boat ride from the Jersey side to the dock on the back of the island. You got a boat, you could come here from anywhere.'

'No security at all during the night?' Mercer said.

'No people anymore. Not since they closed the caretaker's house up,' Fitzgerald said. 'A few surveillance cameras, but if you know where they are, you can come in underneath them.'

'To do what?'

He shrugged his shoulders. 'All Cormac had to do was remove some of the wooden boarding, loosen it up so his friend could pull it aside and sneak in. Then be able to nail it shut again. That's all.'

'Weren't you interested in what this imaginary friend of Cormac's wanted to do here?'

Pete. Fitzgerald looked up at Mercer. 'I figured I knew.'

'And what was that?' Mercer asked.

'I figured Cormac was trying to do the right thing. Trying to help a guy who needed to get out of his uncle's way.'

I stared at him, trying to get a read on his credibility.

Mercer went on. 'Why's that?'

'Emmet Renner's a name nobody wants to hear again, out where I live. Word got around that he had come back, and everybody was scrambling to keep out of Renner's way. He's got a rep for evening scores,' Fitzgerald said. 'Cormac's a good guy. Wouldn't say anything bad about his own family, but he knew he'd become a sort of pariah if Emmet caught up with any of his old crowd.'

'So helping someone hide out over here is what you thought?'

'A union guy, probably. Someone like me, that's what I thought. Someone who just needed to make himself scarce till the grandfather died. By then, Emmet will have to be gone again.'

'How about the woman?' Mercer said.

374

'I'm telling you what I know. Cormac never said anything about a woman.'

'Not even today?' I broke in. 'Not even when you went back to get the sheet?'

Fitzgerald lowered his head. 'Look, we saw you guys come on the island — word got around pretty quick that cops were here.'

'Why was that a problem?' I asked.

'It wasn't a problem for anybody but Cormac. He got jumpy again, all at once. Said he had to go back and check that his friend wasn't still in the fort.'

'And you just volunteered to go along?'

'Yeah. Yeah. I just did.'

'Stupid.'

'That's your opinion.'

'Really stupid,' I said. 'You walked yourself right into a felony, kid.'

'I didn't even go in past the wooden boards, Detective. I swear it. I just waited for Cormac in the hallway.'

'What? To come out with the sheet and the handcuffs?'

'*Handcuffs?* I didn't see any handcuffs,' Fitzgerald said, rattling the arm with the metal bracelet. 'They make noise like this. There were no cuffs. What felony are you talking about?'

'Kidnap, if you're feeling lucky. Murder, if you're acting as stupid as I think you are.'

I was close to the kid's breaking point.

'And his friend?'

'Gone. He said there was no one in there.'

'Was he surprised?' Mercer asked.

'Not surprised so much as relieved.'

375

I took the handcuff key from Jimmy North and held it up for Fitzgerald to see. 'You want me to believe you never asked your pal who he was trying to help?'

'It's true.'

'Or today, that you never pressed him for what he had put himself — and you — at risk for?' I asked, walking toward him.

'I told you. I thought he was doing a good thing, for himself and for everyone afraid of his uncle Emmet,' Fitzgerald said. 'It was over today. I didn't think there was no risk in walking back with him to the fort. Now are you letting me go?'

He watched as I put the key in the handcuff lock. 'Actually, I thought I'd power it up another notch. See if there's anything Cormac said that you might have forgotten to tell me.'

I'd never been into brutality as a means for getting information from a perp. But I thought I might be capable of anything to get Coop back.

Pete Fitzgerald yelped as I turned the metal on his wrist.

'Better?' I asked.

'Make him stop!' the kid screamed.

I knew Mercer was about to shut me down. 'Anything?'

'Cormac was relieved, is all,' Fitzgerald said, as fast as I asked the question. He took one more glance back, in the fading light, to the boat where Cormac was restrained. 'He came out holding that sheet and told me his friend was gone. And . . . '

He paused.

'And what?'

376

'He said something that made no sense, so I ignored it.'

'What was that?' I asked.

'He said, 'Thank God he's gone.' And I asked him where to? 'Cause so far as I was aware, Emmet Renner was still in Woodside. Might not be smart for this friend to be going back,' Fitzgerald said. 'And Cormac's answer to me was 'Manhattan.''

I grabbed his shirt and shook him. 'Did he say where in Manhattan? What about it made no sense to you?'

'The lighthouse. The lighthouse in Manhattan,' Fitzgerald said. 'I would have told you earlier, but it made no sense to me.'

I let go of him faster than he could breathe. I handed the key back to Jimmy North and told him to unlock the cuffs.

Fitzgerald doubled over and started to cry. 'It made no sense because there's no damn lighthouse in Manhattan.'

I started to trot down to the dock.

'What do I do with him now?' Jimmy shouted as Mercer ran after me.

'Take him to the squad with you,' I said. 'Feed and water him, Jimmy. Give him a gold medal and get everything else he wants to say out on the table.'

'Hold up, Mike!' Mercer called out.

I stopped in front of the wooden crates, opened one, and removed half a dozen Roman candles from inside it.

'What did the kid say that turned you around?' Mercer asked.

'The lighthouse in Manhattan. That's where we're going.'

'Why? Where is it?'

'If you'd been any closer to it this morning, you would have bumped into it,' I said, making my way to the Intrepid.

'Where?'

'Jeffrey's Hook, Mercer. The last lighthouse standing in Manhattan is at Jeffrey's Hook.'

45

I jumped onto the deck of the boat and stowed the fireworks on the rear seat. I put the key in the ignition and started to untie the rope at the bow.

'Tell me why,' Mercer said, his hand on the stern cleat.

' 'Cause it's Renner territory, if I'm thinking right. 'Cause I played there as a kid, like I was telling Jimmy this morning, and now the whole picture's coming into focus.'

'Where's Jeffrey's Hook?'

I straightened up and looked at Mercer. 'I'm going to tell you what this is and why I think it might be the place Renner would lure me to. And then I'm going to ask you and Peterson to set the trap, okay?'

'Nothing's okay till I hear you out.'

'Listen up, 'cause I'm moving fast,' I said, turning on the running lights at the front of the boat. 'Jeffrey's Hook is one of the most treacherous points in the Hudson River, right next to Fort Washington.'

'Under the George Washington Bridge?' Mercer said.

'Exactly. The little red lighthouse,' I said. 'But long before there was a bridge, there was this rocky piece of land — the hook — jutting out into the river at a site where there were more shipwrecks than anyplace in the city except for Hell Gate.'

I took the flashlight out of my rear pants

pocket and placed it on the cockpit.

'In the early nineteenth century, the only thought given to preventing wrecks was to hang a red pole with two lights on it out into the river. It wasn't till the 1920s that the city bought this old lighthouse from Sandy Hook, New Jersey. Ten years later, when the George Washington Bridge opened right on top of the spot, there was no longer a need for the little beacon.'

'But it's obviously still standing,' Mercer said.

'Obsolete but still standing,' I said. 'What's the date? Today's date?'

'It's Friday. October twentieth.'

'There's your answer. The lighthouse is open to the public for one week a year every fall. One single week. The rest of the time it's closed. I bet the kidnappers hit the last night of open season on Wednesday — the annual festival. Needed a place to stash their victim for a couple of days.'

'So they had Lonigan create a makeshift B and B inside the old fort for a couple of nights,' Mercer said. 'There was enough activity on Liberty Island, with the concert tomorrow night, to make their comings and goings fit in unobtrusively, no matter what time of day or night they arrived — deliverymen, sound engineers, caterers, crews to erect tents.'

'Fort Washington and that rocky point at Jeffrey's Hook is a comfort zone for Emmet Renner,' I said. 'It's isolated and remote. An easy place to break into, and no one around to disturb him. One of his playgrounds on the Hudson River. It's a dark comfort zone for a dark killer.'

'What else do we need?' Mercer said, about to step on the gunwale and get on the boat.

But I pushed hard with both hands and the bow separated from the dock.

'You're not coming with me, man. You've got better things to — '

'Don't do this, Mike.'

'Throw me that rope,' I said.

'You've got the Lonigan kid.'

'Damn right I do. I swear I'll take good care of him if you work the rest of this with the lieutenant like I need you to do,' I said. 'Now, throw the goddamn rope.'

I had already drifted too far away for Mercer to jump onto the boat. He tossed the line to me.

The engine was idling ten feet off the end of the dock.

'As soon as I take off, you call Lieutenant Peterson. Tell him why I'm sure it's Renner and that I think the red lighthouse is where he's got Coop.'

'I'm dialing now,' Mercer said. 'That much I knew.'

'Tell him no lights and sirens, okay? No John Wayne macho-commando operation at the fort,' I said. 'I think I can surprise him from the water.'

'Dumbest of a lot of dumb things I've heard out of your mouth, Mike.'

'Peterson needs to get Emergency Services on the bridge. There are three or four paths that lead from the surrounding park area to the lighthouse itself. And an abandoned trail across a bridge built in the 1840s for the first railroads. Those would be the logical approaches cops might make because they're pretty well covered by tree foliage — even at this time in the season.'

'Got it.'

'And the Harbor Unit, Mercer. They need to stay back till I give you some kind of sign.'

'With any luck they'll be there before you will.'

It was just after six o'clock and the sun had set.

I switched on the starboard and port lights — green for starboard and red for port — so that I could run the boat safely in the channel without getting hit. I eased the boat away from Liberty Island and circled it once to say one more thing to Mercer.

'No shooting. There's to be no shooting until we see that Coop is alive and well.'

From this point on, once Mercer made the call, I would have no control over any of the decisions being made. But I needed to think that I did.

I pulled back on the throttle and made my way across the river to go north. The water taxis appeared to be full of commuters. I crept along at eight or ten knots because of the traffic, despite my desire to race to Jeffrey's Hook.

I hadn't gotten farther than Battery Park City when my phone rang.

It was Vickee, calling from the press office at One Police Plaza.

'Game's up, Mike,' she said. 'The commissioner wants you to come in to headquarters stat.'

'Have you talked to Mercer?'

'He said he doesn't know where you are.' Her

voice was covered in a crisp layer of frost. 'And I don't believe him.'

Good man, I thought. *Great friend.*

'What's changed?' I said. 'Mercer's not lying. Peterson sent me home.'

'There's a ransom note, Mike.'

I gripped the steering wheel of the Intrepid. I thought I was going to be sick.

'What does it say? What's the demand?'

'No demand yet. A note tucked under the windshield wiper of the district attorney's car when his security detail went downstairs at six o'clock,' Vickee said. ' 'Alexandra Cooper is alive' is what it says. There'll be video proof at ten P.M.'

I pulled on the throttle to ramp up my speed. 'So why does Scully want me? Why does anyone think this is real?'

'He wants you here to protect you from yourself, Mike. From doing something stupid when we've just been offered a glimmer of hope,' she said. I'd never heard an edge in Vickee's voice until just now. 'There's an inked fingerprint on the note next to Alex's name. We're checking it now against the prints in her DA's employment file. Then we'll know if this is for real.'

I heard the word *fingerprint* and I could only think of Westies bosses like Coonan and Renner who had kept fingers that they had cut off their victims. Another wave of nausea swept over me.

'I'll see you at nine forty-five.'

I was cruising past a party boat with revelers celebrating on deck. I didn't think the wake I

383

was kicking up would disturb the large vessel. Speed seemed more important to me at this moment than safety.

'You'd better make it sooner than that, Mike,' Vickee said. 'The commissioner is taking the story public in an hour. He's holding a presser with Paul Battaglia. He knows he can't sit on the story of Alex's disappearance once the video goes viral, so he's breaking the news himself.'

46

I moved the needle up so that I was doing twenty knots, and then twenty-five. I was flying over the water at thirty-five knots, past the piers that held giant cruise ships. I had a distance of about one hundred city blocks to go.

I didn't know this stretch of the river. It seemed to be a straight shot toward the bridge. I could mark my progress by landmarks: the tall lighted spire of Riverside Church near 125th Street and the circular dome of Grant's Tomb. The huge sewage-treatment plant loomed ahead of me, so I checked behind me for other boats, then veered off to the center of the fast-running waterway.

Trains speeding past me on the railroad tracks that ran alongside the river from Penn Station to the north made it impossible to hear almost anything else except the roar of their engines. I checked the depth finder and had plenty of water beneath me for the draw of my boat.

As soon as the detail on the giant gray towers of the George Washington Bridge came clearly into sight, I cut back on the throttle and slowed the boat's speed, gradually, to below ten knots. I cut off the running lights and let my eyes adjust to the blackness all around me, from the starless city sky to the swirling current beneath me.

If it was going to be possible to surprise Emmet Renner, then it would have to be by a stealth-like approach from the Hudson.

I knew there were giant rocks that surrounded Jeffrey's Hook. They were the reason for the existence of the lighthouse, although much of the shoreline had been dynamited to clear the passage for vessels when the GW was built. I needed to be on high alert so that I didn't drive the boat aground before finalizing a plan.

The red paint of the lighthouse reflected the brilliant lights, strung like a necklace, that covered the beams on the great bridge from east tower to west. The sturdy little building was only forty feet high, dwarfed by the six-hundred-foot rise of the steel beams above her.

I caught a break. The lower half of the Hudson River — as far upstate as Troy — was a tidal estuary. The tide was shifting and carrying me northward, taking me closer and closer to the bridge, with only the slightest amount of engine thrust.

I picked up my phone and speed-dialed Mercer.

'Where are you?' I asked.

'On a Harbor Unit boat. About to catch up to you.'

I turned around, keeping both hands on the wheel, and spotted the blue-and-white NYPD vessel about a hundred yards off my stern.

'You've got to stay back, Mercer. That's all I'm asking. Stay back till I signal,' I said. 'How about the lieutenant?'

'He was already on his way to Queens when I called, but he's rushing a team into place.

'There'll be two men in the girders of the

bridge and a crew surrounding the park,' Mercer said. 'And you ought to know that Peterson told Scully everything, including the fact you have your own hostage.'

'Damn it.'

'Since the commissioner knows, there'll be a real plan in play within the hour. Can you hold off one more hour, Mike?'

I didn't know how to answer. It wasn't in me to wait.

'Mike?'

'Can you stay back and douse the lights?' I asked.

I looked around again and the NYPD launch had gone black.

'Thanks for that. Now, as soon as I go past the lighthouse,' I said, 'I'll be out of sight. Your crew can show you on the charts that it's best for me to stay east after passing the main point of Jeffrey's Hook.'

'Okay.'

'There's a stretch of huge rocks there that stand out of the water. Some of them get covered up when the tide comes all the way in, but that's why you won't see me. I'll pull in against those boulders,' I said. 'If you guys are willing to stay back, then I'll wait.'

'You got it, Mike,' Mercer said.

I not only had the current and tides with me. I also had an idea.

I moved the boat as quickly and quietly as she would go, navigating a path around the giant rocks.

Jeffrey's Hook was the narrowest point

between the New York and New Jersey shorelines in this stretch of the Hudson River. That's why it had been chosen as the spot on which to anchor the enormous bridge.

It was for the very same reason that General George Washington selected Jeffrey's Hook as the place to sink his chevaux-de-frise during the Revolutionary War, to try to create a blockade to prevent the British and Hessian soldiers from advancing upriver.

The boulders mined from above Fort Washington were sunk on the wooden chevaux, from riverbank to riverbank, by American soldiers, and the ships that had carried them across the water had later been moored in place above them. It was the only way to secure the position of those vessels and the heavy cargo they had lowered into the Hudson River to stop the enemy.

The massive iron hooks that once held the line of sunken boats in place looked like weapons of war themselves.

I had seen them often, as a kid. They had been buried deep in the boulders by soldiers who would soon after be captured.

They had always fascinated me — hooks the size of the cleats on this boat, forged and fired and bent into shape, looking like the long, arthritic fingers of a witch.

The Intrepid banged up against a couple of the rocks. It didn't sound any worse than a wave crashing against them, buffered by the sound of another passing train.

I didn't want to use the flashlight. Fortunately, the GW Bridge lights offered enough of an outline of the shore.

I knew exactly what I was looking for. There were three boulders, each separated from the next by about ten feet, which were on a spit of land called Ceder Point.

It was on that spit — a huge slab of rock — where the hooks were embedded deep into the schist.

I scanned the area as I tried to idle the boat in place. At the top of a crest there used to be a statue, I remembered. It was a distinctive shape, sort of resembling a snowman, with a round head and a stout belly and bottom. The Daughters of the American Revolution had commissioned it a century ago, with words marking the site: AMERICAN REDOUBT 1776.

I finally saw the stone snowman at the top of the rocky hill.

I held on to the bow rope and crawled off the boat, angled onto one of the boulders. I kicked off my shoes so that I didn't slide back into the water.

It was only a matter of minutes until I found a pair of the Revolutionary-era rusted hooks.

My feet scraped against the rock as I climbed toward them. I was happy to feel patches of moss that made sticking to the surface easier.

When I got one hand on the first hook, I wound the rope around it. Then I reached it to the second hook and made the knot tighter and tighter. I tugged on the line and my little Intrepid seemed to be securely in place.

It was the first step in building my devil's bridge.

47

I sat down on the boulder and moved crab-like back to the boat. I stepped over the side of it and grabbed the metal frame that edged the canvas T-top to lower myself down.

I lifted the cover of the bench and looked down into the head.

Cormac Lonigan — my hostage — was exactly where I had left him.

I pulled him to his feet and told him to walk up the three small steps to the deck. The sock in his mouth would keep him quiet. There wasn't much I had to worry about, but I made him get to his knees.

He was shivering with just his jockey shorts and long-sleeved shirt on.

I bent down in the storage space beyond the toilet. There were a few sets of waders and other boating clothes.

I climbed up next to Lonigan. 'These will be too big for you, but they'll be warmer,' I said.

I helped him pull on the one-piece black rubber overalls. He didn't fight me. I didn't dare remove his handcuffs, so I fastened the clasps over his shirt but decided against letting his hands free for long enough to put on an all-weather jacket.

I had no intention to kill the kid. I just wanted him to be my bait.

I walked to the stern to get the extra length of

rope that was stowed there. I rolled up the legs of my chinos, almost to my knees. When I turned back to Lonigan, I could see him taking in the landscape. He must have recognized the bridge overhead but might have made no sense of the location.

I got back onto the boulder where we were anchored and told Lonigan to follow me.

He hesitated. He had no ability to speak, but his eyes were asking me *Why?*

'Gotta test the water,' I said. 'In case we have to go for a swim.'

His head shook violently from side to side.

'Just sayin', Cormac. Now, take a walk with me.'

He was off-balance from hours of being hunched up on the toilet with his hands behind his back. In addition, he had the bulky waders on, and their footed rubber overalls made walking difficult.

I held on to him to steady him on the slick surface, carrying the length of rope over my shoulder like a lariat.

We were thirty yards or so north of the red lighthouse and walking toward it. We were on much lower ground and hidden by the boulders, so it wouldn't be possible for anyone to spot us. I couldn't see signs of life from within, and I wasn't sure that there were cops in place yet on the girders of the great gray bridge.

To our right, sticking up from the river like a series of large tombstones, was another outcropping of rocks.

I held on to Lonigan's handcuffs, his back to

me, and extended my right leg so that my foot dipped into the water.

'Ooooh,' I said. 'Pretty nippy.' I tugged on the cuffs and pulled him so that his booted feet were standing on the base of one of the rocks, covered up to his ankles by the Hudson.

I talked to him as I laced one end of the thick nautical rope around the links of his handcuffs and then through the shoulder straps of his waders.

'What do you know about hypothermia?' I asked.

Lonigan couldn't speak if he wanted to.

'I didn't think so. It's a dangerous thing, Cormac. Cold water accelerates its onset because body heat is usually lost twenty-five times faster in cold water. It gets to the core of your body,' I said, going about my business strapping the rope around the back side of the naturally made tombstone. 'Gets the brain, the heart, the lungs — all the vital organs. And skinny people like you? Well, it tends to get to them faster.'

I kept my balance as I wrapped the rope around Lonigan's body and then again around the vertical rock.

'Nobody wants you to live more than I do, kid. I'm needing you badly to make a trade, okay? For that woman you don't know anything about, remember? The one your uncle snatched? So in water this cold — and remember, I put these waders on you for a reason — you're good out here for two and a half hours.'

Cormac Lonigan closed his eyes.

'Now, it will get colder, because the tide's coming in and the water will keep rising. Good thing you're nice and tall. And holding still increases your survival time,' I said. 'I took a course once at the Police Academy. A chance to train to be an Emergency Services cop. I got through all the crap about heights and elevator shafts and jaws of life. The one thing I couldn't deal with? It was hypothermia. It was jumping into the frigid East River — like, doing it voluntarily — to save the ass of some drunken fool who had fallen in, who was kicking and screaming and flailing his arms, and more likely to drown by doing that. I gave up on the idea early on. More suited to dead bodies.'

I was knotting the rope at the rear of the rock. My toes were already ice-cold.

'But that's when I learned how important it is, in the case of hypothermia, to keep a positive attitude.'

Lonigan's head was hanging.

'Don't blow me off when I'm talking to you, kid. I'm not joking with you. You need a will to live, and you need to keep as still as possible.'

Cormac Lonigan twisted in place. I thought it was as likely to remove himself from the sound of my voice as it might have been to try to break free.

'Squirming around like that won't help you. If you get loose enough to slide into the river? Well, that's my worst nightmare,' I said. 'The thing about those chest-high waders is that they will fill right up to the top with water and just float you away with the current. Fast and furious as she goes. Most likely you'll crack your head on a boulder before you freeze to death. So take my advice and hold as still as you can.'

There was little chance that Cormac Lonigan could break free.

It was time to talk to his uncle about Coop.

48

I stayed along the very edge of the shoreline, leaning forward on the boulders so that I was angled at almost forty-five degrees.

I couldn't see downriver, so it was unlikely that Mercer and the harbor patrol cops knew I was out of the boat. I couldn't even see the lighthouse, which was blocked from my view by the base of the two bridge towers, so I doubted that if anyone was there he or she could see me.

Slowly and carefully I worked my way around the perimeter of Jeffrey's Hook. The smaller stones hurt the soles of my feet, and the dampness of the large rocks added to my chill.

When I reached the corner of the cement foundation that grounded one of the bridge towers, I stood up beside it. It more than concealed my body from any occupants of the lighthouse, which was not very far away.

I looked up at the massive girders that held the cables and beams that supported the bridge. If there were cops in place — and they should have been by now — they were undoubtedly dressed like ninjas and impossible for me to see amid the hundreds of thousands of pieces of steel and wire.

I opened my phone and clicked on Mercer's number.

'Hey,' he said. 'You still good?'

'Except for lying to you,' I said, whispering

into the device, 'I'm fine.'

'Like there was a chance you wouldn't lie to me?' Mercer said. 'You know about the fingerprint, right?'

'Vickee called me. Told me they were checking.' Every cop, every prosecutor who took a law enforcement job with the city, had to be printed.

'It's Alex. Whoever dropped the note has Alex. That's a confirm.'

'Still no demand?'

'Scully's waiting on that.'

'But going public?'

'Yes. Yes, he is.'

'Can you see the lighthouse?' I asked. 'Can you make it out from where you are?'

'Yes, Mike. We're staying south, but I can see it pretty well with binoculars.'

'There's a glassed-in cupola on top. The lantern room,' I said. 'And then a circular balcony around it and steps that wind down. Can you spot anyone at all?'

'Not even a fly.'

'Are the ESU guys in place?'

'The first team is on location. More men are on the way.'

'Are they communicating with you?' I asked.

'We've got a line open to the sergeant who's with them.'

'Just let them know that I'm the guy at the base of the bridge,' I said. 'I'm barefoot and exhausted and half out of my mind with worry about Coop, but I'm one of them.'

'Will do.'

'I've got an idea to see if Emmet Renner is in there,' I said.

'Please tell me it doesn't involve your gun. There's nobody on site who wants to use a weapon till we know where Alex is.'

'That was my rule to you, remember?'

'Yeah. So what's your plan?'

'I'm going to set off one of Kanye's Roman candles.'

'You're what?' Mercer said. 'You could kill yourself, Mike. Don't do it.'

'It's going to go off from the top of a boulder. Perfectly safe,' I said. 'You just tell Emergency Services and the bridge police that it's not a bomb or anything. I don't want them freaking out when they see the blasts. It's just a couple of pieces of fireworks — just a sound and light display. We'll watch whether anyone comes out to explore. The ESU team needs to stay in place and not even think about shooting.'

'Nobody's shooting,' Mercer said. 'They're just looking for a butterfly net to drop over your head.'

'Keep your eyes on the lighthouse, Mercer,' I said.

I ended the call.

I took the Roman candles out of my pocket. The label said they were eight-shot Thunder Shocks, with maximum loud report. I'd been to enough Fourth of July parties at Breezy Point, the Irish Riviera, to know how to set these off without incident.

I planted the bottom of them in a crevice in a rock near the water, aiming their tops away from the bridge, in the direction of the lighthouse.

I took matches from my pocket and lit the ignition charges. I moved back behind the cover of the base of the bridge.

I waited patiently as the flame worked down to the top pyrotechnic star and the fire spread within each of the candles, which were bound to have a greater impact going off together than each alone.

Boats motored by on the river, but these weren't pointed their way.

Finally, the lift charges were ignited and the candles exploded into the black space of the sky directly south of the lighthouse.

The bright yellow and purple stars burst out of the seam in the rock and kept coming: five, six, seven, eight of them — sixteen in all. The noise of the blast made the train whistle of a northbound express seem like a distant rumble.

I stepped back behind the cement foundation to wait and to watch.

It took less than one minute. The door to the lighthouse opened slowly. A man appeared in the doorway, and backlit as he was, I could see it wasn't Emmet Renner.

He stood there for a few seconds, as though waiting for something else to happen. Then he started to walk down the slope toward the river, toward the source of the fireworks launch.

I could tell that he was younger than Renner. Probably in his twenties, like Cormac Lonigan. I could also see that when he put his hands in the pocket of his hoodie, in his right one he was clutching something heavy, like a gun.

49

The young man who was approaching the far side of the base of the tower didn't seem terribly concerned. The purple and yellow shooting stars and their loud soundtrack had been meant to grab the attention of anyone around, but the fireworks would not have been confused with incoming artillery.

He was dressed for the cool of an early-fall evening, and his sneakers gripped the boulder more readily than my bare feet.

He came down to the water's edge, crouched to pick up some pebbles, and looked around to see if he had any company.

I watched as he tried to skip the stones on the river, still crouching. But the surface was way too busy for skipping them.

Both his hands were engaged in culling stones and tossing them. For at least this moment I had the upper hand.

I stepped from behind the tower's base and onto the top of the slanted boulder. Before the young man heard me, I raced down on my bare feet and pushed him forward so that his face and chest pounded against the rock. His head was almost in the water.

I straddled his back, covering his mouth with my left hand as I grabbed his gun — an old-fashioned revolver — from his pocket.

I held the barrel of the gun against his ear.

'I'm Chingachgook,' I said, 'last of the Mohicans.'

James Fenimore Cooper had stoked my childhood fantasies of Hudson River Valley Indians when I played on these rocks decades ago.

'Say one word and if your gun is loaded, you'll be a dead man. If it's not loaded, I've got my own.'

There was neither sound nor movement from the watchman.

'I'm going to stand up, and you're coming with me.'

He followed orders and got to his feet.

I retraced my route toward the Intrepid, one step behind my new prisoner and the gun tight against his head.

We passed Cormac Lonigan, but I didn't stop to eyeball him, and my companion didn't think of doing anything except looking straight ahead.

When we reached the side of the boat, I had to nudge the guy in his backside to get him to step on board. Once again, I had an occupant for the lone seat on the boat's toilet.

He climbed down the three narrow steps and followed my orders to sit down.

'Take off your shoes and socks and pass them to me,' I said.

I was fresh out of handcuffs, but the good thing about boats was that there was always some kind of line around that would come in handy. I kicked the pile of life preservers aside and there was a blue-and-white nylon rope beneath it.

Once I had tied the man's hands together and shoved one of his own socks deep into his mouth so that he couldn't dislodge it, I speed-dialed Mercer again.

'I got one man out of the lighthouse,' I said.

'What does he say?' Mercer asked. 'Who's in there?'

'Cut me a break, dude. Tell me I did good for a change, will you? I had to get him back to the boat before I could talk to him. But he did have a gun and I took it away,' I said. 'I'm going to put the phone down, on speaker, so you can hear what he has to say.'

'You have an extra set of cuffs, Mike?'

'Nope.'

'A second guy on the boat with you?' Mercer asked. 'Where's Lonigan?'

'Chillin'. Situation under control.'

I rested the phone on the edge of the seat behind me.

'I'm patting him down first,' I said, running my hand over the man's clothes and into his pockets. 'Nothing here. Not even ID.'

I picked up his handgun and checked. Six bullets, locked and loaded.

I held it against his cheek with my right hand as I removed the sock with my left.

'Very softly now, you tell me your name.'

'Paddy,' he said.

'I should have guessed. Paddy what?'

'Paddy Duffy.'

'The luck of the Irish is with me,' I said. 'It's a slight bit of brogue I hear, am I right?'

I thought of what the cop, Officer Stern, had

401

told us that morning, about the redheaded man in the backseat of the SUV with a sleeping woman. That the man had a brogue.

'Yeah. That's right.'

'Where's Emmet Renner?' I asked.

Paddy flinched. Which was all the answer I needed.

'He's in the lighthouse, I'd say. And counting on you to be looking out for him.'

Paddy Duffy nodded.

'There's a woman there, too, isn't there?'

It seemed like an hour between the time I asked the question and his answer.

'Yes. He's got a girl in there.'

'She's alive?'

My breathing was more rapid than his. He knew what to be afraid of, but at this point I wasn't quite sure what I was facing.

'Yeah. She's alive.'

I holstered the gun in my waistband and covered my face with my hands. I didn't speak again until I could compose myself.

50

'Mike? Mike?' Mercer said. 'Are you still there?'

'Hanging by a thread.'

'That's great news, Mike. Now, turn it over to us.'

I resumed my conversation with Paddy Duffy.

'Hold off,' I said to Mercer. And then to my prisoner, 'How many people are in the lighthouse with Emmet Renner?'

'Two. Was just me and another guy, and then the girl.'

'Is she hurt?'

'Not so's I can tell. Emmet's waiting for the cops to show up,' Duffy said. 'He's got a beef to settle. I wouldn't give a nickel for her chances after that.'

'About the same as yours,' I said. 'Guns?'

'You got mine.'

'The other guy?'

'There's a few guns inside.'

'The woman,' I said, 'did you have her on Liberty Island?'

Duffy cocked his head and looked at me. 'Not saying.'

'You don't have to. Cormac Lonigan already gave you up.'

'Cormac had nothing to do with this,' Duffy said.

'You're all singing the same song,' I said. 'I guess Ms. Cooper just kidnapped herself.'

'You're wasting your energy on me.'

'Do you know Cormac?'

'Yeah. You could say that,' Duffy said.

'Come all the way from the other side to hook up with a Renner, did you?' I said. 'Westies redux.'

'I just work with him. Simple as that.' Duffy picked up his head to look at me.

'Don't even think about spitting,' I said. 'It's already been done.'

I put the sock in Duffy's mouth, stepped up, and slammed the lid of the bench.

I picked up my phone. 'Got all that, Mercer?'

'Yes, sir, Detective Chapman. There should be a sniper team in place shortly. Let's ride this one out,' Mercer said. 'Duffy says Coop's okay.'

'You can't do it with guns.'

'What's that about?'

'You can't pick Emmet Renner off with a gun, okay? We've got to see Coop first.'

'I understand that part of it. But the choice of weapons isn't up to you.'

I had the phone in one hand and was swapping positions of Paddy Duffy's gun and my own. I knew my weapon and how it handled. I wanted his for backup, but my own in first place.

'Mike?'

'Almost there,' I said.

'You believe because your father shot Charlie Renner all those many years ago that we shouldn't take this maniac out with a gun? Is that your thinking? That it will change the past?'

'I want to see Coop.' Because if Renner had done anything to hurt her, a bullet to the head

404

would be too easy a death for him.

'So do we all,' Mercer said. 'So do we all. What's next?'

I was as ready as I could get to take on Emmet Renner. As soon as Scully made the public announcement of Coop's kidnapping and the rescue teams were fully staged, there would be choppers flying overhead — police and press — and anything that could float on the river hovering around this desolate point.

'I have one idea, Mercer. A hostage exchange,' I said. 'If I screw it up, then Renner's all yours.'

'Let me in on the — '

I wasn't looking for approval. Nobody was in a position to do better than I was.

I ended the call and climbed onto the giant boulder of Ceder Point. I stayed low and began to circle the rocks on Jeffrey's Hook.

When I passed Cormac Lonigan this time, the swirling current of the river had brought the water well over his knees. I avoided looking at his face. I assumed panic had set in long before now.

I paused when I reached the foundation of the northern tower of the bridge. I had a clear view of the lighthouse, stuck out alone in the Hudson on the very tip of Jeffrey's Hook.

Still no sound from within it. No movement.

I ran to the rear of the bridge foundation and then moved into the space between the towers, staying tight against the twenty-foot-high concrete wall supporting the south tower. The long shadows cast by the bridge lighting on the beams and cables made walking on the rough surface trickier than I had thought it would be. This was as close as I could get to the lighthouse without being seen.

The lantern room on top of the stubby red structure still seemed to be unoccupied. The lighthouse door at its base, the one from which Paddy Duffy had exited, faced the river. There was no way for me to see it from my position.

I thought Emmet Renner would grow impatient when Duffy failed to return. I held as still as I could for several more minutes.

And then there was the sound of footsteps. A hefty man emerged from the lighthouse. I hadn't been able to see the door open, but he was walking around the building, his hand on the wrought iron railing that enclosed it.

'Duff?' He called out with his hand cupped over his mouth. 'Duff, c'mon back.'

I had been prepared by the lieutenant's statement to me about Emmet Renner's plastic surgery. I wouldn't make him, in all likelihood, when we came face-to-face. But this man was no more than my age — probably in his late thirties — while Emmet was over fifty by now.

I let him walk to both sides of the lighthouse and call out for his compatriot. There was no noise except for the waves stirred up by current, lapping against the rocks.

The man was farther away from me now, seeming to be calling Duffy's name a bit more frantically.

I yelled back at him from my position in the shadows behind the bridge tower foundation.

'There's been an accident,' I said. 'Duff's not coming back.'

The man started and flattened his back against the lighthouse wall.

Then a glimmer of light as the door of the building opened and closed again. It must have been Emmet Renner who threw his voice out into the dark. 'You're early, Chapman,' he said. 'I was expecting you'd come looking for her tonight, but you're early.'

51

I could barely stand still once I saw part of the silhouette of Emmet Renner on the edge of the lighthouse walkway. I suppose a sniper in the right position on the water could have picked him off, but half his body — and maybe the hand holding a gun — was inside, where I expected Coop to be.

He was totally out of range of the Emergency Services team positioned somewhere above me on the steel girders.

'I've waited a lifetime for the chance to do this, Chapman.'

'Take your best shot, Renner,' I said. 'I'll step out to meet you if you let Alex Cooper walk out that door.'

'She can't walk right now, I'm afraid.'

'It's about me,' I said. 'Not her.'

'Seems like I've got both of you, Chapman.'

'Not likely. Not likely at all.'

'Then I'll take the bird I've got in my hand,' he said, stepping inside the door.

'Renner!' I screamed as loud as I could. Again, 'Renner!'

He waited a minute or two before coming back outside. Still, his second hadn't budged from his place on the side of the lighthouse.

'I can get you back to Arizona, Renner. No questions asked. One-way ticket.' I was talking too fast and I knew it. 'You've picked the wrong lure.'

'I don't know much about fishing, Chapman, but looks to me like I picked exactly the bait I needed,' he said. 'And I can pretty much write my own ticket where I'm going next.'

'Give her to me and I can make the deal.'

'I give her to you and you won't live long enough to do that. That's the easy part,' Renner said. 'Step out from behind that fortress and I'll show you I haven't lost my touch.'

'So far your only crime is breaking and entering. Liberty Island,' I said. If he released Coop alive and well, then I didn't give a damn about the kidnapping charge. 'And the lighthouse.'

'Don't slight me on the kidnapping, Chapman. We Renners pride ourselves on the big snatch.'

'How about Duffy?' I said. 'I'll give you Duffy back.'

'Duffy's nothing to me.'

'A friend of the family.'

'He's not blood, Chapman,' Renner said. 'And this is all about blood.'

I didn't expect any less from Emmet Renner. But his accomplice, the guy plastered against the side of the lighthouse, took his cue from what he assumed was Paddy Duffy's fate and Renner's icy remark. He bolted.

The man vaulted over the railing and started to run, headed for the bushes of Bennett Park for cover, and then most certainly beyond.

Emmet Renner was stuck in place, unable to shoot the man in the back for fear, I'm sure, that he would expose himself to police fire. I didn't think he'd believe I'd gotten to Jeffrey's Hook by myself.

The runaway wasn't my concern. He would undoubtedly plow straight into a squad of gathering police officers as he tried to make a timely escape from an ungrateful employer, and that left at least one less gun in Coop's little world.

I needed to keep Emmet Renner out of the lighthouse. I needed to keep him from harming Coop — from killing her — now that I was here to witness exactly that.

'Renner! Two men down.'

'Come out where I can see you, Chapman,' he said, turning back — it appeared to me — to enter the lighthouse door.

The silhouette reemerged, and this time he was dragging a bundle across the threshold.

I did a double take. The bundle was a human being, bound and gagged, and being dragged by her long blond hair onto the walkway around the lighthouse.

Now was the time for a sniper to take a shot. All my inhibitions about another shooting vanished in a flash. But the only angle at which Renner would have been vulnerable was from the river, and there was no one in place to shoot.

I pulled out my phone with my left hand, my right hand still holding my gun. I hit redial and when Mercer answered I told him to do whatever he had to — whatever the men could — to save Coop's life. I couldn't even see Emmet Renner as he moved away with Coop.

'Renner!' I yelled again. 'The devil's bridge.'

He stopped moving. The half silhouette reappeared in my sight line. I could see him bend his neck back and look up at the span of the George Washington. I was grateful to have his attention.

'Not that one,' I said. 'Not the one up above us. I've got a better deal for you.'

'Fairy tales now, Chapman?' he said, with a laugh that sounded diabolical. 'I haven't heard about the devil's bridge since my mother died.'

'I've built one just for you, Renner. Just for you.'

'I'm to send Alex Cooper across it and get what in return? What are you offering me?' he said. 'What could you possibly have that I want?'

'I've got your blood, Renner.'

'My what? You've got my what?'

I could see boats passing in the water behind the lighthouse, but I didn't spot the NYPD cruiser.

'Not exactly the first living soul to cross over, but your blood nonetheless.'

'What have you done now, Chapman?'

I had upped the ante and Renner had raised his voice.

'I've got your sister's kid, Renner.'

'No, you don't. You're bluffing me now.'

'I've got Cormac Lonigan.'

It might be bad blood, but they were all Renners.

He was coming around the building, almost into a position opposite me.

'Cormac's home now. I'm sure he's home.'

He was losing it a bit; I could hear that in his

411

voice. He wasn't wrapped that tight thirty years back, and he had undoubtedly unraveled even more.

'You dragged him into this, Renner,' I said. I left out the part about how he had been responsible for his brother's death all those years ago. 'Shauna's kid.'

His roar into the night air was a partial release of his rage.

'Don't do to Shauna what you did to your old man,' I said. 'I'll give you the kid.'

'Where is he?' Renner asked. 'Where's Shauna's boy?'

'You let Alex Cooper go and I'll give you Shauna's son.'

'You'd really kill another Renner kid, Chapman?' he asked, rocking against the wrought iron railing. 'What have you done with Cormac? What have you done with her boy? If you kill him — '

'It's only you who can kill him,' I said. 'You've got someone I love, and I've got Renner blood to trade for her.'

'Where's Cormac?' he shouted at me, rattling the old railing as he pulled on it. 'Where in God's name is he?'

'Not far at all,' I said. 'He's on the rocks, Renner. The kid's on Execution Rock.'

52

'Is he alive?' Emmet Renner asked.

He had taken a few steps back and seemed to be bending over Coop's body. I couldn't see her at all. I couldn't tell whether she was able to move.

'For now, yeah. Maybe in an hour or so he starts hallucinating,' I said. 'You know how that goes. But he's alive now.'

I needed to get Renner out in the open. I needed to move closer and draw him toward me so that whoever was backing me up had a chance to act while I distracted him with his nephew's plight.

'It was your game, the rock,' I said. 'I figure you know what kind of torture it is.'

'You got cops helping you with this?' Renner asked.

'Flying solo. I came here by boat, alone with Cormac.'

'Where the fuck is he?' Renner asked, taking a step in my direction.

'Probably on the very same rock you used, when you used to play in this park.'

I thought I could hear his feet shuffling on the walkway, but I didn't know whether he was moving closer to me or farther away, back to Coop.

'I watched you from the heights above Ceder Point, back before — ' I caught myself just as I

413

was about to insert Charlie Renner's name in the conversation. 'Back when I was seven or eight.'

It was one of the most memorable ways that Emmet Renner and his pals bullied the younger kids, his brother, Charlie, and Charlie's friends, on Execution Rock.

We played in Bennett Park then — all of us little warriors who tracked the bluestone and granite foundation of Fort Washington's ruins. We watched the grown men who staged reenactments of battles on important dates throughout the year. We built our own fortifications on the heights above the Hudson, using tree trunks and branches that had been damaged in lightning storms.

Now I kept backing off, deeper into the shadows and closer to the boat.

There was an old story about the British colonials who controlled New York and Long Island before the American Revolution. I didn't learn it in school. I heard it first from Renner's gang.

When rebels had become unruly and were sentenced to die, the authorities would often chain them to rocks in the river. It was a slow death and a torturous one, as they drowned with the rising water of the incoming tide.

I reached Cormac Lonigan. The water was at his waist. His lips were deep blue and he was shivering uncontrollably.

I'd seen his uncle Emmet play this game with unwitting kids — always the weaker ones, the younger ones. I'd never seen him kill anyone this way, but I was certain he had done just that.

414

The water had risen on the boulder, too, as well as on Cormac Lonigan's body. I waded into it and felt the sting of the cold on my skin.

I reached my arm out toward his face. His head smacked against the rock as he recoiled instinctively.

I took a step closer and reached out again. This time I grabbed on to my handkerchief and sock and pulled them out of his mouth.

The noise that came out of Cormac Lonigan sounded like the cry of a wounded animal. The words he tried to say were *help me*, but it was a great primal scream that shattered the silence of the landscape around me.

53

'You want him, Renner?' I said. 'Come and get him before he starts gurgling Hudson River water.'

Emmet Renner hardly knew the kid. But it wouldn't be easy for him, I didn't think, to face his own sister after returning home and recruiting her son to his murderous ways. That, coming right on top of the death throes of their father.

Cormac was screaming for his uncle now, begging him to save his life. If there was anyone else in earshot, we'd have company soon. It was one of the most sorrowful sounds I'd ever heard.

'People are going to come piling in from the park, Renner,' I said. 'Dog walkers out for a stroll, joggers running by. Only a man with no soul could listen to this howling and not come to help.'

I couldn't see him from where I was standing. I doubted he would leave Coop alone, but the kid made a god-awful noise and if Renner had grown up at all during his years in the desert, he'd have to respond.

'I've got a boat,' I said. 'That's how I brought your nephew here. I'll put you both on it and promise safe passage through the harbor.'

Cormac Lonigan moaned and tried to summon the strength to scream again. But there was no word from Renner.

Then I heard voices shouting, coming from the wooded area in Bennett Park. Then a dog barking. Then two or three dogs.

'Where are you?' one man called out from a point on the heights above me.

'You can't kill them all, Renner,' I yelled to him.

'I'll take the boat, Chapman,' he called back to me. 'Give me the boat and the kid.'

There suddenly seemed to be noises coming from every direction.

I had opened the floodgates by removing the gag from Lonigan's mouth. Now the police units surrounding the lighthouse, the park, and the bridge tower would have to reveal themselves to block the well-meaning citizens from rushing to the rocks.

And Emmet Renner still had Alex Cooper.

I didn't know what to do next. I was overwhelmed by the activity I had put in motion, and now I couldn't figure which one of us was at greatest risk.

I decided to move forward toward the lighthouse again, hoping to get close before anyone else arrived there or lights went on around us. Emergency Services would have no choice but to move in to protect the oncoming good Samaritans. To protect everyone except Coop.

That was when I heard the sound of the Intrepid's engine. I had left the keys in the cockpit and someone had just turned on the engine. Had Paddy Duffy freed himself from the hold? Had Emmet Renner's accomplice circled the lighthouse and found the boat?

I was as close to panicking as I had ever been when I turned away from Renner to find out who was on board.

54

I heard a man's voice say my name. 'Chapman?'

'Yeah.'

'Scuba. It's okay.'

I wasn't shaking as badly as Lonigan, but it was close.

The police diver was in a black dry suit with a full face mask. He'd come to the rocks on a small dark-gray Zodiac that he'd tied up to the Intrepid, then swam ashore.

'Cue me,' I said. 'What do they want me to do?'

'Just what you're doing. Let Renner think you'll give him the boat before backup arrives. That's why I turned on the engine,' the cop said. 'So he'd hear it.'

'But Coop?'

'We'll have you covered.'

'How?'

'Better you don't know, Chapman. You'd unintentionally tip it off.'

'Chapman?' Renner called out to me.

I turned my attention back to him.

'The boat is ready for you. I'm not releasing Cormac until you walk down here and meet me halfway,' I said.

I crossed over the largest boulder, and this time, instead of heading for the shadows of the bridge tower, I stayed close to the shoreline. I was going to the lighthouse.

'I hear the boat, Chapman. Where is it?'

'Just past the rock. Past Cormac.'

The kid was whimpering now, probably out of strength to do anything louder.

'You'd better move fast, Renner. People are coming.'

I almost wanted him to see me. I wanted Coop to hear my voice.

Emmet Renner was really between the rocks and a hard place. His entire plan was crumbling, but he wasn't quite ready to let go of his prey.

'Uncle Em,' Lonigan screamed one more time. 'Come get me.'

For the first time since I had arrived on Jeffrey's Hook, Emmet Renner walked toward me from the small terrace of the lighthouse.

Now to add to the barking dogs was the sound of police sirens coming from the West Side Highway and the streets in the neighborhood.

He knew time was running out. He clearly thought the water was an actual means of escape, and that the only police presence was coming from the park behind him. I was thankful Mercer had convinced the Harbor Unit to stay out of sight.

Emmet Renner stood at the top of the steps that led from the lighthouse to the rocks. His gun was in his hand. He turned his head to look back at Coop.

'I'm here, Renner,' I called out.

He swiveled around to try to find my position, but I couldn't see him clearly enough to try to take him out.

'Step down, Renner.' I lifted my gun and

pointed it in his general direction. 'I didn't think Westies killed broads.'

'She's not a broad, Chapman. She's a prosecutor.'

'Get moving before the dogs come. And the cops,' I said. 'You've got about a minute to go. The key's in the ignition. Walk on by me and I'll cut Lonigan loose.'

Emmet Renner took his first step. 'I don't want the boy, Chapman. I want the boat.'

Bloodless after all. Not even his own family made a difference in the end. Emmet Renner just wanted to save his own skin.

I threw my Glock onto the rock and watched it skid down toward the water.

Renner heard it, must have guessed what had happened, and started to run down the remaining steps and in the direction of the Intrepid.

Before I was able to race across the rock, two more scuba rescue cops in black dry suits hoisted themselves out of the water and onto the boulder.

The first one out tore off his flippers and ran to the lighthouse. He practically threw himself on top of Coop, shielding her from whatever unknown harm still lurked around us.

I was there within seconds, after he ripped the gag from her mouth and as he was cutting the plastic cuffs off her wrists.

I lifted her limp body in my arms, carried her inside the lighthouse, and sat on the floor with her in my lap, cradling her head against my chest as I whispered my apologies to her over and over again.

55

'Nobody died?' Coop asked.

'Nobody,' I said.

'The Lonigan kid?'

'Severe hypothermia. He'll be fine. He's in another wing.'

We were in a private room at Columbia Presbyterian Hospital, just ten blocks from Bennett Park. Coop had been examined in the ER and admitted for observation. It was three o'clock in the morning.

'Emmet Renner?'

'No shots fired,' I said. 'He might need his nose fixed again, but in the meantime he's reacquainting himself with the New York City jail system.'

Coop was in a hospital gown, in bed, with extra blankets to cover her. An intravenous tube was dripping fluids into her arm to rehydrate her. I was sitting on the other bed, dressed in surgical scrubs. Our clothing, damp and dirty, had been vouchered as evidence. I stood up and she reached for my arm. 'Please don't leave me alone.'

'Hey, now. I'm not going far. I just need to borrow something from the cops in the hallway.'

There was a police detail outside Coop's room and would be for as long as she was hospitalized. Probably for a good period of time after her release. I asked two of the guys for their handcuffs.

She was sitting on the edge of her bed when I came back in. Her eyes were moist again and she was dabbing at them with tissue.

I'd never seen her quite this way — so skittish and clinging to me. But she'd never been through an ordeal like the past forty-eight hours.

'Handcuffs?' She seemed startled to see me holding two pairs. I should have been more sensitive to the visual of them after her own experience, but I was out of gas, too.

'I got a problem with hospitals, Coop. There's no king-size beds.'

I unlocked the wheels of my bed and pulled it right beside hers. I reached under the mattress and cuffed the metal frames to each other in two places so they didn't split apart.

It was one of the first times that night I had seen her smile.

She got back under the covers and I put an extra pillow behind her head.

'How about something to eat?' I asked. 'There's room service, you know.'

Renner had given her only a couple of oranges and a few bottles of water in the forty-eight hours she'd been held.

'I can't think about food yet. I'm still kind of nauseated.'

'They've added something for that to your IV, Coop,' I said, stroking her hair.

She turned away from me, onto her side.

'You want to talk?' I asked.

She shook her head in the negative.

'You did a good job filling in a lot of the blanks for the commissioner,' I said.

Coop had confirmed things that we had tried to piece together, like the original abduction. There were parts too hazy for her to have remembered, including the stops to change the license plates on the SUV. She was conscious when they first carried her onto a small motorboat that had been waiting for them at the boat basin after midnight on Wednesday, piloted by a friend of Paddy Duffy's who drove it across the river from a small marina near Edgewater. It was the same boat that delivered Renner and Coop from Liberty Island to the lighthouse. Police were looking for it now.

She didn't acknowledge my comment.

'Dr. Friedman says you've got to talk to me.'

'Maybe tomorrow,' Coop said.

'You didn't let the docs do a rape evidence kit.'

'I keep telling you, Mike. They didn't touch me. Not sexually.'

'You'd never believe a woman who was held for two days and nights by a gang of men and then told you that. You'd make her submit to an exam and figure she'd give it up eventually.'

I moved onto her bed, sitting on top of the covers, face-to-face with her.

'Nobody touched me like that,' she said. 'He just wanted to kill me. Renner wanted you to watch them kill me, and then he'd have killed you, too.'

'Dr. Friedman says I have to give you more time to deal with it.'

'That's not what I need, Mike. I'm done with thinking about that.'

'What do you need, babe?'

'The toxicology results,' she said. 'I'm pretty sure they used chloroform to get me into the car, but the next day they gave me shots of something that put me in the twilight zone. Everything was spacey and vague.'

'Some kind of tranquilizer, Dr. Friedman thinks,' I said. 'Just to keep you subdued.'

There were red marks and abrasions on her wrists, where she had been restrained. But she didn't want to get into that yet, either.

'Who is this Dr. Friedman you keep talking about?' Coop asked, resting her head back against the pillow. 'I'm out of your sight just forty-eight hours and you're taking advice from someone I don't even know.'

'There's a good sign,' I said, leaning forward to kiss her on the forehead. 'The control freak in you is coming back fast.'

'Who is she?'

'The shrink the commissioner hooked me up with yesterday morning. She's the woman I was talking to in the ER while you were being treated,' I said. 'Anyway, she was using me to try to get inside your head. Figure out whether you took yourself out of the action because I'd been mean to you or —'

'That's crazy, Mike.'

'She's smart. It was Dr. Friedman who had the idea that the abduction was all about me.'

'About *you?* I'm the one who was kidnapped.'

'Because of me,' I said, taking both her hands in mine. 'You were kidnapped because of me. Because I love you.'

I didn't expect Coop to start to cry when I said that. But she did. I was dealing with some sort of post-traumatic stress situation. Coop knew more about that kind of thing than I did.

I grabbed the long string behind the bed and pulled on it to turn out the overhead light.

'Please don't cry, babe,' I said. 'I don't know what to do for you.'

It was some kind of release, I guess. She just cried and cried and cried.

'I was all over the map, Alex. I was ready to lock up the Reverend Shipley 'cause I thought he was messed up in this.'

She wiped her nose and looked at me. 'Really? Shipley and me?'

'Yeah. That crap with Estevez the day you disappeared. How he was tied into Shipley,' I said. 'Has anybody told you that they grabbed that Josie Aponte broad?'

'No.'

'Her real name is Rosita Quinones. She took off for Philly right after she did her computer magic. Left the groom all by himself.'

Coop put the tissues down and started asking questions. That was another good sign.

'Who's going to handle the case?'

'I'll get that answer for you by daybreak,' I said. 'Is that good enough?'

She forced another smile.

'Next one to nab is Shipley's pal Takeesha Falls, right, Coop?'

'Who's Takeesha Falls?'

'Whoa, it's been a long couple of days. I forgot you were gone before I even heard her name.

426

Seems like forever ago,' I said. 'Do you remember, when I left Primola Wednesday night, I'd just gotten called on a homicide case? A male victim in a domestic?'

Coop nodded. I was glad of any conversation to take her out of herself.

'It's the girlfriend we're looking for. The dead man's girlfriend, Takeesha Falls. She runs with the Reverend Shipley, too.'

'Oh.' She sounded as though she was getting drowsy.

'Just so you know, I think the commissioner has it in for your boss.'

'What do you mean?'

'You're not alone in thinking that Battaglia has an unholy alliance with Hal Shipley. It all started to come to a head in the meeting we had in Scully's office yesterday.'

Coop's eyelids fluttered. 'Tell me more.'

'In the morning. I'm just saying that when the next election rolls around, District Attorney Paul Battaglia may not be the man on the ballot.'

'That's okay with me, Mike.'

She was rolling from side to side, unable to find a comfortable position.

'The docs gave you medication to make you sleep, Alex,' I said. 'Don't fight it.'

She looked at me and took hold of my hand. 'I'm afraid to go to sleep, Mike. I'm afraid of what I see when I close my eyes.'

I pulled back the covers and climbed in beside her — careful of the IV tube — slipping my arm beneath her neck.

'You know to expect that, Alex. You tell your

victims that all the time,' I said. 'Flashbacks, nightmares. Dr. Friedman said it's only natural that you're — '

'I don't want to hear another thing about what she thinks, Mike, okay? I'm not all that interested in your Dr. Friedman,' Coop said, sounding much more like herself. 'I can't get warm. What do I do about that?'

I held her closer to my side and stroked her arm, bringing the blanket over both of us.

'What's with the Alex stuff?' she asked. 'Why are you suddenly calling me 'Alex'?'

She turned on her side and settled into place with me.

'I can't tell you,' I said.

'What do you mean? Why not?'

'Because it's about Dr. Friedman,' I said. 'She thinks it's a bad thing that I use your surname. That I'm your lover and I can't even manage to call you by your first name. She thinks it's another one of my failings.'

'But I am Coop,' she said, smiling up at me. 'That's who I am.'

Acknowledgements

This is a book I have wanted to write for a very long time. I've been interested in looking at Alexandra Cooper through the eyes of Mike Chapman, professionally and personally. The change in the nature of their relationship seemed to provide the perfect moment to do it.

One inspiration for the setting is *The Little Red Lighthouse and the Great Gray Bridge*, a much-loved children's book by Hildegarde H. Swift and Lynd Ward. For information about my favorite lady, *The Statue of Liberty Enlightening the World*, I relied on Elizabeth Mitchell's excellent book *Liberty's Torch*.

My investigative skills were enhanced by conversations with one of the smartest men I know: Lieutenant Jimmy West, head of the NYPD's Cold Case Squad. He is a great friend and a brilliant detective.

As always, my real-life heroes are the women and men who work in the NYPD; former colleagues who now distinguish the judicial bench, such as Ann Donnelly; and prosecutors under the leadership of District Attorney Cyrus Vance. They include Melissa Mourges, Martha Bashford, Karen Friedman-Agnifilo, Audrey Moore, Kerry O'Connell, Elizabeth Lederer, Larry Newman, and John Temple. I miss that office every single day.

My Dutton family is a happy, steady

professional home for me. Ben Sevier greeted my idea for Coop and Chapman with great enthusiasm. My thanks always to Christine Ball, Jamie Knapp, Stephanie Kelly, Jessica Renheim, Carrie Swetonic, and Andrea Santoro. Best to Brian Tart on his new duties. Gratitude, also, to my Little, Brown UK team as well.

Laura Rossi Totten is my social media guru. She has amazing talent and style and manages to communicate with the world in ways that baffle me.

Esther Newberg — a devoted friend of thirty years — carries that fierce loyalty for which she is revered from friendship to the printed page. She and Zoe Sandler and the ICM Partners are really all one needs to cover your back.

The men of the motor vessel *Twilight* have added great joy to my new life. Captain Michael Cutter promised safe passage through the roughest seas and gave me priceless driving lessons on the Intrepid; Stephens Moss has provided me with the most elegant floating office any writer could imagine — and the perfect cocktail at day's end; and Tom Rogers keeps me way too well fed. Taylor Gandy holds the sharks at a distance — always with a smile — and dances almost as well as Stephens, while Rory Naughton takes some fish bites for the team.

As always, my family and friends are my greatest joy. Cheers to Lisa and Alex! And to David Braunstein, who has shown more courage in one year than anyone I know.

Welcome to the world, Baby Eve.

Justin Feldman, Bobbie and Bones Fairstein,

and Karen Cooper still sit on my shoulders and lift my spirits, always.

Michael Goldberg made the smoothest transition from best friend to best man. And I trust that he will sway with me, always.

We do hope that you have enjoyed reading this large print book.

Did you know that all of our titles are available for purchase?

We publish a wide range of high quality large print books including:
Romances, Mysteries, Classics
General Fiction
Non Fiction and Westerns

Special interest titles available in large print are:
The Little Oxford Dictionary
Music Book
Song Book
Hymn Book
Service Book

Also available from us courtesy of Oxford University Press:
Young Readers' Dictionary
(large print edition)
Young Readers' Thesaurus
(large print edition)

For further information or a free brochure, please contact us at:
Ulverscroft Large Print Books Ltd.,
The Green, Bradgate Road, Anstey,
Leicester, LE7 7FU, England.
Tel: (00 44) 0116 236 4325
Fax: (00 44) 0116 234 0205

Other titles published by Ulverscroft:

TERMINAL CITY

Linda Fairstein

When the body of a young woman is found in a suite at one of the most prestigious hotels in Manhattan, Assistant DA Alex Cooper and Detectives Mike Chapman and Mercer Wallace find themselves hunting for an elusive killer whose only signature is carving a carefully drawn symbol, which bears a striking resemblance to train tracks, into his victims' bodies. When a second body with the same bloody symbol is discovered in a deserted alleyway next to the Grand Central Terminal Building, Alex and Mike must contend with the station's expansive underground tunnels and century-old dark secrets to find a killer who appears to be cutting a deadly path straight to the heart of the city . . .

DEATH ANGEL

Linda Fairstein

In New York's Central Park, Assistant DA Alex Cooper and Detective Mike Chapman race to track down a serial killer before yet another young woman is found dead. Is the body in the Ramble the victim of a deranged psychopath, or could other missing women be connected to this savage attack? The enormous urban park, a sanctuary in the middle of the city for thousands of New Yorkers and tourists who fill it every day, may very well become the hunting ground for a killer with a twisted mind . . .

NIGHT WATCH

Linda Fairstein

New York Assistant D.A. Alexandra Cooper is in France, visiting her restaurateur boyfriend, Luc Rouget, but her holiday is curtailed when a young woman is found murdered. The only evidence: one of Luc's matchboxes promoting his new restaurant in New York. However, Alex is summoned back home to handle a high-profile case. The head of the World Economic Bureau stands accused of attacking a maid in his hotel. Alex is torn between preparing the alleged victim to testify — and a murder case too close to home. When a second body is found — in Brooklyn — with Luc's matchbox, Alex fears that the two cases are connected . . . and that uncovering the secrets of the city's most powerful could cost her and her loved ones everything they hold dear.

SILENT MERCY

Linda Fairstein

When the burnt, headless body of a young woman is found on the steps of a Baptist Church in Harlem, Assistant DA Alexandra Cooper is quickly on the shocking scene. With NYPD cop Mike Chapman, Alex investigates, but soon another woman is slaughtered and found on the steps of a Catholic Church in Little Italy: her throat slashed and her tongue cut out. The killings look like serial hate crimes, but the apparent differences in the victims' beliefs seem to eliminate a religious motive. Convinced that another young woman's life is at risk, Alex uncovers a terrible truth that takes her beyond the scope of her investigation and leads her directly into the path of terrible danger.